# PRAISE FOR MAGGIE SHAYNE

"Maggie Shayne is a bright, shining star that
makes others seem dim by comparison."
—*Affaire de Coeur*

"Maggie Shayne is better than chocolate.
She satisfies every wicked craving."
—bestselling author Suzanne Forster

"Maggie Shayne gifts your holidays with
*Brand-New Heartache,* a sheer delight of a read
with a compelling cast of characters."
—*Romantic Times*

**MAGGIE SHAYNE**

is the author of more than thirty novels, including women's fiction, romance, suspense and paranormal fiction. She has made a name for herself on the *USA TODAY* and *New York Times* extended bestseller lists, and is the winner of numerous awards, including two *Romantic Times* Career Achievement Awards, a National Readers' Choice Award and the coveted Daphne du Maurier Award. She has been nominated seven times by the Romance Writers of America for the RITA® Award. Maggie resides in the town of Otselic in central New York State with her family and faithful bulldog, Wrinkles. Watch for her new romantic-suspense title, *Colder Than Ice,* due out in November 2004 from MIRA Books. Visit Maggie on the Web at www.maggieshayne.com.

# MAGGIE SHAYNE

## STRANGER IN TOWN

Silhouette® Books

Published by Silhouette Books

America's Publisher of Contemporary Romance

 SILHOUETTE BOOKS

STRANGER IN TOWN

Copyright © 2004 by Harlequin Books S.A.

ISBN 0-373-28527-2

The publisher acknowledges the copyright holder
of the individual works as follows:

THE BRANDS WHO CAME FOR CHRISTMAS
Copyright © 2000 by Margaret Benson

BRAND-NEW HEARTACHE
Copyright © 2001 by Margaret Benson

This edition published by arrangement with Harlequin Books S.A.

® and TM are trademarks of Harlequin Books S.A., used under license.
Trademarks indicated with ® are registered in the United States Patent
and Trademark Office, the Canadian Trade Marks Office and in other
countries.

Visit Silhouette Books at www.eHarlequin.com

**Printed in U.S.A.**

# THE BRANDS WHO
# CAME FOR CHRISTMAS

# *Prologue*

*Maya*

Most people in Big Falls, Oklahoma, thought it must have been a case of immaculate conception when they saw me, Maya Brand—eldest of the notorious Vidalia Brand's illegitimate brood—with my belly swollen and my ring finger naked.

Personally, I thought it was more like fate playing a cruel joke. See, all my life, I had struggled to be the one respectable member of my outrageous family. I went to church on Sundays. I volunteered at the nursing home. I wore sensible shoes, for heaven's sake! I *never* aspired to notoriety. I just wanted to be *normal*.

You know. Normal. I wanted a husband, a home, a family. I wanted to be one of those women who make pot roast for Sunday dinner, and vacuum in pearls while it simmers. I wanted a little log cabin on the hillside behind my family's farm, with a fenced-in backyard for the kids, and a big front porch. I wanted to sit down in one of the pews on Sunday and not have the three women beside me automatically slide their butts to the other end.

And it had been starting to happen—before the big disaster blew into town. Bit by bit, I'd *felt* it happening. The PTA moms and church ladies in town had been slowly, reluctantly, beginning to accept me. To see me as an individual, rather than just another daughter of a bigamist and a barmaid. And it wasn't that I didn't love my mother dearly, because I did. I still do! I just didn't want to be like her. I wanted to be like those other women—the ones who were always asked to bake for the church picnic, who did their grocery shopping in heels, and who drove the car pools. The ones who slow-danced with their handsome husbands on anniversaries and holidays, and who took golf or tennis lessons with groups of their friends. They have minivans and housekeepers, manicured lawns and manicured nails, those women.

What they do *not* have are mothers who own the local saloon, or sisters who ride motorcycles or pose for fashion magazines in their underwear.

Still, I was certain my background was something that I could overcome with effort. And, as I said, my efforts had actually been working. Once or twice, one of those other women had smiled back at me in church. The ladies on the pew hadn't moved so far away, nor quite as quickly, and one of them had even returned my persistent "good morning" one Sunday.

Things had been going so well! Until that night...

That night. He ruined everything! Made me into the biggest (literally) and most scandalous member of my entire family! The good people of Big Falls have stopped gossiping about Kara being a jinx—then again, none of her boyfriends have wound up in the hospital from any freak accidents lately, either. They've stopped whispering about Edie, who found the success she chased to L.A. when she became a lingerie model for the *Vanessa's Whisper* catalogue. Mom just about had kittens over that one. The locals used to speculate on Selene, because of her oddball customs and beliefs. Vegetarianism and Zen were not big in Big Falls. And Mel used to generate gossip for being too tough for any man, with her motorcycle and her unofficial job as bouncer at the OK Corral. That's our family's saloon; the OK Corral. Because we live in Oklahoma. Cute, huh?

But the point is, no matter how much I wished that my sisters would conform, or that my mother would suddenly sell the bar and open a sewing shop and cut that wild black hair of hers to a style more suitable to a woman her age, none of their antics did as much damage to my standing in the community as that one night of insanity with that man. That drifter with the eyes that seemed to look right through my clothes. Right through my *skin*.

I suppose, if I'm going to tell you about all this, I should probably start with him, and that night.

See it all started just short of nine months ago....

## Caleb

How was I to know that one night of insanity would change my life forever? I mean, I was respectable, responsible, highly thought of. The Montgomerys of Oklahoma were known far and wide. We had money, and we had power. The name Cain Caleb Montgomery had a long and proud history. My father, Cain Caleb Montgomery II, served two terms as a U.S. senator. His father, Cain Caleb Montgomery I, served *five*.

I am, as you have probably guessed by now, Cain Caleb Montgomery III. And already my political career was well underway. I had just stepped down from my second term as mayor of a medium-sized city. On the day all this insanity began, my entire future was being planned for me. My father and grandfather, and a half dozen other men—men whose faces you would recognize—sat around a large table plotting my run for the U.S. Senate.

They discussed when and how I would declare my candidacy a little before the New Year. They discussed what I was going to stand for and what I was going to stand against. Not with *me*, mind you. They discussed it with each other. I was an onlooker. A bystander. They went on, telling me what I was going to wear, eat, and do on my vacations, as I sat there, listening, nodding, and growing more and more uneasy.

And then they went too far. There we all were, in my father's drawing room. Eight three-piece suits—seven of them straining at the middle—all around a long cherry wood table that gleamed like a mirror. The place reeked of expensive leather, expensive whiskey and cigars of questionable origin. And all of a sudden, one of the men says, "Of course, there will be a Mrs. Montgomery by then."

"Of course there will!" my father says, smiling ear to ear.

And I sat there, my jaw hanging open.

"Got anyone in mind, son?" A big hand slams me on the back, and a wrinkled eye winks from behind gold-framed glasses.

"No? Great. Even better this way, in fact. We can start from scratch, then."

And suddenly they were all talking at once, growing more and more excited all the time.

"She should be blond. The latest analysis shows that blondes hold a slight edge over brunettes or redheads in public opinion polls."

"Of course, there's always dye."

"Medium height."

"Yes, or she'll have to wear heels all the time."

"And of course, she has to be attractive."

"But not *too* attractive. We don't want any backlash."

"Educated. Not quite as well as you, though, but that goes without saying."

"Well versed. She should have a good voice, nice rich tones. None of those squeaky ones. And no gigglers."

"Oh, *definitely* no gigglers!"

"Sterling reputation. We can't have any scandals in the family. That's probably most important of all."

"Absolutely. No scandals."

"We can run background checks, of course. Just to be sure. And—"

*"Wait a minute."*

They all fell silent when I finally spoke. Maybe it was because of the tone of my voice, which sounded odd even to me. I placed both my palms on the table and got slowly to my feet. And for the first time in my entire adult life, I let myself wonder if this were what I really wanted. It had been expected of me, planned for me, even from before I was born. Everything all laid out, private school, prep school, college, law school. And I'd gone along with it because, frankly, it had never occurred to me to do otherwise. But was it what I *wanted?*

It shocked me to realize I wasn't sure anymore. I just... wasn't sure. Giving my head a shake, I just turned and walked out. They all called after me, shouting my name, asking if I were all right. I kept on going. I felt disoriented—as if, for just one instant there, a corner of my world had peeled back, revealing a truth I hadn't wanted to see or even consider. The fact that there might be more for me out there. Something different. Another choice.

Anyway, I went out that night looking to escape my name. My reputation. My identity, because I was suddenly questioning whether it was indeed *mine.* Everyone who knew me, knew me as Cain Caleb Montgomery III. Hell, without the name and the heritage, I didn't even know who I was.

I shed the suit. Dressed in a pair of jeans I used to wear when I spent summers at my grandfather's ranch. God, I hadn't been out there since my college days, and they barely fit anymore. I borrowed the pickup that belonged to our gardener, José. He looked at me oddly when I asked but didn't refuse.

And then I just drove.

Maybe it was fate that made me have that flat tire in Big Falls, Oklahoma, on the eve of Maya Brand's twenty-ninth birthday. Hell, it had to be fate…because it changed everything from then on. Although I wasn't completely aware of those changes until some eight and a half months later.

But really, you have to hear this story from the beginning.

It all began nine months ago, on the day I began to question everything in my life….

# Chapter 1

Maya had always been of two minds about working at the saloon. Of course, it wasn't a five-star restaurant, or even a respectable club. It was where the ordinary folk liked to come to unwind. You would never see the church ladies or the PTA moms on the leather bar stools munching pretzels and sipping beer at the OK Corral. But they didn't have to see Maya waiting tables to know she worked there. It was a small town.

Everyone in Big Falls knew she was a barmaid.

And it probably didn't do her efforts at becoming respectable much good at all. But the thing was, this was the family business. It put food on the table. And it was an honest business, and one her mother had worked hard to make successful. It meant a lot to Vidalia Brand. And respectability or no, family came first with Maya. Always had. That was the way she'd been raised.

So she helped out at the OK Corral, just as her sisters did. Well, all except for Edie. Edie was off in L.A. chasing her own dreams. And respectability didn't seem to be too high on her list.

Anyway, April Fools' night started out like any other Saturday night at the Corral. Kara helped in the kitchen, where her frequent accidents were heard but not seen. Selene waited tables, so long as no meat dishes were ordered. Mel tended bar and served as unofficial bouncer. And Maya did most of the cooking, and gave line dancing lessons, as she did every Tuesday and Saturday.

In fact, the only thing that truly set this particular Saturday night apart from any other was that it was Maya's last Saturday as a twenty-eight-year-old woman. On Sunday, she would turn twenty-nine. And twenty-nine was only twelve months away from thirty. And she was still single, still alone. Still an outcast struggling to make herself acceptable. Still living with her mother and working at the Corral. Still... everything she didn't want to be. Still a virgin.

So she was depressed and moody, and she'd sneaked a couple of beers tonight, which was totally unlike her. As a result, she was just the slightest bit off the bubble, as her mother would have put it, as she walked out of the kitchen. Wiping her hands on her apron, she strained her eyes to adjust to the dimmer light in the bar. Dark hardwood walls and floor, gleaming mahogany bar, sound system turned down low for the moment. Just enough to create a soothing twang underlying the constant clink of ice and glasses, the thud of frosted mugs on the bar, and the low murmur of working men in conversation. The light fixtures were small wagon wheels suspended over every table, a bigger one way up in the rafters dead center. Dimmer switches were essential, of course. The only time the lights got turned up to high beam was when they closed the doors to clean up. The row of ceiling fans over the bar whirred softly and tousled her hair when she walked underneath them.

And then she looked up.

And *he* was there.

He'd just come through the batwing doors from the street

outside. He stopped just inside them, and he looked around as if it were his first time at the Corral. And as Maya looked him over, she thought he seemed just about as depressed and moody as she was.

"Now that looks like a cowboy who's been rode hard and put away wet one too many times," Vidalia said near her ear.

Maya started. She hadn't even heard her mother come up beside her. And though she tried to send her a disapproving glance for her choice of words, she found it tough to take her eyes off the man. "Who is he?" she asked. "I don't recognize him."

Vidalia shrugged. "I don't, either."

He wasn't tall, but he wasn't short, either. Not reed thin or overweight or bursting with muscle. Just an average build. He had dark hair under a battered brown cowboy hat that bore no brand name or markings she could detect. His jeans were faded. His denim shirt unsnapped, untucked and hanging open over a black T-shirt with a single pocket. Even his boots were scuffed and dusty. But none of that was what made her so unable to look away. It was something about his face. His eyes, scanning the bar as if he were looking for something, someone…there was a quiet sorrow about those eyes. A loneliness. A lost look about the man…and it touched off that nurturing instinct of hers from the moment she saw it.

She walked closer without even knowing she was doing it, and those lonely eyes fell on her. Blue. They were deep blue. So blue she could see that vivid color even in this low lighting. His lips curved up in a fake smile of greeting, and she forced hers to do the same. But the smile didn't reach his eyes. They still looked as sad as the eyes of a motherless pup as they latched on to hers as if she were his last hope.

"Can I help you with something?" she asked him at last.

He shrugged. "Can I get a beer?" he asked.

"Well now, this *is* a saloon." She took his arm for some

reason. Kind of the way a mother would take hold of a lost child to lead him home. "Mister, your shirt's wet through."

"That's because it's raining outside."

"Yes, but when it's raining outside, most people stay inside." She took him to a table near the fireplace. It was in the area where the line dancing lessons would be starting up in a short while, but the man was chilled to the bone. He had to be.

He took the seat she showed him and looked at her sheepishly. "I had a flat on my pickup. Had to change the tire in the rain."

"I'd have let it sit there until it let up."

"I hear it hasn't let up in days."

"I suppose you have a point." She signaled Selene, who came right over. "Hot cocoa. Bring a whole pot."

"Um, I asked for a beer."

"Beer will only make you colder. You want to catch your death?"

He blinked up at her, then shrugged in surrender.

"And see if you can find a dry shirt kicking around, will you, Selene?" Maya added.

Selene nodded, tilting her head as she examined the stranger. Of them all, she was the most strikingly different. A throwback to their father's family, Maya supposed. Her hair was long, lustrous, perfectly straight and silvery blond. Her eyes were palest blue, so they, too, often seemed silver. They seemed silver now, as she narrowed them on the man.

"You new in town?" Selene asked him.

"Just passing through," he told her.

Selene's gaze slid from his face, to her sister's. "That's odd. I got the feeling you were here to stay." She shrugged, tipping her head sideways, and said, "Oh, well," as she turned to hurry away.

The stranger sent Maya a questioning glance.

"This month she's convinced she has ESP," she explained. "Last month she was exploring her past lives in Atlantis."

He grinned widely. "Your sister?" he asked.

"How'd you guess?"

"There's a resemblance."

Maya smiled back at him, feeling warm all over just from the light in his eyes. "I'll take that as a compliment."

"You were meant to."

There was something in his eyes that made her heart quiver. She cleared her throat, searched for something to say, and came up with the lamest line in any bar in any town ever. "So, where are you from?"

His smile died. All at once, just like that. He lowered his eyes. Cleared his throat. "Umm...a long ways from here. You wouldn't know it."

"Try me." She wasn't sure why she said it. Curiosity, she supposed. She wanted to know his story. What had hurt him. What had sent him out into the dark rainy night, to a strange town, a strange bar, a strange woman...

He looked up again. Seemed about to say something. Then seemed to change his mind. "Tulsa. I'm from Tulsa."

"Well, now, Tulsa's not far away. And I'm pretty sure everyone in this room has heard of it." She smiled gently at the way his eyes widened, and he looked around. "Hey, don't look so nervous. I'm not gonna tell anyone where you're from if you don't want me to."

His gaze met hers again. Burned into hers. "I appreciate that."

"Are you in some kind of trouble?" she asked.

He shook his head slowly. "I'm not wanted or anything, if that's what you mean."

The reply that popped into her head was that he most certainly *was* wanted. Right now. By her. But she bit her tongue and didn't speak. The fire snapped, and its scent made her nostrils burn. The glow from the flames painted his face in light and shadow, and she took advantage of the chance to explore it more thoroughly. He had a straight nose that began high and was on the large side. It made her think of royalty, that nose. His jawline was sharply delineated, and he hadn't shaved in several hours. A soft dusting of dark whiskers coated his cheeks and his chin. Reaching up, she took off his hat, again moving without thinking first. It was unlike her to be this forward with anyone. But she took the hat off, and it was wet. His hair underneath, though, was dry. Brown and fire-glow red in places, when the firelight hit it. It was thick, wavy, but short. If it grew long, she thought, it would look crimp-curled. But short it couldn't. He kept it that way to keep it tame, she mused. He liked control.

And now who was pretending to have ESP?

"Stealin' my hat, ma'am?" he asked, his voice very soft, very deep, and stroking her nerve endings like callused fingers on velvet.

"Umm…it's wet." Turning away to hide the rush of heat to her face, she hung the hat on one of the pegs beside the fireplace. Then she spoke to him over her shoulder, avoiding his eyes. "Might as well hang that shirt up here, too," she told him.

His reply came from close beside her. "If you say so." A second later, his damp denim brushed her arm as he leaned in close to her to hang it up beside his hat. His shoulder was pressed to hers, his hip…and he looked down slowly, and his mouth was only inches from hers as he turned toward her….

"Ahem!"

Maya jumped, and the stranger spun.

"Your cocoa is here," Selene said, her mysterious silver eyes sliding from one of them to the other. She put the pot on the table, set a cup beside it, and tossed a Denver Broncos sweatshirt over the back of the chair. "It belongs to a friend of mine, so make sure I get it back."

"Thanks," the man said. He took the sweatshirt and pulled

it on over his T-shirt, arms first, then poked his head through and pulled it down around him. He sat down.

Selene stood there watching the two of them intently.

"That'll be all, Selene," Maya said.

Sighing, looking very deep in thought, Selene turned and left them.

"Selene, hmm?" the stranger said. "Fits her."

"You think?"

"Sure. Mystical. Lunar. Isn't it the name of some Greek moon goddess or something?"

"Could have been. Mom used to read lots of mythology."

"So?"

She blinked, saw him looking at her, and, finally, read his eyes. "Oh. Maya. My name is Maya Brand."

His brows went up.

"As in the Earth Mother goddess," she explained.

"And does it fit?"

"Oh, I'm a long way from being anyone's mother. I'm still...that is, I..." She bit her lip. "You haven't told me your name yet."

He averted his eyes. "Caleb."

"Just Caleb?" He didn't answer.

Then she looked at her watch. "I have to go start the line dancing lesson."

He met her eyes, held them. Then, slowly, he got to his feet. "That's great. I've always wanted to learn line dancing."

Oh, hell.

This was not good, whatever it was. She was waiting for a respectable man, with a position of authority. Someone so established that being his wife would set her firmly into the midst of the "good people" of Big Falls and no one would ever think of brushing her off again. She didn't want to get involved with a dirt-poor drifter who couldn't even afford a decent pair of boots. And especially not a man who was just passing through.

Above all else, Maya wanted a man she could depend on. A man who would be there for her, no matter what. One who would climb mountains, swim oceans, if that were what it took to be there when she needed him. A man who would be as honest and loyal and true as…as some TV cowboy. What she didn't want was a drifter or a liar or a cheat. A man like her father, who had never once been around for her mother when the chips were down. A man whose exploits had shamed his entire family so much they were still trying to live them down—even though he'd been dead for over twenty years.

And yet this man—who was already hiding something, keeping some secret behind his blue, blue eyes, and who was obviously a drifter and poor as a church mouse—this man was the one to come along and cause her circuits to overload. Go figure!

It must be physical attraction, she reasoned. But whatever it was, it was powerful. And its timing was damn near uncanny. Especially when she'd only just tonight been bemoaning the fact that she was a year from thirty and still a virgin. Untouched. Untempted…until now. Now she was extremely tempted to forget her morals and her ethics and her goals in life for one brief fling with a man whose eyes told her clearly he would be willing to oblige.

She'd never been so powerfully drawn to a man in her life. Or maybe it was just the beer.

# *Chapter 2*

Maya Brand, he thought as he watched her across the table, pouring his cocoa and stirring it absently and looking at him as if...as if she couldn't look at him enough.

Caleb knew he was running away. Shirking his responsibilities, worrying his father sick, more than likely, and letting a lot of people down. He knew that. And he knew it couldn't go on. He had to go back. To pick up the legacy and carry it forward. It was what was expected of him. His life plan. He'd worked for these goals for years, and it was all coming together finally. In just under a year he would announce his candidacy for the U.S. Senate. He would step into the shoes of his father and grandfather. He would fulfill his destiny.

He didn't know why the hell he'd put on these clothes or borrowed José's pickup or driven clear out into some hole-in-the-wall town. Last minute jitters? A sudden attack of nerves? A desire to sabotage his own success?

Whatever it was, he'd arrived at the door of this little saloon angry, wet, and confused. But this...this was something different.

Maya Brand was an exceptionally beautiful woman. Oh,

not the way most people would think of beauty. Her hair, for example. It just hung there. Not "done" or sprayed. Its color was a deep mink brown. It was very long and wavy, but not curly, exactly. It fell over her shoulders. She didn't fuss with it. Her face...was clean. So clean he could see the slight sprinkling of freckles across the bridge of her nose. Very slight. But there, not covered by makeup. Her shape was not bone thin. She was curvy. Wider at the hip than most women would probably like to be or see as ideal. On her it was good, especially in the snug-fitting jeans she wore. He wanted to rest his hands just above her hips and hold her close to him.

But the most attractive thing about her, he realized with the part of his mind that was still functioning on some rational level, was that she didn't have a clue who he was. She didn't look at him and see Cain Caleb Montgomery III, heir to millions, former mayor, future senator. She didn't see anything but a man in dusty boots and worn-out jeans. And it seemed to him, that she liked him anyway.

Why?

It puzzled him and drew him. What was there about him that she could see to like? He'd been Cain Caleb Montgomery III for so long he wasn't sure who plain old Caleb was anymore. And he found he wanted to know. And he thought maybe this woman might be able to show him.

She went to the center of the floor, where a small crowd had already gathered. Men in their "good" blue jeans and western shirts with pearl snaps. Women in flouncy skirts and cowboy boots. Caleb had never line danced in his life. He figured he would probably make a fool of himself. But it would be worth it just to have an excuse to get close to Maya Brand.

She stepped to the front of the room, looked around, and then glanced at him almost reluctantly. Everyone else had a partner. Everyone but him.

He shrugged. "Looks like you're stuck with me."

She smiled, not just to be polite, he thought. "You say that like it's a bad thing. Come here."

Damn, he liked when she said "Come here."

He moved to stand beside her at the head of the class. Maya waved to the woman at the far end of the bar. The woman at the bar waved back. She looked like a shorter, curvier version of Cher. Exquisite bone structure, dark coloring. Mexican, he thought. She had a head of raven curls that reached to her waist and a few laugh lines around her eyes that only added to her appeal.

Maya called, "Crank it, Mom. Let's start 'em with the Boot Scoot."

Caleb blinked and looked at Maya. *"Mom?"*

"If you're gonna look so shocked, Caleb, you really ought to do it when she's up close enough to enjoy it," Maya told him.

"She's your mother," he said, still not believing it.

"Vidalia Brand, mother of five, and the most notorious female saloon owner in seven counties," Maya told him, and there was an edge of pride in her voice and in her eyes.

"Wow."

The music cranked up, and he had to focus on Maya's instructions and try to imitate her footwork for a time. It was okay, though, because he had to get up close beside her and, every once in a while, hold her hand or slip his arm around her waist, so he didn't mind at all.

And every time he looked down at her, her eyes were sparkling and staring right up into his. And those cheeks were pink with color, lips full and parted as she got a little breathless. He hoped not entirely from the dancing.

Once he had the moves down, they ran through the dance again, without stopping after each step to explain the next one this time. And though he lost himself once or twice, he had it down soon enough, so he could resume the conversation.

"Mother of five, you said."

Maya nodded.

"So the cute one with the short, raven hair, who's tending bar and sending me daggers would be…?"

"That's my sister Mel. She's kicked the stuffing out of some of the baddest men in town. Some of them for far less serious offenses than calling her cute."

He lifted his brows. "But she's so small."

"She's strong, and she's fast, and most importantly, she's mean. Hot tempered anyway. Rides a motorcycle and takes karate lessons. Goes rock climbing. She's a year younger than me, but she kind of sees herself as the protector of the bunch. Guess she figured if our father wasn't around to do it, someone had to."

He nodded, searching her eyes. There had been a flash of pain when she'd mentioned her father. "Would I be out of line if I asked what happened—to your father, I mean?"

She smiled up at him as they moved to the music. "Stick in town more than five minutes and you'll hear all about it. It's the juiciest gossip Big Falls has ever had."

"Yeah?"

"Oh, yeah."

"I'm intrigued."

"Most everyone is."

The music stopped, the dance ended. Maya turned to her group. "Ten-minute break. You know the drill." Some of them wandered off to tables, the rest room, the bar, while others just stepped closer together and wrapped their arms around each other as a slow, sad song came wafting from the speakers.

Before Maya could turn to go, Caleb slid his arms around her waist and pulled her close, started moving her slowly in time to the steel guitar. She tilted her head curiously but didn't pull away. She put her arms around his neck and smiled a little nervously.

"Tell me about your father," he urged her. He wanted to

know all about this woman for some reason. Why did she so intrigue him? Was it because she was exactly the opposite of the political wife his father and the others had described to him? Or was it something more?

She shrugged. "Okay. It's public knowledge, anyway. My father met my mother when she was seventeen. They had a brief affair, and then he went his way and she went hers. By the time she found him again to tell him she was pregnant, he was on the East Coast with a wife of his own. Still, time passed, and he came back. Told Mom things hadn't worked out with his first wife, that they'd split up, and he asked her to marry him. She did."

"Doesn't sound so scandalous to me," he said. He was listening as much to the sound of her voice as to her story. Her tone was deep, rich. Erotically husky.

"Well, that's because I haven't gotten to the scandal yet. See, Daddy wasn't divorced from his first wife. For ten years he managed to get by with two families. He traveled all the time on business—or we thought it was on business. What he was doing was dividing his time between the wife he had in Silver City and the one he had here in Big Falls, Oklahoma."

"He was a bigamist?"

She waggled her brows. "Told you it was scandalous."

"So what happened?" he asked. "Where is he now?"

Maya lowered her head. "He got involved with a bad crowd in Silver City. In the end he tried to mess with the wrong people and was murdered, along with his wife. I never did learn what became of the two kids he had with her. It was only after he was dead that we found out about his other life. By then my mother had five daughters, every last one of us illegitimate. I was young at the time, but I remember it like it was yesterday. It damn near destroyed Mom." She lifted her head, looked across the room with admiration in her eyes. "But she came through it."

"She must be one hell of a woman," he said.

She looked up at him. "She is."

"And she's raised one hell of a daughter," he said.

She lowered her head quickly. "You don't know me well enough to say that."

"I know you well enough to know that I'd like to know you better, Maya Brand. I'd like that a lot."

Thick lashes lowered; then she glanced up from beneath them. "I...think I'd like that, too."

"I'm awfully glad to hear that." He leaned in closer, intending to steal a kiss, but she artfully turned her face away before he could accomplish that. When he lifted his head again, he felt eyes on them from everywhere in the bar, and he thought maybe that was why. Her sisters, her mother—and for some reason, every customer in the place—seemed to be watching them intently.

Okay. So he was going to have to get her alone if he wanted to do anything more than dance with her. It shouldn't be a problem. Nothing he'd ever wanted in life had been difficult for him to have. Especially women.

He stopped himself then. This was different. Always before he'd been Cain Caleb Montgomery. Everyone knew the Montgomerys always got what they wanted. It was a patriarchal dynasty, practically his birthright.

Here, tonight, he was just Caleb. And she was like no other woman he'd ever met.

"I'm sorry," he said. "I was out of line."

She lifted her face to his, and he was tempted to get out of line again. "I can't kiss a man who hasn't even told me his last name, Caleb," she said.

And he got a feeling—a feeling that the way he answered that one, simple question might easily have some great impact he would feel for a long time to come. It was one of those moments when you just sense things looming—like a crossroad. More than anything, he wanted this delicious anonymity to go on. He'd learned more about her—and about himself—

in the last couple of hours than he ever would have or could have as Cain Caleb Montgomery III.

So he made his choice. He chose to lie to her.

"Cain," he said. "My name is Caleb Cain."

She thought he was looking less heartsick than he had when he'd arrived.

And she hadn't minded dancing with him at all. Sure, he was a drifter, on the skids, and from out of town. Sure, he barely had two nickels to rub together, from the looks of him. But tomorrow was her damned birthday, and he was drop-dead good-looking. His touch made her tingle, and she really was getting tired of being good all the time.

No steady boyfriend, no prospects in sight. Hell, one more year and she would be a thirty-year-old virgin. Being the good one was not turning out at all the way she had hoped it would. So if dancing real close and real slow with a handsome stranger was bad, well, then she would be bad. Just for this once.

She ignored the look of surprise on her mother's face when she lifted her head from his shoulder to see her across the room. She ignored the way Vidalia elbowed Mel and pointed at her, and the way Mel's brows came down hard, and the way Selene folded her arms and nodded knowingly. She ignored everything except the man she was with. And how good and strong his arms felt wrapped tightly around her. His breath tickled her ear and her neck, and she grew warmer. Because she might very well be good, and respectable, and pure. But she was also a woman. A Brand woman. And never had she felt it more than she did in this stranger's arms.

At some point later, she realized she was laughing. Laughing out loud up at him, and he was laughing, too. Her skin was warm, and her heart was racing, and she felt incredibly alive.

He walked her back to his table, eyed the now cold cocoa and said, "Am I allowed to have a beer now?"

"Sure you are. In fact, I think I'll join you." She held up two fingers, not even looking toward the bar.

"Think someone saw you?" he asked.

She winked. "Believe me, they haven't taken their eyes off me since you walked in." Then she pursed her lips. "On second thought, I'd better get that beer myself. They're liable to water it down or bring us nonalcohol or something."

He looked surprised but said nothing as she went to the bar.

When she came back, he was deep in conversation with one of her regulars, a local fellow by the name of Jimmy Jones, but they stopped talking the minute she arrived, and Jimmy tipped his hat to her and skulked away, never meeting her eyes.

She set two foaming mugs and a filled pitcher on the table, then sat down and sipped from one. "So what was Jimmy telling you about me?"

"What makes you think he was talking about you?"

She thinned her lips, lowered her brows, gave him *the look.* She'd learned *the look* from her mom, and she was pretty good at delivering it, in her opinion. All the Brand women were.

He smiled. "Okay. You win. He was. He said you come from a wild family. That you Brand girls are the talk of the town."

"Oh, but I already told you about our notoriety."

He smiled. "You left out some things."

She sat down, grinning. "I'm dying to hear. What did he say?"

Tilting his head to one side, Caleb's smile faded. "I don't want to say anything to ruin the night for us, Maya. It's been...too nice."

She drew her brows together, turning to look at Jimmy,

who immediately looked away. "My goodness. It must have been pretty bad."

"No, it really—"

She reached across the table, clasped his hand and said, "I've been putting an awful lot of effort into making myself...respectable in the eyes of the good people of this town, Caleb. It would help me a hell of a lot if you'd be honest with me right now. What did Jimmy say about us?"

He cleared his throat, turned his hand over and closed it around hers. "He seems to think Selene is either a Communist, a Satanist, or both."

She laughed. It came out in a burst, and she clapped a hand over her mouth. Then she took a long drink of beer and said, "She's a vegetarian and a feminist who believes in UFOs, Bigfoot and reincarnation. I suppose that does make her a Communist and a Satanist in Jimmy's eyes."

"You have a beautiful smile, you know that?"

She felt her face heat. "Stop changing the subject. What else did he say?"

He drew a breath. "He seems to think one of your other sisters is...uh...cursed somehow. A 'jinx' is the way he put it."

Again her smile didn't falter. "That would be Kara. She's somewhat accident-prone—and, I have to admit, the men she dates seem to have a tendency to...get hurt. But it's just a string of bad luck." She frowned. "I hope the jerk doesn't let her hear him say something like that."

"If he does, I'll punch him in the nose for you."

She smiled. "You won't have to. Mel will."

"Mel. Right. Jimmy thinks she's a sex fiend. He didn't say it flat out, but he implied she was into whips and dog collars. A dominatrix type."

She rolled her eyes. "It would serve Jimmy right if I told Mel what he said. He's still pissed because she broke his nose last year when he got fresh with Mom."

He nodded. "Then it's safe to say you don't have a sister who's a porn star?"

Her jaw dropped. "Edie is a lingerie model in L.A. Quite a successful one, too. But no, she's no porn star."

"Probably a big relief to your mom," he said lightly.

"Not really. To Mom, there's not that much of a distinction between the two. They haven't spoken since Edie left home."

She pursed her lips, then sipped her beer and set the mug down. "So? What did our friend Jimmy have to say about me?"

Caleb's eyes shifted away from hers. "Nothing."

"Oh, come on, Caleb. Of course he said something about me. What would have been his point in talking to you at all if not about me? Hmm? You're not with Edie or Mel or Kara or Selene tonight. You're with me. So what did he say?"

He shook his head slowly. "He…told me I might as well give it up and go look elsewhere for fun tonight. Told me you don't date, don't even like men."

She leaned back in her chair, took a long pull of her beer. "Well now, this is interesting. I've been wondering what the locals are thinking and saying about me."

He licked his lips, looked away from her.

"What?" she asked, coming upright again. "What's that look?"

"What look?" he asked, still not meeting her eyes.

"*That* look! There it is again! Jimmy Jones said something else, didn't he? He told you what they've been saying about me around town. Didn't he, Caleb?"

Sighing deeply, he finally looked at her. "You don't want to know, hon. Trust me on this one."

"Of course I want to know. I've been bending over backward to become socially acceptable around here. Hell, this is the first real chance I've had to find out how my efforts are panning out. So spill it, Caleb. Tell me what he said."

Caleb pursed his lips. "It's not gonna make you happy,

Maya. And it seemed to me you were starting to enjoy yourself a little bit. You sure you want to ruin all that?''

"Tell me."

He nodded, took a drink of beer, licked the foam off his lips. Made her tummy tighten in response. She took another drink of her own, and he spoke. "He said that as near as anyone can figure, you must be one of two things. Either you're frigid or you're gay."

Maya choked and sprayed beer like a geyser. It hit Caleb square in the chest and rained down on the table between them.

He jumped up automatically, arms out at his sides as the beer dripped from his borrowed sweatshirt.

Maya grabbed a napkin and lunged at him, dabbing his chest, wiping his chin. "God, I'm sorry. I didn't mean—''

He stilled her hands, took the napkin from them and lifted it to gently wipe the beer from her lips. Maya went still, lowered her eyes.

"I shouldn't have told you," he said softly.

"No. No, I needed to know the truth."

"If it helps any, I told Jimmy that if he said another word, I'd knock his teeth out."

She smiled, but it felt weak. "I appreciate that."

"Why does this hurt you so much, Maya? Why do you care what some ignorant fool like Jimmy Jones thinks of you, anyway?"

Closing her eyes, she shook her head slowly. "I've been trying to be the good one. The responsible one. Trying to be good enough for the upper crust residents of Big Falls." She closed her eyes, shook her head. "Trying to be something I guess maybe I'm not and never will be." She sat back down. So did he.

"Hey. Maybe you don't fit in with those kinds of people, Maya, but don't ever think it's because you aren't good enough."

She looked across the table at him, smiled a little. "Thanks for that."

"I meant it. But for the rest of it—I know what you're going through."

"You do? You've been trying to be respectable, too?"

He shrugged and seemed to think about it. "More like I've been trying to live up to other people's expectations of me."

"While I've been trying to live them down."

He smiled at that. "And the results so far have been pretty lousy."

She drew a breath, sighed. "I'm a saint. I live like a nun, but nobody gives me any credit for it."

"I'm expected to live my whole life according to someone else's plan. I've never even questioned it, so they assume I never will."

She drank her beer, surprised to see the bottom of the glass so soon. She was even more surprised when he refilled it for her. "I, um…I don't drink very often," she said.

"Me neither," he said. "But tonight I'm going to do what I want, instead of what other people want me to do. If I want to drink, I'm going to drink. So there."

She pursed her lips, tilted her head. "Yeah. You know what? Me too."

She took a nice long drink. Then she glanced out at the floor, where her dancers were getting ready to begin again. "Ready for round two?" she asked him.

"You lead, lady, and I'll follow."

She did lead. She led him out onto the dance floor, then back to the table for two more beers when the line dancing was done. And then she was on the dance floor with him again when a slow song came on, and everything was different.

He held her closer, tighter, than she had ever been held in her life, and he said softly, "I'm liking this way too much, Maya."

She said, "I am, too."

"Yeah?"

She nodded, looking up into his eyes, liking what she saw there. Feeling the sting of all her efforts to be respectable having failed, the depression over her impending birthday and the effects of too much beer, she knew she was in trouble tonight. And she didn't even care.

"You want to get out of here?" he asked her.

She nodded. "Yeah...I do."

His smile was slow, but gentle somehow. "Your family...?"

She glanced toward the bar. Her younger sister, Mel, was looking decidedly violent just now. Leaning on the hardwood, watching them through narrow eyes. Her short, dark hair and pixielike features hid an explosive temper and a body to match.

Maya felt warm all over in spite of that cold surveillance. Then she frowned at Caleb as a thought occurred to her. "Are you okay to drive?"

"I've only had two beers all night, hon. And the second one's still half full." He nodded toward his mug on the table. "But how about you?"

"It's my birthday," she said, and that was her only reply.

He frowned. Then he looked at her empty mug on the table, and she could almost see him mentally counting how many beers she'd had tonight. Then, licking his lips and sighing deeply, he looked at her again. He said, "As much as I hate to say this, Maya Brand, I think we ought to call it a night. Tell you what. You show me where I can get a room for the night, and we'll continue this tomorrow."

She lowered her head, thinking that she didn't want the night to end so soon. But it was a good sign, she thought. It said a lot about his character. "You're a real gentleman, aren't you, Caleb Cain?"

"I try to be."

She nodded. "Okay, it's a deal."

*   *   *

"So who, exactly, is that stranger?" Mel asked, when Maya carried the empties back to the bar. Caleb had gone to the fireplace for his hat and his shirt, and gone out to start up his truck.

"Hell, sis, he was just a man. Had a flat, changed it in the rain and came in to get warm."

"Well, shoot, since when do we have body heat on the menu?"

"Melusine Brand, you hush up!" Vidalia said. She came out from behind the bar, slipping an arm around Maya's shoulders. "You okay, hon? You look a bit flushed and flustered."

"Fine. Tired, but fine."

"That young man...he new in town?"

She sighed. "Just passing through," she said. And if her regret were audible, she couldn't help it. "He's looking for a room. I said I'd show him the way to the boarding house."

They all looked up at her, silent, eyes wide.

"I'll show him the freaking boarding house," Mel said, balling up her apron and slamming it down, starting around the bar.

Maya grabbed her shoulder, halting her in her tracks. "I'm pushing thirty, Mel. If I want to spend some time with a man, it's my choice to make."

"But...but..."

"She's right, Melusine." Vidalia spoke with authority, and Mel calmed down. She didn't like it. But she backed off.

Then Kara popped out of the kitchen and said, "What's going on? Did someone call a family meeting and forget to tell me?"

"Maya met a handsome stranger," Selene said. She was sitting on a bar stool to the right, playing around with one of those decks of cards she was always messing with. "And now she's going to show him the way to the boarding house."

Kara's eyebrows went up. "The one I saw you dancing with, Maya?" she asked.

Maya nodded.

"Wow. What a hunk."

"Shut up, Kara," Mel snapped.

"He's your soul mate, Maya."

They all turned at once, to see Selene leaning over and staring down at her tarot cards, which she'd laid out in some strange pattern on the gleaming mahogany bar.

"Oh, for the love of..."

"The cards don't lie," Selene said softly.

Maya rolled her eyes. "I'm going now. You all have given me a headache."

Each and every one of them eyed her speculatively as Maya grabbed her coat off the peg near the door, put it on, hoisted her purse and sent them a final wave. She knew what they were thinking...and she didn't particularly care.

"Be careful, sweetheart," she heard her mother say just before she stepped out into the rain. "Don't do anything you'll be sorry for later on."

Those words echoed in Maya's mind and sent a little shiver down her spine. She shook it off, ignored it, pretended not to hear her mother's words over and over again in her head as she tugged her collar up around her, ducked against the rain and ran across the wet parking lot to the battered pickup that waited with its wipers flapping madly and its headlights shining through the rain onto the road sign that said Leaving Big Falls. Come Back Soon!

## Chapter 3

He got out of the truck to run around to her side, open her door and help her in. It was no small distance from the pavement to the pickup floor, after all. And she wasn't long legged.

Funny, he hadn't noticed that before. He usually liked leggy women, taller and thinner than this one. More coiffed. More "done." Or maybe he only thought that was what he liked because he hadn't met Maya Brand.

He stood there watching her the way a scientist would watch an unknown species. She settled into the seat, flipped back the hood of her dark blue raincoat, thrust her fingers into her hair and shook it. He had no idea what that little ritual was, but he liked the result.

Then he realized she was staring at him.

"You're getting all wet again, standing there in the rain, Caleb."

He was, he realized. His shoulders were damp, and a steady drip was running from the brim of his battered hat. He closed her door and ran around to the driver's side to get in. Then he put the truck in gear and prepared to pull out of the parking lot, into the wet, shining, deserted road. "Which way are we headed?"

"South," she said.

He frowned at her, and she smiled. Damn, what a smile she had. "That way," she told him, pointing a finger toward his side of the vehicle.

He turned the wheel to the right, and they were off.

He hated being this noble. But she had been drinking a little bit tonight. And then there was her reaction to the remark that jerk had made about her sexuality. Caleb had been all prepared to take Maya Brand somewhere private and explore that question for himself. But he couldn't do that to her now. So he'd just stick around in this town for a day longer, see her again when she was clearheaded and he could be sure she was with him because she wanted to be.

She told him where to turn off the main road, and he found himself driving over what was little more than a muddy path, barely wide enough for one vehicle. He worried where he would go if another one came along.

"Are you sure this is the right way?" he asked her.

"Uh-huh. I sure am. Just keep going."

He flicked the wipers down a notch as the rain seemed to ease off, and he kept going.

"See that turnoff there?"

"You mean that deer trail?" he asked, sounding skeptical.

She laughed. It was a deep and throaty sound that made him squirm with awareness. "Trust me," she said.

She had, he mused, an honest face. So he turned. But he didn't find a boarding house when he drove in through the tall red pines lining the path. What opened out before him was startling enough to make him hit the brake pedal. Then he put the truck in Park, shut it off and just looked.

He'd driven right up to the face of a waterfall. So big that about all he could see through the windshield was a wall of froth. He didn't say anything, and after a moment, he realized he was holding his breath.

"No one should come to Big Falls without seeing...well, the big falls," Maya said. As she spoke she was opening her door, sliding out of the pickup truck.

Caleb followed suit, stepping out of the truck onto a flat, stony bit of ground that seemed solid enough. Tipping his head back, he looked up to where the falls began, high above. In front of him, about ten feet, the ground ended, and when he looked down over the drop he saw a river unwinding a few yards below. That river was all that stood between him and the massive waterfall.

"This is incredible," he told her.

"I thought you might like it." She walked away from him, and he turned to see what she was up to. He watched her as she looked around, then she frowned, shaking her head.

"What's wrong?"

"Look."

He did, seeing what she was pointing out. A ring of stones, surrounding the charred remains of someone's campfire. Around that, on the ground, a dozen or more beer cans and soft drink bottles were scattered. She bent and started picking them up. "This is a favorite spot for partying." She carried an armload of cans to the truck and tossed them in the back. "We can dump them in the bin back in town."

"Sounds like a plan." He went to pick up the rest of the cans and took them to the truck. Then they both stood there, beside the pickup. He pretended to be looking at the falls, but mostly he was stealing sideways glances at her. He didn't really know what to do next...what she'd had in mind when she'd steered him way up here.

Licking her lips, seeming just as nervous as he was, she said, "The rain's letting up."

He tipped his face up to the sky, then took off his hat and shook the water off it. "Looks like it's stopped altogether."

He opened the pickup door, tossed the hat inside, didn't bother closing the door again. Maya was right, it had stopped raining. The only moisture hitting his face now was the spray from the falls. He watched the clouds skitter away from the tiny sliver of the waning moon above. A few stars managed to shine, too.

When he looked down again, it was to see Maya staring at him, her face tipped up to his. Licking his lips, and knowing he shouldn't, Caleb slid his hands around her waist anyway. "I'm going to kiss you now, Maya Brand," he said.

"It's about time, Caleb Cain," she replied, and her palms slid up the front of him to curl around his shoulders.

He lowered his head and pressed his mouth to hers, pulled her closer, kissed her. It was good. He'd been wanting to kiss this woman for hours now, and it was every bit as good as he'd imagined it would be. Her lips were soft and willing to do whatever his suggested. So when he nudged them apart, she complied right away. She shivered against him just a little when he touched the soft curve of her upper lip with his tongue, and he felt the breath stutter out of her mouth into his. Encouraged, he delved deeper, tasted her fully. She tasted like beer. And that was a reminder to him that none of this was a very good idea.

But then her hips arched against him, and he groaned and kept kissing her. His hands slid down to cup her backside, and when he squeezed her closer, she wriggled against him in a way that almost made him roar as loudly as the falls were doing.

He lifted his head and stared down into her glittering, heavy-lidded eyes. "If you want to stop, Maya, now would be the time to tell me."

She shook her head once from side to side and shucked off her jacket, letting it fall to the rain-wet ground.

"You...you've had a few beers."

"Not *that* many." Her hands came to his chest, her fingers

flicking the snaps of the denim shirt open and pushing it down over his shoulders.

"You were upset by what that redneck said in the saloon."

"Was I?" Her hands went to her own blouse now. It was white, button-down, clean. She undid the buttons one by one, opening the blouse. She wore a white cotton bra...which she filled to overflowing.

"It's...it's cold and d-damp out here."

The blouse came off. She tossed it to the ground with the coat. The bra came next. "You're right, it is."

"Oh, hell." His hands covered her breasts before he could give them permission. Weighty and full, nipples taut with the bite of the chilly air. He ran his thumbs over them and watched her catch her lower lip between her teeth and close her eyes.

"You're an adult woman," he said. "Who the hell am I to tell you what's good for you?"

Her hands again, tugging his T-shirt over his head, and he didn't want to let her breasts go long enough to take it off, but he did, and when he touched them again he used his mouth. The hell with nobility. She'd only had three beers. He'd counted several times in his head since they left that bar. Three beers. She was not incapacitated. And she was not young or innocent or naive. And he was only human.

Warm flesh and stiff nipples on his tongue made him hungry for more, and when her fingers tangled in his hair to hold him to her, he suckled her harder, nipped with his teeth, tugged and pulled at her nipple until she made whimpering sounds and fell back against the side of the pickup. Her nails dug into his back. He attacked her other breast, pressing her back to the cold metal of the truck as his hands tugged at her jeans, found the button, found the zipper, shoved them down hard and fast, baring her from waist to ankles in one hurried motion. She kicked the jeans off, tearing free of her boots at the same time. He looked her over and shivered. Then he closed his hands at her waist and lifted her, set her bare bottom on the seat of the pickup, shoved her legs apart and bent to bury his face in between. He tasted her. Salt and woman coated his tongue, and he delved deeper, spread her wider, tasted every part of her, until she was quivering and moaning and tugging at his hair and shaking. So close to ecstasy. But he didn't take her there…not yet.

He fumbled with his jeans, freed himself, and again clasped her waist and lifted her, pulling her forward this time, and down. Wrapping her legs around his waist and settling her over him, he managed not to move for one brief moment. Teeth grated, he whispered, "You sure, Maya?"

Her answer was a pleading sound from deep in her throat as she rocked her hips. So he pulled her lower, sheathed himself slowly inside her heat. And it was so good his knees nearly buckled. And when she moved lower and cried out, his knees did buckle, and he lowered them both to the ground, because he couldn't do otherwise.

Her coat was his bed as he fell backward, pulling her with him. They moved together, and he forgot to think, to perform, to do anything, as they rolled and clung and twined around each other. Until at last he lost himself to his climax as she trembled and murmured his name and then screamed it out loud.

Breathless and weak, he enfolded her in his arms, and they lay there on the damp ground for a few moments, sated. But then their body heat cooled, and she shivered in his arms.

"Let's get you out of the cold," he told her.

She didn't reply. He pulled back so he could look at her face. Closed eyes, relaxed features, maybe a hint of a smile. And another shiver.

"Sound asleep," he muttered. "Guess that says a lot about my technique, doesn't it?"

He got to his feet, and began to put her clothes back on her. Her pretty white blouse was stained with mud here and there, but he pulled it over her arms as she hung like a rag doll in his. Then he buttoned it up with no small amount of regret. Her coat was going to be a real mess, once they got off it and picked it up off the wet ground. But before he could do that, he had to replace her panties, which were easy, and her jeans, which were not.

She stirred when he wrestled her into the jeans, opened her eyes and smiled crookedly at him. And it occurred to him for one, panicked moment that maybe she'd had more than three beers tonight after all. Maybe she'd been drinking before he'd ever arrived on the scene.

A rush of guilt swamped him, and he closed his eyes. Please, fate, he thought, don't let me have taken advantage of a woman too inebriated to consent. He was a lawyer before he'd ever been a politician. That was the way it was done in the Montgomery family. And he knew damned good and well what a rape charge would do to his political career.

"Caleb," she muttered.

He looked at her, at the pure honest goodness of her. "I'm an idiot. You're not the vindictive type, are you, Maya?" He asked the question as he put on his own clothes.

"Hmm?"

He cupped her chin. "Tell me you wanted this."

She smiled. Then she hiccuped. Caleb closed his eyes tightly and felt a bit ill. "Oh my God," he whispered. "How much have you had to drink tonight, Maya?"

She shrugged. "I don't drink," she said.

"Not ever?" He blinked in surprise.

She shook her head. "It wouldn't look good...you know, to the church ladies."

"Church ladies, huh?"

He wrapped his arms around her and helped her get to her feet. She leaned against him as he picked up her coat, but it was soaked almost clear through. So he put the denim shirt he'd been wearing around her shoulders, and walked her toward the passenger side of the truck.

"Caleb?"

He looked down at her. "What, hon?"

"Is sex always...so...so...you know? Good?"

Caleb stopped walking. "Well...no. Not always. At least, it hasn't been for me. How about you?"

Her grin was shy and beautiful as she lowered her head. "I wouldn't know," she said very softly.

She might as well have picked him up over her head and tossed him into that river. "What do you mean, you wouldn't know?" She reached for the door handle. "Maya? Are you telling me that this was...that you were a...a...?"

"Virgin."

She said it flatly.

"Oh, hell."

She shrugged. "Tomorrow's my birthday," she said. And she smiled a smug little satisfied smile as if that were supposed to mean something quite profound. Then she stepped up into the pickup, only she missed the step and almost fell face first—would have, if he hadn't caught her.

What the hell had he done here? He could see the headlines now.

Senatorial Candidate's Night On The Town:
Montgomery Deflowers Virginal Good Girl After
Getting Her Too Drunk To Say No!

"Oh, hell," he said again. He helped her into the truck. Closed the door. Then he went around to the other side and got in himself. He started the engine, then sat there a minute resting his head on the steering wheel.

"Are you all right, Caleb?" she asked him.

He glanced sideways at her. Wide eyes just as blue as the sky on a clear summer day. That sprinkling of freckles. The look of pure relaxed contentment. She was *not* a political disaster waiting to happen. She was an angel who'd given him a night he would never forget. Smiling crookedly, he reached out, cupped her face with his hand, and said, "Probably you'd do well not to tell anyone about this."

She smiled back at him. "I might be tempted to.... I mean, just to prove that the current theory is wrong."

He knew what she meant. What that redneck at the saloon had said, that she was either frigid or gay. The jerk didn't have a clue. Maya Brand was made for loving.

"I won't tell, though," she said. "Caleb...tonight was about proving something to myself, not so much to the rest of this town." She shrugged. "Besides, I really think I'm starting to make some inroads with the church ladies. No sense blowing it now."

He nodded. "No regrets, Maya?"

She shook her head, then tilted it to one side. "Not a one. You?"

"Not a one."

"You're a good man, Caleb Cain," she told him softly. "I can tell."

"You really think so?"

"Uh-huh."

He backed around, drove down the path from the falls, and turned onto the road to head back the way they'd come.

"Whoever is trying to tell you what to do with your life... don't you let them. I get the feeling a man like you won't be happy unless you're doing what you want to do...not what someone else thinks you should."

"What did you do, Maya? Catch your sister's ESP?"

She shrugged. "Maybe I did. Turn right down here."

He did, driving in silence along Main Street. It was charming, small. Rockwellesque, with an Oklahoma twist.

"That building there on the left—that's Ida-May's boarding house. Our place is another five miles along this road. Think you can find your way back alone?''

''I think so.''

''Good.''

He kept driving. She was silent, but he got the feeling she wanted to ask him something. Finally he pulled into the driveway of the old-fashioned farmhouse, white with red shutters. Every light inside blazing. A small red barn stood off to the left. Maya turned to him and said, ''You *are* staying the night at the boarding house, aren't you, Caleb?''

He smiled at her. ''Of course I am. I'm going to want to see you again, lady.''

She brightened. Then he pulled her close and kissed her, long and slow. And even while a little voice told him this was not possible, his heart kept whispering that it was. That it had to be.

When he lifted his head she flung open her door, jumped out and ran all the way to the house, not even giving him a chance to walk her to the front door. She waved once, then went inside.

Caleb turned the truck around and drove away.

It was late. He was feeling guilty. Decidedly guilty. Running away like a child was a selfish thing to do. Not that he regretted it. But maybe it was time for him to do what Maya had suggested. Figure out what he wanted his life to be, instead of continuing to live by the expectations of other people.

Maybe it was time he made his own decisions.

He flipped open the glove compartment and pulled out his cell phone. He'd had it turned off, until now. But he supposed the right thing to do would be to call his father, tell him that he was having some doubts about his future, and that he would be back just as soon as he decided what *he* wanted to do with the rest of his life.

Maybe he didn't want to tie himself to the city. To a senate seat. To a political alliance instead of a marriage.

He hit the power button on the phone. Glanced down at the lighted number pad. Before he could punch the first number, the phone bleated in his hand, startling him so much that he damn near dropped it.

Frowning, he brought it to his ear. "Hello?"

"Caleb! Thank God we've finally reached you!"

His heart iced over at the tone of the voice even before he recognized it as that of Bobby McAllister, his longtime friend and adviser. And even before Bobby said the last words Caleb had expected to hear.

"You're father's had a stroke, Caleb. We need you to get home right away."

For a moment he couldn't speak. He was too stunned to speak as the information registered. And when it did, his first instinct was to deny it. To accuse Bobby of lying, but of course he knew better. "My God," he finally managed. "Is he...?"

"We don't know anything yet. He's in the hospital. It's... it's serious, Caleb. Please. Get home."

"I'll be there in two hours," he said. He tossed the phone down and pressed the accelerator to the floor.

# Chapter 4

Maya walked into the familiar comfort of the farmhouse with a crooked smile on her face. She sailed past her mother and her sisters, ignored all their questions and demands, and floated up the stairs to her bedroom. She was asleep almost before her hair dampened the pillows.

Twelve hours later, she gradually came to. It was a dull, foggy sort of awakening, and it came with a pounding head and a queasiness in her stomach that grew worse by several degrees when she tried to move.

"Damn," she moaned. "Why am I so…?"

And then memory came. And she sat up fast, despite the rush of dizziness. "Oh my God, what have I done?"

"That's the best question I've heard in a while."

Maya turned toward the sound of her mother's voice. Vidalia had been sitting in a chair by the window, but she rose now. Her waist-long ebony curls were pulled around to one side in a ponytail that trailed down over her shoulder. She wore jeans that showed off a figure no woman her age ought to still have, and a denim blouse with flowers embroidered at the shoulders.

"Oh, Mom." Maya put her hand to her head and fell back on the pillows limply.

"You wanna tell me about it?"

Tears burned at the backs of her eyes, and she kept them squeezed tight. "I don't know what got into me."

She heard soft steps as her mother crossed the room, felt the shift of the mattress as Vidalia sat down on its edge. A comforting whiff of her mother's violet-scented talc reached her senses. As fresh as all outdoors. "Come on, sit up. Sip this," the soothing voice said, and a cool hand stroked her hair away from her face. "I had a feelin' you'd be sick this morning. As little as you touch the stuff, even a beer or two can make you sick."

Maya forced her eyes open and saw that her mother's other hand held a glass of what looked like tomato juice and smelled like the spice aisle at Gayle's Grocery. She grimaced, but she sipped. And when the tiniest relief seemed to coat her stomach, she sipped some more.

"Now I want you to stop beatin' yourself up over whatever happened last night," Vidalia said.

"You wouldn't say that if you *knew* what happened last night."

Her mother smiled. "Well, now, let me take a stab at it, hmm? You got the birthday blues. Lord knows, child, I've had 'em, too. They hit you any time you turn an age that ends in nine. Except for nineteen, of course, which doesn't count."

Maya frowned and lifted her head.

"Drink," her mother said. So she drank. And Vidalia went on. "Oh, people tend to think these crisis points hit us at the round numbers. Thirty, forty, fifty. But they don't. It's the dang nines. By the time you turn thirty, you'll have had a year to get used to the idea of turning thirty. But twenty-nine—well now, that's a shocker. All of a sudden you're looking at thirty seriously for the first time."

Draining the glass, Maya set it aside.

"Better?" Vidalia asked.

"Stomach is. Head still aches though."

"Give it time to work. Old family remedies never fail. Now, where was I?"

"Trying to make me feel like I haven't done something horrible."

"Oh, right." Again, Vidalia smiled. "So you had a couple of drinks last night. And a handsome cowboy came along, and you had a good time with him. It's not the end of the world, you know."

Swallowing hard, lowering her gaze, Maya said, "I took him up to the falls, Mom. I...we..." She bit her lip. "God, what was I thinking?"

Stroking her hair, which was her specialty, Vidalia said, "You had sex with him?"

Maya nodded, feeling as guilty as a schoolgirl caught cheating on a final exam.

"Hon, you're twenty-nine years old. And sex is a celebration of life. It's acknowledging that you're not just a good, decent, upstanding, respectable person, but a woman. A real live red-blooded glorious woman. And that's okay. There's nothing wrong with that."

Maya looked up, sniffling. "You really think so?"

"Of course I do. It's part of bein' alive. So long as you used protection, there's not a thing in the world wrong with a grown woman..." She let her voice trail off, probably because Maya's eyes had flown suddenly wider and her hand had clapped to her mouth. "Maya? Honey? You...you did use protection. Didn't you?"

Her mother pulled Maya's hand from her mouth. *"Didn't you?"* she repeated.

"I...I don't...know. I mean, it was dark, and I was..."

"You were what?"

Maya swallowed hard. "I was...drunk."

Vidalia blinked. "How drunk?" When Maya didn't answer, she slammed her hands to her thighs. "Maya, I'd have never let you leave with him if I thought you'd had more than a beer or two!"

"I just...wasn't thinking last night. God, Mom, I don't know if he used protection or not!"

Closing her eyes slowly, her mother sighed. "I think that's something you might want to find out, child."

Nodding hard, Maya got out of bed and looked down to see that she was still wearing the same clothes she'd had on last night. Her white blouse had mud stains here and there, and her jeans were wrinkled. But there was a new addition to her ensemble. Caleb's denim shirt. "I'll shower, and then I'll go talk to him. He's staying over at the boarding house." Then she paused, and a smile tugged at her lips. "He said he wanted to see me again."

Her mother bit her lip, saying nothing.

"I really like this man, Mom. I mean...he's not what I thought I wanted...not well-off or respectable or any of that... but there's something about him."

Sighing softly, Vidalia managed a smile that looked shaky. "Well now, that's nice, hon. That's real nice. You go shower now. Go on."

Nodding, Maya hurried into the bathroom.

She used the hair dryer, so her brown hair was bouncier and seemed thicker than usual. She wore a pastel blue dress with an A-line skirt and a tab collar. And she even added a hint of makeup, something she so seldom did that she had to borrow it from Selene's room. She looked in the mirror and nodded in approval. She looked perfect. Respectable. Good. Even pretty. If she had time, she thought, she would bake some cookies or something, but that would have to wait. Surely Caleb would be staying on for a little while. Even though she'd been drinking last night, she'd still felt something—something extraordinary—between them. He had to have felt it, too.

He had to.

She took the beat-up station wagon and drove into town, taking her time, humming a little along with the country song on the radio. Then she pulled into the tiny lot at the boarding house. And the first whisper of doubt crept along her spine when she didn't see his rusty pickup parked there.

Still, she got out and went through the front door to the big screened in front porch, and across that to the inner door, where she rang the bell.

Ida-May Peabody answered in a moment, greeting her with raised eyebrows. "Why, Maya Brand. Aren't you looking nice today! Whatever brings you here first thing in the morning?"

"A guest of yours...left something at the saloon last night," Maya said, holding up the shirt. "I've come by to return it."

Mrs. Peabody blinked. "But, hon, I've only got two folks staying here. Maddy Sumner's cousin, Lois, who's here for the wedding, and Ol' Hank."

She shook her head. "This man would have just checked in last night, late last night," she said. "Caleb Cain?"

The woman shook her head.

Fighting a rising sense of unease, Maya rushed on. "He's about so tall, dark hair, blue eyes, early thirties or so...." But Mrs. Peabody just kept on shaking her head from side to side, very slowly. "Are you *sure?*"

"Sorry, Maya. No one like that has been near the place."

Closing her eyes slowly, drawing a deep breath, Maya said, "Thanks, anyway, Mrs. Peabody. I must have misunderstood him. Sorry to have bothered you."

"No trouble, dear." Mrs. Peabody closed the door, and left Maya standing there, holding the stranger's shirt and feeling a little bit used. A little bit betrayed. And a whole lot disappointed.

"I have no one to blame but myself," she muttered, drumming up the will to turn and walk back to her car. She got in, tossed the shirt into the passenger side and told herself she shouldn't be crushed over this. She should chalk it up to experience, hope to God there would be no life-threatening or life-altering repercussions, and move on.

She should.

So why did she have the feeling that wasn't going to be as easy as it ought to be?

Three weeks later, her mother dragged her to an appointment with Dr. Sheila Stone, an ob-gyn in the nearby town of Tucker Lake. And while she knew these things were necessary, Maya hated every second of it all the same. Still, the doctor—a stern, handsome redhead with close-cropped hair and wire-rim glasses—took blood and urine samples, and subjected Maya to a thorough exam and a handful of advice.

"I assume you realize the chance you took by having casual sex with a man you didn't know," Dr. Stone said. "I'm not here to lecture you on morality or even stupidity, Maya. But for the love of God, use a condom next time."

"I told you, I was drinking. This is totally out of character for me, and it won't happen again."

Her face softening, Dr. Stone nodded. "We all do dumb things sometimes, I suppose. Are you worried?"

"Shouldn't I be? Wouldn't you be, Dr. Stone?"

"Yes, I guess I would. And my patients call me Dr. Sheila."

"I don't plan to be one of your patients," Maya said. "This is a one-time visit."

Removing her gloves, Dr. Sheila went to the sink to wash her hands. "Actually, Maya, the truth is you're going to have to come back a few more times."

Maya blinked. "I am?"

"I'm afraid so." She tugged paper towels, wiped her hands dry. "Certain venereal diseases or pregnancy should show up right away, of course. But for HIV...well, you're going to have be tested again in six weeks, and after that in six months, and after that—"

Maya held up a hand. "This is insane."

"That's what I try to tell people. It *is* insane—especially when a ninety-nine-cent item in a foil wrapper would prevent all the worry. Well, most of it, anyway."

Sighing, Maya said, "What if I can find the man?"

The doctor shrugged. "Well, *if* he were willing to be tested, and *if* his test came back clean, and *if* he was the only person you'd had sexual contact with—then we could rest assured you hadn't contracted the virus."

Maya drew a deep breath, held it a long moment, and sighed. "Then I suppose I should swallow my pride and contact him."

"I suppose you should." Turning, she walked to the counter and glanced down at the urine sample to which she'd added chemicals. She was very still for a moment.

"Dr. Sheila?" Maya asked, sliding off the table to pull on her jeans and button them. "What is it? Is something wrong?"

Turning, the woman looked at her. "We're going to need to confirm this with the blood work, Maya...but, um... according to this...you're pregnant."

Maya stopped moving. She was standing there with a paper gown on top and a pair of jeans on the bottom, in her sock feet, and this woman was saying something in a foreign language. It made no sense. It did not translate. It was not comprehensible.

Dr. Sheila came forward and gripped Maya's arms. Gently she led her to a chair and eased her into it. "Are you okay?"

Blinking against the shock, Maya tried to talk, but all that

came out was a whisper, and it wasn't what she'd planned to
say at all.

"I want my mother," she rasped.

"I'll get her."

Caleb spent several tense days at his father's bedside,
racked with guilt over having been out of town when his dad
needed him most. But he was back home now. And if this
episode had taught him anything, it was that you couldn't run
away from your duty. Your heritage. Your responsibilities.
He was expected to play a certain role in life, and he damn
well would.

Running away in search of something simpler, something
better, had only brought on disaster. And the pipe dreams he'd
been indulging in that night? About settling down, about setting up a law office in a little one-horse town. About living
there in a farmhouse with vines up one side, and a big dog,
and maybe a duck pond in back. About marrying a daisy-
fresh wife who had freckles on the bridge of her nose and
looked great in blue jeans. They were just that—pipe dreams.

It was just as well this had happened when it had, if it had
to happen at all. Before he did something foolish. Before he
forgot who he was.

Still, every now and then he would find himself staring out
at a rainy night sky and remembering...thinking again about
that incredible woman he'd met and the night they'd spent
together. Maya Brand. Even her name was one of a kind.

Had she been disappointed to find him gone the next morning? Or just angry? He wondered if he'd hurt her—and hoped
he hadn't. A little voice told him he knew damn well he'd
hurt her. It had been her first time. Women took things like
that to heart. Still, she would be fine, a woman like that.
Smart, capable. Surrounded by family. She would be just fine.
And sooner or later she would find a man far better for her
than he was. Far better.

It was good he'd had to come home, before things got too complicated between them. As it turned out, it had been just a brief interlude. One night of...

What?

That was what bugged him. Try as he might, he couldn't quite think of that time with Maya as a one-night stand or a meaningless sexual encounter between two consenting adults. He couldn't.

Maybe someday he would go back there and...

But no. No. It wasn't meant to be. He had to be here, taking care of his father's interests. Setting his own future into motion. She had to be there, in that little town, with her sisters and her mom. He would probably forget her soon. She would forget him, too.

It was for the best.

Damn, why did that sound like such a lie?

Maya spent the next five weeks just trying to absorb the unavoidable facts. First, that she was pregnant, unmarried and destined to become the most scandalous member of her notorious family. All she'd worked for—the image she'd tried so hard to cultivate as the respectable one, the responsible one, the sane one—all of that was gone—or would be the second word got around town about her condition.

The second fact staring her in the face became cruelly obvious when Mel insisted on trying to locate Caleb Cain of Tulsa to tell him that he was going to be a father. There was no such person. He'd lied to her.

So there it was. And she wallowed in it for those first five weeks, and even for a while after that. She stopped going out, stopped helping at the saloon. She stopped dressing, for the most part. Spent her days in sweats or her nightgown. In the mornings she was too ill to feel like dressing, and in the afternoon, she figured, why bother? She did all her usual domestic tasks, which gave her some comfort. Baking cookies and bread. *Eating* cookies and bread. Sewing and quilting and knitting. But, for the most part, she moped.

Until one bright, sunny morning on the first day of June, when Vidalia marched through Maya's bedroom door, flicked on the bright overhead light and said, "Time's up, daughter. Now get out of that rocking chair, get a smile on that face and put some clothes on."

Looking up, her knitting in her hand, Maya blinked in the light. She liked it dim. Dark. It was easier to dwell on her ruined life that way. "Leave me alone, Mom."

"I will not leave you alone." Vidalia went to the closet, flipped hangers until she found a sunny yellow dress, then tossed it onto the bed. "I've left you alone for long enough already. Thought I'd give you time to absorb this. And like I said, that time's up."

She walked to the rocking chair, took the knitting from Maya's hands and placed it in the basket on the floor. "No more feeling sorry for yourself, girl."

"What would you suggest I do instead?"

"Get up on your feet and act like the daughter I raised instead of some watercolor wimp. You're a Brand, Maya. And you've been given a gift more precious than any other you'll ever know. A child. You should be down on your knees giving thanks, not pouting as if you've been cursed. You want my granddaughter to think she's unwanted? Hmm?"

"How do you know it's a girl?" Maya asked.

Her mother drew her brows together tight and tipped her head to one side, giving Maya the look that said she'd asked a foolish question. Then she gripped Maya's arms and drew her to her feet. "Come on. In the shower. If I can handle five of you all by myself, you can certainly deal with one when you've got all of us to help you."

"I know that."

"Then act like it. You don't need any man to get through life, daughter. You're all you need. *You.*" She poked Maya's chest. "And her," she said, laying a gentle hand on Maya's belly. "That's all. Your sisters and I are an added bonus. Now march in there and shower, then dress and get your tail down to the saloon. Wound-lickin' time is over."

Her mother was right, Maya realized. She had been wallowing in a nice thick mire of self-pity. She'd been lied to, used and left behind. She was pregnant and alone and scared to death, and everything she'd ever wanted out of life suddenly seemed impossible.

But it wasn't. Not really. She could bounce back from this. Somehow.

She pressed her palms to her belly. There was the baby to think about now. What kind of a mother would she be? Depressed, moody, sullen all the time? Or alive and loving and happy?

Sighing, she looked down. "Your grandma's right, little one. Mamma's all through sulking now. Promise."

Vidalia nodded in approval. "Good girl." She left Maya to get her act together.

So Maya showered, and she dressed. She was glad her mother had chosen the sunny yellow dress, rather than something snug fitting, because she felt as if her belly was already beginning to swell just a bit. Her mother insisted that was all in her imagination, but she felt it all the same.

There was a tap at the door, and Maya turned, yellow dress in place, hair still bundled in a towel. Selene stepped in, grabbed her hand and pulled her into the hall. "You've gotta see this!" she said.

"Slow down. Selene! What's going on?"

But Selene ran, tugging Maya behind her, down the hall, into her own room. Then she stopped and pointed at the little table in the corner. It was covered in odd items, that table. Shells, rocks, candles. And, right now, those tarot cards Selene was always playing with. Two of them lay face up on the table.

Maya eyed the cards, because Selene seemed so excited about something, but they made little sense to her. One looked like a clown juggling, and the other was a nude woman with some sort of baton in each hand.

"So?" Maya asked, looking at Selene.

"Maya! You're having twins!"

Maya tried not to laugh, she really did. But it escaped her anyway, in a big gust, when she couldn't hold it in any longer. She held her belly, and snorted and roared so hard her sides hurt. So hard her eyes watered.

"This isn't funny!" Selene said. "I'm telling you, it's twins, Maya. Look at the cards!"

Maya glanced at them again, still trembling with laughter, but neither card had any babies on it, much less two of them. She got her laughter under control, gave her sister a gentle hug and said, "I love you, you flaky little weirdo. Twins." And, laughing some more, she went back to her own room; then, grabbing her shoes, she headed downstairs.

It was good to have a family, even an oddball crew like this—or *especially* an oddball crew like this. She'd needed a good laugh to snap her out of her well of misery. It was time to take charge of her life again.

She needed things. Baby furniture and clothes, a bigger vehicle, just for starters. She needed to get a nursery ready in this old house. There was so much to be done. So many plans to make.

For the first time she began to allow herself to get a little bit excited about the notion of being a mother. And the image her mother had painted for her, of another little girl in the family, warmed her inside. She missed having little girls running around this old house. She'd been a second mom to her sisters, being the oldest of them.

And now maybe she would have a little girl of her own.

Man, one thing was for sure, this baby would be the most spoiled child in seven counties if Maya's sisters and mother had anything to say about things. The most protected, too. And the most loved.

She smiled, shaking her head yet again at Selene and her silly notions. But between the two of them, Vidalia and Selene had managed to snap her out of her state of melancholia. There was so much to be done! She'd wasted far too much time already.

# Chapter 5

*Eight and a half months later...*

Sighing, Maya walked, belly first, to the kitchen window, parted the red-checked curtains and stared out at the snowdrifts and blinding white sky. It was crispy cold outside. In here it was warm and fragrant. She had molasses cookies baking in the oven, a nice stew in the slow cooker. No husband to cook for—not that she needed one. No children. Yet. She really was going to be a fantastic mother, she thought, pressing her palms to her expanded belly. And as long as she lived, she would never, ever do anything to embarrass her children. Not ever. And eventually she would prove to this town that a woman could be a single mother *and* an upstanding citizen. They would accept her into that exclusive club of the respectable and socially acceptable. They *would.*

The back door opened, admitting a rush of frigid wind and bundled bodies. Vidalia stomped the snow off her boots, and whipped off her red-and-white striped scarf and matching hat, an act that set the mass of jet black curls free. She was far too old, Maya thought, to keep her hair so long. Much less dress the way she did. Then again, her mother wasn't old. Not even fifty yet. Vidalia's coat came off, revealing skintight designer jeans and a black spandex top. She kept herself in great shape for a woman her age. She had every right to be proud of her looks. If only she wasn't so determined to be loyal to the memory of her long-dead husband, she might even find love again.

And if she said that out loud, her mother would probably smack her.

"Mmm, molasses cookies, Maya?" Vidalia asked, sniffing the air. "Hot damn, they smell better than a hard man on a hot day."

*"Mother."*

Vidalia shrugged and sent her a wink, her black eyes sparkling. "Still miserable, I see. Just checking."

"I'm not miserable. I'm tired, and my back is killing me, and I keep getting horrible leg cramps that make me want to claw the flowers off the wallpaper, but I am not the least bit miserable." Maya went to the oven, opened it and bent to check the cookies, but couldn't bend very far. Sighing, she gave up and reached for a pot holder.

"Let me get them," Kara said, hurrying off with her coat and coming forward. Towering over them all at five-eleven, she snatched the pot holders from Maya in spite of Maya's protests. Kara was too tall for her own good, and her feet were too big, and she was always tripping over them. Kara the Klutz was the nickname bandied around town, but never in front of her sisters—at least, not since the time Mel had overheard it and left the unfortunate speaker with a bloody nose and a split lip.

"Really, Kara, I can manage," Maya said.

"You should be sitting down with your feet up," her sister argued.

"Kara's right, hon." Vidalia took Maya's arm, and urged

her toward a chair. And Maya could only look grimly back at the damp coats hanging on the peg near the door, snowy boots dripping all over the mat underneath them, and then at Kara and whatever mess would come next. With a sigh of resignation, she sat down as her mother instructed, even as Kara got the tray of cookies out, burned her finger, tripped over her foot and sent cookies flying everywhere.

Vidalia pressed her lips together to keep from saying a word, as poor Kara stared helplessly at the cookies falling to the floor. Then she tossed the cookie sheet toward the sink, turned and ran gracelessly out of the room. Maya heard her feet pounding up the stairs.

She looked at the mess, then at her mother. "What's wrong with her? She usually laughs it off when she does stuff like that."

"Kara had a bad day, hon. Or...her latest beau did anyway." She clicked her tongue. "Poor Billy."

"Oh, no." Maya closed her eyes. "What happened to this one?"

"Bus hit him when he was crossing the street." Vidalia bent to begin picking up the fallen cookies. Her jeans were so tight Maya was amazed the woman could bend at all, but that was her mother. She was nothing if not flexible. "Billy was blaming it on the snowy roads until one of those damned nurses over at General started telling him about Peter and Mike. By the time Kara got to the hospital to see him, he was showing distinct signs of cooling toward her."

Maya started to get up, but her mother held up a hand to stop her, so she settled back in the chair. "So you think he's going to dump her?"

"He dumped her before they even finished his CAT scan." Maya's lips thinned. "Coward."

"Darn straight."

"How bad did he get hurt?" Maya asked.

Vidalia shrugged. "No worse than he deserved. And not nearly as bad as Peter or Mike did. Couple of busted ribs and a few stitches where his head hit the pavement. But it's Kara I'm worried about." Dumping the cookies into the wastebasket, she brushed off her hands, set the cookie sheet down and turned off the oven. Then, turning, she leaned back against the counter, folded her arms over her chest. "But she'll be all right. She's a Brand, and my daughter. Now, how about you, Maya? Any twinges today? Any signs?"

She might be notorious and outrageous and tactless, but Vidalia Brand loved her daughters, Maya thought, smiling inwardly. "Not a one," she said. "These babies seem determined to stay right where they are."

"Well, hon, you're gonna have to stop letting them hear the weather reports out here! I don't blame them for wanting to stay put!" As she spoke, Vidalia came away from the counter. She pulled a chair into position, then lifted Maya's feet onto it. "And speakin' of babies, where's mine?"

"Selene is upstairs in her bedroom doing...whatever it is she does up there. I smelled some godawful incense burning, and she was playing that drum of hers, so I didn't bother her. But tell her when she comes down that those cookies are completely vegan-friendly." Her mother looked at the wastebasket and cocked her brows.

"Not those cookies, Mom. The ones in the cookie jar. I've been baking all afternoon."

"Oh." Then her mother looked at her. "Why?"

Maya shrugged. "Resting all the time makes me tired."

Vidalia grinned. "You sure do look tired now."

"I am. I'm bushed."

"Well, you go on now and have a nap. I'll get dinner, and Mel will be along any time now to help me. Go on. You know I won't take no for an answer."

"I wasn't going to give you no for an answer." Maya put

her feet down and got out of the chair, belly leading the way. One hand immediately went to the small of her back, but she took it away to give her notorious mother a hug. "Thanks, Mom. And as for dinner, it's already made. In the slow cooker."

Her mother released her and hurried to the pot to remove the lid and sniff the steam. "Girl, you ought to be cooking in Paree."

"Yeah. I hear they love stew and biscuits in Paris, Mom." She sent her mother a wink and a smile, then headed through the large living room and on up the stairs. In the hallway she passed her youngest sister's room and smelled the familiar herbal scents coming from beyond the door. The door itself had Selene's idea of a Do Not Disturb sign hanging from it. It read Out Of Body, Back In Five Minutes.

She walked slowly down the hall, past the next door, which bore a sign that used to be funny but today seemed to sting: "Enter at your own risk." Maya heard Kara's voice coming from inside her room. She was speaking to someone, probably on the telephone, so she didn't bother her, either. She secretly hoped the injured Billy had changed his mind about breaking things off.

Shaking her head slowly, Maya finished the trek to her own bedroom and went inside. It was actually a two-room suite, the largest in the house. It was the master bedroom and had been her mother's, but Vidalia had insisted Maya take it so there would be room for the babies.

Already, there were two cribs flanking her own bed. They were in the process of finishing up the adjoining room, which would serve as a nursery. Wallpaper with baby ducks and chicks already lined the walls, but the linoleum floor wasn't quite finished. Carpeting, in a baby's room, Vidalia had decreed, would have been about as practical as whitewash in a chicken coop. Tiles could be washed daily if needed—and it would be, she promised. So Maya had reluctantly agreed.

Maya ran a hand over the smooth rail of one of the old cribs. Both of them had been in storage in the attic. Vidalia's five girls had been born little more than a year apart, one from the other, so she'd needed more than one crib at a time. And she'd kept everything. Growing up, Maya's mother had been very poor. The daughter of migrant workers from Mexico, she'd been named for the crop they were harvesting on the day she was born. And it was a name that suited her, because she had the thick, tough skin and sharp bite of an onion when she needed it. Damn good thing, too. It hadn't been easy, raising five daughters alone.

It was not a path Maya had ever thought she would follow. But as it turned out...

Hell. She'd never meant for it to turn out like this. Sighing, she lay down on her bed, pulled a cozy fleece blanket around her and rested her head on the pillows.

Maya opened her eyes when something tickled her face some time later.

A stuffed bunny with yarn eyes stared at her. She looked past it and saw dark, impish Mel, curled up on the other side of the bed, also staring at her. "You okay?" she asked.

"Why does everyone keep asking me that?" Maya sat up in the bed, picked up the pink terry cloth bunny and squeezed it. It was so soft you couldn't help but squeeze it.

Mel sat up, too, her short, black hair not even messed from the pillows. "Oh, I don't know. Maybe because you're eight and a half months pregnant with twins." She reached behind her, and pulled out another terry bunny, this one blue. "I picked these up in town today. Couldn't resist."

Maya smiled. She couldn't help but smile. "I should assume you're backing Selene's prediction that the newest Brands are a girl and a boy?''

Mel shrugged. "Have you ever known Selene to be wrong about anything?''

Thinking of that long ago night, when her spooky kid sister had told her that Caleb was her soul mate, Maya said, "Yes, actually. I have.''

"Well, not often enough so you'd notice it,'' Mel said. She frowned down at her sister. "This isn't working out the way you had it planned, is it, Maya?''

She only shrugged.

"Hell, if I ever see that no-account phony cowboy again, I'll break his arms off and use 'em to cave his head in.''

"Don't worry, sis. You aren't very likely to see him again.''

Mel averted her eyes. And Maya knew—she just knew— that Mel had learned something. "What is it?''

"Nothing.''

Sitting up, Maya held her sister's gaze. "Don't you know better than to test the patience of a woman as pregnant as I am?''

Licking her lips, Mel finally looked down, and sighed. "You have a right to know. I just...didn't want to have to be the one to tell you.''

"To tell me what?''

Mel got up off the bed and reached into her sweater pocket, pulling out a folded-up newspaper. She opened it, turned it and laid it on the bed facing Maya.

Maya looked, and the babies kicked her so hard she gasped. A grainy black-and-white photo of Caleb Cain stared back at her from the page. And the caption read Will He, Or Won't He?

Blinking back tears of surprise at seeing that face again...at seeing it on the body of a man dressed in an expensive designer suit and tie, with his hair all slicked back, and no battered hat in sight, Maya read the words underneath out loud.

"'Cain Caleb Montgomery III, former mayor of Springville, is still refusing to say whether or not he plans to enter the race for the U.S. Senate, though political insiders say it's only a matter of time before Montgomery makes the formal announcement declaring his candidacy. If that's true, he'll be following in the footsteps of his father and grandfather before him. There is no doubt, that should he enter the race, campaign finances will be the least of his worries. Montgomery is ranked the third richest man in the United States. But just where does he stand on the issues?'"

Mel took the newspaper out of Maya's hands. "Come on, Maya. Do you really care where he stands on the issues?"

Maya closed her eyes. "I can't believe this. He let me think he was a penniless drifter."

"Well of course he did. He didn't want you coming back to haunt him later. Now that we know who he is, however, he's got some explaining to do. When I see him, I—"

"God, no! Mel, you wouldn't. You won't, I won't let you!"

Mel went silent and blinked down at Maya. "Well, gosh, sis, you have to tell him...."

"No, I don't. I'm a Brand, and I don't have to do a damned thing I don't want to. And I don't want to tell him about these babies."

Frowning until her brows touched, Mel said, "But why?"

"My God, Mel, can't you see what would happen? I'd be the biggest tabloid target since Paula or Jennifer or Monica, for God's sake! The man's going to run for the Senate! No. No, if I thought the scandal of being an unwed mother was bad, it's nothing compared to the scandal of being at the center of a sex and politics story. Forget about it...and for God's sake, don't tell Mom."

"Don't tell Mom what?"

They both turned to see Vidalia stepping into the bedroom.

She had a newspaper in her hand. "You wouldn't mean this, by any chance, would you?" she asked, holding it up.

Maya sighed. "Mom, I don't want to be dragged out and flogged by the press. I don't want my babies born in a flurry of political scandal and tabloid gossip. I won't have it."

"I don't blame you."

Maya met her mother's eyes. "Then you...you agree with me?"

"Oh, sure, hon. But that doesn't mean the man doesn't have a right to know he's going to be a father."

Pressing her lips tight, Maya shook her head. "I...kind of thought he gave up that right when he lied about his name and skipped town without a word," she said. She met her mother's eyes. "These are my babies. Not his."

Her mother held her gaze for a long moment, and Maya knew she didn't approve. She might make a lot of tacky, off-color remarks and come off as an irreverent, outrageous woman old enough to know better—but the truth was, her mother's moral code ran deep. Finally, though, Vidalia heaved a sigh and said, "I guess I've got no choice but to let you make this decision for yourself. You're an adult. Soon to be a mamma yourself. I think you're making a mistake, daughter, but that's your right. So we'll do this your way."

Maya sighed in relief. "Thank you."

Vidalia nodded and glanced at Mel. "Agreed?" she asked.

"No. Someone ought to contact that man and make him face his responsibility."

"Mel, it's not your place—"

"I'm the babies' aunt," she said. "Anyone who wants to hurt them or slight them is gonna have to go through me to do it. Why should they be sleeping in...in twenty-year-old cribs or riding in that used minivan Maya bought, while their father sleeps in a mansion and drives around in a limo or something! It's not fair to the babies."

Maya eyed her sister. "We got by just fine without mansions or limousines, Mel. My babies will, too."

Mel pitched the newspaper onto the floor and stomped out of the room. And while Maya looked after her worriedly, Vidalia only sighed. "Give her some time. She's always seen herself as the protector of the family. She'll cool down in a day or two."

"I hope so," Maya said. But deep down, she wasn't so sure.

# Chapter 6

Caleb sat in his father's office, in his father's chair, trying to keep the most prestigious law firm in Oklahoma up and running while his dad slowly made his peace with retirement. But despite the weight of the job, not to mention the decision hanging over his head, or the nip of winter in the air outside, his mind was far away....

It was in a little town in springtime. By a waterfall. With a girl named Maya Brand.

Hell, it had been months. He should have forgotten about her, about that night, long before now. She certainly must have forgotten about him. Then again, he wouldn't know if she hadn't. He'd lied about his name that night. She had no clue who he was. Hell, she'd been worried about him having enough cash for the boarding house, as he recalled.

He sighed deeply. That had been real, that night with Maya. He hadn't spent a real, genuine night with a woman since. He'd been trying, with his frequent jaunts to political functions and state events. But mostly, the women who were on his arm were after something. Prestige, standing, power. Money. Usually money. They were phony, done up, made up, cinched up, dressed up, surgically enhanced, and polished to the point where the genuine parts were too well hidden to detect.

Maya hadn't wanted anything from him. She didn't think he had anything to offer. But she'd liked him anyway. She'd liked him enough to want to spend the night in his arms. It had been so honest, and so simple, and so incredible with her....

Hell, he had to stop thinking about that woman.

He glanced at the stack of memos and unopened mail on the desk, and began flipping through it to distract himself. The sight of a manila envelope with a Big Falls, Oklahoma, postmark caught his attention.

Odd.

He grabbed the envelope, tore it open and reached inside. Then he pulled out an 8 x 10 glossy photo of a woman who looked to be about eleven or twelve months pregnant. He smiled a bit at the sight of her belly, stretched to the size of a beach ball. His gaze moved slowly upward over the figure in the photo. She stood with one hand on the small of her back, a strand of mink brown hair hanging in her face, her eyes....

And then he froze. That face. Those eyes.

An expletive burst from him without warning.

His office door flew open, and Bobby McAllister, his ambitious right-hand man and future press secretary, should he decide he needed one, burst in, looking around with wide eyes. "What's wrong!"

Blinking slowly, licking his lips, his head spinning with disbelief, Caleb turned the photo over. There was one word on the back. *Congratulations.*

Caleb's throat went just as dry as desert sand. All this time...my god, she'd been alone, all this time....

"C.C., what is it?" Bobby asked again.

Caleb bit his lips. "Exactly how long has it been since April first?" he asked.

"April Fools' Day?"

Caleb almost moaned, but instead only nodded.

Bobby thought for three seconds, then said, "About...eight or nine months. Why?"

"*About* eight or nine months? I need to know *exactly.*"

Blinking, Bobby whipped out his pocket calendar, flipped pages and said, "Thirty-seven weeks and two days."

"And how long does it take a woman to give birth?"

"Nine mo—"

"*Exactly* how long?" Caleb said, stopping Bobby before he finished speaking.

Swallowing hard, Bobby turned briskly and left the room. He came back a moment later. "Forty weeks is full term. Boss, why are you asking such odd questions? What's going on?"

He looked at Bobby. Bobby read the look, turned, closed the office door. When he turned back again, Caleb held up the photo. "Thirty-seven weeks and two days ago, I spent the night with this woman."

Bobby's eyes widened to the size of saucers. He strode forward, snatched the photo from Caleb's hand. "According to the date, this was taken the day before yesterday."

"I know."

Flipping it over, Bobby read the back. "This is...this is extortion! *Blackmail.* They can't get away with this!"

Frowning, Caleb said, "Who can't?"

"Jacobson, of course. Your only real opponent for the senatorial race."

"I haven't even declared myself a candidate yet."

"He knows the game. He knows that's just a formality. This is a pre-emptive strike. Who else would want to get this kind of dirt on you, Caleb?"

Caleb shrugged. Silently, he thought perhaps Bobby was

taking his candidacy a bit too much for granted—especially now. But he didn't say that out loud. No sense sending the ambitious young genius into panic mode. "I don't think it's blackmail, because they don't ask for anything. And if it were Jacobson—well, I rather think this envelope would have been delivered to the press, not to me. Don't you think?"

"Well then...who is it? You think it's the woman?"

He shrugged. "Could be. I didn't think she knew who I was, but I suppose she could have found out." He sighed, lowering his head. It hurt, deeply, to think that Maya might have seen through his facade of being an unknown drifter. It had been so special to have someone be attracted to him for him, not for his name or his legacy. He gave himself a shake and went on. "Now she probably figures...I owe her. And I suppose she's right, at that."

"Oh, for crying out—are you saying you think this bull is true? You think you fathered this woman's child in *one night?* For God's sake, she was probably pregnant before you ever met her. She was probably looking for some rich scapegoat to pin it on."

He drew a deep breath, sighed. "No. No, I don't think so."

"Why the hell not?" Bobby was so upset his voice squeaked on the question. He tossed the photo down and awaited an answer.

"First, because she didn't have a clue who I was—"

"Or so she made you believe," Bobby interjected.

"And secondly, because she was...not that kind of girl."

Bobby stared at him as if he'd grown a second head. "Not that kind of girl. She was not that kind of girl? C.C., have you gone out of your mind here or what?"

"She was a virgin."

Bobby just blinked at him. Then he looked at the photo and blinked again. "But...she's...my age."

"I've got to go out there, Bobby."

Bobby's head came up, eyes wide. "Oh, no. No way. That's the worst thing you can possibly do right now."

"I'm going. Make something up. Cover for me. Say I'm sick with the flu and taking a few days off. Or better yet, say I needed some private time for the holidays. There's only a week until Christmas, so that sounds reasonable. Say anything you want, Bobby, but I have to go out there. I have to see her."

Bobby closed his eyes, shook his head. "If this leaks—"

"It won't."

Bobby groaned softly, hand going to his forehead as if to ward off a headache as he paced the office three times. Then, finally, he sighed and faced Caleb again. "Where will I be able to reach you?"

"It's a town called Big Falls," he said. "I'll call you when I get there and give you a phone number."

He tucked the photo back into its envelope, tucked it under his arm and started for the door.

"Boss?"

"Yeah?" he asked, turning.

"Don't let this woman play you for a fool."

He felt his lips pull into a bitter smile. "Don't you worry, Bobby. I'm a grown-up." But he didn't feel like one. He felt sick and queasy and lightheaded.

He left the office, taking the elevator to the basement parking garage and then driving back to the mansion. But the symptoms didn't ease up. His hands were shaking, for crying out loud! His palms were damp. He didn't know what the hell to think. He was so distracted that he drove the Lexus sports car right through two stop signs on the way home, and at the second one, he nearly got hit. He skidded to a stop in the driveway, ran straight up to his rooms and tugged a suitcase from underneath his bed. He whipped open the closet and stared in at the rows of expensive suits, the drawers full of designer shirts.

And then he thought to himself, what if she wasn't the one who sent that photo? What if she still didn't know who he was?

Okay, so it was wishful thinking. But it could happen, right? And if there was even a chance...

He thought about her eyes, the honesty in them. And how sincere she'd seemed when she'd talked about trying to be respectable, to get the town's elite to accept her. He'd believed her.

He still believed her. Damn, what must this pregnancy have done to all her efforts? He winced at the thought.

Slowly he reached for the bottom drawer and pulled out his entire collection of worn-out jeans—all three pairs. He put two in his suitcase and put one pair on. He dug for sweatshirts, found an old fleece-lined denim coat way in the back of his closet, and dug out that stupid battered cowboy hat, as well, for good measure. He wanted to see her as a man—not as a millionaire.

He finished his packing hastily, then carried the suitcase, coat and hat downstairs and set them on the floor near the back door, before forcibly slowing himself down, taking a few calming breaths.

He couldn't just walk out on his father without a word. Look at what had happened last time. Stiffening his spine, he went to his father's study.

The wheelchair turned slowly when he entered the room. Cain didn't use it all the time—only when he was tired or stubborn. He could walk, though his uneven gait required the use of a cane. His stern face was more disturbing now, since the stroke. One side reflected his feelings—that side was looking decidedly pissed off just now—while the other side remained lax and limp.

His father lifted his good hand, and Caleb saw the photograph he was holding. He glanced quickly around the room, half expecting to see Bobby lurking in a corner somewhere, but there was no sign of him.

"No, it wasn't Bobby," Cain said, speaking from one side of his mouth, his words still slightly slurred. "But I did call him. Whoever sent this to you at the office wanted to be sure you got it. Sent a copy here, as well. And I'm glad they did. This is something I ought to know about, don't you think?"

"No. You don't need the stress of this—and I can deal with it. I'm about to deal with it."

"Sit down, son."

"Father, I've made my decision. I have to go out there, see for myself what's going on."

His father glared at him, and Caleb finally sat down. He didn't like upsetting the old man. He didn't want to set off another stroke, or worse. Mean as hell he might be, but he was also in a fragile state right now, though he would rather die than admit it.

"You were a twin, you know."

Caleb sighed, closing his eyes, wishing to God his father would deliver any other long practiced speech than this one. He *hated* this one.

"Your mother carried two of you. Two boys. One bigger, stronger, and the other small and weak. Cain and Abel. Only one of them born alive." He knuckled a button, moving his wheelchair closer. "The doctors said it was just as well. One strong child was much better off than two weak ones. As it was, the stronger of the two survived. And that one was you."

"Right." Caleb had never accepted this, and it was largely why he refused to go by the name Cain. But though he rejected it, hearing it dug deep. "I've heard this story a hundred times, Father, and it has no more merit now than it ever did. Fetuses do not think or plot or conspire. I didn't kill off my weaker brother so I could survive, and the fact that I lived and he didn't is nothing more than genetics."

"Garbage!" his father said in a burst. "You're my son.

Your mother died giving birth to you. You carry my name. So you'll *always* do what you must to survive. You understand?''

He opened his mouth to argue, closed it again, and said nothing, getting up to leave.

''I was a twin, too, you know.''

Caleb, frowning, turned to stare at his father. ''No. I didn't know that. You never told me.''

''It never came up. My birth was just like yours, Caleb. The stronger twin survived, the weaker one didn't make it.'' He shook his head. ''It's genetics, yes, but it's also a marker, Caleb. A reminder that the strong survive, and that we, you and I, were destined for something more than ordinary men. And that sometimes sacrifice is necessary to keep the dream alive.''

''It was a quirk of fate. Not a sign from God,'' Caleb told him gently. ''Dad, you and your destiny had nothing to do with your twin dying. No more than I did with mine.''

Cain shook his head stubbornly. ''Nothing can ruin a political career faster than a woman and a sex scandal, Caleb. Nothing. Now you take my advice. You pay this woman enough to keep her quiet, and then, later on, you get a DNA test done very quietly. If it's yours, you pay her some more. All it takes. Send her and the child away somewhere. But do it all through third parties. Send Bobby out there, or Martin and Jacob Levitz. They're your lawyers, that's what they're paid for. Just don't get personally involved in this.''

Slowly, Caleb went to his father. Keeping his tone low, he said, ''I'm *already* personally involved, Dad. It doesn't get much more personal than this. And I may be your son, but I'm my mother's son, too. God rest her soul. And I think she'd want me to do the right thing here.''

His father's head came up, one eye snapping with anger, the other dull and glazed over. ''She died so you could be born to carry on this family's proud tradition! She would want you to protect that legacy at any cost!''

Caleb smiled, leaned in and clasped his father's hand once, firmly. "If I have a child, won't he be a part of that legacy?" He sighed when his father didn't waver in the least. "I have to do what I think is right, Dad. I'll only be gone for a few days. You've got your nurse and the household staff, and if you need anything they can't handle, call Bobby."

Straightening, he turned and walked out of the room, even though his father's voice shouted after him all the way. He only stopped long enough to pick up his suitcase, and then he headed out.

Two hours later, tired and wary, Caleb pulled into the parking lot of the OK Corral, that saloon he remembered so well, in the middle of Big Falls, Oklahoma. He hadn't been here in the winter before. It was nothing like the city, and he couldn't help feel a little stirring of the senses as José's truck rolled over the narrow roads and in between hillsides that looked wild and ominous. They were almost bare of leaves, some of those trees. There was not a lot of snow yet. But the ground was thoroughly covered, and there had been a fresh inch or two overnight, coating everything like a powdered doughnut.

Pretty.

He wondered why there were no cars in the lot at the Saloon. Then he realized he had arrived in the middle of a Monday afternoon. The Corral likely didn't even open until nightfall.

Great. So how was he going to find Maya?

He looked up and down the road. Saw a few men in red-and-black flannel coats, and some in camouflage from head to toe, hurrying to their pickups with gun racks in the back windows and shotguns in the racks.

Hunting season. This was not the city. Here, if you were a

man, you owned a gun and knew how to use it. And hunting season was the be all and end all of your holiday experience.

Swallowing hard, he got out of the truck and started on a path designed to intercept one burly hunter before he reached the front door of the ammo shop. He paused briefly to snap up the fleece and denim coat, and wondered if the thing looked redneck enough to get him by.

"Excuse me," he said, and he managed to draw the big guy's attention. Jowls and whiskers was the impression he got when the man faced him.

"You lost?" the stranger asked.

"Actually, I, uh...I'm looking for a place to get a room. I didn't see a hotel in town anywhere, so I thought..."

"We ain't got no *ho*-tel," the fellow said, putting the accent on the first syllable.

"That's what I thought when I didn't see one," he said. "I seem to recall there was a boarding house last time I was here, but I've forgotten where, exactly."

The fellow shrugged. "Yep. There's a boardin' house, all right. You might could get a room there. But I don't know for sure."

"Er...right. I might...could. If I knew where it was." The man just stared at him, chewing. "Can you tell me how to get to the boarding house?" he asked, figuring direct was the way to go here.

"End of the road, on yer left. 'Bout a mile up." He pointed.

"Thanks. Good luck with the hunting. I, uh, hope you catch a big one."

"Catch one?" The guy grinned almost ear to ear and strode away, shaking his head. "He hopes I *catch* one," he muttered, chuckling to himself all the way into the shop.

Caleb stared after him, saw him speaking to the fellow at the counter, and then they both looked his way and laughed some more.

Hell. He was fitting in here in redneck land like a duck fit in a henhouse. He was going to have to do better than that.

He turned to go back toward the pickup and came face-to-face with a young woman with short black hair and dark eyes. For a moment they stared at each other as recognition clawed at his mind. And then it seemed to hit them both at once. She was one of Maya's sisters—he'd met her at the saloon that night.

Even as his mind grasped who she was, hers seemed to identify him. Because her eyes went narrow and her lips thinned.

He thrust out a hand in greeting. She thrust out a fist in a right hook that caught him in the jaw and made lightning flash in his brain.

When he shook his brains back into order, he found himself on his butt in the snow, and she was revving the motor of a well-worn minivan and speeding away.

He rubbed his jaw. Hell, he hadn't expected a warm welcome, but he hadn't expected an ambush, either.

The question was, would Maya be as glad to see him as her sister had obviously been? Suddenly he was having second thoughts about finding out. Maybe he'd better try to get the lay of the land just a bit first—rather than waltzing right out to that cozy little farmhouse right away. Maybe it would be wise to make sure there wouldn't be armed infantrymen lining the driveway, with instructions to blow his head off first and ask questions later.

Swallowing hard, he nodded. To the boarding house...then he'd see.

Getting to his feet, he got back into his gardener's pickup truck and twisted the rearview mirror to get a look at his jaw.

Shoot. It was already starting to bruise.

# *Chapter* 7

"Nothing yet?" Mel asked, occasionally rubbing her knuckles as the five of them sat down around the dinner table. Four sat in ordinary ladderback chairs. One had been prodded into the giant recliner someone had hauled in from the living room. Maya sat there, feet up, tray positioned to one side. It would have been in her lap, she supposed, if she still *had* a lap.

"No," Maya said with a scowl. "Nothing yet."

"That's okay, hon. Christmas is coming." Kara grinned, and there was a knowing twinkle in her eye. "Things are bound to get better."

"How are you feeling, Maya?" Selene asked.

"Like a beached whale. Why do you ask?"

Selene shrugged and smiled a secretive smile. "You'll feel better soon."

"I'll feel better when I have these babies," she snapped.

"Oh, come on, don't be so grouchy," Kara said. "This should be a cheerful time for you."

"She can be grouchy if she's of a mind to," Vidalia put in. "It's allowed the first few weeks and the last few weeks.

And you have to admit, she's been a real trooper in between.''
Her mother smiled indulgently at her.

''You all just try carrying a couple bags of feed tied around
your middle for a few months and tell me how cheerful you
are.''

Everyone went silent, and for a moment they just ate while
the tension built. Maya's three sisters kept looking at their
mother sort of…expectantly. Finally Maya picked up on those
looks, and, narrowing her eyes, she said, ''What's going on
that I don't know about?''

Vidalia licked her lips. ''Well, I don't suppose there's any
point in waiting for you to be in a better mood to tell you
this, is there?''

''Not unless it can wait until these kids are tucked in their
cradles, there isn't,'' Maya said.

Vidalia lifted her dark, perfectly shaped brows. ''Fine.
Then I'll just tell you flat out. *That man* is back in town.''

Her sizable stomach clenched—no small task. ''What
man?''

Her mother let her gaze slide down to Maya's belly and
with a nod said, ''*That* man. Ida-May Peabody called. She
said he showed up this afternoon, got himself a room at her
boarding house.''

''Ohmygod.''

''Watch your mouth, young lady,'' Vidalia scolded.

''Mother, really,'' Selene said. ''You say more off-color
things than anyone.''

''But I do not take the Lord's name in vain, nor will I
tolerate anyone else doin' so.''

Maya was pushing her tray away and struggling uselessly
to get out of the chair. And Selene, the silver sister said,
''Hon, it was inevitable, him coming back here. And besides,
it's for the best that he came back. He has a right to know
that he's going to be a father, don't you think?''

''Right? What right? Geez, Selene, he didn't even give me

his real name!'' She pulled herself partway up, then fell back again. ''Will someone get me the hell out of this chair!''

''Your language, Maya,'' Vidalia scolded.

Kara shot to her feet and hurried to her sister's aid, gripping her arms and tugging. She was really leaning into it, too, Maya thought.

''Well, I couldn't care less about his rights,'' Mel put in, rubbing her knuckles again. ''But he does have some responsibilities here, and if you're smart, you'll make sure he lives up to them. You'll feel much better with someone else shouldering part of the financial burden, if nothing else.''

Kara tugged harder.

''I don't need any help from any man. You leave him alone, Mel!'' The moment she said it there was a knock at the front door, about ten feet away from the dining room.

Kara gave one last yank, and the chair sort of thudded into its upright position, launching Maya out of it like a rocket. Kara screamed bloody murder, falling backward to the floor. Maya landed right on top of her like a sack of feed, and poor Kara's scream turned into a burst of air, driven from her lungs by the impact. The others flew to their feet and swarmed, and whoever had been at the front door flung it open and ran inside, no doubt alarmed by Kara's bloodcurdling scream.

''Good God, are you all right?'' a man's voice said.

''Watch your mouth, young man,'' Vidalia scolded.

But Maya barely heard her mother's disapproving tone. Not when that voice had sounded vaguely familiar. Not when she focused her vision to see those scuffed up and battered boots a foot away. And certainly not when two very strong hands closed on her shoulders and gently eased her off her sister, rolling her carefully until she was sitting on the floor, bent knees up and in front of her as if she were getting ready to give birth. Then he crouched in front of her, gripped her underneath her arms and easily got her up to her feet.

She looked up—right into those blue eyes that had melted

her resolve nine months ago, minus a couple of weeks. And in spite of herself, the blood rushed to her cheeks and heated them.

"Hello again, Maya Brand," he said.

"Um…hi." Self-consciously, she reached up to straighten her hair. Then she realized what a wasted effort that was. He was *not* going to notice what her *hair* looked like.

"You okay?"

Her lips thinned. "Fine." She glanced down at Kara. "The more pertinent concern here is, have I flattened my poor sister?"

Kara was already picking her gangly self up off the floor. "It's my fault," she said. "I'm such a klutz."

"I'm sure that's an exaggeration," Caleb said, finally letting go of Maya long enough to reach out, giving Kara a hand up. "A pretty girl like you could never be referred to as a klutz. You look more like a swan."

Kara smiled and lowered her head, blushing furiously.

Selene launched into a "your body believes what your mind thinks" speech. But Maya ignored her. Because Caleb was turning back to her now, and his hands were curling around her shoulders, and his eyes were staring into hers. For a few seconds, anyway. But then they moved, skimming down her body, reaching her belly and widening just slightly. He didn't say "Holy cow," but she heard it anyway.

"Guess I've put on a little weight since you saw me last," she said.

"Uh…yeah, a little bit." He couldn't seem to take his eyes off her belly. So she put a finger under his chin and tipped his head upward until he met her eyes again, at which point he said, "We've got some talking to do, don't you think?"

Drawing a breath, she sighed and looked away. "You don't need to look like that, Caleb. I don't want anything from you, I promise."

He lifted his brows, even as Mel's hand came down on

Caleb's shoulder from behind. He turned at her tug, facing her. "Well, hello again," he said. "Mel, isn't it? Sorry we didn't get more time to talk this morning."

"This morning?" Maya asked. She saw Caleb rub his jaw, saw the slightly bruised skin there, saw Mel's knuckles all red, and said, "Mel, what did you do to him?"

Mel ignored her, her narrowed eyes on Caleb. "Maya may not want any help with this, mister, but you can bet your—"

"Melusine," Vidalia said, cutting her off. "This is between your sister and this fellow! You stay out of it until I tell you otherwise." Then she moved forward, walked up to Caleb, who turned again, facing her this time. And she smiled and said, "But believe me, mister, if I think you're not treating my daughter right, I *will* tell her otherwise."

Kara cleared her throat. "You really don't want to mess with Mom and Mel," she said.

"You all sound like a gang of thugs," Selene said, getting to her feet. "Whatever is meant to happen between these two is going to happen, no matter what you all do or say or threaten. So why don't you just get out of the way and let it?"

Blinking, giving his head a shake, Caleb drew a breath as if about to respond to one or all of them. Then, instead, he just closed his mouth, turned and faced Maya. "Can we *please* talk? Alone?"

She nodded. "We can go—"

"To dinner," he said. "I, um…made reservations."

Lowering her head, Maya said, "I'd really just as soon not be seen with you in public, Caleb. You have no idea how efficiently the rumor mill works around here."

He nodded. "I can guess. That's why I made the reservation in Tucker Lake."

Tucker Lake, the next town over. He had thought this through, then, hadn't he? Maya pursed her lips. "Okay. Sure. I never touched a bite of this anyway."

"Are you sure you should be riding that far, hon? You're carrying—"

"I'll be fine, Mom."

Her mother frowned, but nodded. "Guess you know best, not having ever given birth before. I wouldn't presume to advise you, just because I've been through it *five times over.*"

Selene met Kara's eyes, and they both shook their heads. Mel stood beside her mother as if in full support of her opinion on the matter.

Maya glanced down at her clothes. She wore a pair of pseudo-jeans, big enough for all four of her sisters, held up with a drawstring, and a smock top that looked, in her opinion, like a Christmas tree skirt.

"I was going to say I'd change first, but I basically look the same in any of the assortment of tents in my closet, so it would be pretty much useless. Let's just go, shall we?"

"I'll get your coat," Selene said with a wink. She did so, not handing the heavy woolen coat to Maya, but to Caleb.

"Gee, you're so subtle it's scary," Maya said.

Selene sent her an innocent, wide-eyed look, while Caleb held her coat for her. She slid her arms in and didn't bother trying to button it. She could, but even this super-sized coat was getting snug around the middle.

Taking her arm, Caleb drew her outside, down the steps. She glanced up at his pickup truck, made a face and said, "Listen, I don't know how much you know about pregnant women but—"

"Nothing," he said. "Nothing at all."

She nodded. "Bumpy rides have been known to induce labor. And your truck there doesn't look all that...gentle." Turning, she looked up at him. "I don't want to offend you here, but would you mind terribly if we took my van instead?"

"Hey, no offense taken."

She nodded and led him across to the old barn, some fifty

yards away from the house, which served as a garage. It kept the snow off the vehicles in the winter, anyway. He held her arm the whole way. She reached for the sliding door, but he stopped her with a shake of his head, opened it himself and stood looking at the three Brand family vehicles.

"It looks excessive, to someone like you, us having three vehicles." She watched him as she spoke, knowing to him three junkers like this probably seemed like living at poverty level and waiting for him to admit it. He didn't, damn him. So she just went on. "But even now, we're often short a vehicle. The pickup there is essential out here. And the Bronco sports utility of course, is for when the roads get really nasty. And then there's the minivan. I just bought it. Used, of course, but it's not in bad shape for what I paid. Figured I'd need a reliable vehicle of my own with these...er...with the baby coming."

He nodded. "Good thinking." He escorted her to the passenger door and held out a hand. "Keys?"

"Oh, it's not locked. And the keys are in the ignition."

He lifted his brows but made no comment as he helped her into the van, then went around and got in behind the wheel. He started the engine and drove it out, then got out and went back to close the barn door.

As he drove out the driveway, he said, "You may have to help me find this place. I made the reservations over the phone and got the recommendation from Ida-May at the boarding house. It's a place called Spellini's. Do you know it?"

She lifted her brows and looked at him. "Are you sure you wouldn't rather just stop at a diner? I mean—looking at you, I would hardly think you could afford a highbrow place like Spellini's. There's Polly's Kitchen just off the highway. You can get a whole chicken dinner there for four ninety-five."

He watched her face carefully as she spoke, so much so that she wondered what he was looking for. Had he detected the edge of sarcasm in her tone? But then he sighed, almost in relief. "I've been working pretty steadily since we...I mean, well, you know. I've got some money set aside."

So he was still lying to her. Still willing to let her believe he was some poor drifter, rather than one of the wealthiest men in the state. Why? To protect his millions from his own children?

Drawing a breath, she sighed. It had been stupid to let that hopeful little light flare up in her heart at the sight of him. Served her right.

So she still thought he was a penniless drifter.

Either that or she was a very good actress. Good. He would let her think it a bit longer. That way he could be sure her reactions to him were based on him, and nothing else.

He was pleasantly surprised when they got to the restaurant, a giant-sized log cabin with cathedral ceilings and full-length windows. The bottom floor was littered with tables, and stairs went up to the second floor, where tables lined the perimeter, behind rails. He did not think, however, that those stairs looked like anything he wanted to see Maya trying to climb tonight.

God, she looked so different. So...big. He didn't think he'd ever seen a pregnant woman this large before. But the changes went further than that. Her eyes looked...circled and tired. Not as sparkling or full of life as they had been before. Her face seemed drawn and tight, and he imagined her goal of trying to become accepted by the good folk of Big Falls had blown up in her face, as well. The conservative residents of small towns were not known for being big on unwed mothers.

A waitress greeted them, wearing a tiny black dress with a white apron. "Oh!" she exclaimed upon seeing Maya's condition. "Your first?"

Maya nodded.

The waitress smiled ear to ear and glanced up at Caleb.

"You must be so excited. And you," she said, looking at Maya again. "You look as if you're due any day now."

"Yes," Maya said, at the same time that Caleb said, "Almost three more weeks."

Maya looked at him and frowned. The waitress only laughed. "Sure, I understand! I've had three myself, and I always spent the last few weeks wishing it would happen and get over with."

Maya slowly drew her suddenly suspicious gaze away from Caleb's to look at the waitress. "You've had three? And you got your figure back?"

"Oh, honey, sure I did. You will, too, don't you worry. Now, come on, let's get you off your feet." She led them to a nice table with plenty of room on either side, in a rear corner, with huge windows on both walls.

Caleb took Maya's coat, held her chair, braced her arm as she eased herself into it. God, it must be hard carrying so much extra weight around. She wasn't a big woman to begin with.

"My goodness, he's good," the waitress said. "Does he give you backrubs at night, too, hon?" She sent Caleb a wink. "Believe me, her back has to be screaming by now."

"I believe it."

She took their drink orders at last and promised to hurry back with their menus. But the second she left the table, Maya speared him with those gem green eyes of hers, and said, "How did you know my due date? I didn't even think you knew I was pregnant."

He blinked, searched his mind. "What do you mean?"

"I mean, you just told that waitress I was due in just under three weeks."

"You told her any day now." He leaned forward on his elbows. "So which is it, Maya?"

She narrowed her eyes on him. "Both. Full term would be

January sixth—just under three weeks from now. However, my doctor has no doubt I'm going to go early.''

He blinked and felt a little bolt of alarm. ''You mean…the baby's going to be premature? Isn't that dangerous?''

The waitress came back with their drinks. Milk for Maya. Mineral water for Caleb. She handed them their menus, smiled brightly and hurried on her way.

Maya was still staring at him. ''It's not early enough to be any cause for alarm, Caleb. Actually, early deliveries are common in cases like mine.''

He frowned at her. ''And what kind of cases are those?''

''Caleb…we're getting off the subject here. You knew my due date right to the day. Now how did you find that out?''

He lowered his eyes. ''Forty weeks…from the night we spent together. I was just guessing.'' Lifting his gaze to hers again, he stared hard at her, watched her face. ''It *is* my child you're carrying. Isn't it, Maya?''

It was her turn to look away. ''No.''

''No?'' Shock washed through him like a splash of ice water in the face.

''No,'' she said. ''It's my child I'm carrying. Not yours. Not anyone's. Just mine. Do you understand that, Caleb?''

He felt that ice water come to a slow simmer. ''Hell, no, I don't understand that.''

''Well, then, let me see if I can explain it. You were a stranger, passing through town. We were a one-night stand. There was no relationship. No commitment. I got pregnant, Caleb. My problem. My situation. Not yours. You're still just a drifter passing through. There's nothing for you here.''

There was, he thought slowly, one hell of a lot more going on with this woman than met the eye. He resisted the urge to lose his temper. Not only because she was in a tender state, but because he sensed it would do him no good. ''Maybe I need to rephrase my question?''

She shrugged.

"You were a virgin the night we made love," he said, keeping his voice low, leaning over the table.

Her cheeks went pinker, and she looked away from him, focused on the view outside. Rolling meadows and woodlands beyond.

"And according to the town gossips, you haven't so much as had lunch with a man since. Most of them are going out of their minds trying to figure out how you got pregnant, according to the very talkative Ida-May at the boarding house. Even though a few may have seen us that night, the idea of the untouchable Maya Brand indulging in a one-night stand with a stranger seems to be beyond the realm of possibility."

"It's really none of their damned business, though, is it?"

He let his smile come, even though he sensed she wouldn't like it. He liked her spunk. "One busybody I met in the general store even put forth the theory that you visited a sperm bank and were artificially inseminated."

"Oh, for the love of—"

He covered one of her hands with his own. "Please tell me the truth, Maya. Did I father this child you're carrying?"

Staring down at his hand on top of hers, she said, "Yes." Then, lifting her head slowly, "Now you tell me the truth about something. For once."

He frowned, wondering what the hell that implied. But he said only, "Okay."

"Why did you come back here?"

Ouch. That was not one he wanted to answer. But he'd promised her the truth, and she was damned well going to hear it. "I received a photograph of you taken just a couple of days ago. On the back there was one word. 'Congratulations.'"

She only stared at him steadily. No expression on her face. As if she were waiting for him to finish the story, or to deliver the punchline or something. But when he said nothing, she lifted her brows. "But...who...how...?" Then she drew a breath, and her eyes widened even further. "You thought I sent it, didn't you?"

He sighed deeply. "Hell, I didn't know what to think. But yeah, it did enter my mind that you might have sent it."

"Well. I guess we know where we stand, then, don't we?"

"No, frankly, I don't have a clue where we stand, Maya."

"Caleb, if I'd had any idea how to find you to tell you I was pregnant, I would have called or shown up in person. I wouldn't have sent some cryptic photo with a note on the back. God, what would be the point?"

Good question, he thought. What was the point?

"Listen…it doesn't matter who sent the photo—"

"Oh, it matters. Believe me, it matters. And I have my theories on that. But the point is, I didn't know how to find you. I tried, but there was no such person as Caleb Cain in Tulsa."

He licked his lips. "I…move around a lot."

"You lie a lot."

"Regardless, I'm here now."

"So what?"

He licked his lips. "Well, hell, Maya, I don't know. You're going to be the mother of my child. I guess I'd like to get to know you a little bit. And if you think I'm the kind of man who's going to let you take full responsibility for this all alone, you'd better think again. I'm going to take an equal share of the financial responsibility for this baby."

She leaned a bit forward—not a lot, because there wasn't room between her belly and the table for a lot—and she said, "In exchange for what? Partial custody? Or the whole enchilada? What do you want, Caleb?"

He held up both hands. "Hey, hey, hold on now. Is that why you're so hostile? You think I came out here to try to take your baby away from you? To fight you for custody or something?"

She blinked rapidly. "You'd have to kill me to do that,

Caleb. Just so you know in advance. You'd have to kill me. And I don't care who your father is, or how many millions you have.'' Tears pooled in her eyes.

He was stunned into silence for a long moment. And then he drew a breath, sighed deeply. ''So you do know who I am.''

She nodded. ''I found out yesterday, when I saw your picture in the paper.''

*Twenty-four hours before that photo arrived on my doorstep....*

He shook himself. A tear managed to escape her glittering eye, and it rolled down her cheek. And all of the sudden, not only did he doubt she would try to blackmail him—he didn't care. Moreover, if she did, he wouldn't blame her. ''Dammit, I didn't come out here to upset you.'' Reaching across the table, he covered both her hands with his. ''Please don't cry.''

Too late. The tears were streaming. She snatched up a napkin and wiped angrily at them, even as the waitress came back to take their orders. He hoped to God this entire discussion hadn't ruined Maya Brand's appetite.

Slamming the napkin down on the table, Maya sniffled and said, ''I want the T-bone. The big one. Rare.''

''Mashed or fries?'' the waitress asked.

''Both.''

Smiling, the waitress scribbled and said, ''Gravy or sour cream, hon?''

''Both.''

''Anything on the side?''

''Yeah. The fried chicken.'' She closed her menu with a snap and handed it back to the waitress, who turned to Caleb, pen poised.

''Um...the salmon?'' he ventured.

''Sure thing.'' She scribbled and turned to leave; then, turning back, she eyed Maya's half-empty glass. ''More milk?''

Maya nodded. Her tears were gone now, and as soon as

the waitress was gone, she faced Caleb squarely. "I did not send you that photograph."

"That is becoming painfully obvious," he said. "Frankly, I don't even care who sent me the photo, Maya. If this baby is mine, I want to take responsibility. That's all."

"Then why did you lie about who you were?"

He lowered his head, shook it. "I...had my reasons. What difference does it make, Maya? You know the truth now."

She pressed her lips together. "Not that I trust anything that comes out of your mouth at this point, Caleb, but if you want to spend one more minute with me, I want you to swear you won't try to take my babies away from me. Swear on all you hold dear, Caleb, or leave right now."

"I swear. I'll put it in writing if you want me to. I can have my...wait a minute." He frowned then. "Wait just a minute. What did you just say?"

She bit her lower lip, averted her face.

"Maya, did you just say 'babies'?"

Slowly, she faced him. Then she drew a breath, blew it out again. "Hell, Caleb, you might as well know. I'm carrying two babies, not one."

"Two? Twins?"

She nodded. "That's why the doctor expects me to go early. Twins hardly ever go to term."

He just sat there, stunned to the bone. A deep tremor worked through him, and his gaze fell to her swollen belly. "Are they both...all right?" he said softly.

"If the way they kick is any indication, they're fine."

Those words only made his stomach clench up tighter as his father's words replayed in his mind. *The strong survive, the weak don't. It's our legacy, Caleb. And it's a reminder....*

"What...what does your doctor say? Do they have any way of knowing for sure that they're both...?"

He saw her face then, clouding with worry. And he decided to shut up. She was going through enough without him saying things that would scare her to death. There was no reason to think... Hell, twins were born healthy every day. They were!

"I go in every week for a checkup," she told him. "They listen to the heartbeats, and we've done ultrasounds. These kids are huge, for twins. Over five pounds each already. And they're fine. They're Brands. They can't be anything less than fine."

"They're not just Brands, they're Montgomerys, too."

She shrugged. "So I suppose they'll have politics in their DNA?"

He smiled at her, liking her slightly lighter tone. "Maybe we should ask them to check for it when they do the blood tests."

Her expression changed. Lightness fled. Her eyes became...thunderous. He'd never used that term to describe a facial expression before. But it described hers now.

"A blood test? You...mean a paternity test, don't you? You want the babies to have a paternity test."

He blinked fast. "Well...isn't that pretty standard...I mean, in cases where the parents aren't married?"

"It's standard, all right. In cases where the mother is being called a liar." She glared at him. "Help me up."

"Oh, come on, Maya. I wasn't calling you a liar. I... you're...I..."

"Help me up *now*." She gripped the table and started to rise.

He leapt to her aid but found himself awkwardly unsure where to put his hands. He finally settled on gripping her forearms and pulling, even as he tried to fast-talk his way out of the slam he'd inadvertently delivered. "Please don't leave. Have dinner, come on. You're overreacting to everything I say here."

"I'm not overreacting. And I'm not leaving," she said, once she was upright.

He frowned. "Then...where are you going?"

Tilting her head to one side, she said, "Caleb, there are two hefty babies writhing around on top of my bladder right now. Where do you *think* I'm going?"

"Oh. Uh. Sorry."

She tossed her head and headed across the restaurant to the rest room in the rear. And despite her proud stance, she sort of…waddled when she walked away, which took all the pomp and arrogance out of her exit.

He sat back down, feeling like he'd just been through Round One of a fight with no rules and no reason. The woman was obviously an emotional basket case right now.

And no wonder. Twins. And she was alone.

But why the hell did she seem so determined to see him as the enemy?

The waitress brought the food—Maya's order took up two plates—and a whole pitcher of milk. He waited for Maya to return, and then got up and met her halfway to escort her back to the table. She sat down, looking a bit calmer.

"I did some thinking," she said, "and I've decided that you should go home."

"I should?"

"Uh-huh. First thing in the morning. Leave an address, phone number, something like that. I'll call you when the kids arrive. We'll work out a time for you to come visit them. And I promise I'll be generous about that, so long as you don't try to take them away from me." She shrugged. "And if you want to pitch in on expenses, fine. I won't fight it." She spoke as if it were all decided.

"I see."

She dug into her food as if she were starved. And as Caleb watched her, he thought she looked very smug and superior. As if she made the rules and he had no choice but to obey. He was a freaking Montgomery, for crying out loud. He was the third richest man in the country, a former mayor, and the predicted winner of the senatorial race even though he had yet to declare himself a candidate. And her attitude chafed, big-time.

He picked at his food, while she finished hers. Finally she looked up at him, dabbing her face with a napkin. She'd barely left a crumb on her plate.

"So, are we agreed?" she asked him.

He pursed his lips, crossed his arms over his chest, looked her in the eye and shook his head. "Not on your life."

Blinking in surprise, she stared at him. "Why not?"

"Because you're acting like a little dictator, and I don't like it. So, no, Maya. I think maybe I'd better look into things just a bit more thoroughly before I agree to anything regarding *our* children."

Her brows rose. "Jumping the gun, aren't you? You don't have your precious paternity tests yet."

"No. But I will."

"Oooh, yes. You never know, I might be conspiring to take you for everything you have. Now that I've figured out that would amount to slightly more than a pair of scuffed boots and a rusted-out pickup truck, that is!"

"Why are you so determined to treat me like the enemy here?"

"As far as I'm concerned, you are the enemy!"

"Fine," he said, and he got to his feet. "Then this conversation is over."

"It is *not* over," she retorted, "until *after* dessert!"

His anger seemed to wash away, and something warm and fuzzy rose up to take its place. Only for a moment. But it was there. He lowered his head to hide his amusement from her and tried very hard to regain his anger and indignation. He kept trying, right through the cheesecake and coffee. But the way she tasted the chocolate syrup on the tip of her finger weakened his resolve. And the whipped cream that stuck to her upper lip annihilated it altogether.

She was angry. Okay, he figured she had a right to be

angry. He'd lied to her. And now he was back, and she was afraid. Protecting her babies the way a mother bear might protect her cubs from anything she perceived to be a threat to them. That wasn't a bad thing. In fact, if anything, he ought to appreciate it. It meant she cared deeply about her babies. His babies. It meant she would be a great mother to them, protect them with everything in her.

He just wished she didn't feel they needed protecting from him.

# Chapter 8

Terror was an ice-cold feeling that made him shiver more than the chilly winter wind. Twins. God, twins. Just like he'd been. The cruel joke of the name he'd inherited from his father still twisted in his gut like a blade. And the old man's words echoed like a curse. About how he'd been the stronger, and how he must always do whatever he must to survive.

Hell, he knew, with the rational part of his mind, that a child in the womb couldn't cause premeditated harm. Couldn't even harbor an ill thought. But it dug at him, ate at him. Always had.

And now he was the father, and dammit, there were two babies. Twins. He was scared to death. What if something happened to one of them? What if only one survived?

Standing stock-still in the slowly falling snow outside the boarding house, he blinked at the unfamiliar burning sensation in his eyes, the odd tightening of his throat, the hitch in his breathing.

He still didn't know who the hell had sent the photograph. It suddenly seemed like the least important thing in the world. What he *did* know was that he had to stay here until his children were born. And he had to do everything in his power to make sure they were both strong and healthy. Protected and safe. Cared for, provided for. And those jobs didn't belong solely to Maya Brand. They belonged to him. Because he was...their father. The idea made him stand a little straighter, square his shoulders, lift his chin. All of a sudden he felt...omnipotent.

"Going to stand outside all night or go on in?" a small voice said from behind him.

Caleb turned to see the youngest Brand sister standing there staring up at him. Silvery Selene, with her huge mystical silver-blue eyes and her elfin features. She wore a red hood with a scarf attached and a black wool coat. Her nose and mouth were wrapped up, just her eyes peered at him. But they were enough to identify her easily.

"I'm going in," he said. "You?"

She nodded at him. "Me too. I want to talk to you."

He pursed his lips, then shrugged and led the way up the front steps and onto the glass enclosed porch that stretched the entire breadth of the house. On the large mat in front of the door he heeled off his boots, then shrugged out of his coat and hung it on a nearby hook. Selene did likewise and looked around.

"This is nice, what Ida-May's done out here," she observed.

"It's cozy." Despite the early darkness and chilly temperature, it was pleasant here. And private. Moonlight spilled down over the quiet little town, and he thought it had an almost enchantingly picturesque appeal. Like a Currier and Ives Christmas card. He went to the small round table in the corner, pulled out a chair. "Is this good for our...talk?"

"It's fine. At least it's warm in here." She came to where he was, sat down in the chair he held.

Caleb took his own seat across from her. "So," he said.

She drew a breath, licked her lips. "I'm not sure how to begin."

"Well, maybe I can help. You're about to ask me what my intentions are toward your sister."

She lowered her gaze. "That's...not what I came for...but since you brought it up...are you at least going to stick around a while?"

"At least."

Her gaze rose slowly, locked with his. "I have a confession to make, Caleb. I...I'm the one who made you come back here."

That shocked him into silence faster than almost anything could have. Not only that this innocent-looking baby of the family would resort to sending photographs that could destroy his career in unmarked envelopes, but that she would then come to him to admit it!

"I think you would have come anyway. In fact, I'm almost sure of it, but I couldn't take the chance I might be wrong. It was wrong to make you come back, I know that...and yet...I'd do it again. I'm sorry, though, if it messed up your life."

He closed his eyes, drew a breath, then opened them slowly. "That photograph could have ruined me, Selene. You could have just called me, you know. Anything a bit more discreet than—"

"What photograph?"

He frowned. Huge silvery eyes blinked innocently at him. "What do you mean, 'what photograph?' The photograph that landed on my desk yesterday—the one of your sister, her belly out to here, with the word 'congratulations' scrawled across the back."

Her eyes grew even wider, if that were possible. "Caleb...I don't know anything about any photograph. I just...gosh, I mean, I didn't think it would manifest like that! I'm sorry."

Caleb frowned, because she made no sense. He gave his

head a little shake, but that didn't help. "Selene, if you didn't
send the photo, then just what did you mean when you said
that you were the one who made me come back here?"

She looked so guilty that he almost felt sorry for her. Chin
lowering, she said, "I...performed a little...rite."

"A...rite?"

"A...spell."

He blinked at her.

"Magic," she said. "You know. You burn some herbs,
light some candles, chant some words...."

Light finally dawned. This was the tarot card sister, the
New Age guru. The Aquarian of the family.

"You're not supposed to mess with people's free will,"
she went on quickly. "But I messed with yours. I just wanted
to own up to it. I'll deal with the karma. It'll be worth it
if....well...I mean...if things work out the way I'm hoping
they will."

Caleb smiled. She seemed really upset about all of this.
Her hands fisted together and kneading on the table, teeth
worrying her lower lip every little while. He covered her
hands with his. "You didn't mess with my free will, hon. If
I had known about the babies...I'd have been here long before
now."

"You would?"

"Of course I would. Why does that surprise you?"

She blinked and seemed thoughtful for a moment. "Well...
I guess because you used a false name and everything...you
know, when you came here before. I just assumed that was a
precaution to keep anyone from tracking you down if there
were...consequences to that night."

He sat very still for a long moment. Then he said, "And
is that what your sister thinks, too, Selene?"

She only shrugged. "I don't know what she thinks. But I
think she needs you, Caleb. She's doing just fine at playing
the fearless firstborn of Vidalia Brand, but deep down, she's

scared to death. About carrying those kids, about delivering them, and even more about raising them afterward.''

He nodded. ''She should be. But to be honest, Selene, she doesn't seem any too eager to let me be a part of any of it.''

Selene's eyes speared him. Deadly serious and intense, she said, ''That's got nothing to do with you, Caleb. It's got to do with the past, and our father, and stuff that I don't even remember. I just know it's in her, you know? Like a deep sliver she hasn't been able to dig out.'' She shook her head slowly. ''Maybe she thought it was all healed over, but this thing with you just jammed it in deeper and started it hurting all over again.''

For a moment he thought he was going to learn something real, something meaningful, about the mother of his children. He knew the story of her father. She'd told him, and he'd heard about it again from the local gossips even since he'd come back this time. But he didn't know how Maya felt about it—how she'd felt then, how she felt now.

And it didn't look like he would know any time soon, either. Selene bit her lip, shook her head. ''That's for Maya to talk to you about, not me. Like I said, I don't even remember. But I do know this much. If Maya's unwilling to let you be a part of this, you're going to have to make her let you. You have every right to be involved in the birth of your own kids, Caleb, and you need to say so. Don't take no for an answer.''

''She might hate me for it,'' he said softly.

Selene shook her head. ''Maybe for a while. But she needs you. Trust me.'' Her hand touched his. ''I *know* things.'' Drawing a breath, straightening, she gave a nod. ''And know that whatever happens will be real and coming from the two of you. I'm not going to interfere again.''

He lifted his brows. ''What, no love potions?''

''You're teasing me, aren't you?''

''No, Selene. I might, but there's something about you that makes me wonder.''

She smiled, seeming to take that as a compliment. "Well, that's it. That's what I came here to tell you. Good night, Caleb."

"Night," he murmured. But he barely saw her leave. He was too busy wondering if there were secret wounds festering in Maya Brand's heart...and how he could possibly hope to get close enough to find out.

From his room that night, he called Bobby, spoke to him briefly, only to learn that no further word had come in about Caleb's impending fatherhood. No threats, no demands, no one even hinting that they knew. So if Selene hadn't sent that photo, and Maya obviously hadn't, then the question remained...who had? One of the other sisters? Mel or Kara? Perhaps Vidalia Brand herself? He hoped so. Because if it wasn't one of them, then that meant someone else must know about all of this. And if someone else knew, they were holding the fuse to Caleb's personal political powder keg.

Her back ached. Her head ached. Her stretch marks itched. Her feet were swollen. Her bladder was about to burst, and, oh, hell, she had a leg cramp. "Ow, ow, ow, ow, *OW!*"

The cramp eased. The knotted muscles in her calf relaxed. She stopped yelling and managed to get through her morning rituals without serious damage. The babies were kicking so hard it actually hurt now and then, and she was so big she had to use the long-handled back brush to wash her feet, even though she'd put a waterproof stool in the shower stall.

Ugh!

Finally she chose one of her colorful tent-sized outfits from the selection in her closet and pulled it on over her industrial-strength bra and super-support panties. A pretty kaftan and a pair of stretchy leggings. But she just didn't feel pretty in them.

She sat at her dressing table, brushing her hair, when there was a tap on her bedroom door.

"Come in," she called, not even looking up from her brushing.

The door opened, footsteps came in, falling too heavily to belong to any of the Brand women. And she glanced into the mirror to see Caleb, of all people, standing there with a tray in his hands.

"What in the world are you doing here?" she asked his reflection.

"Good morning, Maya. How are you feeling this morning, hmm?"

She eyed the tray, not answering, because she was so sick and tired of answering that same question every single day a dozen times. "What are you doing here? What is this?"

"Breakfast in bed. Or…it was intended to be. Only, you're not in bed, so I guess I'm late."

Maya set the hairbrush down and turned slowly. "Who let you in?"

"Your mother. I brought enough fresh pastries for everyone, and Vidalia was kind enough to supply the coffee to go with them." He nodded at the cup on the tray. "Decaf for you, of course."

"Of course."

He carried the tray in, right to the chest at the foot of her bed, and set it down. "I found this great bakery in town this morning, just a stone's throw from the boarding house."

"Sunny's Place. I know it."

Picking up a platter heaped with doughnuts, Danishes and muffins, he brought it to where she sat and held it under her nose.

God, they smelled good.

Hell, *he* smelled better. There was a hint of something…not cologne, it was too subtle for that. Maybe it was the soap he used. Sort of a wind and water scent. It tickled a deep part of her that hadn't been tickled in…well, in nine months, give or take a couple of weeks.

"Pretty low trick, bribing your way in here with pastries, don't you think? Why are you doing this, anyway?" she asked him suspiciously.

"Because I want to. Hey, you've been lugging those twins around for nine months now. I figure the least I can do is help you through the last couple of weeks."

"Don't say that!"

He blinked. "Don't say what? That I want to help you out?"

"No. That 'couple of weeks' part. If it's more than a couple of days, I'll die. My belly will explode, and I will just simply die." She sighed, grabbed a yummy-looking Danish and a napkin, took a heavenly bite and closed her eyes in ecstasy as she chewed. "Oh, this is sooo good."

"I know. I ate two myself." He smiled at her.

And he was so damned charming she couldn't help but smile back. But then she thought about what he'd said a moment ago, about helping her through the last couple of weeks, and she tilted her head. "So does that mean you plan to hang around town until the babies come?"

Licking his lips, he seemed to think very carefully about his words before he spoke. "Maya, I'd really like to. I've never been a father before. This is all...well, it's special to me. Scary as hell, totally out of line with my plans...but special. I'm...I'm not the kind of guy who can just walk away from something like this...and I know you probably don't believe that, but I think you will. If you give me a chance. Get to know me...just a little bit." He swallowed hard. "I'd really like you to agree with me on this, but I want you to know that I'm staying, even if you don't. I mean...I'm their father." He looked at her belly. "I'm their father."

The second time he said it, he got a shaky, crooked little smile on his face, and his voice cracked just the slightest bit. She couldn't argue with him when he looked like that. And he was right, she knew that. She'd been feeling guilty about her attitude toward him all night long. It wasn't his fault she didn't want a man in her life.

"I was crabby with you last night," she told him. "I get that way a lot lately. But it's not my normal attitude, you know."

"I know."

She nodded. "I will not exclude you from the babies' lives. I want to make that clear, Caleb. You're right. You are their father, and you can be just as involved with them as you want or need to be. I promise you that."

He smiled broadly and blew a sigh of relief. "I'm glad to hear it." Then he glanced down at her belly. "Still nervous as hell and reeling from all this...but glad."

The babies were kicking like crazy. She had a thought, bit her lower lip, and finally gave in to it. "Give me your hand," she said, setting her Danish down.

He did. She took his hand in hers and laid his palm on her belly, sliding it around to the spot where some little foot had been repeatedly thumping her. He met her eyes, his expectant, excited. It took a moment. But finally there was a succession of rapid and rather forceful kicks.

She never looked away from his eyes when it happened. And she was glad she hadn't, because they widened; then his gaze slid down to where his hand rested, and she swore she saw moisture gather in his eyes. "My God. Oh my God," he whispered.

"You look like you're going to faint, Caleb. It's okay. Babies are supposed to kick. It means they're healthy."

"Are you sure?"

She nodded.

Caleb laughed nervously, gave his head a shake, met her eyes again. "I...it's like it wasn't quite real until just then." Then he frowned. "Does it hurt when they do that?"

"Oh, they give me a good jab once in a while. Enough to make me suck in a breath, maybe, but nothing drastic."

He stared at her for a long moment as if a little awed by her. But then he shook himself and went back to the tray, brought her cup of coffee. "Better drink this while it's still warm."

"You didn't need to do all this, Caleb."

"I wanted to, I told you."

She sipped the coffee. Finished the Danish. Grabbed a doughnut.

"Your mother says you, um…have a doctor's appointment today," he said, speaking slowly.

"Yeah. In an hour actually."

He looked at her, his blue eyes conveying a clear message. She rolled hers and sighed. "Don't tell me you want to come along."

He nodded hard. "Only if it won't make you too uncomfortable," he said quickly.

"When the stirrups come out, pal, you leave the room. Got it?"

He shuddered. "I…think I can safely promise that much." Turning, he went to the two cribs, checked them out, nodding in approval. "Why the mesh on the inside?" he asked.

"The slats were a bit too far apart on the older models. Of course, the five of us survived them, but you can't be too careful."

Nodding, he reached in to touch the soft blankets. "I've never seen a baby quilt like this before."

"That's because I made it."

He turned toward her, his brows arched, then lifted the quilt out of the crib for a closer examination. Building blocks with letters on them, and bunnies and teddy bears, all hand stitched, in various textures and colors, littered the piece. "Wow. This is some intricate work, Maya." Then, grinning at her, he said, "I guess my plan is working."

"What?" she asked.

"To get to know you better," he explained. "Already I've learned something about you. You quilt."

The sound of a throat being cleared made them both look toward the door, where Kara stood looking in at them. Her head was only a few inches below the doorframe.

"She quilts, she sews, she cooks—the woman makes Martha Stewart look like an amateur."

"Oh, cut it out, Kara. I'm not auditioning for anything here."

Kara only shrugged. "Caleb," she said, "I have a favor to ask you."

He said, "Anything at all, Kara. What do you need?"

"Well, with all that's been going on, we haven't even got a Christmas tree up yet."

He tipped his head to one side. "Hell, I can't even remember the last time I had a tree for Christmas."

"Really?" Kara asked. "Why not?"

"I don't know. It's just me and my father, and I guess we…" He shook his head. "I don't know. So, what do you need? Help getting a tree?"

"Yeah. Not that we can't do it ourselves. I mean, we do every year, but the pickup seems to be acting up this morning. It doesn't want to start. So I thought maybe you'd volunteer yours."

"Sure. When?"

"Sooner the better," Kara said with a smile. "How about right after you two get back from the doc?"

"No problem." Caleb smiled. "Actually, I'm kind of looking forward to it."

Kara's smile had enough wattage to light the entire town of Big Falls, Maya thought.

"Hey, we should probably be going pretty soon," Caleb said. "I'm going to go out and start the car, let it warm up." He glanced at Maya. "I'm assuming you want to take the van, right?"

"It's the most comfortable for me."

He nodded and headed out of the room. Maya heard his feet running down the stairs. Her sister sent her an innocent look, and then turned to go.

"Kara, hold it right there."

Stopping, but not turning, Kara said, "What?" in a squeaky voice.

"What did you do to our pickup?"

Now she did turn. She must have thought those fluttering lashes would help her cause. "What do you mean?"

"You did something so it wouldn't run, so that you could con Caleb into coming with us to get the tree. Didn't you?"

Her brows came down fast. "You have a suspicious mind!"

"And you haven't denied a thing."

Kara crossed her arms over her chest. "I *like* him." Then she tipped her head to one side. "Besides, did you see his eyes light up? Did you hear what he said about not remembering the last time he bothered to celebrate Christmas with his father?"

"That's not what he said—he said he couldn't remember the last time he got a tree," Maya corrected.

"So how do you celebrate Christmas without a tree?" Kara shook her head. "He's lonely, Maya. I can see it."

"Yeah, well…maybe."

"Aren't you even curious?"

Behind her, Caleb said, "Curious about what?" Kara gasped and whirled on him. He only grinned, gave her a mischievous wink, and looked past her to Maya. "Your chariot awaits. But you can finish your coffee first. Give it time to warm up."

"I'll take the coffee with me," she said. "The sooner we get this over with, the better." She drew a breath, preparing herself for the inevitable awkward moment when she was forced to get her bulk up out of a chair. But before she could even begin, Caleb was there. He slid one arm behind the small of her back, steadied her with the other, and helped her up so easily anyone would have thought she must be tiny.

She liked it.

And that scared her.

# Chapter 9

Caleb caught himself sliding into a mire of sentimentality more than once on that drive to the small redbrick prenatal clinic in Tucker Lake, fifteen miles the other side of Big Falls. It was a dangerous game he was playing out here. Getting emotionally involved with the babies...insinuating himself into the family and into Maya's life before he even knew for sure that he was the father.

But hell, they were twins. *He* was a twin. His own father had been a twin, too. But, like Caleb's own twin brother, his uncle had been stillborn.

Damn, but it terrified him to think of that. It also verified that these children were his. Maybe not totally, and maybe not legally, but it was all the proof he needed.

He couldn't leave. That was obvious. He didn't *want* to leave. Exactly what he *did* want was as elusive as the meaning of life on Earth. What to do next was a question too deep to even begin to figure out. It seemed all he could do was stumble through, one step at a time. If it turned out that Maya was lying to him, then he was setting himself up for a big fall. The problem was, she wasn't lying to him. He might be a gullible idiot, but he just…believed her. Maybe because he wanted to believe her, an even scarier thought!

That worried him.

They didn't have to wait long. He was glad, because being in the waiting room surrounded by swollen-bellied women and nervous-looking men made him feel like a fraud. As if he didn't belong. As if they could take one look at him and tell he was an outsider, not a real partner to the mother of his kid. Kids.

"Come on in, Maya," a nurse said, only moments after they had taken seats in the waiting room.

Caleb helped Maya to her feet and held her arm as they were led to a small exam room.

Maya seemed to know the drill by heart. She walked in, stepped on the scale, then used a small stepping stool to get up onto the exam table. She lay back, and the nurse whipped out a tape measure and peeled Maya's blouse back and leggings downward to measure her belly. "Any problems?" the nurse asked cheerfully.

Caleb stared at the swollen mound of pink flesh underneath Maya's blouse. Her belly button was turned inside out.

"None," Maya said. "Stop staring, Caleb."

Grinning, the nurse jotted a note and proceeded to take Maya's blood pressure, then her pulse, simultaneously shooting glances at Caleb every once in a while. Curious, pointed glances, but she didn't ask.

He didn't know how much to say, so he said nothing at all.

When she finished, she said, "The doctor will be in soon," and headed out the door.

Maya remained lying down on the exam table, although she did rearrange her blouse. He assumed it was probably too much effort to get up. Caleb paced and looked around the room. Baby scales, baby pictures on the wall. A chart denoting the phases of labor, which he found himself studying intently.

"Sit down," Maya said. "You're making me nervous."

He sent her a sheepish grin and sat down, but the moment his buttocks touched the chair, the door opened, so he shot back up again. The doctor came in. Fortyish, redheaded and female. There were silver frames on her oval glasses and a ready smile on her lips.

"Maya! How are those babies doing this week, hmm?"

"Kicking up a storm, Dr. Sheila," Maya said.

"That's the way we like 'em." She turned to Caleb, offered a hand. "I'm Sheila Stone, Maya's ob-gyn," she said.

"Good to meet you, Doctor. I'm Caleb...er....Cain." Maya shot him a look he couldn't read. "I'm...uh...I'm the..."

"Father?" she asked.

He nodded, not waiting for Maya's permission.

"Well, congratulations. I'm glad to see you're here for the blessed event." She pulled her stethoscope to her ears, leaned over and moved it around until she found the spots she wanted.

"Doctor, is it normal for the babies to kick so much? I mean, they're really...active in there." He saw Maya's curious gaze on his when he asked the question. She had eyes that could hold a thousand emotions, he thought, and he wished he could read every one of them. But they tended to bubble up and swirl and sink again in such rapid succession and unlikely combinations that he thought he never would. He would glimpse something, some glimmer, but it would be replaced by another before he could get a handle on it.

"It's perfectly normal, Caleb," the doctor was saying as he plumbed the depths of Maya Brand's eyes. "It means they're strong and healthy."

Again she leaned over, listening to Maya's belly, and he dragged his eyes away from the depths of the mother to observe the doctor for signs of dishonesty or worry or anything telling at all.

"But...is it safe for them to be so active? I mean...with two babies...it is possible they could...you know, hurt each other?"

"Oh...they may poke each other a bit now and then," Dr. Stone said. "But they're very well protected, Caleb. Completely surrounded and cushioned by amniotic fluid. And while those kicks may seem pretty solid to us out here, the babies aren't strong enough to seriously harm each other. Really, with the quality of prenatal care we have today, twins are barely any more concern to us than single birth babies."

She might be lying to him, he thought. Perhaps because Maya was in the room. Oh, he *wanted* to believe her. But he knew better, didn't he? He'd been told all his life how the stronger twins in his bloodline managed to survive at the expense of their weaker siblings.

"You look worried, Dad," Dr. Stone said. "Come here, let me reassure you." She motioned at Caleb to come closer. When he did, she snagged a second stethoscope from her pocket and handed it to him.

He took it, his hand shaking, and put it on. Then the doctor guided the other end to the right spot. And he heard it. Rapid as the beat of a hummingbird's wings—a tiny, powerful patter.

"Holy...my God, is that the baby's heart?"

"It sure is. Here, here's the other one," she said, moving the business end of the thing yet again.

Caleb closed his eyes as he heard the second beat, every bit as strong and steady as the first. "Are they supposed to be that fast?" he asked, eyes closed as he listened.

"They're just right," Dr. Stone assured him.

When he opened his eyes again, they were slightly blurry, and Maya's were staring right into them. Probing and seeking and surprised and a dozen other things. "It's amazing," he said. "I...I don't even know what to say."

"So are you planning to be in the delivery room, Caleb?"

He blinked and felt his eyes widen as they shot to the doctor's.

Maya smiled. "Don't panic, Caleb. No one expects you to do that."

"But...but..."

"Well, you've got time to think about that. But for now, it's time for the internal, and you need to wait outside."

"Okay. Okay, sure." He reached up and gave Maya's hand a squeeze before he left. Then he met her eyes, held them for a long moment, and without even knowing he was going to, he leaned down and kissed her very softly. Then he straightened, realized what he'd done and wondered why. It had just seemed...like the thing to do. "I'll...be right out there...if you need me."

She stared at him as if too stunned to speak, and he turned and fled.

In the waiting room, he paced. Hell, he didn't like this. He didn't like believing her without question, and he liked even less that he knew right to his toes that he was right to believe her. She wouldn't lie to him. She wasn't up to anything. She didn't even want him around, much less want his money, and even if she did, she wouldn't have to resort to scamming to get her hands on it. She could just ask. He would give it to her. All of it. He would give her everything he had, if she wanted it.

She was carrying two babies, and they were both his. His children. His babies. He wanted to be there when they were born. In the delivery room, right there. She was incredible... that she could do this thing, perform this miracle, give life to his offspring...it was mind-boggling to him.

Minutes ticked by. He spent the time pawing through the pamphlets, of which there seemed to be hundreds. He flipped through all of them, took several. Then added a couple of parenting and natural childbirth magazines to his collection. Finally the door opened, and the doctor called him back in. "It's not going to be long," she said. "I don't think you'll go another week, Maya."

"Thank God. I don't think I can take another week." Maya grimaced at the doctor as she got herself up into a sitting position on the table. "We're going to want a paternity test done as soon as they're born, Dr. Sheila," Maya said.

The doctor lifted her brows. "Sure. But I can already tell you their blood types. Not that it would prove you are the father, Caleb, but it could eliminate you."

Caleb shook his head. "I don't need that. I don't need—"

"I want it settled," Maya told him.

"I believe you, Maya. You don't have to prove anything to me."

She lowered her head, keeping her gaze from his. He couldn't even try to read her eyes. She said, "That…means a lot to me, that you'd say that, Caleb. Thank you."

"No. Thank you."

Lifting her head, meeting his eyes, she drew a breath. "Caleb, you're…who you are. The question of paternity is going to come up, sooner or later—someone's going to want proof. Maybe it won't be you. But it's going to happen. So I'd just as soon we get this done right away."

He thought about what she'd said, realized she was right. It *would* come up eventually. "All right. Okay, you're probably right."

The doctor flipped open the charts without so much as shooting Caleb a curious glance. He liked her. She was a pro. "Well, according to the amnio, the babies are both type O-negative. That doesn't match Maya, so it has to match the father. Do you know your blood type, Caleb?"

He lifted his head slowly. "Yeah. It's O-negative. And it's not a common blood type." He turned to face Maya. "I'd like…very much…to be in that delivery room with you, Maya. If you think you wouldn't mind too much.''

Frowning until her brows touched, she sighed. ''I…don't know.''

Dr. Stone eyed them both. ''When you make a decision, let us know, okay? The hospital needs to be forewarned.''

''Thanks, we will.'' Caleb watched the doctor go and turned back to Maya. ''I didn't mean to put any pressure on you. I mean…if it would make you uncomfortable, then—''

''We have a tree to cut down,'' Maya said. She started to slide off the table.

Caleb reached for her, picked her up and gently lowered her to the floor. Their eyes locked as he did, and Maya's cheeks went pink. Then he grabbed her coat and held it for her. But she shook her head slowly and glanced down.

He looked, too, and saw that she was standing there in her socks. Her warm suede shoes stood nearby. She, too, looked at the shoes. Then at him. Then at the shoes again. She kicked them closer to the chair where he'd been sitting earlier, then sat down and, biting her lip as if preparing to face some great challenge, bent to reach for the shoes.

Caleb got there first. ''Let me do that.''

''I can put on my own shoes.''

''Lean back in the chair, Maya. You bend over any further and my kids are going to be born with no necks. You're squishing them.''

''I am not.'' But she did lean back.

Caleb knelt down. He grabbed a shoe, then slid it gently onto a socked foot. He pulled the laces snugly and tied them up. ''Just like Cinderella,'' he quipped, picking up the other shoe.

''Yeah, but those aren't exactly delicate glass slippers.''

He shrugged. ''Yeah, well, Cindy didn't have to carry her coach-sized pumpkin around with her. It carried her, as I re-call.'' He slid the other shoe on, tied it and got to his feet.

"Last week I could reach," she said.

"Maybe next week you'll be able to reach again."

She closed her eyes fast, turning her head slightly. But not before he saw what flashed through her expression. "Hey," he said. "It's okay to be nervous about this. Hell, I'm nervous and I don't have to do anything." She didn't say anything. He caught her chin, tipped it up. "Are you? Nervous?"

For a long moment she stared into his eyes, and then she said, "I'm scared to death, Caleb." Her hands went to her belly. "I mean, what if I can't do it? One baby is hard enough. I went to the hospital one day just to check out the maternity ward. And I heard some woman screaming in the delivery room. It sounded like a Halloween horror movie on high volume. I thought she was being murdered in there."

He swallowed hard. "Did you talk to your mother about it? I mean, she's been through it so many times."

Maya lowered her head. "I don't want her to know how scared I am. Mom's...she's the strongest woman I've ever met. She thinks I'm like her."

"I think you are, too."

She shook her head. "I can't tell her I'm terrified of something as natural as giving birth. She'd be..."

"Disappointed?"

Maya nodded.

"Don't you think she was afraid the first time? Hell, I'll bet she was afraid every time, Maya. But your dad was there with her, right? And maybe that made it easier."

Maya sighed. "No. Dad wasn't there for her at all. Not for any of us. Mom...she gave birth five times, all by herself. Daddy...well, his job kept him traveling a lot. Or...that's what we all thought at the time."

Frowning as he helped her to her feet, Caleb asked, "But...it wasn't really his job that kept him away, was it, Maya? It was...his other family."

"Yeah," she said, smoothing her blouse, turning her back to him and shrugging into her coat with his help.

He waited, but she said no more.

"Will you tell me about it sometime?" he finally asked.

She shrugged. "I already told you about it, that night at the bar."

"You told me the facts. Not how it affected you or your mother or your sisters. I'd like to hear how you felt about it, when it all came out. How you feel about it now."

She shook her head. "It's irrelevant. It's in the past."

"Then will you tell me?"

She gave a shrug. "Maybe."

He nodded slowly, taking her elbow, steering her out the door, through the waiting room and into the parking lot where her van waited. He opened her door for her, helped her get in, then went to the driver's side.

After he started the engine he sat there for a minute. Then he said, "Tell me this much. What happened between your dad and your mom—is that why you don't trust men very much?"

"Who said I didn't trust men?"

He shrugged. "No one. No one had to, Maya. You've been suspicious of my every move, word and deed since I showed up here."

"Well, who wouldn't be?" She shook her head. "But for the record, it's not that I don't trust men. It's that I don't want to get hurt like my mother did—but, uh, by the looks of things, I didn't miss it by much. I mean, you didn't break my heart, but I sure as hell did end up with a pair of babies and no husband around."

He licked his lips and told himself not to blurt the words he blurted next. "That could be remedied, Maya."

Her eyes got wider than the rings around Saturn, and she stared at him as if he'd lost his mind. "You've got to be kidding me."

"No. No, I wasn't, as a matter of fact." Starting the van, he drove it into the road, and carefully back toward Big Falls.

She was still staring at him. He could feel her eyes on him, huge and probing. "You're out of your mind, Caleb. My God, I wouldn't even consider marrying you!"

The barb sank deep. He felt it clear to his bones. "Why not? I mean it's not like I'm the flat-busted drifter you thought I was before. I could give you anything, Maya. Everything."

Not one word came from her lips, and when he turned to ask why, the look in her eyes almost toasted him to a nice golden brown hue.

"How dare you?" she whispered.

He shrugged. "How dare I what?"

"Try to buy me! My God, do you really think I give a damn how much money you have or don't have? I wouldn't consider marrying you for one reason, and one reason only, Caleb Montgomery! I don't love you. I don't even *know* you."

"And what if you did?"

Her brows bent low, and her eyes burned him. "What if I did what? Know you? Or love you?"

"Both. What then?"

She lowered her head, her cheeks burning red. "This is ridiculous. It's a ridiculous conversation, Caleb. Because it's irrelevant. But the fact of the matter is, if I were in love with a man—any man—it wouldn't matter to me how much money he had, or what kind of truck he drove, or what he did for a living."

He searched her face, looking for the lie, but seeing no sign of it.

"The only thing that would matter," she went on, so earnestly it was difficult to imagine she might be making it up as she went along, "would be how he treated me and the babies. Whether he...felt the same way. I'll never be one of those women tied to a man who doesn't love her. I've seen them—the political wives, the trophy wives, the ones who married because they fit the profile their husbands were looking for, and vice-versa.''

He stared at her for so long he almost veered off the road. Then he looked straight ahead again. Snowflakes, huge and soft as balls of cotton fluff, came floating a few a time from the sky.

''You're right,'' he said finally.

''I know I am.''

He glanced sideways at her. ''I had a profile, you know. Just before I left that night when we first met, my father and his advisers had been filling me in on the woman I was going to have to find and marry. Or should, if I wanted to win the senate race.''

Blinking slowly, she turned to look back at him. ''And I'll bet I missed on every point,'' she said. ''Go on, tell me the kind of woman you were looking for. Let's see, I imagine she should have at least been college educated, which I'm not. Probably her mother should not own a saloon, and I daresay her father being a bigamist wasn't on the list. I don't imagine being pregnant and unmarried showed up anywhere, either.''

He tilted his head to one side. ''I left that night because I didn't want to be tied to the woman who would fit their profile. And you're right—you would have missed it by a mile on one point in particular.''

''What's that? 'Must have class and breeding'?''

''No. It was item number seven, if I recall correctly. 'She must be pretty, but not too pretty.' '' He tried a charming smile on her. ''You're way too pretty.''

She averted her face quickly, stared outside, but her cheeks went pink. ''I'd have missed on a dozen points,'' Maya said softly, her voice raspy. Then she shrugged. ''But you already know I'm not up to your family standards, don't you? Isn't that why you lied about your name to Dr. Stone?''

He stepped on the brake, stopping the van dead center in

the middle of the deserted, snowy road. "Is that what you think?"

She didn't look at him, so he gripped her shoulders and turned her until she did. "Maya, I lied about my name to protect you and the babies and the rest of your family."

This time the message in her eyes was clear. Doubt. Skepticism. She didn't believe a word he said. "Protect us from what?"

"From public humiliation. Scandal. The press. A story like this gets out, Maya, and this town will become a circus. You wouldn't have a moment's peace, and what's left of your reputation would be in shambles."

She tilted her head to one side. "And so would yours."

With a sigh, he nodded. "Yes. So would mine. But that's not what I was thinking about when I gave the doctor a false name."

"And what about the last time—when you lied about your name to me? Was that to protect me, too?"

He swallowed hard, looking away. "I had reasons. They had nothing to do with you, Maya, I just...I was running away from who I was that night."

"That's convenient."

He lowered his chin, shook his head and put the van back into gear again. "I'm telling the truth, Maya," he said as he drove. "You're the one who's lying now."

"Me?" She shot him a surprised look. "What have I lied about?"

"When you said you don't have any problem trusting men."

She looked away. She needn't have bothered. It wasn't as if he had a snowball's chance in hell of reading whatever flashed into her eyes.

An hour later they pulled in at the house, and Maya reached over to blow the horn. Within minutes several bundled-up women came scrambling out the front door. One was carrying a small chainsaw. Mel, of course. She tossed it in the back of Caleb's pickup, then came to the driver's door of the van, tapped on the window. Caleb rolled it down.

"Where do you think you are, Caleb? New York?" she asked him.

"Huh?"

"Keys," Mel told him, holding out a hand, palm up. "You've got that thing locked up tighter than Fort Knox."

"Oh. Right." He dug in his pocket, fished out the pickup keys and handed them to her. "It's not that I think anyone's going to steal that heap," he told her. "Just habit."

"Oh, yeah? I suppose it would be, for a guy used to tooling around in a Mercedes-Benz sedan." Mel wore a blue knit hat with a fuzzy ball on top over her short dark hair. Her bangs stuck out from under it, and a couple of snowflakes had landed in them and clung like glittering ornaments.

"Lexus coupe," he told her. "It's less pretentious."

"Oh, yeah, right. That's downright slumming." But she said it with a smile. "So you may as well drive the van over. I'll take Mom with me in your truck. That is, if you trust me with your wheels."

Already the side door of the van was sliding open, and Selene and Kara were clambering into their seats, snapping their belts. "Sure I trust you," he told her.

"You should," Mel said. "I figure any collisions I might have can only improve the looks of that thing, anyway." She sent him a wink and turned away.

"Hey, I saw yours in the barn, Mel. Makes mine look like a luxury car," he called.

Mel stopped, turned and eyed him.

"And, I might add, mine runs."

She grinned and sent him a mock salute, then walked away. As he rolled his window up he heard Vidalia say, "I told you he'd loosen up once he got to know us."

In the back seat, Kara and Selene were still laughing at his exchange with Mel. As he put the van into motion, Kara said, "I'm so glad it's snowing! It really ought to snow on tree day, don't you think?"

"Oh, yes," Selene said, sobering. "Snow is a great backdrop for murdering a tree."

"Oh, gee, here we go..." Maya muttered.

"Oh, come on, Selene!" Kara cried. "Don't spoil it for us!"

"I can't help the way I feel! I just don't think it's nice to chop down millions of living trees every year just for our own selfish pleasure. Hell, we only throw it out a few weeks later!"

"It's not like we're chopping down *wild* trees, Selene," Kara argued. "These trees wouldn't exist without the custom! For Pete's sake, they are planted and raised just for this purpose! Selling them helps farmers make ends meet. You're so narrow-minded!"

"I am not. Life is life. Trees have spirit, and I don't see the sense in murdering them."

"Dammit, you two, enough!" Maya shouted. They went silent as she glared at them over the seat. "We are going to be joyful and filled with Christmas spirit while we choose our tree, do you understand?" She practically growled the words through clenched teeth. "Now stop fighting and be joyful, or I'll come back there and make you sorry!"

Caleb looked at the two pouting faces in the rearview mirror, then at Maya's angry one beside him. He cleared his throat and very softly said, "Can I...make a suggestion?"

All three sets of eyes turned on him. He swallowed hard. "The ground's not frozen yet. It wouldn't be all that hard to dig the tree up, instead of cutting it down. We could wrap the roots in burlap and soil, put it into a big tub of dirt, feed and water it all winter. Then, come spring, we can take it out and plant it again."

Selene's pout eased into a smile so soft and genuine that Caleb thought she might lean up and kiss him. She looked at Kara, and Kara smiled back and nodded.

Then he looked at Maya. But she wasn't reacting at all to his suggestion. Instead she said, "What do you mean 'we'?"

"Huh?"

"You said *we* could take the tree out and plant it in the spring. I want to know what you meant by that."

"I...well, hell, I don't know."

"Do you plan to be here in the spring, Caleb?"

She said it as if she were issuing a challenge. He decided to rise to it. "Are you and my children going to be here in the spring?" he asked her.

"Well, of course we are."

"Then...then so am I." He didn't know what the hell made him blurt those words. Had he lost his freaking mind?

"Hot damn," Kara said from the back seat. "You go, Caleb!"

"Shut up, Kara," Maya growled.

Caleb glanced at Kara in the mirror and sent her a wink. She smiled, and her eyes sparkled. He shifted his gaze to Selene, whose eyes were knowing, wise beyond their years. She gave him a very slight nod of approval, but the look she sent him said she had known it all along.

Caleb was worried. He'd said something he had no intention of saying. He had no idea if he *could* be around here in the spring. He would visit, of course, but that wasn't the way his statement had sounded. And now it was said. It was out there.

## Chapter 10

The truck and the van were parked side by side in the tree farm's driveway, and Maya was following the farmer up a snowy hill, surrounded by her sisters, her mother and Caleb Montgomery. She didn't know why he'd said what he had. That he would be here in the spring. He couldn't have meant it. He couldn't have. She wouldn't believe him. After all, he'd told her one night, eight and a half months ago, that he would still be here in the morning. But in the morning, he'd been gone. He hadn't so much as mentioned that to her, or offered an apology, much less an explanation. And she would be damned if she would stoop low enough to ask for either of those things. Far be it from Maya Brand to let a man think his presence or absence mattered that much to her.

It didn't. And it wouldn't. Not now, not ever.

She remembered the nights…the soft sounds of her beautiful mother crying alone in her room. She'd felt her mother's heartache as if it were her own, no matter how Vidalia had tried to hide it from her.

No. She wasn't going to let any man hurt her like that. And she would die before she'd subject her children to that kind of pain.

Besides, he couldn't very well run for the U.S. Senate from
Big Falls, Oklahoma. He couldn't serve from here if he won.
He was lying. Just plain lying. And all this concern for her,
for the babies, all this pampering and coddling and chivalry—
putting on her shoes, for God's sake—it was just an act. Jok-
ing with her sisters, respecting her mother. It was false. She
didn't know what the hell he wanted from her—maybe just
to win her over so he could then convince her to keep quiet
about his illegitimate babies. Whatever it was, it didn't matter.
She wasn't falling for it. He wouldn't be here when the chips
were down, when she really needed him. He wouldn't, because in her experience, men never were.

A twinge of pressure tightened around her belly and made
her lower back howl in protest. She stopped walking, her hik-
ing shoes ankle deep in the snow. Beside her, sharp as a tack
and twice as irritating, Caleb grabbed her arm. "Maya? You
okay?"

She blinked slowly, took a breath, and took stock. Nothing.
"Fine," she said. "Just a twinge. Not the least bit uncom-
mon."

They were twenty feet from the van, and there were twenty
more to go, up the side of a steep little hillock, to the field
of perfectly shaped little trees. And in spite of herself, Maya
sniffed the Christmassy scent of them, and felt her spirits rise.

"Smells good, doesn't it?" Caleb asked.

"Smells like a memory in the making," she said, not
knowing why. Her mother was always saying things like that.
But not her. It was a sappy, sentimental thing to say. She
turned to look at Caleb, at the snow falling on his shoulders
and dusting his dark hair. He was staring into her eyes and
looking confused, maybe a little emotional. Hell, it was that
time of year. Everyone was emotional.

"A memory in the making," he repeated. "I've never
heard that before."

She gave her head a shake. "Maybe I'll go back to the truck. Sit this one out."

"Now what kind of a memory would that be?" He moved closer, brushed the snow from her hair. "Come on, before they pick a tree without us."

Without warning, he scooped her into his arms, right off her feet, and started up the hill with her.

"Caleb! You're out of your mind! Put me down!"

"No way."

"I weigh a ton! You'll kill yourself."

"Hey, there are three of you here! And hell, you've been carrying these two kids of ours around for nine months. I think I can handle it for a minute or two."

*Ours.* She didn't like the way the word sounded on his lips, or on the air, and she liked even less the way her tummy tightened in response to the sound of it.

They reached the top of the hill and the tree lot. Caleb stopped trudging, but he didn't put her down. She was looking ahead at her sisters, running around like excited children from tree to tree, examining them from all angles. But now she drew her gaze in, turned it upward and focused it instead on the man who held her as if she were not the size of a small hippo. He wasn't even out of breath. And he was looking at her like...like...

"You're beautiful, you know that?" he said.

She lowered her lashes. "Stop."

"You are. Snowflakes on your lashes. Cheeks all pink and glowing. But it's more than that. I've been trying to put my finger on what's different...but it's not something I can name. It's something from inside."

"It's a pair of somethings from inside," she told him.

He smiled at her. Then he leaned down, and he kissed her. Long, slowly, tenderly. His mouth was warm, and he tasted so good she wanted to kiss him forever. Yet the kiss terrified her, partly because she wanted it so very badly. And then he lifted his head away.

She blinked rapidly, because there was moisture in her eyes, and she stared at him. ''Put me down.''

''What do you want for Christmas, Maya?''

She looked away fast when he said that. Because images of her childish wishes and dreams popped into her mind. A rambling log cabin. A dog to lie by the fireplace. A cat to sit in the window. Her own kitchen to fill with the smells of baking bread and Christmas cookies. Her children's wide sparkling eyes as they watched for Santa's reindeer on snowy Christmas Eves. And a loving, devoted husband coming through the front door, stomping the snow off his boots, his arms filled with presents for the kids. His eyes filled with love—for her.

''Maya?'' he asked.

She cleared her throat. ''Let's go get a tree before we start worrying about what to put underneath it.''

He set her down on her feet, and she trudged forward.

An hour later, a huge tree with roots enough to fill the entire back of Caleb's pickup was on its way to the Brand place. It was wrapped in burlap, and a half acre of the tree farm seemed to be coming with it. It had taken all that time for Caleb, Mel and Ben Kellogg, the farmer, to dig it up. And once they removed it, they had to fill in the hole and smooth things out as best they could. The farmer charged extra for the privilege of digging up a living tree. Caleb insisted on paying, since it was his idea.

It took a giant washtub to hold the thing. But Maya watched Selene's eyes light up when they finally got the tree home and standing upright in the living room. Her small hands were black with soil and her hair full of pine needles. She'd been underneath the tree, smoothing the soil they'd added to the tub, pouring in water and tree food, holding the base as they straightened it and tied it off to keep it in place.

And talking to it as if speaking to a puppy. The tree's lush branches completely hid the baling twine they'd used to support it, thank goodness.

Maya stood back and looked at it, shook her head at the dirt all over Mel and Caleb and the living room floor.

"My, my, but that's the nicest tree we've ever had," Vidalia said, shaking her head in awe.

"You say that every year, Mom," Maya told her.

"And every year it's the truth. We just keep topping ourselves." She smiled. "Well go on, now, Caleb, Mel, Selene, get washed up. Dinner in an hour, and there's plenty to do before that. We'll need all hands on deck for hauling out the decorations. Lord knows we're already late getting them up." She clapped her hands twice.

Maya looked at Caleb, closed her eyes. "That's my mother's way of inviting you to stay for dinner."

He smiled at her. "I figured that out. But I'd feel better if you were the one issuing the invitation."

"Would you really?"

He nodded. And he looked at her with those big eyes of his like a puppy dog. She felt something soften inside her. In spite of herself, she heard herself asking, "Would you like to stay for dinner, Caleb?"

His smile was fast and blinding. "Oh, yeah."

She rolled her eyes as he raced off to the bathroom to scrub his hands like an excited youngster. Vidalia came close to her, slid a protective arm around her shoulders. "He seems like a decent man," she said.

"Yes. He does, doesn't he?"

"He's your soul mate, Maya," Selene whispered from nearby.

"Hell, Selene, you just like him because he didn't support the tree killers of the family."

Selene shook her head slowly, coming closer, slipping her arm around Maya on the other side. "I do like that about him.

But, if you recall, I told you he was your soul mate that night a long time ago, in the saloon, when you first met him.''

Maya frowned and turned to the side.

"She did,'' Kara said, coming from the kitchen. ''I remember she told me the same thing.'' She sidled up to her mother, slung an arm around her. So there were four now in the link.

"What made you think it?'' Maya asked.

"Something in his eyes…and in yours. Plus I pulled a tarot card from my deck when I first noticed the sparks between you two. The Lovers.''

"You know I don't approve of those cards, Selene,'' Vidalia said.

"Not now, Mom, please. Come on, it's Christmas.''

Vidalia looked sideways at her, and her frown eased. She smiled and began to hum a carol, and in a few bars she began to sing the words, and they all joined in. At some point Caleb and Mel reappeared, and Mel slung an arm around Caleb's shoulders, dragged him to the tree and linked with the others. They both joined in the singing.

The timer bell from the oven pinged, and Vidalia stepped out of the arms of her children, dabbed at her eyes, and turned to hurry into the kitchen, muttering, ''Lord, it's almost perfect.''

When she was out of sight, Caleb sent Maya a questioning glance. ''Almost?'' he asked.

She nodded. ''There's one more of us,'' she said. ''I told you about her before, didn't I? Edie. Mom misses her most around the holidays.''

"We all do,'' Selene said, eyelids lowered.

"She doesn't come home for Christmas?'' Caleb asked.

Maya shook her head. ''She and Mom aren't on…the best of terms.''

"Not even speaking, you mean,'' Mel filled in.

They had broken ranks and were drifting toward chairs, the

sofa. Kara bent to paw through a box of ornaments Vidalia had brought down from the attic.

"But why?" Caleb asked.

Maya had settled into the corner of the sofa, and she noticed that he didn't hesitate to take the spot beside her. Awfully sure of himself, wasn't he?

Mel said, "Edie ran off to the West Coast with stars in her eyes, Caleb. But when she got there, she found a thousand other girls just as pretty and just as bright with the same dreams. Her biggest break to date was landing a gig as a model for *Vanessa's Whisper.*"

His eyes widened just a bit. *"Vanessa's Whisper?"* he asked. And when Mel nodded, he said, "Wow, I had no idea. Maya told me she modeled lingerie, but I didn't realize she was that famous. Why didn't anyone say anything sooner?"

Maya blinked at him. "You think we go around advertising it?"

"Hell, if it were my sister I'd erect a monument in the middle of town to her success."

"Success, Caleb? My sister poses in her underwear. And the closest thing to a monument to her in this town is Wade Armstrong's body shop, where my sister's photos, clipped from the pages of the catalogue, are the basic wallpaper pattern."

Caleb's brows came together. *"Vanessa's Whisper* is big time, Maya. Your sister had to have competed against hundreds of models to land a contract with them. Do you know how many actresses got their starts as models? This is a big deal."

"That's what I keep trying to tell them," Selene said. "Edie's gorgeous, and the beauty of the female form is nothing to be ashamed of."

"Nor is it something to spread naked on the walls of body shops for dirty minded men to drool over," Maya said primly.

"She doesn't pose nude, Maya, and you know it," Mel put in.

Kara looked up. "I don't care what she does. I think you and Mom have been too hard on her, and I just want her to come home."

Maya lifted her brows in disbelief, then slid a glance toward Caleb. "And you agree with her?"

"Well…yeah, frankly, I do. I think you ought to be congratulating your sister, not condemning her."

Maya thinned her lips. "And how would you feel if it were your daughter posing in an eye patch and a rubber band, airbrushed, glossed over and sent to thousands of pairs of horny eyes all over the country?"

He blinked, and she knew she had nailed him on that score. "I…hadn't thought of it that way."

"Well maybe you should."

"Shssh! Mom's coming," Kara said.

"Dinner in a half hour," Vidalia said, smiling. "Then we'll decorate this tree."

Maya lifted her brows and parted her lips to protest. It was bad enough her family had conspired to get Caleb to escort her to the doctor, then dragged him into their family tree expedition. And invited him to dinner. But to invite him to actually help decorate the tree was going just a bit too far.

"I'd be intruding, Vidalia. That's…that's a family thing. I've already been hanging around here too long."

He looked almost sad to have to say so.

"Bullcookies!" Vidalia squawked. "Are you the father of my grandbabies or aren't you?"

"He's not gonna answer that one until after the DNA tests, Mom," Maya said softly.

That earned her a sidelong scowl from Caleb. "I am," he said to Vidalia. "Though the idea of you being a grandmother is almost as stunning to me as that of me being a father."

Vidalia smiled and sent him a wink. "That makes you family. Period." Then she leaned closer to him and said, "That doesn't mean you need to ease up on the efforts to flatter your way into my good graces, however."

"I wasn't planning to." His smile came slowly. First one side of his mouth pulled upward, and then the other. "It's been a long time since anyone's called me family, Vidalia," he said. All humble and sweet looking. The big phony. "Thank you."

Vidalia looked as if she were going to melt right into a puddle of pudding at his feet. And as Maya glanced around at her sisters, she saw that he'd wrapped them all around his fingers, as well. Even Mel looked at him without snarling.

Hell.

"You okay?"

She frowned and saw that the man of the hour was addressing her, still sitting beside her on the sofa. "My feet are swollen and my back aches and I have cramps in my calves that would down a bull moose."

He smiled softly and lifted her feet up off the floor, draping her legs across his lap and proceeding to rub her calves with his big hands. As he massaged the cramps away, she released a breath.

"Go on, relax. You know you want to," he said. "Lean back. Breathe, for crying out loud."

"I am breathing."

But she did lean back and let go. Hell, it felt great, what he was doing. She was only human.

"Sheesh, when did that start?" Kara asked from across the room. She stood with curtains parted, staring out the window. The snow was falling harder than before. The gently floating fluff of earlier in the day was now slanting downward at an alarming rate.

"I'd heard we might actually get an inch or two tonight," Vidalia called from the kitchen. "Come on, Kara, Mel, Selene, you three get upstairs and start bringing down the ornaments and lights, while I set the table.'' She glanced in at Maya, then Caleb. ''You two stay right where you are,'' she added with a wink. ''I've been trying to get that girl to lie down and relax for days but she's been just like a jitterbug on a hot plate lately....'' Her brows rose, and she tipped her head to one side. ''They used to say it was a sign the time was near, when a woman takes to acting all nervous and jittery like that.''

''We can only hope,'' Maya groaned, letting her eyes fall closed.

It was nine o'clock by the time he headed back to the boarding house. In a small town like Big Falls, that seemed like midnight. The town only had a handful of streetlights, and those were dim. But it was enchanting, all the same: the moon straining to shine through the thick night clouds, giant snowflakes falling like an invasion of tiny paratroopers.

He stomped the snow off his boots, then crossed the closed-in porch area and heeled them off. He carried them inside— then stood still as the man in the living room rose from the chair where he'd been sitting, apparently having tea with Mrs. Peabody, and turned to smile at him.

Caleb almost cursed aloud. Jace Chapin was grinning like a Cheshire cat. ''Well now,'' Caleb said slowly, wishing to God he could make the man disappear. ''What's the world's sleaziest tabloid reporter doing way out here in Big Falls?''

''Came to find out what the richest candidate for the U.S. Senate is doing way out here in Big Falls,'' Jace replied.

''I haven't declared my candidacy, Chapin. But getting the facts straight has never been your strong suit.''

The man shrugged and pursed his lips. ''Oh, but the facts this time are too good to resist,'' he said. ''I mean, the background on this unmarried pregnant woman you've been running around with is better than anything I could have invented, I gotta tell you.''

Caleb tried to look unconcerned, but he kept his eyes averted as he walked past the man, stood near the fireplace, set his boots down. "You're going to have to explain to me why the background story on a friend of mine would be of any interest to your readers, Jace. Because, frankly, I'm clueless."

"Oh, come on, Montgomery. It's your kid. I have photos of you escorting this woman into the clinic in the next town. Having dinner with her. Carrying her up a snowy hill to pick a Christmas tree."

"That's quite a leap of the imagination, even for you. From dinner to fatherhood."

He shrugged. "I've got more. Just wanted to give you a chance to comment before the story runs in tomorrow's edition."

"Run this story, Jace, and I promise, I'll bury you."

Jace's brows lifted. "And what will you do for me if I *don't* run it, Montgomery?"

Caleb narrowed his eyes on the man, finally reading him. "You're slime, you know that, Jace? How much do you want?"

He shrugged. "Five hundred grand...for now."

"Fine."

"Fine? You mean you'll pay it?"

Caleb had his hand on his cell phone already. "Just tell me where to transfer the funds and I'll call—"

A click made him stop speaking. Jace had one hand in his pocket, and he pulled out a minirecorder. "That's all I need, Montgomery. If this wasn't your kid, you wouldn't be so desperate to keep it quiet. I can name my price for this story."

Caleb reached for the little weasel, but he ducked, and ran for the door. Caleb ran after him, only to stop at the porch, sock feet already damp, as he saw the man slam his car door, and lurch into the narrow street.

"Son of a—"

"Oh, my. Oh, dear. Oh, my, what are you going to do? Poor Maya! Poor, poor Maya. That dear girl..." Ida-May Peabody wrung her hands and paced behind him. "I had no idea! I should never have let that man in here. Oh, my."

"Now, Ms. Peabody, you know this isn't your fault. You had no way of knowing," Caleb assured her.

She didn't look too relieved.

He had to get to his room, call Bobby, see what could be done about damage control. And then...then he had to warn Maya.

Damn, if she didn't already dislike him enough...

"He'd make a real nice addition to this family, you know," Vidalia Brand said softly. She and Maya were sitting in front of the fireplace. Maya had her feet up. Her backache had been growing steadily worse all day, and now it was really hurting. The dishes were done, and her sisters had all gone to bed. The tree winked and sparkled magically.

"He will be a part of the family," she told her mother. "As the babies' father, he'll be as much a part of it as he wants to be."

"Looks to me like he wants to be...even more than that."

"Mother, please..."

Vidalia shrugged, sighed a surrender. "Not easy, you know. Raising a family alone."

Looking up, Maya saw her mother's eyes. The lines at the corners, the hard-worn contours. "You are a hell of a woman, Mamma. Did I ever tell you how much I admire you? No, really. I mean it. You did fine by us. No man could have done better. And I know it was hard. Probably the hardest thing you ever did in your life, raising us alone."

"No, child. The hardest thing I ever did was saying goodbye to your father."

Maya closed her eyes, lowered her head. Her father had

been a two-timing slime bag. But damn, her mother's loyalty ran deep.

"I think that man could love you, girl."

Lifting her head, she met her mother's eyes. "I don't want him to…. I don't want to—"

"To believe in him? I know. You're afraid he'll let you down, break your heart, the way your father did to me."

"I don't want to talk about it," she corrected.

"It was worth it, Maya. The time we had together—it was worth the hurting later on. And just because you admire me for having survived the raising of a family without the help of a man, doesn't mean you should wish it for yourself, because it's no kind of rose garden."

Reaching out, she covered her mother's hand with her own. "There's a difference, Mamma. You had nobody. I have you. And Kara and Selene and Mel."

"And Caleb," her mother insisted stubbornly.

"No. The babies will have Caleb. I won't."

"But, Maya…"

"Mother, that's enough. I'm not going to discuss this. There is no way I'll let myself get tangled up with any man I can't depend on."

"But…but how do you know you can't depend on Caleb?" she asked, seemingly dumbfounded.

"He already left me once. Just walked out, without a word. And eight and a half months later, he waltzes back in again like nothing's happened. Just like…" She bit her lip.

"Just like your father," Vidalia finished for her.

"Oh, Mom, I didn't mean—"

"Yes, you did. I'll remind you, daughter, that you are talking about the man I love." She got to her feet and stomped away, up the stairs, and Maya heard the bedroom door slam.

Damn. She hadn't meant to insult her father or hurt her mother's feelings. What was wrong with her, anyway?

She strained to her feet and waddled through the house,

checking locks, shutting off lights. She paused at the window to glance outside. Then she let the curtain fall back into place and sent a sidelong glance at the telephone. She told herself that she was not hoping he would call to say good-night.

One hand on her aching back, she turned to go upstairs. And then the telephone rang, and she knew it was him before she even picked it up.

"Hello?"

"Maya?" he asked. "Why aren't you sound asleep by now?"

She pursed her lips. "How do you know I wasn't?"

He hesitated. Then, "Oh, God, I'm sorry. Did I wake you?"

Her lips pulled into a smile in spite of herself. "No. I was just on my way up."

"Well…well good. You, um…you need your rest."

"You sound like my mother. Why are you calling, Caleb? Is something wrong?"

"No. I mean…yes." He sighed.

She heard it and frowned. "You're leaving, aren't you?"

"What?"

"It's all right. I've been expecting it. I never asked you to stay, Caleb. Hell, at least you're calling to let me know…this time."

"Maya…I'm not going anywhere. I'm calling because… Wait a minute, what do you mean, 'this time'?"

She closed her eyes. "Nothing. Just tell me why you're calling."

It took him a moment. She wondered why. "I can't tell you how sorry I am about this, Maya, but there's been a leak. The story's out. There was a tabloid scumbag waiting here when I got back to the boarding house tonight. Apparently he's been following us around, snapping pictures. God only knows how much dirt he thinks he's dug up on us."

Maya closed her eyes in relief, which was so odd that she

felt like smacking herself in the head for feeling it. But she felt it all the same. A wave of relief that he hadn't called to say goodbye. And while the actual news should seem far more serious than the latter would have been, it felt small in comparison.

She must be losing her mind. Maybe it was hormonal.

"Maya?"

"Yes. I'm here. I'm just…well, I'm just not sure why you're telling me this. What can I do about it?"

There was a long pause. "I just wanted you to be warned. It'll hit the tabloids tomorrow, and the press will be stampeding into town in droves."

"Well…then you'll be able to tell your side of the story, won't you?"

"I'm afraid my side of the story isn't exactly going to help matters."

She sighed. "This is liable to ruin your chances for the Senate, isn't it, Caleb?"

"I don't know. It might."

"It will. If they go digging for dirt in my background, they won't have to dig far, Caleb. My family is…rolling in it." She licked her lips nervously.

"It's not me I'm worried about here, Maya. It's you, your family. I don't want this upsetting you—you're in no condition to—"

"Everything upsets me in this condition," she said. "But I'm getting used to it."

"I'm going to fix this, Maya. I'm going to find a way to make it all right again. I promise."

"Don't make promises, Caleb. I don't like when they get broken."

"I promise," he said again. "Try to rest, Maya. I'll be there first thing in the morning."

"You will?"

"Yeah. I will."

She pursed her lips, bit them to keep from making some remark about the last time he'd promised to be around in the morning, and whispered good-night. Then she hung up the phone and went up to bed. But she didn't sleep for a very long time, and when she did, the dreams that plagued her were odd and frightening.

She wore white and walked into the church on a fine summer Sunday, with two gorgeous toddlers clinging to her hands. But she found the church doors blocked by a crowd of her neighbors, all of them pointing at her and whispering words that blended together. *Trash. Sinner. Harlot.* And then they aimed those fingers at her children, and the whispers grew louder. *Bastards. Fatherless. Illegitimate. Bastards.*

Beyond them all she saw Caleb, his suit impeccable, turning away and sneaking out the church's back door.

She looked down at her pristine children, but they wore rags now, and their faces were coated in tear-streaked dirt. And her own white dress had turned to scarlet.

She sat up in bed with a gasp and a sharp pain in her middle. But then it eased, and she lay back again. "Just a dream," she said. "This is the twenty-first century, for God's sake. They don't tar and feather fallen women anymore."

Maybe not literally, a little voice inside her whispered. No, the ways of making people feel less than worthy were far more subtle these days. The whispered remarks, the constant slights. The invitations that didn't arrive, and the distasteful looks of those who considered themselves better.

She'd grown up with all of those things. They had hurt her, because she'd been too smart a child to not be aware of them. She did not want her children to feel the sting of nasty people and their nasty attitudes.

And yet she didn't know how she could prevent it.

# Chapter 11

The telephone rang at 7:00 a.m. Maya had finally fallen into a fitful sleep, but the sound woke her instantly, and even as she rolled over, covered her head and decided to ignore it, she heard her mother's voice from downstairs as she answered the call. But when she spoke again, Vidalia's tone made Maya's eyes blink wider, and all thoughts of sleep vanished.

"Exactly where do you get the nerve to call my home and ask me something like that, mister? Don't you dare call here again!" There was a bang, no doubt the sound of the phone being slammed back into its cradle.

Maya got up, tugged on her industrial-sized bathrobe and went into the hall barefoot. She was halfway down the stairs when the phone rang again. And by the time she got to the bottom her mother was slamming it down just like before.

"What is it, Mom? Who was that?"

Her mother looked at her as Maya crossed the living room. The angry look on her face immediately eased, and she replaced it with a false smile. "Nothing for you to worry about, hon. Just some kid playing pranks on us, is all."

Her mother was lying, trying to protect her. She knew that.

Maya reached the kitchen, eyed the filled coffeepot and longed for some real caffeine, and the phone rang yet again.

She snatched it up before her mother could.

"Hello, is this Maya Brand?" a strange voice asked.

"Who wants to know?" She walked to the coffeepot, took a mug from the tree and filled it.

"I'm Ben Kylie, a reporter for the *Herald,* ma'am. Do you have any response to the story in this morning's *Daily Exposé*?"

"I don't read trash, Mr. Kylie, so I have no clue what story you mean."

She eyed her mother, who was sending her a look of pure worry.

"You mean…you haven't seen it?"

"No, I haven't. And I'm very busy today, so if you could get to the point…"

"Sure. The point is the *Exposé* says you're carrying the child of Cain Caleb Montgomery III, as the result of a drunken one-night stand last spring. It claims you yourself are the illegitimate progeny of a bigamist with connections to organized crime and a barmaid, and that your family's main claim to fame is that you have a sister who poses nude for men's magazines. Is this basically accurate?"

Her mouth had fallen open as the man spoke, and now she drew the phone away from her ear to stare at it in disbelief.

A firm, warm hand took the telephone from her, and she looked up through welling tears to see Caleb standing there. "Ms. Brand has no comment at this time. However, rest assured that her team of lawyers are even now preparing their libel suit. I would be extremely careful about what I printed if I were you." He clicked the phone down, held it two seconds, then picked it up again and laid it on the counter, off the hook.

His eyes met Maya's. "I'm sorry. My God, Maya, I'm so sorry."

She held his gaze, even though hers was swimming now. "Did the *Daily Exposé* print what that man said it did?"

"I...what did he say?"

"Don't avoid the question, Caleb. You know what he said. Have you seen the story or not?"

He licked his lips. "Yes."

"And do you have a copy with you?"

He shook his head side to side, hard. Too hard.

She held out her hand.

"No."

"Fine. I'll go to the general store and buy my own copy." She reached for the door.

"Maya, for crying out loud, you're barefoot and in your pajamas!" her mother said, reaching past her to press a palm to the door.

"So what, Mom? You afraid the neighbors will talk?" Her voice broke just a little with the irony.

"Look, it doesn't matter what that rag sheet said or didn't say, Maya. All that matters is how we respond to it."

Maya sank into a chair at the kitchen table, lowered her head onto her arms. "If it doesn't matter, then why won't you let me see it?"

Her voice sounded muffled, even to her. But he could hear her. She knew he could.

"Maya...try to understand." He sat down in the chair beside her, and his hands closed on her shoulders. "You're carrying my babies. I want to protect you from this kind of garbage. I want to stand between all that ugliness and my family."

Very slowly, she lifted her head. She knew her eyes were probably wet and red, and her hair was likely sticking up all over. She hadn't even showered yet this morning. And yet he looked at her with nothing more than kindness, tenderness, caring, in his eyes.

"Isn't that what a father is supposed to do?" he asked her.

"It's what a mother is supposed to do, too, Caleb." She sat up a little straighter. "Thanks for reminding me of that."

"Well, hallelujah," Vidalia said, smiling. "I wondered where my daughter was hiding for a minute there."

"She's back, Mom." Maya sent her mother a loving smile. Then turned to face Caleb again. "I'm Vidalia Brand's eldest daughter. I need to see the newspaper, and I promise you, I'm not going to fall apart when I do. No matter what it says."

Caleb lifted his brows and turned to glance at Vidalia. She gave him a nod. Looking as if he thought better of it, he reached inside his jacket and pulled out a folded-up tabloid newspaper. On the front page was a photo of Maya and Caleb walking into the clinic, obviously taken the day before. The headline said Front-Running Candidate's Dirty Little Secret.

She lifted her chin, folded the paper back up. "I'm going to shower and put on some decent clothes. I'll take this with me."

"Maya, don't worry. We're going to fix this. I promise."

She looked at Caleb, so strong, confident, sure of himself. "You really do care about these babies, don't you?" she asked. Because it was suddenly so crystal clear to her that he did.

He held her gaze. "I didn't know it was even possible to care this much, Maya."

She smiled a bit unsteadily. "I know."

"Do you need help...with anything?"

She shook her head. "My sisters are still upstairs. I'll, um...I'll call them if I need them." Then she frowned as a thought occurred to her. "Mom, if Mel catches any reporters snooping around, there's going to be trouble."

Her mother looked worried, then looked at Caleb. Good Lord, why was everyone suddenly turning to him for answers? They'd gotten along just fine without a man forever!

"No reporters will be near the place. I was on the phone half the night getting things set up. We've got security men stationed out front. No one's going to get past them. My top aid is on his way here with my legal team. They'll help us formulate our response. And by the time you get out of the shower, Maya, you'll have a new private telephone number.''

She tilted her head. ''You work fast.''

''I've been in this game a while.''

She got to her feet, but before she turned to go, he stopped her, placing his hands tenderly on her swollen belly. ''I'll make it all right…for all of you. I promise.''

She laid her hands over his. ''I honestly believe you'll try, Caleb.''

He was looking very deeply into her eyes just then, and there was something else. ''All this…all that's been happening…there hasn't been time to talk about…anything else.''

She lowered her head. ''What else is there?'' And before he could answer, she turned and hurried away.

By the time she came back downstairs, dressed in her prettiest maternity clothes, back throbbing and clenching in protest, Maya's home was crawling with strangers. Men with radios and headsets sipped coffee and munched on crumb cake in the kitchen, and the dining room table was surrounded. Mel, Selene, Kara and Vidalia lined one side of the long oak table, while three men in dark blue suits lined the other. Caleb sat at the head, and the chair to his right was empty.

''I'm telling you, Caleb,'' one animated man in his late twenties was saying. ''I can spin this thing into solid gold, for both you and Ms. Brand.''

''She's not going to like it, Bobby,'' Caleb said.

''What won't I like?''

Everyone looked up to see her. The men rose, and Caleb pulled out the empty chair for her. ''Gentlemen,'' Caleb said, ''meet Maya Elouisa Brand, the mother of the heirs to the Montgomery fortune.''

She blinked in surprise. "That's a far cry from my former title—'the slut who destroyed the Montgomery legacy.'"

"Thank you," the impeccably dressed, almost boyishly good-looking Bobby said.

She frowned at him. "Why are you thanking me?"

"For the compliment on my work. 'Mother of the heirs to the Montgomery fortune.' That's mine. It's what I do," he explained. "You're status is soon going to be the American equivalent of royalty, Ms. Brand. I'm the best spin doctor in the business. And you…well…" Shaking his head, holding his palm up toward her, he smiled. "Hell, with you to work with, this is going to be a cakewalk."

She frowned. "I'm afraid I don't follow." She went to her chair, took it, and the men sat down.

"Well, *look* at you. You're gorgeous. And you have that clean, natural, healthy look about you."

"I'm not sure whether to thank you or offer to let you check my teeth," she said.

Bobby smiled even harder. "Perfect. Wit, too. You're perfect."

"Perfect for what, Mr.…um…?"

"Bobby McAllister. Just consider me your new right-hand man."

She glanced at Caleb, who looked uncomfortable, and then at her mother and sisters, who sat there wide eyed and uneasy. "So what is this plan I'm not going to like?" She looked to Caleb.

He reached out, took her hands and drew a deep breath. "Believe me, this is not the way I would have…gone about this, given the choice, Maya. But…" He paused, looked at the men around the table, then at Vidalia. "Maybe it would be better if I could speak to Maya alone."

"Good thinking, son," Vidalia said with a smile of encouragement. "The family room is empty."

Caleb drew a breath so deep it made his chest expand. Then

he blew it out again, got to his feet and reached for Maya's hand. Frowning, she took it and let him help her up. "This better be good, Caleb," she told him. "Getting up out of a chair is no small effort, you know."

He shot her a look and a slight smile. A nervous one, though. And he kept hold of her hand as he led her through the doorway to the left, into what they called the family room. It held a wall of bookshelves, a sewing machine and several baskets full of half-finished projects, a writing desk, and an air hockey table. A smaller table in the corner held a propane burner and a double boiler. Strings tacked to the walls like miniature clotheslines had hand-dipped candles suspended from them to dry. And in yet another small alcove, a TV/VCR combination sat near a rocking chair.

Caleb stood in the center of the room, looking around at the odd collection and smiling.

"It's..."

"No, no...let me. The sewing stuff is yours. My crafty, talented baby-quilt maker. The candle making setup has to be Selene's. Actually, I'm surprised it's not a Ouija board or something."

"Mom makes her keep that in her room."

He smiled. "The air hockey has to be for Mel. And the books and television must be Kara's."

"She lives for fantasy," Maya said.

"The desk is your mother's."

She nodded. "Getting to know this family fast, aren't you?"

"I hope so." He walked to the most comfortable chair in the room, turned it slightly and nodded at her to sit on it.

She did. "What's Bobby's brilliant plan, Caleb?"

He stood in front of her for a minute. Then, finally, he took her hands in his and dropped down to one knee. "Maya..."

"Oh, come on—" She tugged her hand against the grip of

his and wished he wouldn't say what she thought he was going to say.

He held on tighter and said it anyway. "Let's get married."

She closed her eyes. "That's got to be the most ridiculous thing I've ever heard in my life."

He licked his lips, lowered his head. "Not *exactly* the reaction I was hoping for, Maya."

"Caleb, we barely know each other!"

"Maya, you're having my kids. Two of them. And…and, hell, if I had to choose a wife today, I can't think of anyone I'd rather marry than you."

"If you had to. The point is, you don't have to."

"No. I don't have to. And neither do you. But if you'll just listen to my argument here, I think you'll see that it's the logical thing to do."

"The logical thing to do would be to get up off the floor, Caleb."

He frowned at her, but got up. Pushing a hand through his hair, he turned and paced away, then paced back again.

"So, present your case, already. I can't wait to hear this."

"Okay. Here it is. Marrying me will be the difference between you being seen the way Bobby described you out there and the way that tabloid rag did. It is the difference between you being the most notorious member of your family or the envy of every woman in town. It's the difference between those babies you're carrying being legitimate or illegitimate. Between them being snubbed or respected as…practically as princes. And it will be the difference between our story being a dirty little scandal or a classic American fairy tale."

She pursed her lips. "And it will make the difference between you winning or losing the senate race."

He gaped at her. "My God, I don't even know if I'm going to run! Maya, that is the last thing on my mind, I swear to you."

She narrowed her eyes on him, not sure she believed that. But she did know he cared for the babies. Deeply.

"I...I don't know, Caleb. This is...this is very sudden and I...well, I don't..."

"Is there someone else?"

He asked the question so suddenly she almost hurt her neck snapping her head up. "Someone else?" she asked. "Are you out of your mind? Have you *looked* at me lately?"

He muttered something that sounded like, "In my sleep," but she couldn't be sure. "You're beautiful, smart, sexy as hell."

"I'm a heffalump."

He smiled then, broadly, widely, and came back to her. He ran a hand over her hair, cupped her cheek. "Tell me there's no one else."

She rolled her eyes. "There's no one else."

"Then why not me? Hmm? Maya, I can give you everything."

"I don't *want* everything." She bit her lip, sighed heavily. "I want to live here, not in Tulsa or D.C. or wherever you'll end up if you win this thing."

"You'll be able to do that. I promise."

"Yes, I imagine I will." But where would he be? She didn't voice the question. "I don't want my kids getting their hearts broken, Caleb. I don't want them giving their whole hearts to a father who's going to walk out on them and leave them bleeding. I can't do that to my babies."

His eyes widened, and they seemed wounded, way down deep. "That's what your father did to you, didn't he, Maya?"

She closed her eyes, nodded. "I really did love him. And Mom...oh, God, she still adores the man. But he was cheating on her, cheating on all of us, and it hurt me, Caleb. It tore my mother apart, and it broke my heart. He was never around when we needed him, and we never knew why until he was dead and gone." She lifted her eyes to his, knowing they were tearing up again. "I know it almost killed my mother. But she was a strong woman. I was just a little girl, and I can't even begin to tell you how the truth ravaged my whole world. Everything I knew, believed, had been a lie. Now I'm the mother. And I'm strong, and I can take anything this world can dish out. But I won't subject my kids to that kind of heartache, Caleb. I won't let you hurt my children the way my father hurt me."

He stood there for a moment. Then he sank to the floor again, just sitting down in front of her chair. He drew a deep breath and sighed heavily. "I've been meaning to explain some things to you. So much has happened that it just keeps getting pushed aside, but I can see now that it's important."

He looked up at her. "When I came out here that night, last spring, I was running away from who and what I was. I told you that, but I didn't explain it to you. Not really. I was running from what was expected of me. When I saw you in the bar that night, all I could think was whether a woman like you would give a guy like me a second look—without the name, without the legacy. And then...you didn't recognize me. You didn't know who I was. And you...you liked me anyway."

She tilted her head to one side, studying him, seeing sincerity in his eyes. "Yeah, well...what's not to like?"

"I'd never had that before, Maya. Everyone in my life wanted something from me. No one just wanted me...for me. And I needed that so badly that night. So I didn't tell you my real name. It was stupid, Maya, and I've regretted it ever since."

She lowered her head. "And yet...you left that night. You said you'd stay...and then you left."

"Just like your father did," he said softly. He lifted a hand to her cheek, and she closed her eyes at his touch. "Maya, it wasn't like that. I got a call that night. My father had a stroke."

Her eyes flew open, met his, saw the truth there.

"You can check it out. Hospital records—hell there was even a piece in the paper about it. I rushed home…and I decided to stop running from my destiny and live it. I didn't contact you again…because I was afraid of what you'd think of me. Running out on you, lying about who I was. I figured I'd already blown any chance I might have had with you. I figured you were better off without me, anyway."

She sighed, shook her head. "You're such an idiot, you know that?" But she said it softly. "If only you'd called."

"I know. I know. I screwed it up…badly, Maya. But there was something between us that night. I know there was." He put a hand gently on her belly. "I think…there's something between us now. Something more than just the babies. And I think we owe it to them, and to each other, to find out what."

"Finding out what is a far cry from getting married, Caleb."

He nodded. "I know. But…marriage is just the legal part of this. The paperwork part of it. It's got nothing to do with what's really happening here."

She averted her eyes, felt her cheeks heat all the same as she asked, "Then…you're talking about a…a marriage in name only. Just for the sake of the babies…."

"No," he said. "Not necessarily. Unless…that's what you want."

She couldn't look at him, couldn't answer him.

"Listen, let's do this. Let's get married, officially, on paper, for the record. For the kids and the press and the public. But between you and me, Maya…let's just take this one day at a time. See where it leads." He took both her hands in his. "I can promise you this, Maya. I'd walk through fire before I'd hurt these babies. I swear it on my mother's grave."

A tear finally fell onto her cheek and rolled slowly down. She wanted to believe him more than she had ever wanted anything. But she was so afraid he would let her down. All the same, she knew his solution made perfect sense. "Okay, then," she said. "Okay."

"Yes!" someone shouted.

Maya and Caleb both turned their heads sharply. The door was opened just a crack, and Selene smiled sheepishly at them and, backing away, pulled it closed.

A second later it burst open again, but this time it was Bobby, in his extremely expensive suit, who appeared, smiling and rubbing his hands together. Maya could almost see his mind clicking away behind his eyes like some high-tech piece of equipment.

"It's agreed, then?" he asked. "That's great. Listen, neither of you talks to the press. Not yet. We'll go the righteously indignant route for today. Of course, I'll arrange a couple of leaks. Get people wondering. Then we'll grant some lucky reporter an exclusive. Meanwhile, we need to get our story in place. So…" He paused there, probably because Caleb was frowning at him, and finally Bobby glanced at Maya. "I'm sorry. Um…congratulations, Ms. Brand. I don't mean to come on like a steamroller here."

She wasn't sure what he meant to come on like, but she was thinking more bulldozer than steamroller. "I'd just as soon leave the plotting to the two of you, if that's okay," she said. "Maybe you could just fill me in later?"

Getting to his feet, Caleb nodded and gave her a nervous, encouraging smile. "We'll handle everything. Just don't worry. It's not good for the babies."

She nodded, and hurried—as much as a woman her size and shape *could* hurry—out of the room. Her sisters and her mother were waiting in the dining room, all of them on their feet, all of them grinning ear to ear, and only her mother's eyes shadowed by a hint of worry.

"I guess you already know the big news," she said.

Vidalia came forward then, pulled her close and hugged

her tight. "My baby. Are you sure this is what you want to do, hon?"

Forcing a brave expression, she pulled away just enough to look her mother in the eye. "I think it's...I think it's the right thing, Mom." And then she waited for the reassurance she needed to hear right now.

"No you don't, girl," her mother said. "You're scared to death. But, honey, I think you're doing the right thing. I do, Maya. I honestly do."

"Oh, yes, of course you are!" Selene chimed in, coming closer. "You wait and see. It might not seem perfect right now, but...oh, it will be."

"It better be," Mel said, eyeing the closed family room door. "He hurts you or those babies, and I'll personally kick his—"

*"Melusine!"*

Mel frowned at her mother, then sent Maya a wink. "But don't worry. I think he might be an okay guy."

"I think this is the most romantic thing in the world!" Kara said, wiping at her eyes.

"There's nothing romantic about it, Kara. We're doing what's best for both our sakes and for the babies'. That's all."

"Landsakes," Vidalia said, slapping her hand to her forehead. "Do you have any idea how much there is to be done? Why, there's the dress, the church, flowers and food—and here we are standing around.... Do we even have time for invitations? These babies could come at any moment!"

# *Chapter 12*

Her mother, her sisters and Bobby seemed to have bought every newspaper in print the next morning. It was the day before Christmas Eve. A time when she should be bustling around in excited holiday preparations. Not worrying about the press. At first Maya was almost afraid to look at the newspapers scattered across the table. The ones she'd seen the day before had been horrible. Mean-spirited, and filled with attacks on her character and personal life. Some went so far as to suggest she'd deliberately sought Caleb out and gotten pregnant with his child, all as a means to get her hands on the coveted Montgomery fortune.

Hesitantly she picked up one paper, glancing at the headline.

More Than Meets the Eye?

Her gaze skimmed to the lines someone had highlighted.

Sources close to Montgomery suggest there is far more to this story than meets the eye, and that it is, in fact, more a tale of star-crossed lovers than a political scandal.

Frowning, she set that paper aside and glanced at the one beneath it, which also had lines highlighted in yellow.

The Reverend Robin Mackensie, of the Big Falls Christian Church, claims that despite what the press has had to say about Miss Brand, her character is beyond reproach. In fact, all the residents of the small town seem to have positive opinions about Maya Brand. Far from the party girl some sources have depicted, residents claim she has rarely even been seen in the company of a man, much less dated one. She goes to church every Sunday and is good to her mother and sisters. Doesn't drink, doesn't smoke, doesn't swear. So what is the real story here? At the moment, Montgomery remains stoically silent on the issue, refusing any comment at all.

She set the paper down atop the rest of the stack on the kitchen table when she heard the now familiar pattern of Caleb's footsteps. Heavy steps, trying hard to be light. Measured, but not hesitant. Pausing, always, when he got a certain distance from her. She wondered about that.

"Morning," he said softly.

She looked up. He was whiskery this morning. His hair tousled, his eyes sleepy. He'd been up half the night plotting with Bobby and the two lawyers her mother insisted on calling Oompah and Loompah. Not to their faces, of course. The lawyers and Bobby had taken up residence at the boarding house. Caleb had spent the night here, in Edie's old room.

"Morning," she replied. Then she held up her coffee mug. "You want some?"

"I'd love some, thanks." He took her mug, took a sip, licked his lips and handed it back to her with a smile that told her he knew full well that wasn't what she'd meant. "That's so good I think I'll get a cup for myself."

"That was the whole idea," she said.

He crossed the room, poured his mug full, sipped again and said, "Caffeinated?"

She turned to look at him. "Half. I swear it won't hurt the babies. But I might have collapsed without it."

He frowned at her. "Not sleeping well?"

"No."

He lowered his head fast. "It's all this stress. I knew it would be bad for you—"

"It's only partly because of the stress, Caleb. Mostly, it's these kids of yours, wriggling around. I swear they're break-dancing in there."

Smiling at her, Caleb returned to the table, set his mug down and moved behind her chair. "It won't be much longer, Maya." His hands closed on her shoulders, squeezed, pulled, released. "Lean forward, hmm?"

She sighed deeply and, folding her arms on the table, laid her head on them. "You don't have to do that," she said, and didn't mean a damn word of it.

He rubbed between her shoulder blades, then down her spine, and finally made small, delicious circles right at the small of her back where it seemed all the tension of the past eight and a half months was centered.

"Oooh, yesss," she moaned very softly.

His hands stilled, but only for a moment. Then he went right back to rubbing again. "We, um…we've got an interview scheduled with Dirk Atwater, today at noon. He's with the *Oklahoma Times*. They're putting out an evening edition, and we're the lead story."

She lifted her head a little. "Do I have to be there? I mean, you're the celebrity here. Can't you do the interview?"

He stopped rubbing. "I can. Sure I can, if you want."

"Keep rubbing."

She almost heard him smile, but he started massaging her again.

"It would be better if I was there, though, wouldn't it?" she asked.

"It'll be fine either way."

"Is that what Bobby would tell me if I asked him?"

He hesitated. His hands stopped moving on her back. So she sat up and turned to look over her shoulder at him. "You don't have to protect me, you know. If it's better for me to be there, I can be there. It's not my dream come true, but it won't kill me, either."

"I just...don't want you doing anything you'd rather not be doing right now."

She smiled. "Tell me that when I'm in labor. Speaking of which—I'll make a deal with you."

His brows went up. "A deal?"

"Yes. I made a little appointment of my own for us today. You come to mine, and I'll come to yours. Okay?"

He narrowed his eyes on her. "Do I dare to ask what I'm agreeing to here?"

"You said you wanted to be in the delivery room, didn't you?"

Very slowly, he nodded.

"Well, then you should come with me today."

He didn't realize what he was agreeing to. And he didn't regret it, exactly, he just hadn't been prepared. He drove. And he pretended not to notice the number of vehicles that fell in behind the rather weather-beaten van as he left the Brand farm behind.

"We're going to have to get a new van," he commented.

She swung her head toward him. "What's wrong with this one?"

"Nothing!" he answered quickly, because she sounded slightly defensive. "I mean, it's just odd, the wife-to-be of a multimillionaire, driving around in a...er...an older... vehicle."

She pursed her lips, crossed her arms over her belly. "I worked hard for this van. It's a *nice* van."

"I know you did, and I agree. It's a *very* nice van."

She pouted a little, then sighed. "I suppose a newer one *would* be safer. For the babies, I mean."

"Oh, yeah. Lots safer. Side impact protection, built-in baby seats—you know, they say a lot of kids get hurt because their car seats aren't fitted correctly for the kind of vehicle they're in."

She frowned at him. "Where did you hear that?"

"Read it. One of those parenting magazines I got from the clinic. See, the seats of various vehicles are shaped differently, so the baby seat that's perfect for one car might be totally unsafe in another."

"You actually read all those magazines you took home?" she asked him, her eyes curious.

"Sure I did. Research. I bought about a dozen books in town, too."

He glanced at her as he pulled to a stop at a red light, the only red light in town. She was smiling. "I'm really glad you believe in doing your homework, Caleb."

"Why?"

"Because that's what we're doing now. Turn right here. It's at the house around the corner."

"We're going to someone's house?"

"Uh-huh. Nancy Kelly. She's the nurse who gave the natural childbirth classes I attended. I called her, and she agreed to give us a quick refresher course, since you missed the first round."

He felt his eyes widen. "Childbirth…classes?"

"You want to be in the delivery room, don't you?"

He nodded mutely.

"You want to know what to do while you're in there, don't you?"

"I kind of thought being there would be the extent of my... duties."

"You thought wrong, then."

She said it with such a sweet smile that he almost stopped being nervous.

Fifteen minutes later, though, the nervousness was back and then some. He was sitting on some woman's living room floor, legs stretched out in front of him, with Maya reclining in between them.

"Come on, Maya," Nurse Nancy said with a scowl. "Lean back and relax. You know how this is done."

"It was a hell of a lot different with Mom as my partner," Maya said, but she did lean back.

She reclined against Caleb's chest, and her hair was under his chin, and the scent of it reached up to tickle his nose and his memory. It smelled the same as it had that night, all those months ago. But wait a minute, he wasn't supposed to be thinking thoughts like that. Certainly not at a time like this.

"Put your hands on her belly, Caleb. No, no, like this." Nurse Nancy bent to take his hands and place them strategically on the lower part of Maya's swollen middle. Then she paused and looked up. "My goodness, Maya, the babies certainly are riding low today."

"I thought something felt different. Does that mean anything?"

Nancy smiled. "It might mean you're getting ready to deliver."

"You think?" she asked, eyes widening.

"Well, if I were a betting woman," Nancy said, "I'd lay odds you'll go within forty-eight hours." She shrugged. "Of course, I could be wrong."

Maya looked up at Caleb, her eyes shining with a combination of nerves and excitement. Nancy replaced her hands on Caleb's, moved them slowly. "Now rub very gently, in soft, slow circles. It's going to soothe her through the contractions. See?''

He moved his hands over her. It was intimate. Almost sensual. When he glanced down at Maya, he saw that she had closed her eyes. This was the most relaxed he'd seen her since he'd been back here. ''Am I doing it right?'' he asked softly.

Her lips curved into a smile. ''You're a whole lot better at this than Mom was.''

''Yeah?''

''You're not doing the breathing, Maya.''

''I'll hyperventilate and pass out.''

''Then you're in the perfect place for it,'' Nancy said. ''Now breathe. Hee hee hee, whoo. Come on.''

''Hee-hee-hee-who,'' she breathed, only she managed to do it to the tune of Beethoven's Fifth, and Caleb burst out laughing.

''Oh, sure, encourage her!'' Nancy said in exasperation.

Maya opened her eyes to grin up at him, her head moving up and down with his laughter. He looked back at her, and for just a moment their eyes locked. He stopped laughing. Her smile faded. And something inside her reached out to touch something inside him. At least, that was what it felt like.

''Now, Caleb,'' Nancy said, ''I'm going to explain to you what happens when we get to the actual pushing.''

He almost grimaced in pain at that thought.

Maya said, ''Don't worry. As my mamma used to say before a spanking, 'Darlin', this is gonna hurt me a whole lot more than it's gonna hurt you.'''

''I wish it wasn't.''

''My mamma also used to say to stop whining and be a Brand. Don't you worry, Caleb. I'll be fine.''

He hated the black fear that crept up inside him when he thought of the ordeal ahead. His mother had died, hemorrhaged to death with the doctors right there, helpless to save her no matter how they tried. And one of her children stillborn. The day of his birth had been a black day of despair and grief, rather than one of joy and celebration. He damn well didn't want the Montgomery family curse visiting itself on this woman...on these babies. But he didn't know what to do about it.

He noticed the nurse looking at him oddly, tried to shake the dread out of his expression, and forced a smile as he continued with his lesson in how to coach the woman who would be his wife through labor and delivery.

But later, when they'd finished and Maya had gone to visit the rest room before they left for home, the woman handed him a pamphlet. "Everything we've been over is on here. So you can review things before the big day."

"Great. I was beginning to regret not taking notes."

She smiled, but it didn't reach her eyes. "So what is it you're worried about, Mr. Montgomery?"

"Caleb. Please, after the things we've discussed today, I think we ought to at least be on a first-name basis."

She lifted her brows, gave a nod and waited. "You looked scared to death once or twice."

He nodded, licked his lips and glanced nervously in the direction Maya had gone. Not seeing her, he looked back at Nancy again. "I was a twin. My mother hemorrhaged—they couldn't save her."

"I'm sorry."

He held up a hand. "My twin brother was stillborn."

"I see," she said. "But, Caleb, that doesn't mean—"

"That's not all of it. My father was a twin, as well, and his brother didn't make it, either." He'd let his gaze sink slowly as he spoke, but now he lifted it again to see if there was any reaction in her eyes.

There wasn't. She was a nurse, though, and trained to hide her emotions from frightened patients, he told himself.

"Listen to me, Caleb. In the years since you were born

there have been more advances in neonatal care than you can even imagine. We have babies born under three pounds today. Babies so tiny I've held them right in the palm of my hand.'' She cupped her hand to demonstrate. ''Babies who did just fine. Now Maya's had ultrasound exams done. We already know that both babies are of good, solid size, and that they're healthy. Maya's healthy, too. And you've got to take her family history into account as well as your own. Her mother gave birth five times—the first time when she was only in her teens. And she was on her feet telling the other new moms in the ward to stop their whining in a matter of hours.''

He smiled at that. He couldn't help it, it was such an accurate visual he was getting of Vidalia Brand.

''Maya's strong. The babies are strong. There's no reason to think they won't be just fine.'' She looked at him again, smiled. ''But if it will make you feel any better, I'll give Maya's doctor a call and bring her up to speed on your family history. Okay?''

He nodded. ''That's good. I wanted to do it myself, but I didn't want Maya to know any of this.''

Nancy nodded. ''That's for the best. No sense getting her as terrified as you are.''

''That's what I thought, too.''

She nodded. ''I'll keep it to myself—at least until after your kids are born safe and sound.''

''Thanks. You're a good woman, Nurse Nancy.''

She made a face, rolled her eyes. ''Gee, that's the first time I've been called that.'' Her tone was sarcastic but teasing. Reaching up, she tucked the pamphlet into Caleb's shirt pocket. ''See you in the delivery room, Dad,'' she said with a wink.

His stomach clenched all over again. ''Bring smelling salts, in case I pass out, all right?''

''Oh, you wouldn't be the first,'' she assured him.

Which didn't make him feel any better for some reason.

# Chapter 13

Maya sat beside Caleb in the dining room, which looked as if it had been polished up for a royal visit. A photographer toyed with his camera at the far end of the table. Bobby sat in a chair, tucked away in the corner. Lurking in the shadows like a happy frog who would snap into action if a fly happened by. And he didn't seem the least bit concerned. He seemed as if he knew full well that everyone would fall easily into line with his plan and be better off for it in the long run. The guy had spunk.

She didn't particularly like spunk today, feeling almost completely devoid of the stuff herself. Although the time she'd spent with Caleb at Nancy's house had been...it had been bliss. That was not a good thing, she reminded herself. She couldn't forget that this was a game. A political game. She would be Caleb Montgomery's wife because that was the role she needed to play for the good of all concerned. It didn't mean anything, and she couldn't let herself slip into believing that it did.

Everyone else seemed to be lying low somewhere. Caleb's lawyers, the Levitz brothers, were apparently still out at the boarding house. Vidalia and the others had gone out to order a wedding cake. The house was empty, except for the five of them. Dirk Atwater, the well-known reporter, was adding cream to his coffee in the kitchen, while his photographer frowned at the overhead light, and changed his camera lens.

"If you get confused, just follow my lead, okay?" Caleb said in a low voice, leaning close, squeezing her hand.

She nodded. But she felt sick with nerves.

"And remember, the closer we stick to the truth, the better."

"Right."

"If you get confused about any details involving the wedding or arrangements, just make them up."

"I'm no good at making things up on short notice, Caleb," she said quickly.

"Well...then don't make it up. Fall back on what you dreamed about as a girl. Okay? Every young girl dreams about her wedding day and what her married life will be like, doesn't she?"

"Well...yes, sure, but—"

"Then use that. You'll be fine, I promise."

She nodded again. The reporter came in from the kitchen with his coffee, sandy blond hair styled with some kind of miracle mousse that made it look silky soft but prevented it from moving even a fraction of an inch out of place. His eyes were too blue to be real. Colored contacts, she thought. He was fairly well known in Oklahoma, did TV spots all the time in addition to his print columns. He looked like he should be an actor or a model.

He sat down with his coffee, looked from one of them to the other. "Are we ready?"

Caleb glanced at her, brows raised. She smiled and gave him a nod. "As ready as we'll ever be, Dirk. But before we begin, I do want to make one thing clear. Maya is very close to her due date. If anything said here seems to me to be upsetting her in any way, the interview is over.''

The reporter's brow quirked just a bit, but he nodded. "Fair enough.'' He took a small tape recorder from his jacket pocket, set it on the table, clicked it on. "But, uh...I understood the baby wasn't due for a couple of weeks yet.''

"Well, here's where you get the first of several scoops on your competitors,'' Caleb said, his gaze brushing over Maya before returning to the reporter. "We're having twins.''

Dirk Atwater's eyes widened, then he grinned. "Twins!''

"Yeah. They run in my family.''

"You never told me that,'' Maya said, sending Caleb a frown.

His smile faded, and he licked his lips. The reporter's eyes sharpened, and he watched every move they made so closely that Maya felt as if she were under a microscope. "I've been meaning to,'' Caleb said softly. "We've been so busy, with so much going on, there's barely been any time.''

She nodded in agreement with that.

"At any rate,'' Caleb went on, "twins normally come early, and Maya's doctor expects them to make their entrance into the world any day now.''

"Holiday babies,'' Dirk Atwater said, scribbling a note. Then he sat back in his seat. "You won't mind my making the observation that you two seem...close. Far from the relationship that's been depicted between you by some of the tabloids.''

Maya frowned. "I don't know how those people could even pretend to know anything about Caleb and me. They've never even spoken to us.''

"That's why we invited you here today, Dirk. We want to set the record straight,'' Caleb put in.

"For the sake of your senate campaign?'' Dirk asked.

Caleb frowned. "At this point, I don't even know whether there will be a campaign.'' The reporter looked skeptical.

Caleb sighed. "Right. I don't expect you to believe that. But for now, let's keep this on the subject, all right?"

"All right. Fine. This young woman is carrying your children, Mr. Montgomery. What do you intend to do about that?"

Caleb smiled then, not at the reporter, but at her. "I intend to marry her, just as soon as we can make arrangements."

The reporter blinked in surprise, looking from one of them to the other. "You're...getting married?"

Maya nodded at him. "On Christmas Eve, as a matter of fact."

Dirk Atwater glanced at his photographer, who shrugged at him. Then he looked back at Maya and Caleb again. "That's...tomorrow." And Maya nodded. "So...let me get clear on this," Atwater said. "You're getting married just to make things legal...to, uh, legitimize the babies, correct? Then, Caleb, you'll head back to the mansion in Tulsa, while you, Ms. Brand, will continue on just as before."

Caleb started to speak, but Dirk held up a hand. "If you don't mind, sir, I'd like to hear Ms. Brand answer this one." Caleb nodded, and Dirk focused on Maya. "So tell me, Ms. Brand. What happens after the wedding?"

Every eye turned on her. She fumbled, searched her mind, but damned if she knew what to say. She and Caleb hadn't talked about what would happen after the wedding. Not in any detail. But then she recalled what Caleb had told her— fall back on her dreams if she got confused. And that should be easy enough. Lord knew she'd nurtured those dreams for long enough that she knew them by heart.

She smiled at Dirk, got to her feet, belly first, and managed to accomplish the task even before Caleb leapt to his feet to help her. She walked to the window in the rear of the room, parted the curtain. "Come here, Mr. Atwater." He did. And she pointed. "See that level spot, at the top of the hill, right back there?"

Dirk nodded.

"That's the piece of this farm that belongs to me. It's where we'll build our home. A big cabin, made of pine logs. With a huge cobblestone fireplace, and knotty pine window boxes, where I'll grow pansies and geraniums. There will be a big room in the back for all my crafts and sewing. I'll give lessons in my spare time. No one in this town is as good at crafting as I am." She smiled, felt her cheeks heat just a little, but it was the truth.

"I didn't know that," Atwater said. And he looked around the room, taking in the décor—the wilderness scene hand-painted on the blade of an old crosscut saw, hanging over the picture window. The embroidered samplers, the needlepoint table scarves. He glanced at her again, brows raised. "These are all yours?"

She nodded.

"You ought to see the baby quilts," Caleb put in, and she thought she heard pride in his voice but reminded herself he was playing a part. For the reporter.

"There's going to be a huge front porch on the cabin," she told Atwater. "And a fenced yard in back, so the kids can't wander too close to the woods. In the summertime, that hillside is just alive with wildflowers and songbirds...and the deer come out at twilight to nibble the tender grasses." She sighed wistfully, visualizing it all just the way she'd always done. "And we'll have a dog. A big, oversized, long-eared, shaggy mutt of a dog."

She was smiling broadly as she let the curtain fall and turned to glance back at the table at Caleb. He was sitting there very still and very quiet, his face expressionless, and she felt her smile slowly die. Maybe she'd shocked him. Maybe her dreams didn't fit in with his plans at all.

"So this is for real, this marriage of yours? It's not just for appearance's sake?" Dirk Atwater turned away from the window to address Caleb.

Caleb stared at Maya, and she stared back.

Bobby got up and came over to the table. "Look at the two of them," he said to Atwater. "Does that look to you like it's for real?" The cameraman fired off a series of shots.

Maya felt her stomach clench and quickly averted her eyes.

But there was no stopping Bobby once he got started. "Over eight months ago, these two met by chance. Or maybe it was fate. The middle of a rainstorm, a flat tire, a man looking to get warm and dry walks into a charming little roadhouse and meets the girl of his dreams. It was love at first sight."

And as he spoke, Caleb never took his eyes off Maya. She wanted to look away, but found she couldn't.

"Through a series of misunderstandings and bad decisions," Bobby went on, "they fell out of touch. Ms. Brand didn't want to be labeled a gold digger—a fear that was justified, if the tabloids are any indication. And Mr. Montgomery didn't even know about the babies. Now these two have managed to get past all of that and put things together again. Not for the sake of the press, Mr. Atwater. They've done this *in spite of* the press. In spite of public opinion. In spite of irresponsible journalists who see fit to drag Miss Brand's family and her character through the mud to sell papers. In spite of the whole damned world, Mr. Atwater, these two star-crossed lovers have found their way back to each other. This is not a political scandal. This is a love story, Atwater. A Christmas story. A miracle."

Maya blinked back her senseless tears and wondered if Bobby were about to burst into a chorus of the "Star Spangled Banner" or "Silent Night." She thought Dirk Atwater might very well shed a tear of his own at any moment.

But then he pursed his lips, met her eyes and said, "So then there won't be any prenuptial agreement?"

Bobby's jaw dropped, and Caleb said, "Don't you think

that's getting a bit too personal, Atwater? That's over the line.''

Maya held up a hand. "Actually, I'm insisting on one." She sent a gentle smile Caleb's way. She'd been watching Bobby, and she thought she got it now. This art of "spinning." "I know you're against it, Caleb," she said, though she had no idea if he was or not. In fact, she rather thought he would be nuts not to ask for a prenup. "I just see no other way to prove to the world that all of this isn't an elaborate conspiracy to get my hands on your family's money."

"You don't need to prove anything to anyone, Maya," Caleb told her.

She sighed, nodded, but from the corner of her eye she saw Bobby's slight nod of approval. Good. She'd done her job, and maybe she ought to quit while she was ahead. "I'm a little tired," she said, rubbing the small of her back.

Caleb was beside her in a flash, arms sliding easily around her as he eased her back to her chair. The camera went off. "Do you need anything? A drink? Something to eat?"

Bobby cleared his throat. "I think this is going to have to conclude the interview. Dirk, you have the exclusive on the impending marriage and the twins until tomorrow morning. Then we'll issue a press release. That's all."

Atwater clicked off the tape recorder, nodded once and gathered up his notebook. "Thank you both," he said. "I appreciate this, and I think you'll see that when my story runs tonight." He shook Caleb's hand. Gave Maya a gentle smile. "You take care, Ms. Brand."

The photographer snapped another shot, and then they left.

Maya blew air through her lips and let her head fall backward in the chair. "God, I'm glad that's over."

"Oh, come on, don't tell me that was tough on you," Bobby chirped, smiling. "You sailed through it like a pro! Hell, where did you get all that stuff about the log cabin and the dog and the pansies? I couldn't have made that stuff up if I'd tried!''

She brought her head level again, saw Caleb searching her eyes. He said, "You fell back on your dreams, didn't you, Maya?"

She shrugged. "Maybe I'm just a good liar."

"I don't think so."

Looking away, she said, "So do you think he bought it?"

"We'll know in a few hours, when the evening edition hits the streets," Bobby said. "You two ought to go into town between now and then. Be seen together. Pick out some baby clothes or something. Great photo op, with all the press in Big Falls."

Maya tried not to grimace at the thought.

Caleb said, "No. I think maybe a quiet, healthy meal and then a long nap would be a better choice. Don't you, Maya?"

"Sounds like heaven to me," she said. "You must be reading my mind."

"I wish. Come on, let's get you someplace more comfy than this hard chair. Sofa or bed?"

"The easy chair will be sufficient. I can't be dozing with a wedding to plan."

Caleb brushed a lock of hair off her forehead. "Hey, trust your mom and sisters and Bobby and me to take care of all that, will you? You need your rest. You've got a pair of babies to deliver, you know."

She smiled a little nervously. "I want it simple, Caleb. No doves or violins or…or goose liver."

He made a silly pout. "Bobby, call the Pope and tell him we won't need him to perform the ceremony after all, will you?"

"Very funny," she said. But she saw the odd, speculative look Bobby sent them.

Caleb was already helping her to her feet, walking her into the living room and lowering her to the sofa. He tucked a stack of pillows behind her before ordering her to lie back, and then he stuck a few more under her feet. "I read that elevating the feet can ease the strain on the back." Even as he said it, he pulled off her shoes, let them thud to the floor.

"When you have time to do all this reading is beyond me," she muttered, deciding to give in to the pampering. She was achy and tired, and it felt good to be babied. That tiny voice of doubt whispered at her not to get too used to it, but she brushed it aside.

"Wait till you hear what I've learned about potty training." Caleb winked at her. And she thought that it wouldn't be so bad to live with this guy. At least...if that were what he intended.

She wondered if it was. Wished it could be. Hated herself for daring to wish such a big wish.

She fell asleep on the sofa in spite of her determination not to, and the nap was easily a couple of hours long. But the commotion in the kitchen woke her up at once. The deep booming voice belonged to some man who had no qualms about speaking at full volume. "Are you out of your mind! What are you thinking?"

"Hey, just a gol'darn minute, mister fancy-suit! Who in all hades do you think you are, storming into my kitchen yellin' like a lunatic, anyway!" Vidalia's tone was just as loud and twice as mean.

Maya started to get to her feet just as Kara reached the foot of the stairs. "What's going on out there?" Kara asked.

"Damned if I know," Maya said. "Help me!" She held out a hand. Kara took it and pulled her to her feet. The yelling was still going on when the two of them walked into the kitchen. A man in a calf-length black wool coat stood just inside the door, having apparently just come in from outside. He still had snow on his shiny shoes and at the bottom of his gleaming brass-handled walking stick. He had a face like a mountain of solid granite, after it had been blasted through to make room for a road to pass. Chiseled and lined and hard... but only on one side. The other side seemed oddly lax. The man towered a good six feet tall, even though he was leaning over just slightly, weight on the walking stick. He was waving a newspaper around in his other hand and saying, "Get out of my way, woman! This doesn't concern you!"

Vidalia was in his face, her forefinger poking him repeatedly in the chest to emphasize her words, "It's my house, mister, and you'd better believe anything in it concerns me!"

Behind her, Caleb shrugged. "You gotta admit, she has a point, Dad."

Maya gasped, and the three of them turned around, spotting her there. Caleb quickly took Kara's spot beside her, his arm sliding protectively around her shoulders, his gaze doing a quick scan of her face. One she was getting used to. He was always looking at her like that, as if checking to be sure she was okay. As if he could see in her eyes if she wasn't.

"Maya, I'd like you to meet my father, Cain Caleb Montgomery the Second." She looked from Caleb to the older man, who was scowling hard. "Dad, this is Maya. Soon to be your daughter-in-law and the mother of your first grandchildren."

"Over my dead body," the old man growled.

Vidalia leaned up into his face. "*That* can be arranged."

He glared at her, one eye narrowing slightly more than the other.

"Mother, please," Maya said, moving out of Caleb's embrace to place a calming hand on her mother's shoulder. Her mother moved aside at Maya's urging, and Maya stood before her future father-in-law. A more intimidating presence she couldn't even begin to imagine. Even with the obvious damage the stroke had dealt him, he was an imposing man. But she lifted her chin and looked him in the eye. "I understand your being upset about this, Mr. Montgomery. But I promise you, I would never do anything to hurt your son or your family.''

His brows went up. ''I'm not sure if you're a good actress, woman, or if you're as clueless as you pretend to be, but trust me, the harm has already been done. And continues to be done.''

''Father—'' Caleb began, a deep threatening tone in his voice.

''No, Caleb, let him speak. Please. I want to hear how he thinks I've harmed your family.''

''Our reputation! Our line! By God, girl, we can't have a girl of your background muddying up our family tree!'' He shook the newspaper again. ''Illegitimate, they say! Father was a bigamist, for landsakes! Ties to organized crime. Mother who—''

''Mother who what?'' Vidalia asked, gripping the front of his shirt in her fists.

He stopped talking, looked down at the woman. ''You? You're the saloon-owning mother?''

''You're damn straight I am, mister, and I'm about to forget my manners and toss your sorry carcass out into the nearest snowdrift.''

He blinked down at her, his eyes wide.

''Mom,'' Maya said, ''at least this one didn't call you a barmaid.'' Not that she expected it to help.

''Dad,'' Caleb said firmly, ''your mother was a waitress at a truck stop when your father met her. Or have you forgotten that?''

''My father wasn't running for the U.S. Senate when he met her.''

''That's totally irrelevant.''

''That's the only thing that *is* relevant! Don't you know what this girl's background is going to do to your campaign, son? And this—'' glancing down at the newspaper he tossed it onto the table ''—this fairy tale Bobby's trying to sell the public—it's never going to work. Voters don't care about sappy stories, they care about their bank accounts." He shook his head slowly, then closed his eyes and pressed a hand to them.

Vidalia gripped his arm. "Sit down, you foolish old windbag, before you fall down." She guided him to a chair. "Kara, get some of Selene's calmin' tea brewing. That with the chamomile and valerian root." As Kara shot into action, Vidalia eyed the older man. "You had a stroke last spring, didn't you?"

He looked up, defensively. "I'm completely recovered from that."

"Maybe. Didn't learn anything from it, though, did you?"

Maya pulled out a chair and sat down beside the old man. Caleb sat beside her and turned the newspaper around so he could examine the story. Maya watched him reading it over and saw his lips pull into a smile. Then he pushed it toward her. "It's good," he told her. "It's very good."

"Good? Bah, it's fiction! Any fool can see through that sorry excuse for a cover story," his father said.

Kara put a teacup down in front of the older man, and then Selene appeared with a big amethyst in one hand and a bowl of mixed herbs in the other. "I heard yelling. What's up?" She set the amethyst in the middle of the table. The glittering purple stone winked and glimmered.

"My father arrived," Caleb said. "You can call him Cain. Dad, this is Selene, Maya's sister, the one you haven't insulted yet tonight. The two you have are Kara, her other sister, and Vidalia, her mother."

He lifted his brows. "Vidalia? Like the onion?" He stopped short of sniffing in derision.

"That's right. They named me that because I'm so good at making arrogant jackass men cry like babies."

"Easy, Mom," Selene called from the range, where she was fiddling around. "The negative vibes are going to be cleared out of this room in just a few seconds." She poured the remaining water from the tea kettle into a saucepan, lit the burner underneath it and stirred it slowly while sprinkling her herbs into the water.

"What the hell is this? You have some kind of witch doctor in the family, too?"

"Careful, or she'll turn you into a toad," Caleb told his father. "Drink your tea."

His father sipped. "Bad enough about the stripper in the family! Now we have voodoo!" His brows went up, and he licked his lips; then he sipped some more of the tea.

"We do not have any strippers in this family, Mr. Montgomery," Vidalia huffed.

"Actually, Maya's older sister is a highly successful model," Caleb said.

His father grimaced but kept sipping his tea. "I don't care if she's an Oscar-award-winning actress," he muttered. "This marriage can't happen. I won't let it happen."

"You don't have a choice in the matter, Father."

"Son, don't you see what's going to happen here? You'll lose your shot at the Senate."

"I'd rather lose my shot at the Senate than lose my shot at being a father to these babies."

His father's head came up, and his eyes seemed frozen. "Babies? There are two?"

Maya saw the look Caleb sent his father. There was a message in it, one his father seemed to see and read. He said, "Yes, twins. It was in the article."

The old man's gaze slid toward Maya, then lower to her belly, and she could have sworn there was something new there. A hint of...could that be concern? Worry? At least it wasn't blatant hostility.

"I got so wrought up I never finished reading the whole thing," he said.

Steam was rolling off Selene's brew now, and she was waving a hand at it as if to send it around the room. It gave off a pleasant, woodsy aroma. Then there was a tap on the door. Bobby came in, Mel right behind him. Both of them were smiling as they shouldered their way into the crowded kitchen.

Kara looked at them. "Where did you two meet up?"

"Just now in the driveway," Mel quickly told her. She had a bag of groceries in her hands, which she handed off to Vidalia, before bending to tug off her snowy boots. "Bobby says he has good news." She got out of the way, sniffing the air as she went to check out Selene's concoction.

"I sure do. Dirk Atwater's paper ran a telephone poll in the same issue as the story. Caleb, your numbers have gone through the roof since they last ran this same poll, two weeks ago. Then you were neck and neck with the other likely candidates. Now you're leading them by more than thirty percent."

Caleb's brows rose. That was his only reaction. His father, on the other hand, looked stunned. "You've got to be kidding me," he said. "The voters are actually falling for this nonsense?"

"Voters have hearts, Cain," Bobby told the older man. "I tried to tell you that years ago, but you never wanted to hear it."

"Well the voters in this family have stomachs," Vidalia said firmly. "And if I hope to feed them, I'm going to need the bunch of you to take your hides out of my kitchen."

Maya nodded and started to get to her feet, but Caleb put a hand on her shoulder and shook his head. "Stay put. Have some tea. Relax," he told her. "I'm gonna take my father over to the boarding house, get him settled in. I think I, uh... need to have a talk with him. Get some things...straight."

She nodded. "Don't be hard on him, Caleb. He's your father, no matter what."

Caleb glanced at his father, who must have overheard that

remark. Maya wondered if the man was still scowling at her but didn't turn to look.

"Maya, we have all the arrangements in place. I don't want you fussing or worrying about anything at all. All you have to do is wake up in the morning. We're getting married at ten o'clock."

She felt her brows shoot upward. "But...how did you pull everything together so fast?" She looked from Caleb to her mother and back again.

"Your mom can fill you in on the details. Okay?"

She nodded. "O-okay. I guess. Caleb, there's so much I want to talk to you about before we...you know...do this thing."

"I know." He looked at her so intensely she could almost feel the touch of his eyes. "I know. I'll come back early, I promise. We'll have time to talk. All the time you want. Okay?"

She nodded. Then sucked in a breath of surprise when he leaned down and pressed a kiss to her mouth. It was quick, brief, but not a peck. It was firm and moist. A kiss that... seemed to *mean* something. But what?

Then he was gone, Bobby and his father with him.

"See that?" Selene said, still wafting her steam with her hands. "Cleared away the negativity so well that it even chased the old grouch away!"

"He's not as bad as he seems," Maya said.

"No one could be as bad as he seems," Vidalia said.

"Gee, what did I miss?" Mel asked.

Kara grinned. "It's just as well you did miss it, Mel. Otherwise that old goat would have been carrying his walking stick in a new place."

"Kara!" Vidalia scolded—or tried to, but it was ruined when the grin she tried to suppress broke through.

Everyone laughed. Then Maya said, "So my wedding is all planned?"

Vidalia smiled at her. "I'm under strict orders from that man of yours to get your approval on everything first. But I'm supposed to do that without giving you the slightest cause for stress or tension." She shrugged. "Guess he's never been around too many brides before if he thinks that's possible." She turned to pull her notebook from the top of the fridge and, flipping it open, sat down at the table. "It's amazing what that man manages to do with a few phone calls. I'm telling you, hon, having all that money and clout is not a bad thing."

Neither, Maya thought, was being so popular in the polls. For some reason, though, that news didn't make her as happy as it should. Because it meant he would probably decide to run after all, even though he'd said repeatedly that he hadn't made that decision yet. He would make it now. He would run, and he would win. And he would have to spend half his time, or maybe more, in Washington, D.C., and the other half in the state capital, or traveling around doing…political stuff. If she did get her dream house, she would be in it alone.

Well, she thought, a hand on her belly, not entirely alone. Just not with him. And for some reason that felt like the same thing.

Then again, he hadn't promised they would be together constantly. Even live together at all. That was one of the things they needed to talk about. Their living arrangements. Because she had no intention of moving away from her family. Especially when they might be all she and the kids had, if Caleb turned out to be the kind of man who would break his word, let her down. The kind of man who wouldn't be there when she really needed him.

More and more, she doubted Caleb was that kind of man at all.

If only she could be sure….

# Chapter 14

"Maybe…it can work after all."

Cain Caleb Montgomery II spoke the words as if they were being forced from his lips. And he had a grimace on his face while he did it. Caleb had been sitting before the fire in the parlor of Ida-May Peabody's boarding house, talking with his father for the better part of an hour, hearing all the same arguments and keeping his father's teacup filled with tea steeped from the little packets Selene had handed him on his way out of the Brand house tonight. He didn't like the gray tinge to his father's skin. He didn't like the dizzy spell the old man had had earlier. And he didn't like it that his father refused to admit to feeling even slightly less than peak.

Now all those things faded to background worries as shock took precedence. He stared at his father, wondering if he'd heard him wrong. Maybe he'd fallen asleep and just dreamed it. "Did you just say you might have been wrong?"

His father glared at him. "Don't expect to be hearing it again any time soon."

He sipped the tea, his third cup, and for just a moment Caleb wondered what sorts of herbs mystical Selene had put into it, and whether they were fully legal.

"That woman, the mother with the onion name..."

"Vidalia," Caleb corrected.

"That's right, Vidalia. She's tough. I gave her my worst, and she didn't even flinch. Most females would've been weeping." He puckered his lips in thought, rubbed his chin. "I like that about her. If your Maya has any of her mother's gumption, she might just make you a decent wife. She doesn't know how to dress or act, and that hair will have to go, but all that can be corrected. She seems bright enough to learn as she goes. I suppose she has all the raw material to be molded and shaped into—"

"I don't want her molded or shaped into anything, Father. I like the way she dresses, and I like the way she acts, and I'd fight any man who tried to get near her hair with a pair of scissors."

His father's brows went up, and he studied his son's face. "She'll never survive in our world as she is, son. She'll have to change, adapt to it."

Caleb looked away, because he didn't want to argue with his father. Not tonight. Not when that statement made so much sense, even if nothing else his father said tonight had. His world would be difficult for Maya. Maybe impossible for her.

But he wasn't even clear on things in his own mind just yet. No, there was no sense upsetting his father by arguing with him, especially when the old man wasn't feeling up to par.

"How...er...are the babies?" his father asked, his tone gruff.

For the second time tonight the old man had surprised him. Caleb got to his feet and walked to the fireplace, bent to toss a log onto the flames and stayed there, hunkered down, as it began to burn. "The doctor says they're both fine and strong. No sign of any problems."

"You're worried, though."

Turning, he looked at his father over his shoulder. "Hell, yes, I'm worried. They're twins. Like I was...like you were." He felt too much showing in his eyes, so he jerked his head around, focused on the flames again.

He heard his father get up, heard his steps but didn't turn. A hot tear burned behind Caleb's eye, but he blinked against it. Then a hand fell on his shoulder. "I've been there, you know."

Caleb's brows came together. Stunned, he turned to look at his father.

"It's like a nightmare, where you can only watch what happens, but you can't move to stop it, or do a damn thing to help. You feel the dread right down deep in your gut, but you're paralyzed."

Blinking, Caleb said, "That's exactly what it feels like."

"I know." Lowering his head, shaking it, his father went on. "We knew there were problems with one of you long before the time for the birthing came, son. The doctors felt all along that one of the twins was not developing at a normal rate." He lowered his head. "It felt like a personal insult to me. Hell, man, I never failed at anything before! And when your mother didn't make it, either...Caleb, I was never the same. I felt responsible. If not me, then who? I was her husband. I was supposed to protect her, take care of her."

Caleb rose slowly. "So you blamed me for it."

Meeting his son's eyes, Cain nodded. "Maybe...maybe a part of me did, son. That's true. But that ended long, long ago. Since then it's just been...a spin."

"A spin?"

Cain nodded. "All my rubbish about the strong surviving, the weak falling by the wayside, sacrifice for the greater good. Hell it was how I dealt with the loss. By putting a spin on it. By pretending it was a sign of strength. Because if I could make myself believe that about you and the brother you never had, then maybe I could make it true about myself and my brother, as well." He clasped Caleb's shoulder hard. "But it's not true and never was. Your twin didn't survive because he didn't develop normally. As for my own, I'll probably never know. But that doesn't mean these twins of Maya's have to suffer the same fate, son. If they're both strong and healthy this late in the game, then chances are—"

"They're going to be fine. Both of them. They have to be."

His father drew a breath, sighed. "My great-grandmother had twins, and both survived. Did you know that?"

"No."

They stood side by side now, both staring at the fire. "Maya, she's strong. Healthy. Comes from good stock, if that harridan mother of hers is any indication," Cain told his son.

Caleb nodded. "The woman gave birth five times without problems," he said.

"That's good. That bodes well." Cain didn't turn. He said, "Your mother used to quilt. Did I ever tell you that?"

Caleb looked at him in surprise.

"I read in that article that Maya does that sort of thing, too. Just thought you'd like to know it was something she had in common with your mother. She was talking about giving it up. Said it was too rustic a hobby for a woman in her position. She never did, though. Just kept it to herself." Turning, he set his empty cup down. "Guess I'll head up to bed now. Big day tomorrow, with the wedding and all." He started toward the stairs.

"Dad."

The old man stopped but didn't turn around.

"Thanks."

"Good night, son."

"Night." Caleb sat down again, alone now with his thoughts. His fears. And the new, confusing things circling his mind like sharks. He was glad his father had reached out to him tonight, tried, in his way, to mend old wrongs. But he couldn't help but think he should have been having a long conversation with someone else tonight.

With Maya.

Because, dammit, there was so much he needed to work through where she was concerned. So much he was confused about. Mostly he wanted to know why she'd agreed to marry him. Had it been for the reasons he'd laid out? Because, frankly, he'd been making those up as he went along. It scared the hell out of him to admit it, even to himself, but he had to know. They were at zero hour. Mostly he'd just wanted to lock on to her and the babies in some way that assured him they wouldn't just vanish from his life, fall through his tenuous grasp someday. Coming out here, he'd discovered that they were precious to him...*she* was precious to him. He could understand feeling that need to hold on to the babies. They were his, after all. But why that desperate need to cling to Maya Brand?

She was the mother of his kids. That had to be stirring some kind of primal instincts to life inside him. There were probably all kinds of psychological reasons why a man would feel drawn to a woman who was about to bear his children.

Weren't there?

And why didn't it feel as if that was the answer? Why was he suddenly dreading the thought of taking her with him, into his world, watching her evolve into the perfect political wife, seeing her change...and maybe cut her hair? Or...give up quilting?

He stayed up by the fire for a long time, thinking, searching his mind. But all he kept seeing when he imagined the future was a dark-colored log cabin on a hillside above a wildflower-strewn meadow. A couple of kids, and a big shaggy dog bounding through the blossoms. Maya on the front porch, in the sunshine. A doe and a pair of spotted fawns feeding out back.

He fell asleep, and the images wove into dreams. Vivid, achingly wonderful dreams.

Maya had pleaded exhaustion and gone to her room just to get out of the sight of her mother and sisters before the tears came. And once they started, they didn't seem to want to stop. She buried her face in her pillows and thumped her mattress repeatedly with her fist, but it didn't help.

After twenty minutes she forced herself to sit up, reached for a tissue and caught a glimpse of herself in the vanity mirror. Red puffy eyes, wild hair, streaks on her face and a runny nose looked back at her. "You are a basket case, Maya Brand," she told herself. "Why don't you get a grip?"

"Because you're going to become a wife and a mother of two all in the space of the next few days, darlin'." Her mother's voice made her jerk her head around. Vidalia sat in the chair beside the bed. In her hands she held a big bowl of vanilla ice cream, with chocolate syrup drizzled over the top, and a generous dollop of whipped cream...and two spoons.

Maya sniffled. "How long have you been sitting there?"

"Long enough for the ice cream to get just soft enough. I figured I'd let you cry it out. It's cleansing, a good cry. Sometimes you just need to let it rinse you clean."

She held out the bowl.

Maya eyed it. "I'm not hungry," she said.

"Since when do we eat ice cream because we're hungry?" Vidalia asked, and set the bowl in her daughter's lap.

Maya picked up the spoon and took three consecutive bites.

"You came upstairs before I got to tell you about the wedding plans that man of yours managed to put together."

She sniffed, ate another bite, looked at her mother.

"He spoke to Reverend Mackensie, and the reverend says he'll personally take care of getting the church ready. He even offered to have the full choir turn out, and Mrs. Sumner is practically begging to be allowed to play the organ." Vidalia sneaked a quick taste of the ice cream with her own spoon. "And get this, Mrs. Mackensie and the Ladies' Auxiliary volunteered to see to it the flowers arrived and take care of the decorations. Well, you know, Mrs. Mackensie's sister is the only florist in town, so I suppose that makes sense, but—"

"But, Mom, the church ladies don't even like me."

"Oh, honey, they do now."

Maya thrust out her lower lip. "I don't think I want them at my wedding."

"That's what Caleb told them. He said he just wanted use of the church, thank you very much. Said he had his own florist in mind, and that he didn't want anyone there who wasn't specifically invited. Told the reverend his next sermon ought to be on loving thy neighbor and the dangers of false pride." She smiled. "The reverend laughed! He said it was about time someone put that bunch in their place, and he thought Maya Brand was just the one to do it."

Maya's eyes widened as she stared at her mother.

"It's true, hon. Oh, don't you see, child? You're getting what you've always wanted. Respectability. Why, you're marrying into a family who could buy and sell this town and everyone in it. Every person who ever snubbed you is gonna be kissing up full force, just hopin' to get invited to have a cup of coffee with you."

Maya's face puckered, and her lower lip quivered. "Y-you're right. That's wh-what I've always w-wanted. But I wanted to earn it...not marry into it."

"You'd already earned it, Maya. That's the point. Those women are forced now to give you the respect you already deserved. You should be happy to see them so firmly put in their places."

"I...know I should."

Her mother tilted her head to one side. "Well, then, how come you're crying?"

"I don't know!" she wailed, and the tears flooded her face, and she shoveled in some more ice cream.

"Darlin'," her mother said after a moment, "I do know. And so do you, deep down. And you'd best get busy thinking it through and figurin' it out, because you're gonna be married in a few hours, and it would be a darned good notion to have your head on straight when you do."

Blinking several times, sitting up straighter, she thought very hard. Her mother snatched tissues from the box and wiped Maya's face, her nose.

"Well?"

Maya stared down at the melting ice cream in the bowl. "I'm afraid I'm not good enough to be a senator's wife."

"You're a liar. You're good enough to be any thing you want to be, and you know it. Now think some more. What's really wrong?"

Maya frowned. "Maybe it's…that I think *he* may not think I'm good enough—"

"Bullcookies. He wouldn't be marrying you if he thought that way. Try again."

"His…father. Yes, that's it, his father hates me, and—"

"His father is a teddy bear trying to act like a grizzly. I can't believe a daughter of mine didn't see through that stuff and nonsense at first glance."

Licking her lips, Maya nodded. "I did. He's just lonely and feeling left out."

"Uh-huh."

Drawing a deep breath, Maya sighed, took a big bite of ice cream and thought some more. "Maybe it's…that I don't know what's going to happen. I mean, I don't want to move away from here. But he's going to have to, if he becomes a senator. And I don't want to go with him, but I don't want to be left behind, either."

"Why not?"

Her brows went up. Another bite. "Well, I…I…the kids.

It would be hard on the kids, and hell, I don't want to be raising them all alone. I mean, I've seen how hard that is.''

"We've been just fine alone, Maya. You know you could do it, and do it in spades, if you had to.''

"But this is different. I mean...okay, it's not that I don't think I could raise the kids alone, I mean, I could. Of course I could. I know I could.''

Vidalia nodded and dipped her spoon in for another bite.

"It's just that I don't want to be alone.''

"You were fine alone, a year ago,'' her mother pointed out.

"That was before I met Caleb...'' Maya blinked and went very still, with a spoonful of ice cream halfway to her mouth. She lowered the spoon. "Oh, no,'' she whispered. "What if I love him?'' She turned to stare at her mother through eyes gone wide with horror. "Landsakes, Mom, what if I *love* him?''

Maya's mother sat beside her, stroking her hair and talking to her until she finally fell asleep. A restless, fitful sleep, but still, she needed the rest. And she did rest, just fine, until about 1:00 a.m., when something woke her. She wasn't sure whether it was the howling wind outside or the sensation of being soaking wet from the waist down. She only knew that the house was freezing cold and pitch dark, and that her water had broken.

"Mom?'' she called.

And then a giant hand closed tight around her middle, squeezing her front and back, inside and out, and she gripped her belly and yelled louder, pain and fear driving the single word out of her with far more force than before. *"Mamma!''*

An insistent, howling sort of cry shook Caleb out of sleep. At first, in his drowsy state, he thought it was Maya's voice, crying out to him for help. He came awake with a start, surprised that when he opened his eyes, the only light to be seen was the orange red glow of the coals in the fireplace, a few feet from him. And the cry he'd heard was only the wind, shrieking abnormally outside. Blinking away the sleep haze, Caleb realized he'd fallen asleep on the sofa in the living room of Ida-May's boarding house. Still, there was usually a light left on down here at night.

Sitting up, he rubbed his shoulders, suddenly chilled. Then he reached for the big lamp on the end table.

*Click.*

Nothing. He tried again, but it was no use. Either the bulb was blown or...

"...or the power's out," he said aloud. And that was when that wailing wind outside drew his attention again. And there was rattling, too. He half expected to see a death wagon come thundering into the room with a banshee at the reins, singing her funereal dirge.

He shook that image away with another shiver, a full body one this time. "It's the wind," he muttered. And he went to the fireplace, added three chunks of wood, then rose again and tried the wall switch. Still no lights. But as the flames grew, they illuminated the room for the most part. He could see around him. Orange and yellow, leaping shadows.

Then another light appeared. A small flame, floating closer out of the shadows, until it morphed into Ida-May herself, carrying an old-fashioned kerosene lamp. "Caleb?" she asked, squinting at him, then nodding in answer to her own question. "Power's out," she told him. "And it's storming to beat all." She set the lamp on a high shelf and quickly went to the hearth to light another lamp—one Caleb hadn't even noticed sitting there. Come to think of it, there was a candelabra on that marble stand in the corner.

Caleb went for that, brought it to the fireplace and reached for the matches there on the mantel. "Does this happen often?" he asked, lighting the candles one by one.

"Oh, once or twice a year at most. This is a big one, though. My goodness, listen to it rage!"

He didn't need to listen to hear the fury of the storm. The wind whistled and moaned, and branches skittered against the windows and walls. He went to the nearest window, parted the curtain and tried to look outside. Dark as pitch. The entire town was black, and even the whiteness of the snow didn't break it. "Looks like the whole town's blacked out." Then he turned. "I need to check on Maya."

"Oh, my, yes!"

Footsteps thundered, and in moments Bobby reached the bottom of the stairs, with Cain at his side. In the fireglow, the old man's face looked downright mean. "Dad, here, take the sofa." Caleb helped his father to a seat, then yanked a blanket off the back and draped it over his shoulders.

"It's colder than the hubs of hell in this place," Cain growled, pulling the blanket closer and hunching into it.

"The power's out, Mr. Montgomery," Ida-May explained. "But we have the fireplace. You'll be warm as toast in no time." Then she looked at Bobby. "Someone should wake the others, those two lawyer fellows and Ol' Hank. Have them come down here where it's warm."

"I'll get them," Bobby said. "Along with some more blankets."

"Why's the power out?" Cain demanded. "And what's that infernal racket?" Then, blinking, he looked toward the windows, then at Caleb. "Snowstorm?"

"Yeah, the whole town is without power, by the looks of things." Caleb tried the telephone, but there was only dead air. He clicked the cutoff several times, to no avail. Then he went to the foot of the stairs and called up them, "Bobby, bring your cell phone down."

Cain was shaking his head. "How bad is it out there, son?"

"I don't know, Dad."

The old man pursed his lips. "That Brand girl...she hadn't

ought to be out there at that farm without heat, or even a telephone.''

''I know.''

''I have a radio, some batteries. I'll get them,'' Ida-May said, and taking one of the lamps, she hurried away. Caleb went to the door, yanked his coat off the rack and pulled it on. ''I'm gonna take a look outside. Maybe it's not as bad as it sounds.''

''Good idea, son.''

He stepped out onto the porch, pulling the door closed behind him. The howling here was louder, almost deafening, and a rhythmic thumping worried him. He pulled up his collar and went to the door, opened it. The wind hit it, yanked it from his hand and slammed it against the wall. Caleb ducked his head, brought his hands up in front of his face and, squinting, stepped out onto the stoop. Icy barbs of snow slashed at his face like razors. The snow on the ground was level with the top step and still coming. He tried to see up and down the road, but only snow, gray with darkness, shadowy drifts looking like miniature mountains and wind-driven snow were visible. Everything was covered, every rooftop and porch, every vehicle and tree. Telephone poles, those he could make out in the darkness, were tilted and leaning. Wires, laden with snow, drooped low.

He backed onto the porch and forced the door closed against that insistent wind. It was an effort, but he managed it. He took off his coat, shook the snow off it, stomped off his shoes and went back inside. ''It's a freaking nightmare out there.''

His father and Bobby were pushing all the chairs nearer the fireplace. Martin and Jacob Levitz, Caleb's lawyers, stood huddled over the radio as Ida-May turned the dial from static to static. The boarding house's permanent resident, a grizzled fellow Caleb only knew as ''Ol' Hank,'' sat in a rocker looking confused.

Finally Ida's radio dial hit paydirt. ''...the unexpected blizzard is raging through Big Falls and surrounding areas with winds up to sixty-five miles per hour and temperatures well below freezing. Twenty-four inches of snow have already been dumped in the area, with another eighteen inches possible before morning. Residents are advised to remain in their homes if at all possible. Use fireplaces, woodstoves, kerosene heaters if you have them. If not, light all the burners on your propane or natural gas ranges. If you have none of those, then you need to dress warmly, stay dry and keep moving until daylight. All roads are closed. Emergency personnel cannot get through. Phone service is out in three counties, and power in more, though the full extent of the outage is not known at this time. Rescue personnel will be out in force at dawn, when the storm is expected to abate. If you need emergency assistance, hang a red flag from a front window or door of your home.''

Caleb swallowed hard and looked at his father. "I have to get to Maya."

"Son, they said to wait until dawn." He glanced at the old-fashioned pendulum clock on Ida-May's mantel. "It's only five or six hours away, at the most. Surely she'll be all right until then."

He met his father's eyes. "What if she isn't?"

"Caleb, you could get killed out there in this mess. It's a good five miles out to the Brand farm."

"Dad, the nurse we saw yesterday predicted she'd give birth within forty-eight hours. Anything could be happening out there."

"Come on, Caleb, what makes you think—"

"I don't know. I don't know. I just…I feel it in my gut. I have to get out there." He paused, searching his father's face. "What if it were my mother out there? What would you do, Dad?"

Thinning his lips, the old man nodded. "All right." Then

he turned. "Caleb's going to need flashlights, with good batteries, and some damn warm clothes."

"Flashlight, hell," Ol' Hank grumbled. "What the boy needs is one o' them there snow machines. You know, like Joe Petrolla's got."

Caleb blinked and turned slowly to Hank. "A snowmobile?"

"Yep, that's what I mean. A snow-MO-bile."

"Hank, does this Joe...fellow live near here?"

"Lives a half mile south. Turn right at the light, if you can find the light—it's the only light in town, you know. Turn right onto Oak Street. It's the first house on the left."

"I know where that is," Caleb said, remembering every trip through this town. Picturing the street in his mind, hoping to hell he could find it in the pitch dark, in a blizzard.

"Caleb, there are guardrails along the edge of the road between here and there," Ida-May said. "Only on the left hand side, though, cause that's where the steeper drop is. You go out, and you find those guardrails. Let 'em guide you so you don't get off track. Hold right on to 'em, till you get to the traffic light. You hear?"

He nodded. "That's good advice, Ida-May, thank you."

She nodded, picking up a lamp. "Now you come on upstairs with me. My late husband's clothes are still packed in the closet. We'll get you bundled up proper."

## Chapter 15

The sounds of thundering feet in the upstairs hallway of the Brand farmhouse, immediately following Maya's shout, were loud enough to drown out the noise of the storm outside. In between the pounding feet, there were bangs and bumps and crashes, and voices asking what was wrong with the lights, and more rattling and clanking, and more footfalls. It only went on for a matter of perhaps two minutes, but Maya felt as if it was taking her family *hours* to complete the simple task of getting from their rooms to hers.

But then they were all stumbling through the bedroom door. Selene in her floor-length black silk nightgown looked even more like a Gothic heroine due to the black wrought iron candelabra she carried, with its spiderweb design. Her silvery hair spilled over her shoulders, and she looked so damn skinny Maya suddenly wanted to growl at her. Right behind her came Mel, with a baseball bat in one hand and a flashlight in the other. She wore flannel pajamas, and her short dark hair stuck up in several directions. A fighting mad hen with wet feathers. She made Maya want to laugh. Behind her, Vidalia burst in, wearing her red satin bathrobe with the black lace collar and cuffs. Maya had always referred to this as her dominatrix robe. She carried an old tin and glass hurricane lamp, its globe in need of cleaning, but it gave off some light all the same. Her masses of raven curls were bound in one long braid that twisted down her back. The fourth one in was Kara. She had no light and came bursting into the room so fast she ran into Vidalia, who bumped into Mel, who shouldered Selene, who fell onto the bed and managed not to set the blankets on fire with the candles.

There were several "oomphs" and "ughs," and then Kara said, "Sorry. What's going on?"

"Power's out."

"Big snowstorm."

"Maya yelled."

Three voices gave three answers. Then Maya gave the fourth. "I'm in labor."

There was one brief moment of stunned silence, and then everyone started bustling at once. Kara muttered something about boiling water, and Mel said something about dialing 911, and Selene said, "I think I have a spell for this somewhere!"

Then Vidalia shouted, just once. *"Stop!"*

And everyone went still and silent. "That's better. Now calm down, all of you. Mel, take this lantern, go on out to the barn and get the generator fired up." She handed the hurricane lamp to Mel. "Dress warm, now. There's no big hurry. First babies take their time. Kara, you go on downstairs and call Caleb over at Ida-May's. Tell him it's time. And, Selene, you go on out with Mel and start up the van. Pull it right up to the door here. We'll let it get nice and warm." She smiled and took Selene's candles, setting them on the bedside stand. "You'll find some more lamps and candles in the kitchen closet, third shelf. Matches with them, as always. Go on now. I'll stay here and mind your sister."

Nodding, they shuffled out, Mel's flashlight guiding the way.

Maya tried to slow her breathing, tried to be calm. It wasn't easy. She was actually trembling. Drawing a breath, she sat up and flung back the covers. "I'm soaking wet," she said. "I think my water broke."

"Not to worry, hon. I'll just get you some clean, dry things." Vidalia went to the dresser, pulling open the top drawer, and hauling out an oversized flannel granny gown with pink flowers all over it.

"That thing's big enough to shelter the homeless," Maya moaned.

"And just think, this will be the last night you'll need to wear it. Come on, now, up on the edge of the bed."

Maya moved with no small effort, and her mother helped her peel off her wet nightgown. She brought a washcloth and towels for Maya to wash herself up, and helped her into the clean, warm nightie. Then she wrapped her in the extra blanket and set her in a chair beside the bed.

It took all of five minutes. And then the next contraction came, and it pulled tight, and Maya wrapped her arms around herself and bowed her head, and made a sound from down deep in her chest.

Vidalia was peeling the wet blankets and sheets off the bed, but she stopped, and her head came up. "Is that the second contraction?"

"Mmm." Maya managed that and nothing more, but accompanied it with a fierce nod.

"And the first was when you called out?"

"After," Maya told her. And she knew damn well it hadn't been very long. She pried her eyes open, saw her mother look at the wind-up clock on the bedside stand. She didn't look away until Maya sighed her relief and sat a little straighter. Her mother finished stripping the bed, carried the bundle of covers to the bathroom and came back with fresh linens. How she managed to be so fast and efficient in almost total darkness was beyond Maya. She thought her mother could probably do just about anything. Thank God she was here!

"There now," Vidalia said. "I'll throw fresh blankets on there, and it will be all ready and waiting for you when we come home from the hospital."

Maya licked her lips. "Dammit, I was supposed to get married today," she moaned.

"Watch your mouth, dear."

"I don't want my babies illegitimate."

"Oh, for heaven's sake, child, it's the twenty-first century. What kind of a modern woman are you if you still think a baby needs its father's name to be considered legitimate? I mean, really, who made that rule? When did the mother's name become so unimportant?"

"Mom, this isn't exactly the time for feminism or politics."

A throat cleared, and Maya looked to the doorway, seeing Kara and Selene standing there, looking frightened. "Um... Mom, can we talk to you a minute? Out here?" Kara asked.

Vidalia lifted her brows. Maya held up a hand. "No. Whatever's wrong, you spit it out right here, right now. I've got a right to know."

Kara looked at Maya. Then she looked at Vidalia. Vidalia heaved a mighty sigh, and gave a nod. "Go on, what is it?"

"Mom, there's a blizzard going on out there. No power, no phones, at least two feet of snow piled up, and some of the drifts out there are higher than my head. Wind's blowing something fierce. I can't even see from the house to the barn."

Frowning, Vidalia went to the window, parted the curtain. "Where's Melusine?"

"She went out anyway. Bundled up and said she thought she could make it to the barn, get the generator started,"

Selene said softly. "We told her not to go, but you know Mel."

"Lord have mercy," Vidalia whispered.

Maya bit her lip, but the cry was wrung from her anyway. Tears sprang to her eyes this time, the pain was so intense. Her sisters huddled around her, and Vidalia looked at the clock. "Four minutes," she said. Shaking her head slowly, she looked at the ceiling. "Lord, if you're still owin' me any favors, now would be a fine time to pay up on 'em." Then, she stood straighter, lifted her chin. "All right, all right, we have what we have, we may as well deal with it. Kara, get that mattress cover from the hall closet, and get it onto this bed. Bring extra blankets, too. Selene, did you gather up the lamps and candles?"

"They're right here. I brought the whole box." As she spoke, she turned back into the hallway, bent to pick up a large cardboard box and brought it into the bedroom.

Vidalia went to the round pedestal table by the window and, taking the tablecloth by its edges, gathered it at the top, lifting a dozen framed photos, trinkets and knickknacks all at once. She set them in an out-of-the way corner. "I want you to put every one of those lights right here, in this bedroom window, and fire them up. We'll need the light to work by, and if they're bright enough, they might help Mel keep her bearings."

"What if they don't, Mom?" Selene was already unloading candles and kerosene and oil lamps from the box onto the table.

"Don't you worry, Selene. Vidalia Brand is not goin' to let any blizzard take one of her girls. Now you just do what I told you, quick as you can. There's work to be done. I need rubbing alcohol, scissors, that ball of string from Maya's sewing basket...."

Caleb thanked God for Ida-May's suggestion about clinging to the guardrails at least a hundred times before he made it to the traffic light. The snow was blinding, the wind constantly driving his body off track. He could have veered off course and not even known it. It was impossible to tell the road from the ditches. There was nothing but snow. White, ice-cold snow, crotch-deep and stubborn as hell. With every step he took, his legs and borrowed boots were pushing massive amounts of the stuff. It was unbelievable.

He had to let go of the guardrail and cross the street now. The rail was on the left-hand side, and the street he wanted was on the right. He turned, aimed the flashlight Ida-May had given him, hoping to pinpoint a spot on the other side so he could have something to aim for. But the light couldn't cut through the wall of slanting snow. He started forward anyway, but a gust caught him and sent him stumbling sideways. He fell over, snow in his face, even inside the fur-trimmed hood of the late innkeeper's parka. Shaking himself, Caleb rose to his hands and knees, got slowly to his feet. He was off track, turned around already. He'd lost his sense of which way he'd been facing, which way he wanted to go.

Tipping his head back, he turned in a slow circle, aiming the flashlight upward, until finally he saw it reflected back at him from the traffic light above. And when he found it, he realized he could just manage to make out the shapes of the cables that held it suspended above the street. He'd been on the left, so the shortest stretch of cable was where he'd been. The longest stretch was a map pointing the way to the other side of the road.

Bowing against the wind, he walked, stopping every three or four steps to look up at the traffic light and its cables to keep his bearings. And eventually he reached the spot where the cable ended. Again he shone the light. What now? Nothing to go by, no guardrails. He battled his way forward, facing directly into the biting wind now, took a few steps, then a few more. And at last his light gleamed on what turned out to be the reflective numbers on the door of a house. He was looking for the first house on the left. Joe Petrolla's place. He didn't know if this was the first house, or if it were on the right or the left. It was as close as he could guess, though.

His entire body shaking, he managed to get up the sidewalk to the front door, and then he banged as hard as the oversized mittens would allow.

It was only moments before the door opened and a man in a plaid housecoat pulled him inside, then slammed the door closed behind him. "Great jumpin' Jehoshaphat, who in their right mind would be out on a night like this? You all right, fella?"

Shivering, Caleb yanked off the mittens, so he could loosen the scarf and the strings that held the hood—no easy task, since they were caked with snow and ice. But after a few seconds his cold fingers managed to accomplish it, and he pushed the hood down. "I'm Caleb—"

"I know who you are!" the man said. "Honey, it's that politician fella from the newspapers. The one who's gonna marry Maya Brand!"

Caleb hadn't noticed the woman huddled near a potbellied wood stove on the other side of the room. He did now. "Well, I'll be," she said.

"Listen, I don't have a lot of time to explain, but I'm looking for Joe Petrolla. Are you him?"

The man frowned and shook his head. "No. Name's Cooper. Tom Cooper. This is my wife, Sarah."

"How far am I from this Petrolla's house?"

The man scratched his head, looked at his wife.

"Only Petrolla I even knew moved to Texas five years back," the wife said.

Caleb closed his eyes, lowered his head.

"Must have been some important, to bring you clear out here on a night like this," Tom Cooper said.

"It is important. The roads are blocked, power's out, as

you probably already know, and the phones are dead. Maya is all alone out there at the farmhouse, and I don't have any way of even knowing if she's all right." He bit his lip. "Just yesterday a nurse predicted she'd have the babies within a day or two at most."

"Someone ought to go on out there and check on her," Tom Cooper said slowly.

His wife, who'd crossed the room, smacked him on the arm. "Well what did you think this young man was doing, Thomas, taking a stroll?" She rolled her eyes and looked at Caleb. "What did you want from this Petrolla, anyway?"

"Ol' Hank, at the boarding house, told me the guy had a snowmobile. I thought I'd stand a better chance of making it out to the farm if I could borrow it."

She sighed heavily. "Well, we don't have a snowmobile."

"You'd never make it on a snowmobile in this storm anyway," her husband said.

Then the wife's head came up. "Could you make it with the bulldozer, Tom?"

Tom blinked twice and turned a horrified stare at his wife. "What the—do you think I'd just hand over—that thing cost more than this house, woman!"

"Tom's in the construction business," she said, as if that explained his reaction. "His equipment is as precious to him as if it were attached." She turned a narrow glare on Tom. "But there is a pregnant woman and twin babies at stake here, so of course he'll realize there's only one right thing to do."

Cooper set his jaw and shook his head.

"Mr. Cooper, you said you knew who I was," Caleb told the man. "So that must mean you know what I'm worth."

The man's brows drew together in a brief frown, then rose as his mind processed this new data.

"Tom, please...if you help me tonight, I'll buy you a brand-new dozer tomorrow. Any kind, any size, any price, you name it."

Tom Cooper rubbed his chin. "Don't need a dozer," he said slowly. "Got one." Then, tilting his head to one side, he said, "Could use a backhoe, though."

"Deal. You have my word, and your wife is our witness. The minute the roads are cleared, you go out and you order the biggest, shiniest backhoe in existence, and I'll foot the bill." Caleb thrust out a hand.

Tom pursed his lips, then reached out and shook on it. Turning, he said, "Hon, I'm gonna need my wool union suit and my Carhartt overalls."

"Hey, wait a minute. I didn't say anything about you going with me," Caleb said. "It's not safe out there."

Tom lifted his brows. "You ever run a dozer, mister?"

Caleb shook his head.

"Didn't think so. I'll be ready in ten minutes." He glanced at the window, shook his head. "Nope, you'd have never made it out there on a snowmobile. Never."

"I wanted to do this in the hospital! I wanted a freaking epidural!" Maya's voice carried all through the house. But as the contraction eased and she relaxed back on the pillows, her focus changed again. "How long has it been?"

"Only an hour," Vidalia said.

"Mom, you gotta go after Mel. Dammit, if I could, I'd go myself."

"Mel's the toughest of any of us," Vidalia said. She couldn't hide her fear from Maya, though, or from anyone else. It showed on her face. She was terrified for Mel.

"Let me go. Mom, she's right. We have to get to Mel," Kara said.

"I can do it," Selene put in. "You have to let one of us try, Mom."

Vidalia looked again at the window. "Just give her a few more minutes. I don't want to risk either of you getting lost out there.'' She wiped the sweat from Maya's brow with a soft cloth.

Kara had brought up the small portable kerosene burning heater from the basement, and it was almost too warm in the small bedroom now. Or maybe it only seemed that way to Maya.

She clasped her mother's hand. ''You have to let one of them go, Mom. Mel might be in trouble.''

''Maya—''

''Listen...oh, hell....'' The pain was coming again, she clenched her jaw and her fists, and spoke through it. ''Tie a rope...to the porch rail. Tie...the other end...around her waist.''

Vidalia nodded hard. ''Do your breathing, Maya. Come on, breathe through it.''

She panted out the breaths as she'd been taught, while her mother joined her. When it passed, Vidalia stroked her hair. ''Good girl, you're doing fine, honey.'' Then she turned. ''Your sister's right. Kara, I want you to get the rope from the hall closet. Tie one end around your waist and the other to the porch rail. Go out as far as you can reach and see if there's any sign of Mel. Bundle yourself, girl. Cover every bit of skin, take the flashlight and don't linger. You get out there, and if you don't see her, you get right back in.''

''Why not me?'' Selene demanded.

''Because you're younger and you're smaller. The wind would whip you around like a dandelion seed. I want you to stay on this end, every bit as bundled as Kara. You keep watch that the rope doesn't come loose. And don't you even think of leaving that porch, you understand me?''

Selene scowled, but nodded. She moved to the head of the bed and leaned over to kiss Maya's cheek. ''Be okay, hon. I won't be long.''

''Hey, I've got your childbirth herbs in my pillowcase, your protection incense burning and your power stone being crushed to dust in my fist, sis. What could go wrong?''

Kara came to the other side. "Will you two be okay without us?'' she asked.

"Mom's done this a few times, don't forget,'' Maya said breathlessly. "Go on, bring Mel back.''

Kara nodded, and she and Selene hurried out of the room. Another pain hit, and Maya's head came off the pillow at the intensity of it. *"Is it supposed to hurt this much?''* she growled.

"Breathe, baby. That's it. You trust me, when we ask you about this later, you're gonna tell us it was nothing at all. This part leaves your mind like it never happened.''

Panting through clenched teeth, Maya said, "That's bull.''

"If it were bull, darlin', you'd be an only child.'' Vidalia smiled gently at her. "In fact, I think everyone would be. Well, everyone except for twins and triplets and such special little angels as those.''

The pain ebbed. Maya stopped panting, blew a sigh, dropped her head to the pillows once more. "Can you see out the window, Mom?''

"It's damn near black as pitch,'' Vidalia said, but she went to the window all the same and stood looking out. "Well now, wait a minute…what in the world?''

"What is it?'' Maya twisted her head to try to see, but couldn't.

"Why…there's a light, way off to the north. Looks to be coming this way, too. Who on earth…?''

"Is it Mel? Maybe she got turned around and wandered—''

"No, it's too far away to be Mel. Besides, that little flashlight wouldn't shine so far, not in this weather.''

Maya closed her eyes. Maybe it was Caleb. God, she wanted him so much right now. And it made no damn sense whatsoever, but there it was. He'd been her first thought when she'd felt the initial pangs. And he'd been on her mind constantly ever since. She'd been lying here foolishly fantasizing that he would show up, like some knight in shining armor. That he would fight his way through a storm that even emergency workers couldn't penetrate just to be with her. She kept envisioning him bursting through the bedroom door.

She was hopeless. If he had a clue how she really felt about him, he would probably take his offer of marriage and run screaming back to Tulsa just as fast as his feet could take him. She'd always been so practical. When had she turned into this emotional, needy, lovesick basket case?

But she knew the answer to that. She'd been that way since she first laid eyes on Caleb Montgomery. And she didn't think there was any cure in sight.

And yes, she needed him tonight, and no, he wasn't here. But she knew now that she couldn't judge him by that. If he knew what was happening, he would be here. If there were a way to get here. His not being here didn't mean he would turn out to be a man like her father was, or that he would let her down or walk out on her children. It didn't mean that at all.

"Whoever it is, they're coming this way," Vidalia said.

"I hope it's a team of paramedics with radios and a whole suitcase full of drugs," she said, as yet another contraction tightened its fist around her.

"You are such a liar," her mother told her. "You hope it's Caleb." She licked her lips, shook her head slowly. "And frankly, daughter, so do I."

The bulldozer moved at the speed of molasses, and with every snowdrift it crushed beneath its tracks, Caleb felt more certain that something was wrong. Terribly wrong. His stomach was tied up in knots, and the cold wasn't the only thing causing his shivering.

What if something happened to those babies?

What if something happened to Maya?

A shaft of red-hot pain sliced right through his frozen body to lay open his heart. Damn, he was a mess, wasn't he?

"Shouldn't we see the house by now?" He leaned close to Tom Cooper, and shouted the question. Between the noise of the dozer and that of the storm, he wasn't sure the man could hear him even then. Besides, they were both wrapped in hoods and scarfs and a solid half-inch layer of snow at this point.

Cooper turned slightly and yelled back, "Maybe. If there were any lights on."

Hell, if there were no lights on, then what the hell did that indicate? Nothing good, he bet. A brief image of Maya lying frozen in her bed, still and white, her skin like glass, crystals forming on her eyelashes, floated into his mind. Like Sleeping Beauty, he saw her. He squeezed his eyes tight and gave his head a hard shake to rid himself of that image.

She was okay. She had to be okay, and the babies, too.

Cooper held up one mitted paw, sort of pointing.

Caleb squinted into the cutting snow to try to see what he did and finally made out a dim speck of light in the distance. "Go toward it!" he yelled.

It probably was an unnecessary instruction.

The dozer belched and bucked, inch by inch, nearer the light. And the light didn't move. More and more it seemed to be coming from ground level, and the fear in Caleb's belly churned tighter. Then the spotlights mounted on the dozer were pointing directly at the smaller light, so it vanished altogether. But the edge of the house came into view, and he could see lights at last in one of the upper windows.

"Thank God," he whispered. "Thank God." At least it looked as if someone were alive in there.

The dozer rocked closer, and its lights picked out a lone form, struggling against the wind...with what looked like a rope tied around it. Turning to face the dozer, the form waved its arms frantically, held its hands flat out, made a pushing motion.

"Stop, Tom," Caleb shouted. "Shut her down, but keep the lights on."

Cooper did so. Caleb climbed off the machine, amazed at how difficult it was to bend or unbend anything. Every joint in his body seemed to have frozen over. His legs sank hip deep in snow as soon as he hit, but he waded forward, fumbling in his big pocket for the flashlight, grabbing it as clumsily as a bear cub in boxing gloves, and finally flicking it on.

The figure with the rope around it was bundled beyond recognition, until he got all the way up in her face. Then her eyes, peering over the top of a scarf gave her away as a Brand woman, and her height told him which one.

"Kara? What are you doing out here?" he said, loudly, over the wind.

"Caleb?" she asked. "Oh, thank God!" She hugged him, totally ineffective in all the layers of clothing.

"What's wrong?" he shouted again, clasping her shoulders, and backing her up just a few inches.

"It's Mel! She went out to the barn—for the generator— but she never came back."

His heart did a little spasm in his chest. "How long?" he shouted.

"Almost two hours!"

He didn't like it. Damn, Mel out in this for two hours? Why the hell hadn't someone gone out after her sooner?

"Go back to the house," he yelled. "I'll find her."

Kara shook her head. "Not without my sister!"

He started to get mad, then remembered the faint light he'd seen before. It hadn't been Kara's. It had been further out than that. He patted Kara's shoulders. "Wait here!" Then he dragged himself back out to the dozer, where Tom Cooper waited. "Turn off the lights and come with me."

Cooper cut the lights, clambered down, and the two of them hunched their backs against the storm and made their way through the snow once more. When they reached Kara, Caleb said, "I think I saw her. I'm going out. You two stay right here. If I'm not back in ten minutes, Cooper, you take this girl back to the house, whether she wants to go or not. It's at the other end of her rope."

Cooper nodded. Kara argued, but Caleb didn't take time to listen. He started out through the drifts, praying to God he would see that little beam of light again.

And then he did. Ten feet from the barn, with an inch of snow already covering it. He raced closer, dropped to his knees, and pawed the snow away rapidly, digging out the light, and the gloved hand that clung to it. Mel's hand. Then her arm, shoulder and the rest of her. Lifting her upper body, he shook her. "Mel! Mel, come on! Talk to me!"

There was a very slight movement of her lips. Maybe a moan, but if so, it was lost in the wind. At least he knew she was alive. He gathered her up into his arms, turned and started back the way he'd come. He homed in on the glow spilling from the upstairs window and trudged with everything he had.

He reached Kara and Tom Cooper with what felt like the last ounce of strength in his body. He was so cold he couldn't even feel his hands or feet anymore.

Cooper took Mel from his arms, turned toward the house. Caleb took a step toward it, as well, and Kara put a hand on his chest to stop him. "We still need the generator," she said.

Cooper turned back. "Don't walk it, Caleb! Take the dozer. No one out there to run over by accident now!"

With a sigh of relief, he nodded. "Get back to the house, Kara. I'll be in with the genny in a few minutes."

She looked him in the eye and said, "Hurry, Caleb. We need you in there." Then she turned and trudged away.

In only seconds she was swallowed up by the storm. Drawing himself up, Caleb started toward the dozer.

# *Chapter 16*

He hadn't thought about how he was supposed to get the generator to the bulldozer. The thing was huge, and it would have taken two or three men at the very least, to pick it up. But he discovered chains on the back of the dozer, attached them to the machine, and even thought to make sure it had gasoline in its tank, so he wouldn't have to make this trek again to syphon some from one of the cars. The tank was full, though, so he remounted the bulldozer and ground it into motion. And he thanked his lucky stars Tom Cooper hadn't just handed it over earlier tonight or he'd never have gotten here. He'd been watching for five miles, and he still just barely managed to make it go where he wanted. There was a definite knack to this thing.

He dragged the generator right up to the front door, then shut the dozer down, got off, and, finally, after what seemed like an endless, freezing journey, he stumbled on frozen stumps into the house.

Cooper met him at the door "I'll start the genny and get her plugged in the second I get thawed out here. You'd best get out of those things. You're needed elsewhere."

He thought of Mel and rapidly, clumsily, started tugging at the snow-encrusted scarf and mittens. The parka's zipper was frozen, and there was so much snow frozen to his legs that he could barely tell where the boots ended and the overalls began. Snow scattered everywhere, but eventually he got shed of most of the layers and limped into the living room on numb feet.

Mel lay on the sofa, her clothes on the floor, her body wrapped in blankets. Kara and Selene worked fiercely, rubbing her hands and feet. Mel's hair was wet but thawed out. The fireplace burned full blast, giving off blessed heat that began to make his own hands and feet burn as the feeling came back to them.

"How is she?" he asked, leaning over the other two.

Mel's eyes opened. Her teeth were chattering and her body shaking, but she managed a weak smile. "I'll b-b-be fine. Thanks t-t-to you."

"Hey, that's what brothers-in-law are for, isn't it?"

"Caleb...I...need to tell you something." Mel was so cold her teeth were chattering. "I...the photographs. It...was me. I sent them."

He leaned closer to her, looked right into her eyes and said, "Then I know who to thank, don't I?"

Her smile was wavering, but heartfelt, he thought. Then she frowned. "W-what are you waiting for? You should be upstairs," she told him.

Caleb frowned. "Upstairs?" Then he glanced at the other two.

But before either of them could speak, a heart-ripping shriek tore through the house and right into his soul. He thought it might have cracked a few windows. A rush of dizziness hit him so fast, he almost fell down. "Maya?" he asked stupidly.

"You better get up there, Caleb," Selene said. "We'll take care of Mel."

Caleb didn't want to think what he was thinking, but he didn't take time to verify it. Instead he lunged to the stairs, and his half-functioning, damp sock-clad feet stumbled and slammed into steps on the way up. They would hurt like hell later, when the feeling came back.

"God, Mamma, why does it have to hurt so much!" Maya's voice cried brokenly.

He lurched down the hall, burst into her bedroom and stared in shock at the scene being played out in front of him.

Maya lay propped up on pillows. Her knees were bent and pointed at the ceiling, and her bare feet pressed down into the mattress. Her mother, looking about as terrified as Caleb felt, was at the foot of the bed. Then, looking up at her daughter, pasting a calm and confident smile in place, Vidalia Brand said, "All right now, honey, it's time. When the next contraction comes, I want you to push."

For one brief instant he thought he might pass out cold. He shook that away and thought he might throw up instead, from sheer terror. But he shook that off, too. The look of unmitigated fear on Maya's pale face was all it took to snap him out of it. It was fairly easy to size up the situation. The babies were coming, and they were coming now. There was no choice about it. His own fears didn't matter. Hers did. His job here was to get her through this. Not add his own worries to hers.

"Now, Maya Brand," he said, "I thought I told you I wanted to be in the delivery room. What are you thinking of, trying to get started on this without me?"

Maya's head turned fast, and her eyes met his. And he saw something that almost floored him all over again. The look in her eyes when she saw him standing there…he'd never seen anything like that before. He'd never felt so wanted, or so needed. Or so loved.

He felt himself grow an inch or two taller.

"Caleb," she whispered, sounding exhausted already. "My God, you're here. You're really here."

"I'm here." He moved closer, trusting his legs not to buckle.

Maya's eyes widened. "Caleb, my sister...Mel...she's—"

"Safe and sound on the sofa downstairs. Kara and Selene have everything in hand down there. And a friend of mine ought to have that generator running in a few minutes or so. I want you to stop worrying about all that. You've got plenty to do right up here."

She heard his voice and thought it was her mind, weaving more fantasies. She'd been lying in the bed, in pain, terrified for her babies, for her sisters, for herself...wishing with everything in her that Caleb would walk through her door and somehow make her believe everything was going to be okay. So powerful was the image in her mind that when she turned her head and saw him there, she almost didn't believe he was real. And then she did, and everything she'd been feeling for him seemed to spill from her pores and beam from her eyes.

His face changed—something moved over his features. But she couldn't tell what. Then he was moving closer, and she noticed his odd gait—he was limping or—

"Caleb, what's wrong?"

He shook his head, pausing to warm his hands over the small portable heater. "Nothing a little warming up won't fix," he told her.

Vidalia frowned at him. "How in the world did you manage to get out here, Caleb Montgomery?"

He winked. "Would you believe I hitched a ride on a sleigh with a guy in red and eight tiny reindeer?"

"It's a day early for that," Vidalia said. Then Maya saw her mother look down at Caleb's feet, saw her brows draw together in concern. She started to twist around to have a look for herself, but another contraction hit.

Caleb came to the bedside, and the second his hand was within reach, she clutched it in hers. Cold. His hand was still so cold.

"Time to push, honey," her mother told her. "You remember the drill."

"Come on," Caleb said, sliding an arm around her shoulders to brace her up. His face was close to hers. "Push now. That's it, one, two, three, four..."

When Caleb reached ten, she stopped pushing. Rested. He let her lie back and stroked her hair away from her face. Vidalia ran to the bedroom door and shouted down the stairs. "We need a bowl of ice chips up here," she called.

By the time she was back in position again, another pain had Maya in its grip, and she pushed again while Caleb held her and counted.

Selene arrived with the requested bowl of ice chips and set them on the bedside stand. In her other hand she held a pair of wool socks. "Put these on, Caleb," she said, handing them to him. "We warmed them by the fire for you. Your feet look about frozen."

"That was really sweet of you. Thanks." He tugged the damp socks off, and quickly pulled the warm ones on, just barely finishing before the next contraction came.

It went on and on. Caleb holding her, counting with her, wiping the sweat away from her brow, feeding her ice chips in between. She pushed until she thought she couldn't push anymore. She felt her body being torn apart. And then, finally, a rush of relief.

She fell back on the bed, breathless and limp. Panting, she looked at Caleb, and saw his gaze directed toward her mother, at the bed's foot. His look was intense, and for the first time, she saw the fear in his eyes showing through the confident facade. The only sound from the foot of the bed was that of her mother's hurried movements.

"Mamma?" Maya whispered. She tried to lift her head

from the pillows to see. Her heart seemed to slow to a stop in her chest, and she held her breath. Caleb's hand tightened around hers.

Then, softly, a hoarse and snuffly cry. Like the bleat of a newborn lamb. And then her mother was at her side, holding a tiny, messy, squirming, red-faced bundle, wrapped in a small blanket. "A boy," Vidalia said. "Your son, Caleb." And she handed the baby into Caleb's waiting arms.

Maya couldn't take her eyes off the baby. Her mother helped her sit up farther, plumping the pillows behind her, which she'd pretty well flattened, as Caleb sat on the edge of the bed holding the baby. He hadn't said a word. Not a word.

As soon as Maya was upright, Caleb gently placed the baby into her arms. Filmy, unfocused eyes squinted at her, and when she touched the tiny hand, it gripped her finger and her chest contracted with a kind of wonder and joy she'd never experienced. Lifting her head, she looked at Caleb.

His face was wet. His eyes, his cheeks. He met her gaze, and smiled at her. "My God, Maya, look what you did. You're...incredible." And then, leaning closer, he brushed his lips over hers, very gently. She closed her eyes, sighed very softly. His hand threaded in her hair, and he kissed her again. Then he drew back and just stared at her, as if he'd never quite seen her before.

She looked at the baby. "Cain Caleb Montgomery the Fourth," she said softly. "Such a big name for such a little thing."

Caleb lowered his forehead to hers, and the tears on her cheeks mingled with those on his.

The sound of a motor reached Maya, and only then did she tear her eyes away from her baby. Then the lights flickered on, blinked off, came on again, and stayed this time.

"Thank the Lord," Vidalia said. "Now, darlin', if it's okay, can I take my grandson for just a bit?"

Maya nodded, and Caleb gathered the baby from her arms

and handed him carefully to Vidalia. She turned toward the doorway, and for the first time Maya looked beyond Caleb to see that Kara and Selene were crowded there, peering in. They were both damp eyed, too.

"Well come on in here and close the door, this little one needs to be kept very warm just now," Vidalia said.

"Mel's resting," Kara explained. "Tom Cooper's gonna sit with her so we can help out up here."

"I turned the furnace way up, Mom, and I brought diapers and baby clothes, and blankets," Selene said.

"Yeah, and even a little hat." Kara held up the tiny little cotton skullcap. "They always put hats on them in the hospitals."

Vidalia looked at the baby, obviously not relishing the idea of handing him over. But then another contraction came, and Maya, caught by surprise, cried out. Vidalia shot her a worried glance and handed the newborn off to Selene, complete with a set of instructions, which she spoke rapidly even as she resumed her position at the foot of the bed.

"Oh, God, not yet," Maya moaned. "I can't do this again." It hit her that that was exactly what was about to happen.

"Yes, you can. Come on, Maya, you can. I know you can," Caleb told her.

Panting, she waited for the pain to pass, then looked up at him. "I need to sit up. I need something to brace against."

He didn't hesitate. He lifted her shoulders and positioned himself on the bed behind her, just the way they had done at the childbirth class. He bent his knees so she could brace her hands on his thighs, and his chest was solid behind her.

"Better?" he asked.

She let her head fall back against him and nodded. "I think...oh, God!"

"Another one? Okay, okay, it's all right. Breathe through it." His hands were on her belly, rubbing circles that were supposed to be soothing. But it was his breath, and his voice, so close to her ear that gave her the most relief, the most comfort. He was here. He was actually here for her, when it had been all but impossible to be. He was not like her father, and he would never be. He might not love her, but he would always, she sensed, be there for her. And for her children.

He held her like that all through the wee hours. He breathed with her, talked to her, held her. A few feet away, her sisters took turns holding the baby, their body heat his incubator. And as the sun came up, breaking through the storm clouds, and climbing steadily higher, Maya pushed with all the strength she had left in her.

And finally the second baby emerged into the world.

She collapsed against Caleb. And his arms tightened around her. She heard the fear in his voice when he spoke. "Vidalia…? Is he…?"

Opening her eyes, Maya looked up at Caleb's face, seeing the stricken expression. Fear hit her hard, and she shifted her gaze to the foot of the bed, where her mother was working. But she couldn't see the baby.

But then Vidalia smiled, and she knew it was okay. Everything was okay. The baby started to cry gustily as Vidalia wrapped it in a blanket and held it close to her. "You men just tend to jump to conclusions, don't you?" she asked Caleb as she brought the little bundle and placed it in Maya's arms. "Your daughter is just fine," Vidalia whispered.

"Oh…a girl?" Maya breathed. "A little girl? Just like Selene said…."

"Was there ever any doubt?" Selene asked softly. "Help ought to be here soon. At first light Mr. Cooper headed back to town. Said he'd go straight to the sheriff's department and let them know the situation."

Maya frowned tiredly. "How was he going to do that?"

"Same way he got out here with Caleb," Kara said. "On his bulldozer."

Maya blinked in shock, tipping her head backward to stare up at Caleb. "You came all the way out here last night on a bulldozer?"

He shrugged. "Hey, I was looking for a snowmobile, but I figured I'd better take what I could get."

"But it must have taken over an hour—and in that storm... God, Caleb, it was a crazy thing to do."

"Walking would have been crazier," he told her. And his eyes got that look again. All...deep and potent. "But I would have, if that was the only way to get to you last night."

Her brows came down. "How did you know?"

He shook his head. "I didn't.... I just had a feeling that I had to get here. That you needed me."

"I was sending a telepathic 911," Selene confessed from across the room.

But Caleb's gaze never moved from Maya's, as she whispered, "So was I, Caleb. I was wishing for you so much...and you came. You came."

"I always will," he promised her. And for the first time, she believed it with all her heart.

## Chapter 17

She'd been resting in the hospital all day. Heck of a way to spend Christmas Eve. Caleb had been in and out a half-dozen times, each time seeming a little more tense. He brought flowers the first time, candy the second, a pair of giant teddy bears the third. He kept saying he had a very busy schedule today, but that he couldn't stay away from her and the babies for more than a couple of hours at a time.

She wished he wouldn't say things like that unless he really meant them—at least, the way she wanted him to mean them. She was sure he was utterly sincere where the babies were concerned, but she was sure he could bear to be away from her just fine, if need be.

At any rate, he certainly was heroic. She'd had the TV on for the past hour, and the coverage of the storm told her more than she'd already known about how bad it had been last night. He'd literally risked his life to get to her.

Her admiration for him—her love for him—grew even deeper at the knowledge.

The door opened, and she looked up, wondering which of her frequent visitors would appear there. Selene, Kara, her mother, Caleb—or Mel, who was in a room down the hall recovering from her brush with hypothermia. Aside from a touch of frostbite, she was going to be just fine. They'd promised she could go home today. Maya and the babies would be released on Christmas morning.

But the visitor was none of those people. It was, instead, Cain Caleb Montgomery II. He hesitated in the doorway, peering in at her, leaning on his cane. "I can come back later, if you're resting," he said.

"No, no, please come in."

He did, his cane thumping the floor with every other step.

"Have you seen the babies yet?"

He looked at her with a smile...an actual smile. She hadn't seen one on him until then. "I've been in the nursery for the past half hour." The smile grew. "They let me hold them. I didn't want to put them down."

"I'm glad I'm not the only one," she said. "Come in and sit down, Mr. Montgomery."

"Oh, now. You call me Cain." He sat down, pursed his lips. "Actually, I'm hoping that, down the road, you might want to call me Dad, instead. I mean, you know, since you're marrying my son."

Her hand touched her chest involuntarily—in response to a small flutter there. "I haven't called anyone that in years."

"Yes, well..." He cleared his throat. "I owe you an apology, Maya. I came here judging you, insulting you and your family, and the truth was, I was only reacting out of fear that you were going to take my son away from me. Instead, you've given me...oh, such a precious gift."

She didn't know how to respond to that, so she said nothing.

"I want you to know that Caleb and I have had a long talk. I've told him already that whatever he decides to do or not do with his life, is fine with me. Just so long as I have plenty of time with his...his family."

"Oh, my goodness." She had to dab at her eyes. "That must have meant so much to him. And it does to me, too. Thank you Cain...Dad."

His smile was quick and bright. "Well, I won't keep you. We have lots to do tonight, after all. But, um...I have a little gift for you first. Two, actually, but, um—"

Caleb came in then, glanced at his father, then at Maya, and smiled warmly.

"Good, good, you're here. You should be," Cain said. "Would you kindly get the package I left outside the door there, son?"

Caleb frowned, but did as his father asked. He came back with a huge package wrapped in gleaming gold foil, with elaborate ribbons. "It's for Maya," Cain said.

Caleb brought the package to her and laid it across her lap on the bed.

"My goodness, it's almost too beautiful to open."

But she opened it anyway. She tore the paper aside and took the cover off the large box it had concealed.

And then she felt her mouth fall open and tears spring to her eyes as she stared down at the wedding gown of ivory satin and lace. She looked up at Cain, who hurried forward and took the dress from the box by its shoulders, holding it up so she could see it better. The full skirt spilled free, and Maya caught her breath. "I don't know what to say. It's...it's beautiful. The most beautiful gown I could imagine."

"I knew you were planning to have the ceremony before the birth," Cain said. "So I thought you probably didn't have a dress—at least, not one that would fit you now."

"Well, you were right," Maya said, still admiring the gown.

"This was...this was Caleb's mother's."

Her gaze shifted to Cain. "Oh...oh, my..." Pushing aside her covers, sending the box and wrappings to the floor, Maya got to her feet, went to the older man and kissed him softly on the cheek. "Thank you. You don't know how much this means to me."

He grinned and handed Caleb the dress. "I'll go now, so you can give her the other present."

"Thanks, Dad. Or should I say Grandpa?"

"Grandpa is a title I'll bear with great pride." He winked at his son and limped out the door, with a decided bounce in his step.

Caleb opened the small closet and carefully arranged the dress on a hanger. Then he turned to where Maya was still standing.

"You should be lying down. Resting."

"I've been lying down all day, Caleb. I'm fine, really."

He smiled. "You sure are."

Feeling her cheeks heat, she averted her face, walked to the chair beside the bed and sat down. Caleb went to the bed, sat on its edge. "I want to talk to you about our...um...our arrangement."

Her head came up fast. "You do?" Worry gnawed at her. Had he changed his mind? Had he decided he didn't want to marry a woman he didn't love after all?

"Things have changed, Maya. And...well, I just don't think it would be fair to let you go through with this marriage without being perfectly honest with you."

Lifting her chin, bracing herself, Maya looked him in the eye. "All right. I'm listening."

Drawing a breath, he took her hands in his. "First of all, I've decided not to run for the Senate. In fact, I'm pulling out of politics altogether."

It was not what she'd expected to hear.

"I thought I'd go into private practice. Open a law office right here in Big Falls. How would you feel about that?"

She knew she was gaping, but she couldn't seem to stop. Shaking herself, she finally let her relief show. "I'd feel...

wonderful. God, Caleb, that's almost everything I've been hoping for.''

"Really?" He smiled. "Why didn't you say so?"

She shook her head. "I...I didn't want to start making career decisions for you, Caleb. I don't have the right to do that.''

He came off the bed, still holding both her hands. "You have every right. Maya...." He hesitated, bit his lip. "Maya, you said that was *almost* everything you'd been hoping for. What else was there?"

She looked away fast. "Nothing. It doesn't matter, Caleb.''

One hand rose, palm gentle on her cheek, turning her to face him again. "Come on, Maya, tell me the truth. Please. Because...I'm hoping for more, too.''

She felt her eyes widen as she searched his. "Caleb?"

"I'm in love with you, Maya. I don't want to marry you for the sake of the babies, or to save your reputation or mine, or anything else. I want to marry you because I don't ever want to have to spend a day of my life without you. And I'm sitting here like a big idiot hoping to God you feel the same way about me.''

Her lips trembled, and tears spilled onto her cheeks. "I do, Caleb. I have all along.''

He cupped her face and kissed her, long and slow and deeply. And when he straightened away again, he took a small velvet box from his pocket. "This is the other gift Dad mentioned." He opened the lid to reveal a glittering diamond engagement ring, its large teardrop-shaped stone utterly flawless. "This was my mother's, as well. And I know she'd want you to wear it.''

Taking the ring from its nest, he slipped it onto Maya's finger. "Will you marry me, Maya? For real?"

"Yes," she whispered. "Yes, Caleb, I will.''

He kissed her softly again. "In an hour?"

"I..." Her eyes flew open. "An hour?"

"What did you think I'd been running around planning for all day?"

"But...*an hour?*"

"What's wrong, darling? Do you need help getting ready that soon?"

"Maybe a little," she said, her tone sarcastic.

He grinned at her, gave her a devilish wink and one last kiss, then went to the door and pulled it open. "Would all my pending in-laws please come in now?"

One by one, her sisters came in the door. Selene, and then Mel, and then Kara. Her mother came in last and let the door go.

"No, no, no. That's not everybody," Caleb said, snatching the door before it closed all the way, opening it wide once more. "I said *all* my pending in-laws."

Several confused frowns were aimed at him. And then it became clear.

Edain Brand, the prodigal daughter, walked through the door, looking even more beautiful than she had when she'd left home two years before.

"Edie? Oh my God, Edie?"

Kara, Selene and Mel mobbed her with hugs, and when they parted, Edie faced Vidalia.

Their eyes met, and for just one brief second Maya wondered if the old tension would rise up yet again between them. But then Vidalia smiled, and opened her arms, and Edie rushed into them.

Maya met Caleb's eyes across the room. "You did this, didn't you?"

"Merry Christmas," he said.

Edie and Vidalia pulled apart, and Edie went to Maya, hugged her gently, and said, "I can't believe I'm an aunt twice over."

"It's so good to have you home, Edie."

"It's good to be home, hon."

They separated, and again Maya looked toward the door. Caleb blew her a kiss and slipped quietly out of the room.

An hour later, Caleb waited in the elaborately decorated hospital chapel as his bride walked toward him. His children were held in the loving arms of their grandmother and grandfather, and every time he looked at them, he felt his chest swell with pride.

When he looked at their mother, it was more like awe. He couldn't believe he'd gotten so lucky. But maybe...maybe luck had nothing to do with it. Selene kept insisting that it was no coincidence that caused him to have a flat tire in front of the OK Coral almost nine months ago. She kept saying it was something far more powerful. Something like fate.

When Maya stood beside him and slipped her hand into his, smiling up into his eyes with love shining from hers, he thought maybe his bride's kid sister was wiser than any of them.

He slid a glance toward where Selene was sitting.

She gave him a nod as if she knew exactly what he was thinking.

# *Epilogue*

So that's the whole story. Well, not the whole story, but that's how it began. I'm sitting here now on the wide front porch of my log cabin. The snow finally melted; spring came as it always does. From here, I can look down on the farmhouse on the far side of the wildflower-dotted meadow below. It's within shouting distance. Not that shouting is ever needed. My mom and sisters are up here as often as Caleb and the babies and I are down there. But we always were a close family. Always will be, too.

Edie's still here. She's been quiet and moody, and I think Mom has been letting her get away with that for the past few months, but her patience is wearing thin. Any day now I expect her to tell Edie enough is enough and it's time to stop licking her wounds and tell us what went wrong out there in La-La-Land.

My dream house is almost exactly the way I pictured it. I say "almost" because I never pictured it this big and sprawling, but I guess that's what happens when you marry a millionaire. Caleb got rid of the Lexus sports coupe, though. Bought a minivan for me and an Explorer sports utility for him. Eddie Bauer Edition, of course, but that's okay. He managed to rent office space in town, just around the corner from Sunny's Place, and he hung up a shingle that says Montgomery Law Office. He takes all kinds of cases—and many of his clients can't afford to pay him. But he says that, luckily, he *can* afford to represent them.

He's a hell of a guy, my husband.

Here he comes now, walking across the meadow from Mom's house, a baby in each arm. Look at him, smiling and talking to them as if they can understand every word. Sometimes, the way they look at him, I almost think they can. We named our little girl after my mom. Vidalia. But we call her Dahlia for short. You know, like the flower. Mom insisted. Said as much as she might deny it, it wasn't easy growing up with an onion for a name. As for little Caleb, we call him Cal, just to avoid confusion. Tough having three men in the family with the same name. And Caleb's father is around enough so that he finally broke down and rented a house in town, so he has a permanent residence out here. He could stay with us when he visits, of course, but he's too stubborn to want to appear dependent. Still, he's out here more than he's in Tulsa. He took Caleb's decision not to run for office far better than either of us expected him to. The old goat is so madly in love with his grandchildren that there isn't much Caleb or I can say or do to upset him. But if he brings any more toys to the house, I don't know where we'll put them.

Caleb's halfway to the house now. He just looked up and caught my eye. And the breeze is ruffling his hair. Gosh, when he looks at me like that, my stomach still clenches up. I love that man more than I ever thought possible. He healed my old wounds for me…and I like to think I helped mend some of his. And he gave me something more precious than gold— those babies. And his love.

At any rate we're happy—deliriously happy with our little family. And I think we will be for a long, long time.

\* \* \* \* \*

# BRAND-NEW HEARTACHE

# *Prologue*

It made him sick that he liked her so much. In Wade's mind, she represented everything he hated about this town, this high school. When he passed her in the hall, she looked right through him, just like most everyone did.

Wade Armstrong lived in a rusty, lopsided trailer with three junk cars, none of which ran very often, in the driveway. His old man was the town drunk and got tossed into jail at least once a month for being disorderly at one of the local bars. Even, every now and then, the one her mother owned. He didn't remember his own mother. They said she hanged herself when he was three.

He didn't think Edie Brand was so much better than him. Sure, she had a mother, but her old man wasn't in the picture. Folks said he'd had another family on the side. Wade heard he'd been shot down in a gangland execution. That might be way more romantic than hanging yourself, but the old man was just as dead.

Of course, there was more standing between him and Edie Brand than that. Edie's mother owned a saloon, kept her daughters in decent clothes and shoes. Wade's father spent most of his time in saloons and most of his money on whiskey. Wade's own clothes never looked like much and were rarely a perfect fit. He couldn't afford to be fussy. His part-time job at the garage in town barely paid enough for him to keep the power and heat turned on in the trailer and buy a few groceries now and then.

Edie lived in a house. No mansion, but it was worlds above his place. Still, her family was almost as scandalous as his own. She just had a way of outshining her background. A way that almost made him jealous, though he would die before he would admit it out loud. Why the hell couldn't *he* breeze through life as if he were just a hair short of royalty, despite the truth?

Hell, he knew why. Because guys were different. The jocks in this school detested him, and they never let him forget how far above him they saw themselves. It wasn't overt. Just the looks they'd send. The way they would huddle in a group and watch him pass, talking softly, then laughing aloud. Matt McConnell was the worst offender. In various little ways over the years, he'd managed to make Wade feel about as important as a piece of gum on the quarterback's shoe.

Wade turned, leaned against his locker, and watched Edie Brand as she walked away from him, hangers-on milling around her like gnats around a bug light. Everyone wanted to be near her—as if she gave off some kind of magnetic energy that drew them. He didn't know what the hell it was. True, she was beautiful. More than just your normal, garden-variety prettiness—Edie Brand was *beautiful*. Movie star beautiful. Her smile made people act like idiots, tripping over themselves to get closer.

That could easily include him, unfortunately. It was a constant effort to appear as if he didn't give a damn whether she was on the planet. God, he was pathetic.

She didn't even know he existed. He was sure of that much. When he met her in the halls at school, she never looked him in the eye, always kept hers averted. Never said hello, and he would be damned if he would speak first. He was invisible to her. Her whole crowd—the jocks, the cheerleaders, the popular kids—ignored him. They didn't mess with him, but they didn't speak to him, either. He didn't exist in their world. They were content to keep it that way.

He would show them someday. He would show them all.

For now, though, he just watched, and willed her to look his way as she stopped at her locker, faced it and began spinning the dial on the lock while smiling and talking to her admirers. His fantasy spun out in his brain the way it always did. This was his senior year. The prom was coming up. She was only a sophomore. Not that it mattered—he wouldn't go anyway. But in his fantasy, he did. He rolled up to her farmhouse in a long black limo, and he got out wearing a tux. She came to the door in a white dress that reached the floor, looking just like an angel. Smiling with those baby-blue eyes, right up at him.

Hell. It was a dumb dream. He couldn't afford a tux or a limo. He would be lucky to get one of the junk heaps on the lawn running long enough to drive to the school gym and back, and a tux would be out of the question. He'd been idiotic enough to check the prices for rentals. Then there would be tickets, a corsage, dinner out somewhere beforehand, like all the socially acceptable couples had. Maybe if he didn't eat for a week...

A squeal of girlish laughter shook him out of his thoughts, and he looked again at Edie Brand, as her friends nudged her and giggled. Matt McConnell was standing near Edie, holding her hand, smiling at her, waiting.

She parted her lips to speak, and Wade found himself straining to hear, moving closer without even realizing it.

"Sure, Matt," she said. "I'd love to go to the prom with you."

Something burned like acid in Wade's chest as he watched the confident high-school quarterback lean close and plant a kiss on Edie's cheek. And he vowed he would hate that girl forever.

# Chapter 1

*Thirteen Years Later...*

"Hey, boss, you hear the latest?" Jimmy rolled out from under a red Taurus headfirst, faceup, wiping his hands on a grease rag.

Wade stopped halfway between the tiny office attached to the garage and the communal coffee urn, a cup in his hand. "What news?"

"Your favorite pinup girl is back in town."

He managed not to spill the coffee. In fact, he was pretty sure he managed not to show any reaction at all. It shouldn't be difficult. Hell, he barely thought about Edain Brand anymore—or Edie B., as she was known in the media. He only had her sexy catalogue photos pinned up all over the shop because she represented everything he hated, everyone who had ever brushed him off as unworthy. Looking at her reminded him of all the things he had to prove to the upper-crust folks in this town. That he was as good as they were. That he wasn't anything like his old man. That they had been wrong to judge him as if he were. That he could be successful.

He wouldn't be happy until he was the most successful person in Big Falls. And he had a damn good start on it, too. Armstrong Auto Repair & Body Shop had four full-time employees. Wade didn't even have to work on the cars anymore. He still did once in a while, just to keep from going soft, but he didn't *have to.* He was even thinking of opening a second garage over in Tucker Lake. And by week's end, he planned to buy the nicest house in Big Falls, just to drive his point home.

"Boss? You hear me? I said Edie B. is back. Shelly saw her in town today."

"I heard you. What makes you think I care?"

Jimmy frowned at him, glanced at the catalogue pages lining the walls, the calendar that had gone out of date five months ago but still hung there. Then he looked at his boss again. "I don't know. I just thought you'd want to know."

"Already knew," he said. "She's been back in town since her sister got married, last Christmas. Just been keeping to herself." It wasn't as if he had been paying attention or anything. Nor had her brother-in-law Caleb, Wade's only real friend, breathed a word. He'd just happened to see her name in one of the celebrity gossip rags at the checkout counter of the local grocery store when he'd been picking up snacks and beer for the Super Bowl, and he'd picked it up to read the article. The piece said Edie B. had left L.A. when her contract with the sexiest lingerie catalogue in the world, *Vanessa's Whisper,* had expired in December, then dropped out of sight. There had been all sorts of speculation as to where she'd gone and why, from plastic surgery to a secret marriage to a dread disease. Even more questions were posed about her plans for the future. Would she renew her contract with *VW?* She was their top model, but it was common knowledge her price had been dropping over the past year, as hot new faces and lean new bodies arrived on the scene. Would she continue modeling, the paper asked, or maybe move on to acting?

That theory had made him smile. Those tabloid writers sure had short memories. Five years back or so, Edie B. had landed a bit part in an action flick that had gone straight to video. It hadn't been easy to find a copy. Wade had to hunt it down on the Internet to get his hands on one. Just out of curiosity, of course.

He'd almost winced for her when he'd watched her acting debut. She was terrible. *Terrible.*

"She's been holed up at her mother's place this whole time," he went on as Jimmy watched him with arched brows. He knew that because he'd been kind of keeping an eye out for her ever since he'd read that article, back in January. And he'd glimpsed her once or twice. Checking the mail, shoveling the walk. He'd seen her out mowing the lawn one day last week. "She's been hiding out like a whipped pup."

"What do you suppose happened to make her want to do that?"

Wade shrugged. "Don't know, don't care." He wondered about it, too, though. She'd always been in the spotlight, right in the center of attention and loving every minute of it. For her to retreat so well that none of the locals even knew she'd been in town for five months was damned out of character. But what the hell did he know? "Apparently, whatever it is, it's over now."

"Then why isn't she back in L.A.?" Jimmy asked.

"Jimmy, how about we stop gossiping about the local underwear model and get on with fixing this car, huh?"

Jimmy shrugged, grinned and slid his creeper back underneath the car.

Wade headed for his office again. But he paused on the way to glance up at Edie Brand on her hands and knees, back arched, hand making a claw like a cat scratching at the camera. She wore a push-up bra and thong panties made of fake leopard fur. Her blond hair was teased and perfectly tousled, and her teeth were bared between shiny pink lips.

Damn, she looked good.

*    *    *

Edie B. looked into the camera as if it were her secret lover. Her face was flawless, her hair piled and curled and gleaming like gold. Her practiced smile was unwavering as she answered a TV entertainment reporter's questions regarding her daring outfit for the Couture Network Fashion Awards, where she was presenting that night. Who designed it? Were there sequins involved? What color would it be? And what was really going on between her and the drummer from that hardcore band?

She answered every question without giving away a thing. And she looked good doing it. She'd been at the top of her game that day.

Her mother came into the living room, looked from Edain, slouched on the sofa, watching herself on TV, to the television, where the year-old taped interview rolled on. Then she looked back at Edie again. "I thought I told you the pity-party was over, daughter?"

Edie thumbed the stop button and dropped the remote control onto the sofa beside her. "I went out today," she said, a little defensively. "I even did my hair and makeup first. Ask Mel, if you don't believe me."

"It's true, Ma," Mel called from the kitchen. "She bought cute little outfits for the twins and some fresh flowers for the dining-room table."

Vidalia Brand nodded slowly, eyeing Edain as she did. "Well, that's a start, I suppose. Too bad you came home and resumed wallowing in ancient history so darn fast."

"I know how little it means to you, Mom, but I was at my best in that piece I was just watching."

"Oh, you were, were you?"

"Yes. I was."

"That piece aired the day after a schoolroom shooting. A

six-year-old girl died, Edain. And you were on the TV talking about your clothes. It was far from your finest moment.''

Edie looked up slowly. She honest to God had a love-hate relationship with her mother. She loved the woman, respected her for having managed to raise five daughters on her own. And she owed her own good looks to her mom's genetics, if not her coloring. God, even now, Vidalia Brand didn't look half her age. She had a killer figure, and thick, raven hair with a few strands of silver just starting to line it, and the cheekbones of a royal.

Unfortunately, though her love for her mom was requited, the respect was not. Vidalia had never gotten over Edie's career choices. And she probably never would.

''The shooting hadn't happened yet when we taped the interview,'' Edie said slowly, trying to hold her temper.

''It had happened when they ran it, which ought to tell you a lot about the values in that make-believe world where you've been living for the past ten years.''

Edie looked down at her hands in her lap, unable to answer that. It was true. She knew that.

''I like to think there was a reason you left that life, Edain. Like maybe that you finally realized you didn't belong there. And if you think *that*—'' she snatched the remote up and hit Play, then paused it on Edie's perfectly made-up face and false smile ''—was your finest moment, then you are sadly misinformed.''

''I was at the height of my career.''

''You were pretty. It didn't matter what you thought or how you felt, just so you looked good, and you did. To you, that's some kind of peak?'' Sighing, Vidalia shook her head. She shut the TV off, tossed the remote down. ''Are you going back to modeling underwear for a living or not, daughter? It's time you made a decision.''

''Don't you think I've been wrestling with that question for the past five months? Don't you think it's killing me, not knowing?''

"No, I don't. You've got too much money, that's what your trouble is. You can afford to mope around the house, licking your wounds and pouting, for just as long as you want. No pressure to get off your backside and earn a living.''

Edie bristled. "I'm pitching in more than my fair share around here! I even work at the bar after hours.''

"Uh-huh. And that's what you're gonna do for the rest of your life? Mop floors after hours and spend your days watching old tapes of yourself on TV? Hmm?''

"No! Of course not!''

"Then what *are* you gonna do?''

"I don't—''

"Don't you tell me you don't know. I didn't raise any airheads, Edain Brand, contrary to public opinion and TV spots like that giggling, vacant-eyed one you call the peak of your career. So don't you tell me you haven't given this some thought. You always knew your good looks wouldn't sustain you forever.''

Edie crossed her arms over her chest, refusing to meet her mother's eyes. "I always thought retirement would be another ten years off.''

Her mother made a noise.

Edie said, "Well, at least five.''

"And?''

She shrugged. "I don't know.''

"You don't know.'' Vidalia said the words as if they made her stomach hurt. Then she stomped away, up the stairs.

Edie sighed in relief, thinking the conversation was over, but that was a mistake. Because seconds later Vidalia came down again with Edie's big black camera case in one hand. She placed it carefully on Edie's lap. "Lie to your mother, will you?''

Edie shook her head, confused. "This doesn't mean anything. It's just a hobby."

"The hell it is, girl. I saw the photos you've taken since you've been home. Maya's twins. Your sister's wedding, such as it was. The Falls. The snow on the trees after that freak storm. You're good, Edie. And you know about a camera. Goodness knows you've spent enough time in front of one."

Edain licked her lips, hesitant to admit to something she knew her mother would leap on. "I...*have* toyed with the idea of opening a photography studio of my own."

Vidalia Brand smiled, nodded once, firmly, and said, "Then do it."

"I don't know, Mom. I'm not sure I—"

"Moping time's over, daughter. Get out of this slump you're in and start making a life for yourself, or I will personally kick your backside all the way back to La-La-Land. If you think I'm not serious, you just try me."

"I know you're serious."

Vidalia nodded again. "You'd better." She drew a breath, blew it out again, then sat on the edge of the sofa. She glanced just once toward the kitchen, but Mel had the good sense to keep out of the line of fire, though she'd peeked in a few times during the discussion. "What are you running from, Edain? Something sure chased you home in a hurry. You haven't been yourself at all since you came back. You barely see anyone besides family. You keep to the house as much as possible. What is it?"

After a long pause, Edie said, "Maybe I'm not myself because I'm not sure who that is anymore."

"Bullcookies."

Edie sniffed, lowered her head a little. "No. It's true. You always used to tell me there was more to me than a pretty face, Mom, but I didn't bother to find out what. That pretty face was all I needed to get where I wanted to go. Where I...thought I wanted to go. Now, I...I don't know. I'm close to thirty. Models fifteen years younger are taking the slots that used to be mine. It's getting harder and harder to keep up with them.'' She shook her head. ''Something scared me, you're right about that. I thought that was the only reason I left, but I just can't drum up any enthusiasm for going back. I don't want to work out until I drop or live on carrot sticks anymore. You know I've put on ten pounds since I've been home?''

''Ten? You could use another twenty. You're nothing but bones. A grown woman is not supposed to have the body of a prepubescent girl and the breasts of a nursing mother, you know. It's unnatural.''

A snort came from the kitchen.

''Shut up, Mel.''

''Sorry. Frog in my throat,'' Mel called.

Her mother sighed, because the body image that Edain's work perpetuated was another sore subject with her. Along with morality and dignity and about a hundred other issues. Still, she softened and searched Edie's face. ''What scared you, honey? You tell me, and I'll see it gets removed from creation, whatever it is.''

That made Edie smile. Her mother meant every word of it, she knew that. The woman would fight a pack of rabid wolves bare-handed for her daughters. Even the one she so disapproved of. ''It doesn't matter, Mom. It's been months. I think it's over.''

Vidalia looked doubtful, but nodded all the same. ''So, you gonna get on with your life or what?''

She smiled gently. ''I suppose I could go see Betty Lou at the real estate office. At least see what's available that might make a nice photography studio someday. In case that's the decision I make.''

''That's a start,'' Vidalia said. Then she turned to look through the dining room into the kitchen. ''It's safe to come in now, Melusine. You can stop pretending to check on my pot roast. We all know you can't cook anyway.'' She glanced at Edain with a smile. "Bring the cordless phone along, will you, Mel? Your sister wants to call Betty Lou Jennings, over at the real estate office.''

Mel came in, telephone in one hand, phone book in the other. She was the toughest pixie ever to live in Big Falls, tiny and dark as an elf, strong and hot-tempered as a Brahma bull. She sent Edie a sympathetic look as she handed her the phone. Edie took it with a sigh.

"I suppose now is as good a time as any.''

Two hours later she was driving her SUV into a curving driveway, where another vehicle was already parked. She came to a stop and stared at the tall, darkly stained house. It had a modified A-frame center, with two wings angling back on either side. There were huge skylights on both sides of the steeply pitched center roof, and floor-to-ceiling windows in the front. It was huge. And it sat on a hilltop, with the falls providing a stunning view from a short distance away.

When she'd spoken to Betty Lou, describing what she wanted—something large, airy, open, with plenty of natural light—she hadn't expected the woman to tell her she had the perfect place, much less that she was showing it to a client that very afternoon. Edie had to wonder if her mother had cooked this up ahead of time with the real estate agent, who was an old friend.

Still, the place was spectacular. God, if she knew for sure she were going to stay in Big Falls, she would buy it this minute, without even having seen the inside.

This was it, Wade thought, walking slowly through the house he'd been all but drooling over for the past ten years. A Tulsa architect had built it here, planning to retire in it, but the isolation had proven too much for him to handle in his old age. He'd longed for tropical climates, so now the place was vacant and up for sale.

It was a dream. And the way it sat slightly above the rest of the town appealed to him for its symbolism. No one could look down on him up here.

He heard a car pull in, figured Betty Lou had arrived. She'd left a key in the mailbox for him, told him to come on up and look around, that she would meet him here. He couldn't help but show up a little on the early side. He'd been waiting a long time for this. He already had a buyer for his little place in town. He planned to close on that deal by week's end. That would bring enough for the down payment, and he had a good enough credit rating to finance the rest. Everything was in place. He was ready.

Footsteps came up the stairs from the lower-level foyer. He turned, expecting to see Betty Lou Jennings, whose shape and demeanor reminded him of a bumblebee. Instead, he saw *her*.

She met his gaze, seemed a little startled, but hid it quickly enough. "I'm looking for Betty Lou—"

"She's running a little late," he managed without stammering, because, damn, she looked better than in her photos. The fact that she had clothes on didn't take a thing away from the sex appeal that wafted from her like musk. It had only been hinted at before she'd left high school and Big Falls all those years ago. Now it was full grown, and so was she. Eyes so big they could swallow him whole. Skin like satin. Her hair was pulled back, pinned up, nothing like the bedroom styles she wore for those sexy photos. But her lips were just as plump, and he knew that wasn't collagen. They'd always been that way.

"I'm sorry," she said. "I don't think I—"

So she didn't remember him. No wonder. She'd barely noticed him. "Name's Armstrong," he said quickly, cutting her off.

Her brows drew together briefly, but then she was busy

glancing around the room, and he didn't think she was checking the place out with the eye of an interested buyer. She looked more like a woman alone with a snake, searching for something to whack it with.

"Betty Lou will be along any minute," he said.

"I'm sure she will." She shuffled her feet, looked nervous.

"So are you looking to buy this place?"

Her eyes shot back to his. "I was thinking about it. Of course, I haven't even seen it yet, so it's hard to say."

"Well, we can remedy that right now." He moved closer to her, almost against his will, curved a hand around her elbow, felt a shot of pleasure at touching the woman whose naked flesh had fueled so many of his nighttime fantasies. He had to forcibly remind himself of his goal here. Eliminate any competition he might have for this place. Quickly. "This is the living room. The fireplace is my favorite part." He led her toward it, trying to resist the catalogue page that flashed into his mind. Her, sprawled suggestively on a bearskin rug in front of a fireplace a lot like this one.

When she looked at him, he wondered if he'd groaned out loud or just mentally. He tried to cover by getting back to his goal. "Of course, it's a huge risk, having a natural fireplace. Easy as hell to burn the place to the ground if you don't know what you're doing."

"Good thing I grew up with wood heat, then, huh?" she asked. She made it sound completely innocent, but he could tell she had guessed what he was up to. "You looking to buy this house for yourself, Mr. Armstrong?"

He shrugged, turning away from the fireplace. "Then, of course, there are the windows. Floor to ceiling," he said in his best tour guide voice.

"I can see that," she said. Almost as if she were talking down to him.

He bristled but tried to hide it. "They'll make it damned

uncomfortable in here. Roast you right out in the summer, I imagine.''

"Unless you turn on the AC," she returned.

He pursed his lips. It was going to take more than questioning the house's merits to get rid of her, wasn't it? Fine. He had more. He had plenty more. "It'll take a creative mind to figure out how to cover them. For privacy, I mean. Then again, I don't suppose you worry about that too much."

She narrowed her eyes on him. "And why do you suppose that, Mr. Armstrong?"

He shrugged. "You don't seem like the shy, retiring type."

"Because I was a model?" She faced him now, hands on her hips, and he could see she was angry.

"Because there's not much of you that hasn't already been seen by everyone who cared to look."

"That was my job, caveman. It doesn't mean I'm going to parade around in my underwear in front of open windows."

He lifted his brows and his hands. "Hey, don't get defensive on me. I didn't mean anything. Hell, I'd be the *last* one to complain about your work. Ask anyone in town." He turned away again. "Now, as you can see, this main area could double as a dining room. The kitchen is right through—"

She stopped him, a hand closing tight around his upper arm as he started toward the kitchen. He winced in pleasure. God, he liked her touching him. "What do you mean, you'd be the last one to complain?"

He turned an innocent look on her. "Only that your photos provide a valuable service to a great many men on cold, lonely nights, Edie B. Myself included."

"When you can't get a real woman, you mean?" she snapped back.

"Exactly. Sometimes there's just no one to keep a fellow company besides you, and good old Rosy Palm."

She frowned. "Rosy Pa—" She went silent, her mouth

gaping. She was only speechless for an instant, though. A second later she clamped her jaw, smacked him across the face and turned on her heel. She was out of the house so fast it must have been some kind of record.

Her tires spat gravel in their wake when she left.

Wade smiled broadly, rubbing his cheek. "For a second there, I was afraid I'd never get her out of here," he said to the empty room.

He probably shouldn't have been quite so mean. But it served her right for not recognizing him. She should at least have found him vaguely familiar. But no. She was the same arrogant little brat she'd always been. Still thought she was better than him. Just like so many others in this town.

Screw it. He would show them all. The minute Betty Lou Jennings arrived, he was going to tell her to mark this place sold. To him.

# Chapter 2

She spun her tires as she tore out of the driveway onto the curving dirt road that twisted away from the gorgeous house and got about a hundred feet before she realized what that manipulative SOB had done. He had driven her away on purpose—because he wanted the place for himself.

She was so furious she damn near had steam coming out her ears. Wade Armstrong. He had *always* been trouble. Everyone knew it. And he had *always* managed to intimidate the hell out of her. Dark, brooding, moody—she had been as turned on by him as every other girl in high school. But she had been equally afraid of him. Rumors about Big Falls' own bad boy had abounded back then. They said he could make a girl do anything he wanted her to. And that he always did just that, on the very first date. They said he only went out with older women, because girls her age couldn't keep up with his appetites, and there was a ton of speculation about him and the young English teacher who had only kept her job for one school year. She had taken a special interest in Wade Armstrong, and the next thing everyone knew, she was gone.

Edie had been completely intrigued by him. And convinced

that if she so much as looked him in the eye, he would see that in her eyes and approach her. And if he asked her out, she didn't think she had it in her to say no. And then she would be in big trouble, her reputation ruined, her popularity in the toilet, and her virginity another trophy in Wade's collection. Her mother would have *killed* her.

So she only looked at Wade Armstrong when he wasn't looking. She avoided him as if he were poison. And she remained afraid of him.

"Well, not anymore," she muttered, jamming the brakes. "I'll be damned if I'll let some sexually depraved grease monkey chase me away from something I want."

She was going to turn around and drive right back there. She was going to stomp up to the arrogant bastard and tell him exactly what she thought of him. She was going to...

A car came around the bend, slowing as it drew nearer. Edie saw the magnetic "Betty Lou Jennings Real Estate" placard on the side, cranked her window down and waved. Betty Lou stopped so the two cars were side by side, facing in opposite directions. It wasn't a problem on a winding dirt road like this one. No traffic to worry about. Edie bit her lip, hoping Wade Armstrong would stay right where he was for a few more minutes. That was all she needed.

Wade was standing in the living room, choosing a spot for the big-screen TV that was so sorely out of place at his little house in town, when he heard a vehicle's tires rolling over the gravel driveway. He tensed a little, and his belly went tight. He shook the reaction off—it wasn't Edie Brand. She wouldn't be back after the way he'd sent her packing. Pacing to the window, he glanced outside, just to make sure. And it puzzled him that he found himself half-hoping it *would* be her in her little powder-blue Jeep out there. He liked sparring with her. Liked to watch her face heat with color and her eyes spark with anger. Liked it when her lips parted and no words came out. Loved it when she touched him.

But then, so would any red-blooded American male between the ages of ten and dead.

By the looks of things, she was planning to stay in Big Falls for a while. Maybe a long while, or she wouldn't be looking to buy a house. That knowledge kept digging at him for some reason. He would brush it aside, but five seconds later he would be thinking about it again, as if it meant something to him, when in fact he couldn't care less.

Betty Lou Jennings got out of her station wagon and came up the steps, and Wade opened the front door before she reached it. She looked up fast, startled, and then a troubled V formed between her eyebrows.

Well, his news ought to put a smile on her face. "I'm taking the house," he announced. "I made up my mind yesterday. Got my little place in town sold already, and it's more than you need for a down payment. Rob at the bank says my loan is going straight through, no problems. It'll take about a week to get the official papers signed, and then we can close the deal."

"Oh." She wasn't smiling. She wasn't looking him in the eye, either. "You sold your place, you say?"

"Signed the contract yesterday," he said. She did not look happy. Her short, round little frame was perfectly still, her eyes staring straight ahead. "Sorry about not using your agency, Betty Lou—it was just one of my employees who bought it. He's getting married. I made him a decent deal."

"It's...not that."

"Well, then, what's wrong?" He watched her force herself to meet his eyes, and he got a bad feeling in his belly.

"I'm so sorry, Wade. I...the place is sold."

He blinked, repeating the word in his mind, and then aloud, because he didn't think he could possibly have heard her right. "Sold? It's *sold?*"

Betty Lou nodded, her short brown hair bouncing with the jerky motion of her head. "I've been waiting for you to make up your mind for a month, Wade, and I had no reason to believe you wouldn't keep dragging your feet for another one. I have kids to feed, you know."

"Yeah, but—" He turned slowly, pushing a hand through his hair, totally blown away.

"She wrote me a check, right there on the spot, for the full amount. No haggling, no banks, no questions. She just took it. Just like that."

Wade stopped with his back to Betty Lou, one hand on the back of his head. He froze there for an instant, then slowly lifted his head, eyes narrow. "It was Edain Brand, wasn't it?"

"I...well, I...yes. It was."

"That bossy, arrogant, egotistical little—"

"Wade, really. There are other houses in town. I have at least three I can show you this very afternoon."

"I don't want any other houses," he said, enunciating each word and keeping his tone completely level. "I want *this* house. She doesn't. She only bought it to stick it to me."

Betty Lou lifted her brows. "Don't be ridiculous, Wade. No one drops two hundred thousand dollars just to get revenge."

"That's pocket change to her."

"Well, what on earth did you do to make her angry enough that you think she would do such a thing?"

He looked up then, having nearly forgotten Betty Lou was there. He had been talking mainly to himself. So what *had* he done to make the great Edie B. angry? Not much. Just called her a slut and told her that men around the world enjoyed manual stimulation while looking at her pictures—himself included. Not in so many words, of course, but he supposed he'd been less than tactful.

"Guess I insulted her."

"Guess you must have." Betty Lou glanced at her watch.

"Look, I have to run. Don't worry about this, okay? We'll find you a great place in no time, I promise. Okay?"

"Yeah," he muttered. "Whatever."

She turned and hurried back down the flagstone path to her car. Wade followed her outside, pulling the door closed behind him. Betty Lou had forgotten to ask for the key back. Not that it mattered. Not now. Damn. *Damn* that woman for showing up and screwing up his plans.

He was furious, fuming as he drove back toward town. And then he saw her little Jeep parked on the shoulder of the road. He told himself to keep right on going. That it was a foolish, stupid thing to do, stopping when he was this angry. But he stopped anyway. He got out of his pickup and walked up to her car, glanced inside. She wasn't there. He hadn't expected her to be. There was a footpath here that led out to the falls. You could drive right up to them from the other side, but from this end you had to walk. And it looked as if that was what she had done.

Wade squared his shoulders and marched onto the meandering path, fully ready to tell the woman just what he thought of her high-handed tactics and the way she threw her money around. He followed the narrow trail through the woods. It wound downward, ending at the riverbank, near the base of the falls. And that was where he found her.

She was sitting on the rocky bank with her knees drawn to her chest, head lowered on her crossed arms. Crying. Not a soft, quiet, delicate kind of crying, with a sniffle and a few tears. No, she was really bawling. Hiccuping, with sobs in between, her shoulders shaking with the force of it.

He didn't know what the hell to do. He sure as hell couldn't confront her now, tell her off the way he'd intended, not when she was like this. His throat felt oddly tight—he couldn't seem to swallow for a while.

He froze, just watching her there for a long moment. Then, silently, he withdrew. He made his way back to his pickup and drove back the way he'd come until he found a place where he could park reasonably out of sight. Then he sat there, and he waited. An hour went by before she finally came dragging back up the path, got into her car and headed for home. Only then did Wade return to the garage.

"Well, I hope you're happy," Edie said as she stomped through the door of the farmhouse. She heeled off her suede walking shoes and sank into a kitchen chair. "I bought the place."

Her mother looked up from the coffee she'd been sipping, a stack of open mail beside her, peered over the tops of the glasses she refused to wear in public and said, "Maybe you should go outside and try coming in again with a better attitude."

Edie sighed, lowering her head. "Sorry. It's not your fault. Not really."

Her mother laid the letter she'd been reading aside and got to her feet. She leaned through the doorway into the dining room, and called, "Selene, you still around, sweetie?"

"Yeah, Mom?"

"Go on up to your room and get us some of that calming tea you brew. I think your sister could use a batch."

Selene's footsteps pounded away, up the stairs. At that moment the kitchen door burst open again, and Maya stepped through it, carrying a baby on each hip.

"My land, you'll be crippled before they start school!" Vidalia scolded. But she smiled as she hefted little Dahlia away. Turning, she handed the five-month-old to Edain, then relieved Maya of the other one. "CC, boy, you get any bigger, you'll have to start carrying me instead," she said, laughing. "Yes, you will. Yes, you will," she chirped as she carried the baby to a chair and sat down with him.

Edie held Dahlia on her lap and tried to be cheered by the huge blue eyes and spit bubbles, but it wasn't helping much.

Maya hung her jacket on a peg near the door and came in, poured herself coffee. "So what's new around here?"

"Well, your morose sister finally got herself out and about today," Vidalia said, her attention fully on her grandson.

"I thought I saw you driving out this afternoon. What did you do, Edie?"

"Not much. Bought a house I hadn't even fully seen, is all."

Maya blinked, looking from Edie to her mother and back again. "You...you bought a house?"

"Yeah. The big A-frame on the hill overlooking the falls."

"Oh, gosh, that place is *fabulous!* But...so...does that mean you're staying?"

Sighing, Edie shrugged. "To tell you the truth, I hadn't even really made up my mind what I wanted to do. I only went out there to look at the place, just in case I decided to stay."

"She's thinking of opening a photography studio," Vidalia filled in.

"That's a wonderful idea!" Maya exclaimed, clapping her hands together.

The baby in Edie's lap smiled and clapped her hands together, too.

"It was just a thought. I really don't know if that's what I want to do."

"Well, then...I don't get it," Maya said. "Why'd you buy the place if you still haven't decided?"

She drew a deep nasal breath, lifted her head, met her sister's eyes. "I ran into Wade Armstrong out there. He wanted to buy the house himself, and he insulted me and pissed me off and—"

"Language, Edain," Vidalia cut in.

Edie bit her lip. "He *ticked* me off so badly that I left. And then I realized that was what he intended, to chase me off before Betty Lou got there so he wouldn't have any competition for the house. So when I met her on the road, I stopped her, and I...I bought the house.''

Maya just sat there staring at her. She finally glanced at her mother. ''Is she kidding?''

''I don't think so. And we always thought Mel was the hot-tempered one.''

Selene came trotting into the kitchen then, her silvery-blue eyes curious, a mason jar half full of finely ground herbs in her hands. ''Hi, Maya. Hey, Edie,'' she said, waltzing through the kitchen. She paused to lean over each of the babies, cooed and tickled them hello, then turned to put water on to heat. She found her metal tea balls in a drawer and began measuring herbs into them. ''How many for my calming brew?''

''Just Edie,'' Vidalia said.

Looking over her shoulder, Selene lifted her brows. ''What's got you all out of sorts, sis?''

Edie sighed, saying nothing. Vidalia answered for her. ''Edie just dropped four years' income on a house because some man made her mad.'' At Edain's glare, she amended. ''Sorry. Four months' income for her. Four years to anyone else—more than that to most folks.''

Selene lifted her brows, glancing at Edain. ''Wade Armstrong, I'll bet.''

Maya closed her eyes, shaking her head slowly. ''Knock it off, would you? That really creeps me out.''

Selene shrugged. ''So what happened, Edie? Did you go into his garage and see all the—''

''Selene, your water's boiling,'' Vidalia said quickly, a sharp edge to her voice.

Edie heard it. She frowned and looked at her mother, who looked away.

''He insulted her,'' Maya said, hurrying to fill in the tense silence. ''And he wanted the house himself, so she bought it right out from under him, to get him back.''

Selene lowered her head quickly, but not before Edain saw

the smile. "Bet he didn't expect that. Heck, he has most people around here believing his big bad scary routine. They're
too intimidated by it to mess with him."

"He hasn't changed a bit then, has he?"

"Since high school?" Selene asked. "Nope, not a bit. He's
still a loner. Still carries a big chip on his shoulder and walks
around as if daring anyone to try and knock it off." She
carried a steaming cup of fragrant tea to Edain and set it down
in front of her. "And he's still nuts about the most popular
girl in town."

"I pity her, whoever she is," Edie muttered as she lifted
the cup to her nose to sniff the contents.

Selene smiled crookedly. "So, now that you have a house,
you gonna move out and leave us, sis?"

"Not right away. I mean, I need to think about furniture—
the whole place needs to be decorated. And besides, I like
being close to the babies." As she said it, she bounced Dahlia
on her knee and tickled her underneath her chin.

"Well, there's no hurry," Vidalia said.

"Nooo," Maya said, drawing the word out. "But it will
sure burn Wade Armstrong's buns to see the place sitting
empty. I mean, he must know you bought it just to spite him."

"He's an arrogant jerk who thinks the only thing I'm capable of doing is posing in my underwear. He had it coming."
Her sisters and her mother were looking at her. She pursed
her lips. "He *did*."

"Okay. He did. The question remains, what the heck are
you going to do with a house you're not even sure you
want?" Maya asked.

"Oh, she wants it." Selene spoke slowly and with an authority that seemed out of place coming from the youngest of
the sisters. "Deep down, some part of her knows that. Ticking
Wade Armstrong off was just an excuse."

Vidalia tipped her head to one side. "I never can figure out if you're more witch doctor or headshrinker, girl. But you do make a good point. Don't you think so, Edain?''

"No, I don't think so.''

"Neither did I, when she said I was going to have twins,'' Maya muttered, half under her breath.

Edie pursed her lips and sipped her tea. It was good. It was delicious, but she wasn't going to give her know-it-all kid sister the satisfaction of saying so.

"No need to make a decision now, anyway, Edain,'' Vidalia said, patting her daughter's hand. "You can stay right here just as long as you want to. Just so long as you don't try to hole up in the house like a hermit. You're a beacon, girl. You need to shine, or you'll just flicker out.'' Then she glanced at the clock on the wall. "I have to go. Kara's all alone over at the Corral, and it'll start getting busy soon.'' Getting to her feet, Vidalia set her grandson back in his mother's lap.

"I'll ride over with you, Ma,'' Selene said, snagging a light jacket from one of the pegs beside the door. The two headed out without another word, and Edie was certain they would be discussing her all the way to the family business—the OK Corral.

"I have to get home,'' Maya said. "I left bread in the oven.''

"You're gonna make that man of yours fat,'' Edie said. She got up, though. "Come on, I'll help you carry the rug rats up the hill.''

"Thanks.''

Together they put the babies' sweaters and hats back in place. It was May, but it was also evening, and there was a breeze. As they walked along what was now a well-worn path that led up the hill a hundred yards from the farmhouse to the dream house Maya and her husband, Caleb, had built, Edie couldn't help but admire the place. It was large and homey. A log cabin fit for *Home Beautiful,* big enough for a big shot like Caleb—whose father was one of the richest men in the country—yet cozy enough for Maya, the original home-body. There was still some work under way. The driveway hadn't been paved yet, and the two-car garage was still un-finished. But the wide front porch was just what Maya had always talked about, and there was already a swing set in back, though the kids were way too young to enjoy it yet.

As they neared the house, Caleb's car pulled into the long gravel driveway that wound from the far side of the house down to the road. He got out, spotted them coming, and started toward them, a warm smile on his face. Edie still couldn't get over the way that man's eyes lit up whenever they fell upon Maya or the babies. He was hopelessly in love with his little family. God, Maya was so lucky.

He met them halfway, wrapped his wife in his arms, baby and all, and kissed her deeply. Then he took little CC from her, smooching the baby's cheek until the kid laughed aloud. He relieved Edie of her niece in the same manner, then grinned. "Hello, Edie. Heard you bought a house today."

She blinked at him. "My goodness, news travels fast around here."

"Oh, not really. I just had some inquiries as to whether there were any legal actions that could be taken to block the purchase."

"What?" She blinked at him, then understood. "Wade Armstrong?"

"I really can't say. But it doesn't matter, anyway. There's nothing in the law to stop you from going ahead with it. If you…you know, want to."

"You sound as if you think I shouldn't!"

He shook his head quickly. "I didn't say that."

"He and Wade are friends," Maya said. "But this is fam-ily. Right, Caleb?"

"Well, yeah. Sure. I mean, I…"

"And Wade Armstrong can just find himself another house. Right, Caleb?"

He hesitated. "Technically," he said at length, "either one of them could probably find another house."

"Caleb..."

"Come on, Maya, I don't want to disagree with you on this. But...it was kind of mean, what your sister did. Wade's been getting things lined up to buy that place for a month now."

"Well, he didn't move fast enough."

"Because someone richer came along and used her money like a weapon," he said. And it hurt. Edie winced.

*"Caleb!"* Maya sent him a scowl.

"No, Maya. Caleb's right," Edie said slowly. "That's exactly what I did. Wade made me angry, and I struck back. With my money. Just exactly like a weapon. And it wasn't very nice." She sighed, lowered her head.

"I only know because I've been there," Caleb said, his voice gentle. "It doesn't make you a bad person. You just had a brief flash of temper, is all."

She nodded. "So he's really been planning to buy the place for a whole month?"

Caleb nodded as his daughter pulled his hair and his son stared at him as if transfixed. "He sold his own place, too. I don't know what he'll do about that."

Edie swallowed, lowering her head. "God, why do I let my temper get away from me like that?"

"Nobody's perfect."

She sighed. "I suppose I could undo this thing before it goes any further," she said with a sigh. "It would probably be the fair thing to do. He did see the place first."

"He's not a bad fellow, Edie. But he does have a bad attitude about people lording it over him. Thinks he has something to prove. This really hurt."

She nodded. "Thanks, Caleb. I suppose if I'm staying in

Big Falls, I shouldn't start out being known around town as that bitch who throws her money around to get her way." She drew a breath, stiffened her spine, told herself it was no big deal. She could afford to have a dream house built to her own specifications if she wanted to. But it wasn't the idea of letting the house go that was bothering her. It was the idea of admitting her mistake.

Caleb read her face. "I can call him for you if you want."

"No. I'll, uh, I'll do it myself. I'm an adult."

He nodded, turned and started toward his own dream house with a baby on each hip. Maya leaned closer, hugged Edie hard. "I'm sorry he's so darned..." She seemed to search for the right word.

"Ethical? Moral? Fair-minded? Decent?" Edie asked. "You're right, he's all those things. He's also right. The rat."

"Just don't do anything unless you're sure."

"It was a temper tantrum, Maya. I'll think about it some more, but I suppose if I don't have that house, I'll get over it. See you tomorrow, okay?"

Maya nodded, then turned and hurried after her husband. Edie sighed, squared her shoulders and began marching back down the hill to the farmhouse, the phone and the meal of crow she was about to devour.

She knew, deep down, that she had reacted to far more than just Wade Armstrong's petty little insults and slams. It wasn't him at all, she reminded herself. She had become hypersensitive to men who saw her as a sex object. And that had nothing to do with Wade Armstrong. He was just your garden-variety lech. Just one more who saw her as nothing more than an airbrushed, glossy bit of flesh in sexy clothes.

No, her reactions were because of one particular man, one who'd taken it too far. Crossed the line. Frightened her so badly she'd left L.A., left the business, left everything behind. But that man, she reminded herself, was a part of her past. History. He was a sick, disturbed nobody who had only been able to get to her because she was so much in the public eye. Now she was home. Her life was her own again. *He* wouldn't even know where to begin to find her now.

She walked the rest of the way down the hill to the friendly back door, hauled it open and stepped inside. Then she paused. A small brown cardboard box sat on the kitchen table. Exactly in the center. For a minute a chill whispered down her nape, and she shivered. But then she told herself that was ridiculous. It was a simple delivery. This was Big Falls, Oklahoma. If you weren't home and your door wasn't locked, delivery guys routinely set their packages just inside the door. Especially if they knew you. And *everyone* here knew everyone else. This was not a big deal.

She walked up to the table, her steps slow, her eyes darting through the doorway into the dining room, her ears straining to hear any sign of anyone else inside the house. She looked at the box. It had her name on it.

"No postmark," she whispered. "No address."

It hadn't been left by any delivery guy. She swallowed the dryness in her throat, edging along the counter until she reached the knife drawer. She slid it open, closed her hand around the largest handle in it, pulled a cleaver out.

Still looking, still listening, she moved silently closer to the table, and with her free hand she reached out and flipped open the lid of the box. Leaning closer, she peered inside, her gaze darting downward only briefly, in case someone came at her from elsewhere in the house. She thought of just running back up the hill, shouting for help. But not for the world would she put Maya or those babies at risk.

Inside the box, unwrapped, lying loosely, were a pair of handcuffs.

Then, very clearly, she heard two solid footsteps coming through the back door, stopping right behind her.

# Chapter 3

Wade strode up the path to the wide-open back door of the Brand house. He'd seen Edain Brand go in that way only a minute ago, and she had left the door swinging, so he assumed she was still lingering nearby.

When he paused at the entrance, she was standing with her back to him, looking at something in a box on the kitchen table. When he took a step toward her and opened his mouth to announce his presence, she spun around before he got a word out, brandishing a meat cleaver.

He ducked reflexively, bringing up one arm in self-defense—even though she didn't follow through on the swing once she saw his face.

"You!" she accused. At least it sounded like an accusation to him. Just what she was accusing him of, he couldn't begin to guess. "You did this, didn't you? You sick, vile—"

"That's about enough, Edie." He reached out and clasped her wrist, rendering her cleaver-bearing hand harmless. Then he took the cleaver away. "Now, just what is it you think I've done? Let me guess. Maybe I did something really horrible—like swooping in to buy a house I didn't even want just so you couldn't get it." He frowned. "No, wait. That was you."

"You're not one bit funny. And if you think this twisted little *gift* is, then you're more warped than I realized."

"Gift?" For the first time, he took a good look at her face. She was pale, not her usual flawless color, and her eyes had an expression in them he hadn't seen before. "I didn't send you any..." He looked past her, at the box on the table; then he moved toward it.

She stepped into his path, but he put a hand on her shoulder and moved her aside without a hell of a lot of effort. He looked into the box, saw a pair of handcuffs in the bottom. He turned, lifted his brows. "Secret admirer?"

She averted her face so quickly that he found himself frowning again.

"You didn't send it?" she asked. "This isn't some kinky little insult to get revenge on me for buying your house?"

"No."

She closed her eyes quickly, whispered "damn" on a soft breath.

"Disappointed?" he asked. "You were actually hoping I harbored some sexy little bondage fantasies about you?"

"Shut up."

"'Cause I do. I mean—of course I do. But I didn't send the handcuffs." He glanced at them again. "Nope. In my version we use silk scarves. Red ones. And—"

"*Shut up,* Wade."

He shut up. Not because she said so, but because she'd called him by his first name, and he felt it all the way to his toes.

"You haven't changed a bit, have you?" she asked him. "Still trying to intimidate people, just like in high school. Well, I may have been scared to death of you then, Wade, but I'm not anymore. So just knock it off already."

He couldn't speak for a minute. He had been so certain she

didn't remember him at all—that she hadn't even noticed him
in high school. "You...were scared of me?"

"Everyone was scared of you."

"So what are you scared of now?" he asked.

She shook her head. "Look, what did you come here for?"

"Doesn't matter. What are you scared of, Edie?" He
glanced at the box. "The guy who sent you those?"

"How can I be, when I don't even know who it was?"

He frowned. Then he had a thought and reached for the lid,
intending to flip it down and check out the label, the address,
postmark, that sort of crap. Edie closed her hand on his wrist,
moved it away from the box, and placed herself between him
and the table that held it.

"It's none of your business, Wade."

He studied her face, blinked slowly as he tried to figure her
out.

"You came here to try to talk me out of buying that
house," she said slowly. "You wasted your time. Not only
am I going ahead with the deal, but I'm moving in tomorrow."

"And rubbing my nose in it tonight, apparently."

"Get out, will you? I want to be alone."

"You're a lousy liar."

She walked to the door, stood beside it, waiting for him to
leave.

"What was with the meat cleaver, Edie? Tell me that and
I'll go."

"You startled me. That's all."

"That's all? And you were standing there looking at a pair
of handcuffs with a meat cleaver in your hand because...?"

"Because I freaking felt like it."

He studied her, wondering if he could be mistaken. But no,
he was certain she'd been scared witless when he had stepped
in here. And Edie Brand had never been anyone's fool, despite her public image. If she were scared, there was a reason.

"I'll tell you what," he said. "I'll leave. But first I'm gonna have to go on up the hill and tell Caleb about your anonymous gift."

She stabbed his eyes with hers. "Don't do that."

"Why not?"

She licked her lips, looked away, seeking a plausible lie, he was certain. "Look, I don't want anyone to know about this. I need you to keep it to yourself, Wade. I mean it."

"All right. I will. On one condition."

Her head snapped toward him. "If you think for one minute you can blackmail me into giving back the house..."

"Uh, no, that's not the condition I was thinking of."

She went silent for a moment. Then she looked at him, and her eyes widened and her cheeks heated.

"Neither was that," he said, before she could accuse him. Damn, she thought awfully little of him. Then again, so did most of the locals. "I was going to say, I'll keep quiet if you'll let me take you somewhere."

"Where?" she asked, her eyes suspicious.

"Anywhere," he said. "Your sister's place, the saloon, I don't care. I just don't feel right leaving you here alone when you're scared half to death of some anonymous pervert, okay? Maybe I'm an idiot, but that's the way it is."

She blinked and kept looking at him as if she'd never seen anything like him before. Finally she nodded, her head moving in short, jerky motions. "Okay. Fine, you can take me to the saloon. I, um—" She glanced at the box.

"You want me to throw it away?"

"No. I should keep it."

He frowned at her, tilting his head. "Come again?"

"They teach you these things when you start getting a following. Any oddball gifts like that should be tucked away, in case a problem surfaces later on. I'll just...take it up to my room." She turned away, grabbed the box and started for the dining room with it, but her steps slowed, and he read her fear again.

For God's sake, did she think there might be someone in the house?

He didn't ask. He just fell into step behind her, even putting a hand on her elbow. And he figured he must have guessed right, because she didn't jerk away or snap at him. He walked with her through the dining room, into the living room and up the stairs. She went into her bedroom, knelt down and shoved the little box under the bed.

He knelt down, too, peeking under there. He saw a larger box but couldn't see what was inside it. Sighing, he got up and moved through the bedroom, checking the closet, the bathroom; then he strode out of the room and down the hall, and checked every other room, as well. She didn't yell at him or tell him to stop. He checked every room upstairs; then they went down, and he did the same again, even to the basement. When he finished, he took her arm and led her out to his truck. She locked the house when they left. No one locked their doors out here. No one.

She swallowed hard. "That wasn't actually necessary."

"No, I didn't really think it was."

They were both lying. And he was more curious than ever as to what kind of trouble Edie Brand had dragged home from L.A. with her.

She sat quietly in Wade Armstrong's tow truck as he drove. It was nice, for a glorified pickup truck. Leather seats and lots of room. It was black, bigger than normal pickups, with a boxy nose and a chrome grille that looked like a leering grin. To her, anyway. He had a pair of those headlights that looked like the eyeballs of a giant bug mounted on the hood. As if his normal headlights weren't bright enough all by themselves. In the back, where the box should have been, there was a towing contraption instead. She sat there, feeling awkward, unable to come up with anything to say. She hadn't played fair. She had bought his house out from under him, and he had returned the slam by coming over just when she was more scared than she had been in months and making everything all right.

Not that she would ever admit that. But maybe it wouldn't hurt to be halfway civil to him. Considering. She slid a sideways glance at him.

He sat there behind the wheel, looking straight ahead. He was as good-looking as he'd always been. Better, maybe. But not in a handsome way. More in a dark, brooding kind of way. He had a hard face. Skin that was dark and shadowed with stubble. Eyes that tended to be too narrow and squinty. Brows that were too thick and usually bent in a scowl. His jaw was square. She wondered for a moment just what it was that made the whole package seem attractive to her. Then she decided it had to be his mouth. He had a great mouth. Lips on the full side for a man, and coral colored and moist, the dip above the upper one a little deeper than usual. His mouth was wider than the average, too, and he had nice teeth. Big and even and strong-looking.

His neck wasn't bad, either. Corded and thick. She liked that. And she liked that he didn't cut his black hair off severely but let it curl over his neck just a little. Kept that wild image of his alive. The nonconformist. The rebel. It curled over the tops of his ears, too. But it was definitely his mouth that drew her eyes back again. Yeah, his mouth was his winning feature. If she photographed him, she would have him biting into a juicy peach, a little trickle on his chin, those lips on the fruit as his teeth sank in.

"Damn, woman, you keep staring at me like that, I'm gonna think you mean it."

She blinked and jerked her gaze away from his lips, fixing it on his eyes. Only she couldn't, really, because he had put on a pair of dark sunglasses the second they got into the truck.

"Think I mean what?" she asked.

He shook his head slightly, licked his lips, and she wanted to tell him to do it again. But she resisted, as he focused on the road. The sun was going down now, aiming at them right through the windshield. Edie reached up automatically and folded the sun visor down to protect her eyes.

He did the same. And that was when she saw the tiny, dashboard-size calendar there. One of those peel-and-stick numbers, with pages smaller than business cards, and a single photo on the top.

In this case, it was a photo of her. She was wearing a black push-up bra and a pair of thong underpants to match. She had a black furry cat in her arms and cleavage to spare.

"Come on, Wade, don't do this."

"Do what?" He glanced at her, then followed her gaze to the calendar. "Oh. I kind of forgot it was there. Does it embarrass you, Edie?"

"No. Well, yes, but—" She sighed, shook her head. "It was a catalogue shoot. I didn't even know it was going on a calendar until six months later."

"They put it on the big wall calendar for '99. April. Then they recycled the same shot for this little dashboard model for 2000." He shrugged.

"Yet here it is, almost 2002, and the thing remains on your visor."

"What, you think I put it up there so I'd know the date?" She looked away, felt her face heat.

"If it really bothers you, I'll take it down. Right now."

Stiffening her shoulders, she lifted her chin. "It doesn't bother me. Why should it? I looked great." She licked her lips. "At least, I did for a while. By the time that cat got through with me, it wasn't so pretty."

"Didn't take to being photographed, hmm?"

"He didn't mind that so much as he did the poodle that

some twit brought onto the set. It let out one yap, and all of the sudden I felt as if I'd fallen into a paper shredder.''

He laughed softly. She liked the sound, in spite of herself. And when he glanced sideways at her, she realized she was smiling at him.

"Don't think this means I'm over the whole house thing, Edie. I'm not.''

"I didn't expect you to be. For what it's worth, I know it was a lousy thing to do.''

"Yeah? So why don't you undo it, then?''

She licked her lips. "I can't.''

"What do you want? A profit? I can probably—''

"No. It's not…look, I can't go into the reasons, but maybe I can find some way to make it up to you.''

He lifted his black eyebrows. "Baby, I like the sound of that.''

Her good humor fled instantly. "That is not what I meant. Pig.''

He pulled into the parking lot of the bar and came to a stop. "Can't hate a guy for trying.''

"Yeah, actually, I can. You know, there's a lot more to me than the way I look, Wade Armstrong.''

"Oh, I'm sure there is. Like any red-blooded male, I just don't happen to care.''

She pursed her lips tight, shoved her door open and slid out of the truck. "Thanks for the ride. Slug.'' She slammed his door closed.

Wade looked at her, shrugged as if he were completely innocent of any wrongdoing, and then backed out of the parking lot with a wink and a wave.

He was in his little house, which was located around the corner from the garage, and was just big enough for a guy to be cozy. Two bedrooms, but he only used one. The other had become a weight room for him and the guys who worked for him. He had a Nautilus machine in there, weight bench, dumbbells, a treadmill and a punching bag. His mountain bike hung on the wall, boxing gloves underneath it. And there was a mini-basketball hoop fastened to the inside of the door.

The living room was just a place to watch sports on TV, although his roommate, Long Tall Sally, thought of it more as a place to nap. She was stretched out on the floor now, snoring happily, and he figured it was easily five feet from her hind legs to her forepaws when she lay like that. Maybe more. The kitchen was basically the place where the beer and junk food were stored. Sally pretty much agreed on that, he thought, only for her it was Great Dane chow and water. It was nothing special, his little saltbox in town. But now he was wishing he didn't have to let it go.

He leaned over, idly scratching Sally's head. She sighed contentedly in her sleep, twitched a long ear. Maybe he didn't have to let the place go, he thought. Hell, Tommy Hall was a friend as well as an employee. Wade could probably explain things to him. Yeah. That was what he would do. He would call Tommy and tell him what had happened, that he couldn't go through with the sale. Tommy would tear the contracts up. Sure he would, he was a friend.

Wade reached for the phone.

Someone knocked at the front door, bringing Sally's head up fast. She scrambled to her feet, tripped, got her footing and loped to the door, tail wagging. Frowning, Wade set the phone down again and went to answer the door. The young man he'd been about to call stood there grinning at him. Sally barked hello, and he petted her automatically.

"Hey, Tommy! I was just gonna call you, buddy. How you doin'? C'mon in. You want a beer?"

"Yeah." Tommy came inside as the dog danced beside him. He was a tow-headed, crew-cut fellow, too big for his own body. He wasn't from Big Falls, but Wade knew he'd been an outcast as a kid, just like himself. Wade could tell.

He could spot another social reject from across a crowded room. There was a scent they gave off, though you couldn't exactly smell it. Maybe it was an energy. Or just something in their eyes. But it was real.

Tommy scuffed his feet over the doormat, then headed straight to the sofa while Wade ducked around the corner into the kitchen to pull two beers from the fridge. He popped the top on one, handed it to Tommy, then opened his own. He didn't sit down. He was too nervous to sit. And feeling a little guilty too for what he was about to do. Sally came and sat so close to his side that her body was pressed to his leg from ankle to calf. She did that when people came by. Her way of showing her loyalty, he supposed.

"You, uh…you aren't packed," Tommy observed, looking around the place.

"Uh, no. Not yet."

"The closing's the end of the week, though," Tommy said, looking around. "Right?"

"That's what we said, yeah." Wade took a sip of his beer, paced away from the kid. Sally moved with him.

"That's good." Tommy said it with a sigh that sounded relieved. "I promised Sue we could move in over the weekend. She would have my hide if I had to go home and tell her I got the date wrong." He shook his head, grinning. "You don't know how stir-crazy she's getting in the apartment, Wade. She's just about climbing the walls."

Tommy's wife-to-be, Sue, was usually a pretty easygoing sort. At least, Wade had always thought so. Laid-back, never snappy or mean, didn't care for gossip. Wade liked her. "Since when is she so miserable in the apartment?" he asked. "I thought she liked it?"

"She did, but…" Tommy licked his lips, took another swig of beer, then looked Wade in the eyes and got all serious. "That was before we knew we were having a baby."

Wade blinked and felt his heart drop to waist level. "Baby?"

Tommy nodded, his face splitting in a smile. "You look as shocked as I did when she first told me. I thought I was gonna pass out cold." He turned his head, glancing down the hall to the two doors that stood opposite one another. "The weight room's gonna be a nursery. And she's just about dying to get in there and measure it up for wallpaper and curtains and carpet." He licked his lips, a shadow flitting across his eyes.

Wade picked up on the reason for that shadow immediately. Wallpaper, curtains and carpet could be summed up in one word. Money. "Sounds to me like you're gonna need a raise to go with this baby, Tom."

Tommy's eyes snapped to Wade's instantly. "I wasn't try-ing—"

"I know. Trust me, you've earned it." Wade lowered his head, found the dog's deep-gray speckled face staring right back up at him. It almost seemed she knew there was a prob-lem. "I don't suppose that apartment of yours is gonna be available once you leave?"

"Nah, the owner's got a waiting list." Then he frowned. "Why, Wade? I thought you were gonna buy that big place up by the falls."

"Someone beat me to it," he said. Then he plastered a smile on his face quickly. "Nothing to worry about. I'll just find a bigger, better place to buy."

"Not in this town, you won't." Tommy leaned forward, elbows balanced on his knees. "If you don't have anywhere to stay, Wade—"

"Look, this is not your problem. I'll be fine. I can room at the boardinghouse until I find what I want."

"But what about Sally?"

At the sound of her name, the dog spoke. "Ree-rah-roo," it sounded like. She was always doing that, and Wade always thought she knew exactly what she was saying, even if no one else did.

"I'll take care of Sally, don't you worry. It's not a problem, Tommy."

"Are you sure, Wade?"

Wade nodded, keeping his smile firmly in place, petting his dog reassuringly. Then he took a large bracing drink of beer and followed it up with an exaggerated belch that had Tommy laughing and shaking his head, and made Sally look at him with her head cocked to one side.

"If you're sure," Tommy said finally.

"Sure I'm sure. A deal's a deal."

Tommy drained his beer, got to his feet. "Then I guess I'll see you Saturday. Let me know if you need help moving any of your stuff out."

"I will. Same goes for you, moving stuff in. And I imagine putting a crib together is gonna be a bit different from re-building a carburetor, so I'll help with that, too, when the time comes."

Tommy got a funny look in his eye. "I can hardly imagine it. Me, a father."

"Think how the poor kid's gonna feel." Wade chucked him on the arm as he said it.

"Thanks a lot, Wade. I mean it. Thanks."

"Go home and tell your wife no duckies in my weight room. I never liked duckies. I want something rugged on that wallpaper or the deal's off. Teddy bears, something like that."

"Roo-roo!" Sally chimed in.

Wade nodded at her. "Right, girl." Then to Tommy, "Puppies would be acceptable, too, she says."

Tommy grinned. "I'll tell Sue." He crushed his beer can in his fist, handed it to Wade and headed for the door.

After he was gone, Wade wandered down the hall with Sally walking so close he almost tripped over her big feet.

He looked at his weight room and shook his head. "I'm gonna have to strangle that Edain Brand."

His phone rang, and he turned and walked back to the living room, plunked down in his favorite recliner, yanked the cordless off the end table beside it and said, "Yeah?"

"Wade, it's Caleb. Just wanted to let you know who to thank, pal."

Wade lifted his brows. Caleb was a good friend, a talented lawyer and an all around nice guy. It had taken Wade a while to see that, because he tended to dislike rich bastards like Caleb on sight. But although Caleb was rich—filthy freaking rich—he was not a bastard. However, none of that applied to this situation. Caleb was married to the enemy camp here. "Who to thank for what?" Wade asked.

Sally seemed to be getting tired of following him. She returned to her spot in the middle of the floor, in case he needed something to trip over, and stretched out again.

"For Edie changing her mind about the house," Caleb said. "I'm the one who made her see logic. Not that I want any gratitude or anything, but, uh—"

"She changed her mind?" Wade came to his feet. "She changed her mind? When?"

"Earlier tonight. Hell, I thought she'd have told you by now. It was before you showed up at the house, and then took off with her. Where did you take her, anyway? Date?"

He released a sharp burst of air that could have been a laugh but wasn't quite. "I took her to the saloon and dropped her off. And she didn't say a word about having changed her mind about the house."

Caleb was silent for a moment. "She told me she was thinking seriously about canceling the purchase. Even said she was going to call you herself to tell you."

"She told *me* she'd be moving in tomorrow."

"Well now, Wade, that just doesn't make any sense. What could have changed her mind from the time she walked back down the hill from our place to the time you pulled in the driveway? Hell, it couldn't have been more than five minutes.''

Wade pursed his lips and thought about the box on the Brands' kitchen table, the handcuffs inside it, and the way Edie had acted scared half out of her mind when he'd come up behind her. Beyond that, he'd been ninety-nine percent sure she had been afraid there might be someone in the house. She sure as hell wouldn't have left with *him,* of all people, if she had felt safe there. ''I think something's going on with your sister-in-law, Caleb.''

''Something like what?''

''I don't know, exactly.'' Wade had given his word he wouldn't tell anyone about the gift. Now he wished he hadn't. But he had, and he couldn't break it. ''Has she said anything about why she left L.A.?''

''Nope.''

''You think it could have been a guy? You know, an overbearing boyfriend, bad breakup, anything like that?''

''I don't think so. At least, she hasn't mentioned it to Maya, and they're not the kind of sisters who keep secrets from each other. Why, Wade, do you think someone's giving her trouble?''

''Maybe.''

''And what would that have to do with her changing her mind about the house?''

''Couldn't say.'' He could speculate, though. Whoever she thought had been around was someone she didn't want around her family. The Brands were a tight bunch. Notoriously tight. Maybe she wanted to keep the sender of that odd gift away from her homestead. Hell, she'd damn near panicked when he had threatened to tell Caleb about it. Maya and Caleb had twin babies, just a hundred yards from the farmhouse. And the sender must have the mailing address....

Unless the package had been hand delivered.

Which would explain her reaction to him coming up behind her even better.

He nodded to himself. "I'm gonna look into this, Caleb."

"Yeah? Why is that, Wade?"

He tipped his head to one side. "Well, hell, I want my house back."

"Uh-huh. And?"

"And nothing." But he knew there were other reasons— the main one being that he was the only one who knew about the gift. And since he had promised not to tell, he couldn't hand the information off to anyone else. So until he could wriggle out of that promise, no one else would know as much as he did about what was going on. Even though what he knew was damn little.

"You sure about that?" Caleb asked.

"Get over it, Caleb. Just get over it. And listen, keep an extra eye on things around the place for a while, okay?"

"I have kids, Wade." The reminder came in a low, serious tone of voice.

"I know you do. I'm on this, okay? No reason to be worried. When there is, I'll let you know. All right?"

"All right."

"Talk to you later." Wade hung up the phone. Sighing, he got to his feet, picked up his empty can and Tommy's crushed one, and carried them into the kitchen to drop them in the recycling bin. Sally followed him with her eyes but didn't get up. Then he opened the fridge and stared inside, wondering what he ought to eat for dinner. But as he stared, he wasn't thinking about food. He was thinking about Edain Brand and the handcuffs in that box and the fear in her eyes.

He swung the fridge door closed and said, "Guess I'll get dinner out tonight. Wonder what they've got on the grill over at the OK Corral?"

# Chapter 4

The OK Corral was hopping by 9:00 p.m. The place was damn near packed, and Edie found wending her way through crowds of mostly male bodies while carrying mugs of beer was far more difficult than she remembered. Her sisters made it look easy. Except, of course, for Kara, but she stayed mostly in the kitchen in back, grilling up finger foods. They didn't serve full meals at the Corral, but they kept the deep frier churning out mozzarella sticks, chicken fingers and onion rings at a steady rate. And Kara, still laboring under the assumption that she was both a full-fledged klutz and something of a jinx, preferred manning the frier to carrying breakable tumblers and spillable liquids.

She wasn't a klutz, of course. She had a body some of the models Edie had worked with would kill for. Six feet tall, slender as a reed, with a neck like a swan's and legs that didn't seem to end. She just hadn't learned to be comfortable in her own skin yet. But she would; Edie was working on that. If there was one thing she could do besides pose in skimpy lingerie, it was teach a tall gangly young woman how to walk.

She delivered drinks to a table full of men who looked at her as if they were trying to see through her clothes, then took the empty tray back to the bar and set it down.

"Watch yourself out there, Edie," her mother said as she topped off a frosted mug from the tap.

"It's packed." Edie brushed a wisp of hair off her forehead with the back of her hand.

"It's a Friday night, and it's springtime. Those young men are randy as billy goats. We got twice as many males as we do females in here tonight, and adding booze to that mix is like tossing it right onto an open flame. Watch yourself. And don't serve anyone you think has had enough."

Edie nodded slowly. "They're just locals, though. No one dangerous."

"Honey, just 'cause they're local don't mean they're saints. Big Falls has its share of jackasses, just like any other town."

As if to punctuate the warning, Edie felt a body slide up close beside hers, and when she glanced up, she saw a vaguely familiar face grinning at her. "Hey there, Edie B.," he said slowly. "You wanna dance with me?"

"No room for dancing in here tonight," she said. He was the son of the guy who owned the drugstore, she thought, searching her brain for a name to put with the face. "Besides, I'm not much of a dancer."

"Sure you are. You were in high school."

"Yeah, well this isn't high school." Pete, she thought. Peter Dunnegan. That was his name.

"No kidding." He put his hand on her hip. She caught it at the wrist before it could slide around to cup her backside, tugged it away and dropped it like garbage.

"Grow up, okay?" She saw her mother on the other side of the bar, reaching underneath for something, and she knew the baseball bat was going to come out momentarily. She held up a hand. "I've got it covered, Mom. I didn't survive a decade in L.A. without learning a thing or two."

Her mother frowned but straightened again. Edie's admirer said, "You sure did learn a thing or two, I'll vouch for that. Hell, from the looks of you in those catalogue spreads, I'll bet you learned a lot. Why don't you come over to my place and show me, hmm?"

"It's time for you to leave," she said. She gripped his arm, started pushing him toward the door. "Let's go."

"To hell I will!" he yelled. The place went quiet as he jerked his arm away and whirled on her. "No trashy little slut like you is gonna tell me what to do."

Vidalia came around the bar, baseball bat in hand. Mel vaulted over the top of the bar with murder in her eyes. But neither of them had the chance to do what they intended, because someone else grabbed Pete by the collar, spun him around and smashed a fist into his face.

He went down like a sack of feed, a startled expression on his face, his nose spurting blood.

Edie looked up to see Wade Armstrong standing there, rubbing his knuckles. He gave her a wobbly smile. "No need to thank me."

"Thank you? *Thank you?*"

"You're welcome. But really, it was nothing."

"You're right, Wade. It was nothing, and I had it under control." She rolled her eyes and looked down at Pete. "You all right?"

"Screw you," he spat, and scrambled to his feet; then he turned and headed out of the bar.

"Dammit, Wade, that was a paying customer. One of Mom's regulars."

He gaped at her. From behind him, Vidalia said, "Edain, hon, I don't think he'd have come back anyway, once I whaled on him with Babe, here." She slapped the baseball bat into her palm a few times to make her point.

"That was a nice job, Armstrong," Mel was saying. "I'd

have used an uppercut to the chin, but that right cross was nicely done.''

"Thanks.'' He wasn't looking at Mel, though. He was looking at Edie, and he seemed confused and maybe a little insulted. "You'll have to watch out for him,'' he said. "He probably won't try anything again, but his pride's been wounded—and in public, to boot. He may give you some trouble down the line.''

"He wouldn't be the first,'' she said. Sighing, she lowered her head. "Well, come on and sit yourself down. I should at least buy you a drink.''

"Don't put yourself out.'' But he did move through the bodies to the bar, then took the stool the idiot had formerly occupied. The guy next to him immediately got up and moved, and when he patted the vacant stool, Edie took it.

Her mother shoved a glass at her. "Go on, drink it down. You've been as tense as a bowstring, girl, ever since you got in here tonight.'' She drew a beer and slid that across to Wade. "Your usual.''

As Vidalia moved away, Wade leaned close to Edie, speaking so near her ear that his breath sent a shiver through her. A good shiver. But the effect was ruined by his next words. "Did you tell her yet? About the package?''

"No.'' She looked toward her mother to make sure she was out of earshot, felt like clubbing Wade for bringing it up here. "And I'm not going to, either.''

"Okay, okay. Drink your whiskey.''

She put the shot glass to her lips and downed the whiskey in one quick swallow. It burned like fire in her chest, but it warmed her, too. She set the glass down.

"How about the fact that you're moving out tomorrow? Did you tell her that yet?''

She averted her eyes, shook her head. "That's not a conversation I want to have in a barroom full of people. I figured we'd talk about it after closing time.''

He nodded, sipping his beer thoughtfully. "I had a phone call from your brother-in-law earlier," he said matter-of-factly.

"Did you?" She asked it as if she could not possibly care less.

"Yeah. He somehow got the idea that you'd decided you didn't want the house after all. He called to find out if you'd told me yet. Hell, I was confused. Especially seeing as how I saw you five minutes after he says you made that decision, and you had totally changed your mind by then."

She ran a forefinger around the rim of the shot glass, looking at it rather than at him. "Don't I have the right to change my mind?"

"Sure you do. I'd just like to know why, is all."

"Well, you're not going to. I have my reasons. They're private. And that's all I have to say on the subject."

He nodded slowly, lips pursing. "It had to do with the package," he said. "Or the fellow who sent it."

She shrugged. "Not necessarily."

"I wasn't asking. This much I know, not being blind or a fool. You're moving out to keep whatever you're afraid of from getting too close to your family."

She frowned at him as if she thought him insane. Inside, she was reeling at his accuracy. "You have a really big imagination, Wade. That's one of the things I don't remember about you from high school."

He smiled slightly. His lips were even tastier looking when he smiled. "I didn't think you remembered anything about me from high school, to be honest."

"Oh, I do. I remember a lot." She had to force her eyes not to linger on his mouth. Why it intrigued her so much, she couldn't even imagine.

"Tell me," he asked. His tone had changed. His eyes, too, in some indescribable way.

"Someday maybe I will. For now, though..." She slid off the bar stool and stood up. "I've got drinks to sling."

She walked away, but she felt his eyes on her from then on, and even though she avoided having to talk to him again, she continued to feel them all night long.

They closed up at midnight, when the last of the patrons had left. Legally, the Corral could remain open till 2:00 a.m., but they rarely did. Once things wound down, they tended to push the stragglers along toward home and lock the place up for the night. They split up into two vehicles, Vidalia's pickup truck and Mel's Jeep, and headed home. Then they all trooped in the back door, kicking off shoes as they entered.

Selene stepped inside, heeled off one shoe and then stood still, lifting her head and looking around. "What the heck is that?" she asked.

"What?" Everyone else looked, too, listened. Edie even sniffed the air, wondering what her baby sister was referring to.

"Don't you feel it?" Selene asked. Then she rubbed her arms and gave her head a shake. "Someone or...something has been in this house."

"Someone or some*thing*?" Mel rolled her eyes. "You've been watching that vampire slayer show again, haven't you, Selene?"

"Never miss it. But that's beside the point." She heeled off her other shoe and started through the house. "I can't believe you guys can't sense the negative energy."

"Oh, for crying out—"

Vidalia held up a hand. "Be nice to your sister, Melusine. Selene, hon, if you feel something's wrong, you feel it. Nine times outta ten you're right." She nodded to the girls. "Split up, check the house, make sure all the doors and windows are locked up tight while you're at it."

"I'll take this floor," Kara said. She opened a drawer and

pulled out a rolling pin, then went creeping toward the living room.

"I'll come with you, hon," Vidalia said. "Mel, Edie, you two take the basement."

"I don't think it's still here," Selene said. "But I'll check upstairs."

"Not by yourself, child," Vidalia said, but before she finished, Selene was off, jogging through the living room, tromping up the stairs.

"Go after her," she told Mel and Edie. "Kara and I will do the basement once we finish here." Vidalia glanced at the cellar door. It was locked, and that seemed to reassure her.

Mel and Edie ran upstairs after Selene, who was already opening doors and closing them one by one. They caught up to her as she checked the third bedroom, but she was already shaking her head slowly. "No. It was never up here."

"That's reassuring," Edie said. She wished she could bite the words back the minute she said them, but too late. Mel just sent her a funny look.

They checked Selene's room last, with Edie wishing the whole time she could just tell them that Wade Armstrong had already checked the entire house, and that the vibes Selene was sensing were from someone who'd come and gone hours ago. But she couldn't. Telling them that much would necessitate telling them more, and if they knew she was being harassed by some perverted, obsessed fan, they would never let her move into her own place. They would want to protect her. They would put themselves in danger.

Selene's room, like the others, was undisturbed.

In fact, even if the intruder had gone through every room in the house, Edie thought idly, he wouldn't have bothered Selene's room. It was the most peaceful place Edie could imagine. Little fountains bubbling here and there. Low-wattage bulbs kept it softly lit, and the ever-present aroma of incense clung to everything. There was no clutter in Selene's room. It was like a miniature temple.

Selene opened her closet, fumbled around inside, and came out again with a tiny bundle of twigs in her hand. "Sage," she said, when they looked at her with their eyebrows raised. "I'll just smudge the house a little and get rid of the bad energy."

"Oh, man," Mel said, tipping her head skyward. "That crap smells like pot. You know what people will think if they come by and smell that stuff?"

"If I don't do it I'll never sleep. Besides, who's going to come by at this time of the night? And it does not smell like pot, it smells like sage."

Mel threw up her hands, shaking her head as she stalked out of the room. "I'll go check the basement. If I'm lucky the boogie man will get me before your stinky smoking weeds do." She headed out of the room in a hurry.

Edie glanced at Selene. She felt bad about letting the kid take so much ribbing when she was dead-on accurate in whatever she was sensing. How that could be, she didn't know, didn't even try to guess. Her sister had something. She always had.

"You all right, Edie?" Selene asked, voice soft, eyes probing.

"Yeah. I, um...I should go help Mel."

"All right." Selene flicked a long-nosed lighter and touched the flame to her tiny bundle of twigs. They flared up for a moment; then the flame lowered, waned and died. Smoke immediately started wafting from the smoldering ends of the twigs. Selene set them into a copper bowl and picked up a fan made of feathers. She was always picking up feathers when she found them lying around outside, from wild turkeys, crows and whatever other large bird happened to drop one for her collection. She followed Edie down the stairs, waving her fan and sending smoke into the shadows and nooks and crannies of the old house.

She was a strange one, all right. Edie picked up the pace and caught up to Mel halfway down the cellar stairs.

Mel had a flashlight in one hand and a tire iron in the other.

"Gee, you're not nervous, are you?" Edie asked.

"Not really. But if Wanda the witch up there is right, I'm thinking a tire iron might have a little more impact than smoking stinkweed."

They reached the bottom of the steps. The stair light was on already, and Edie reached out to flip the switch that would light the rest of the basement. It worked; the lights came on. She'd been half expecting the switch to have no effect, like in some horror film. Then again, sometimes in those kinds of movies the lights went off *after* appearing to work just fine.

Edie walked close to Mel, glad of the tire iron her scrappy sister carried. They both pretended to be unconcerned, but they were both a little scared. Even Mel couldn't deny Selene sometimes nailed things in ways that defied explanation.

They traversed the entire basement, though, and found nothing amiss. Then they headed back up the stairs, much more relaxed than before.

The scent of Selene's sage lingered but wasn't overpowering. Still, Mel made a show of waving the air in front of her face and wrinkling her nose. Selene smirked at her. Her sage and bowl were gone, apparently returned to her bedroom. And no doubt Vidalia had already made some comment about how a recital of the Lord's Prayer would have been just as good and asking why Selene insisted on such heathen practices. Selene had probably already responded that sage had been used by indigenous cultures for centuries to ward off negativity, and that since God put it on the planet in the first place, using it couldn't possibly be in any way sinful.

It was a conversation repeated so often, with various twists, that Edie could have recited it almost verbatim. She was glad she had missed this round.

"Do you suppose we could all go to bed now?" Kara asked, leaning against the door frame between the kitchen and dining room. She yawned.

"I think so," Selene said.

"I know so," Mel put in.

Edie opened her mouth but closed it again without saying a word. She needed, at some point, to sit down with her family and tell them she had decided to move into her own place. The suddenness of it would worry them. They would ask questions. But despite their tendency to hover and be overprotective of each other, they also did their best to respect each other's privacy. At least, that was the stated policy, she thought with a pained smile as she headed up the stairs to her room.

She would break the news at breakfast. That would be soon enough. That would be *plenty* soon enough.

She changed clothes, cleaned and moisturized her face, brushed her hair and teeth, and went to bed. She stopped thinking about how infuriating Wade Armstrong was. About how insulting Peter Dunnegan had been. And about breaking the news to her mother that she was moving. All those musings quieted as she lay there, hovering on the edge of sleep.

But when the other things went still, that left room for the one thing, the big thing, to take center stage in her mind.

She chased it away, but her eyes were heavy. It was late. She slipped into sleep without warning, and she was there again.

*Her newly hired bodyguard a half step behind her, Edie walked unsteadily along the wet sidewalk that led from the nightclub where she'd been partying toward the car that waited at the curb. Inside the club there had been a crush of people, shoulder to bare shoulder. Music pounded and sweat scented the air. Outside, it was nice. Quiet in the wee hours, or quiet by L.A. standards, anyway. No one around to speak of, light traffic, just headlights gliding past every now and then, with the sounds of tires hissing over wet pavement. She got halfway to the car and stopped dead.*

*Mike closed a hand on her elbow. "You okay?"*

*"I left my purse." She looked up at him sheepishly, and maybe a little drunkenly. Mike was old enough to be her father, a short, stocky man with a face like a bulldog. As bodyguards went, he was one of the best. He came highly recommended.*

*"Would you...?" she began.*

*"Not till you're safely locked in the car." He kept hold of her, kept moving forward. He held out his hand to the valet who waited by the open passenger door. The valet dropped the keys into his hand, and he tucked them into his pocket. "In you go."*

*Edie sank into the front seat of the plush sedan. It was not her own vehicle. It was Mike's car. He'd insisted. He was bossy for a bodyguard. After all, he was supposed to be working for her, right? So where did he get off being so bossy? She wasn't even sure she honestly needed a bodyguard. Hell, aside from a few kinky anonymous gifts and some really graphic letters, there was nothing. Certainly no physical risk, despite the threats. But her agency had insisted she hire someone once they caught an eyeful of those notes.*

*Mike locked the car door and closed it, sent her a smile and headed back to the entrance of the club. The valet stood at attention, his back to her door. Mike must have told him to stand guard. Great.*

*She leaned her head back against the softness of the seat, folded her hands in her lap.*

*A hand slid around her face from behind, clamping tight over her mouth before she could scream, even as another one gripped her wrists so hard she thought they would break. Her eyes flew wide, but she could see nothing. A face rubbed against her cheek, and a voice whispered near her ear, "Did you get the gifts, Edie? And the letters? Did you?"*

*She twisted and pulled in his grasp.*

*"Answer me!" He made a whisper seem like a shout. "Did you get them?"*

*Edie nodded, her eyes wide, growing wet now.*

*"Then you know what I'm going to do, don't you, Edie? Yeah. You've been waiting. That's why you sent your goon back inside. Isn't it?"*

*She shook her head side to side, tried to kick her feet.*

*"Stop!" he barked in her ear. "Do you want me to have to kill you, Edie? Do you?" Something cold encircled her wrists and snapped in place. Handcuffs. Oh God. Then his hand was free again. It vanished and returned with a knife, its blade sharp and deadly. "I'll kill you. Now you sit perfectly still like a good girl. Don't make a sound, Edie baby. I just want to see, that's all. We won't have time for more. Not tonight."*

*His blade moved, easily snapping the buttons off her silk blouse one by one. He used the knife to push the blouse open, exposing the black lace demi-bra she wore underneath.*

*She felt him shaking his head slowly, side to side. "You've been a bad girl, Edie. I told you in the last note, I didn't want you wearing bras anymore. Not outside the shoots. When you're not posing, I don't expect any underwear at all, do you understand? Do you?" He dug the point of the blade into the rounded, soft part of her breast.*

*She nodded fiercely, but the blade pricked her anyway. She felt blood, just a trickle. "I'm going to have to punish you, Edie. You've got to do what I tell you or face the consequences. Do you understand?"*

*She nodded again, her eyes shifting toward the club and the rigid back of the useless valet. How long would it take Mike to get the purse? How damn long in that crowd of idiots?*

*His mouth attacked her neck then, wet and sloppy. She felt his tongue, and his teeth bit down cruelly. And all the while that damn knife was pressed to her throat. Her stomach turned. She wanted to vomit. "Get off me," she whispered. "Just get off me and go. I won't tell, all right?"*

*He stopped lathering her neck and sat up. "Get off you?" He asked the question as if incredulous. "Oh, Edie, why did you have to go and ruin it, hmm?" He dropped his knife and closed his hands around her throat so fast and so hard she couldn't breathe, much less cry out. She thumped the window once, and he jerked her to the middle of the car so fast that she couldn't hit it again. Her head was pounding, her eyes straining, her entire body shaking in need of air. He was going to kill her. She was going to die.*

*And then he was gone. Just like that, the pressure was off, the hands were gone, and she collapsed against the seat, sucking in huge, choked breaths. She lifted her head to look in the rearview mirror and saw the back door standing open, the back seat empty.*

*Tears rolled hot and burning down her cheeks. She clawed for her door handle, found it and shoved it open. The valet turned as she started to get out of the car. Then his eyes went wide as Edie fell to her knees on the sidewalk. She glimpsed Mike coming out of the club, running toward her, and then she passed out cold.*

Edie came awake with a start, her eyes wide, her hands on her throat. Then she lay there for a full minute, trying to convince herself that she was home, in Oklahoma, not in L.A. That her monster was a long way away from her.

But he wasn't. He had been here, in her haven, she could feel it. She reached for her light, turned it on and sat up in the bed. She probably wouldn't sleep another wink tonight. Reaching under her pillow, she pulled out the present Mike had given her as a parting gift. It had been tucked away in her closet since she'd been home. But now she felt she needed it again. It was snub-nosed, deadly black and fully loaded. Mike had been the only person in L.A. who had taken her fear seriously. Her agent had been just barely sympathetic, his most memorable comment being, "Hey, you pose half-naked for a living. You telling me you didn't *expect* something like this?"

That had hurt most of all, because it reminded her, painfully, of her mother's warnings, her disapproval, and her constant reminders that you reaped what you sowed. Edie had considered Vidalia Brand a judgmental, prudish pain in the backside at the time. Now she wondered if her mother had been right all along. If maybe, in some way, she had brought it all on herself.

And now, Edie mused, she had brought her problems back home to share with her family. God, the thought of that animal touching one of her sisters the way he had touched her...

She was going to have to make sure word got around town that she had moved out of her mother's place tomorrow. It wouldn't be hard in a small town like this. The rumor mills worked with amazing—even alarming—efficiency.

But in the meantime... She glanced at the clock, calculated the time in L.A. and then reached for the phone beside her bed. She dialed Mike McKenny's home number, and he picked up on the third ring. Just the sound of his voice helped a little. He was a strong, sharp man. A good bodyguard. And he sounded glad to hear from her.

"Hey, Edie, my favorite former client. How are you?"

"I don't know, Mike. That's kind of what I'm calling to find out."

She could almost see his expression changing from light to serious. "What's going on?" he asked.

She drew a breath, sighed. "Look, I know you said he would never trace me back here, but I think maybe he has."

"Why?"

That was Mike, straight to the point. "I got another package. A pair of handcuffs. No return address. The box was left on the kitchen table.''

"Describe them,'' he asked.

She sighed, not wanting to think that much about her troubling gift. "Standard, like maybe police issue?''

"Uh-huh. And the note?''

"No note. There was nothing.''

He sighed deeply, and she thought she heard his fingers drumming in time with his thoughts. "I don't think it's him, Edie.''

She released her breath in a rush. "Really? Oh God, I'm so glad. Why not, Mike? Convince me.''

"He always leaves a note, for one thing. For another, his toys usually come from the sex shops. He would be more likely to send you a pair of satin-lined or leopard-fur-covered love cuffs than cold steel handcuffs. It's not his pattern.''

"So then, this is what? Another insane fan?''

"Look, you did do that spread with the bondage overtones last year. Weren't there handcuffs in that piece?''

"Hanging from the bedpost. But I wasn't wearing them.''

"The implication was there. It may not even be a dangerous fan, Edie. Maybe just a horny one. They could be a gag gift, even. Have you pissed anyone off since you've been home?''

She blinked and thought of Wade Armstrong. "Yes, actually, I have.''

"Uh-huh, I thought so. Listen, do you need me to come out there?''

She took a breath, sighed. "How's Richie doing?''

"His T cells are down a little. It's not serious yet.''

She nodded at the phone. "You stay where you are, Mike. You're probably right, it's probably a pissed-off redneck. God, I can't believe how scared I was.''

"Don't get overconfident here. Take precautions, be on your guard. And call me if anything else happens, okay?''

"I will, Mike. And thanks. You're one in a million."

"Any time," he said.

Edie hung up the phone and lay back in the bed, feeling a lot better than she had been. Then she started thinking about Wade Armstrong. He had arrived only seconds after she had found that box on the table. Maybe he'd been there the whole time. Maybe he just put the box there, then went out front and waited for her to have time to find it. He had probably only come back to enjoy seeing her scared witless.

She mulled that over. He hadn't *acted* as if he were enjoying her fear. Then again, he didn't know about the stalker she had picked up in L.A. He probably hadn't expected her to react with more than disgust at the suggestive gift. Maybe he even felt a little guilty after seeing how much it upset her. Yeah, that was it. No wonder he had given her the ride and defended her against Peter Dunnegan. Guilt.

The bastard.

On the other hand, what if he *hadn't* been the one to send the lurid present to the house? What if...?

No. It wasn't her stalker. It wasn't.

She was almost glad now that she had stolen Wade Armstrong's house out from under him, the lowlife. She was going to enjoy rubbing it in his face every chance she got.

# Chapter 5

"I don't get it. I just don't get it, Edie."

Edie hadn't planned on Maya and Caleb and the twins being present when she made her big announcement at the breakfast table. She knew their presence would make things a little more complicated the minute they arrived, but she was out of time. And the entire family was going to have to know sooner or later anyway.

"What's to get?" Edie asked, as casually as possible. The others around the table were quiet. Mostly just looking at her as if she'd lost her mind. Her mother wasn't. She was searching, her eyes narrow and knowing. "I bought the house, and I want to be in it. Why should I wait?"

"Because just last night you were on the verge of changing your mind and letting Wade Armstrong take the place," Maya said.

Edie shrugged, sipped her coffee. "That was just guilt talking. Wade Armstrong's a big boy. Why should I give up something I want just so he can have it? We're not children sharing a sandbox here. We're both adults. I was the first one to come up with the money and sign on the dotted line. That's the way business is done in the real world. And Wade Armstrong, of all people, understands that.''

"Why do you say that?" Caleb asked, his voice careful, level.

"What?"

"'Wade Armstrong, of all people,'" he repeated. "Why would he understand it better than anyone else?"

"Because he owns his own business. Competition is an everyday event for him. What did you think I meant?"

Caleb shrugged. "Maybe that he would understand more than most because he's been getting jerked around by people with more money than him his entire life. That's all."

"You should talk, having more money than God and all," Edie said, knowing full well she was being unnecessarily snarky to her brother-in-law, and that he really didn't deserve it.

"I try real hard not to club people over the head with it, Edie. I think you tend to keep friends longer that way."

"Well, lucky for me, Wade Armstrong is not my friend."

"He's not?" It was Selene who voiced the question around a bite of French toast, a cup of herbal tea halfway to her mouth. "I thought he gave you a ride to the bar last night? And then wasn't he the one who decked Peter Dunnegan in the face for insulting you?"

Edie pursed her lips, sent her sister a glare. "He only drove me in so he would have more time to badger me about the house. And I really don't have any idea why he decked Pete. Maybe they had other things going on between them. But the fact remains, Wade Armstrong is not now, nor has he ever been, a friend of mine."

A tap sounded at the back door, and everyone looked up to see Wade Armstrong peering through the glass. Vidalia waved him in, so he opened the door and stepped inside. "Hello, Mrs. Brand," he said, greeting her first, then nodding hello to the others. He looked Edie straight in the eyes. "I figured you could use an extra vehicle today,'' he said. ''To help with the move.''

Selene sent Edie an ''I-told-you-so'' look, lifting her eyebrows and tipping her head to the side.

Edie rolled her eyes. ''Just what good do you think a tow truck is going to do, Wade?''

''I didn't bring the tow truck. Brought the Explorer.''

''Man, am I glad to see you,'' Caleb said, getting to his feet to greet his friend. ''I figured I'd be the only guy around for the grunt work.''

Mel rolled her eyes. ''Why is it men always assume women can't lift a heavy object or load items into a vehicle?'' she asked.

Kara nudged her with an elbow. ''Hush now. Don't you remember when all Edie's stuff arrived from L.A. in the moving truck? It took us hours to get it all unloaded and stacked away out in the barn. You want us to do it alone?''

Mel crossed her arms over her chest and leaned back in her chair. ''I'm not saying we can't *use* the help. Just that we don't *need* it.''

''How about just saying we're grateful for it, daughter?'' Vidalia asked, a stern edge to her voice. Then she nodded at Wade. ''Pull up a chair and have some breakfast, Wade. After that...'' She looked at Edie. ''Well, if you're bound and determined to move today, then we'll move you.''

Her eyes said more, though. Her eyes said that she knew perfectly well there was more going on than Edie had told her, and that she would find out the truth, one way or another.

Edie believed it, too.

Wade took off his shoes without being told and made his way to the only empty chair in sight, and everyone at the table scooted one way or the other to make room for him. Edie felt a toe connect with her shin hard enough to make her jump, so she got up and got him a plate and silverware. Even poured him a cup of coffee.

He smiled at her, but it didn't reach his eyes. He was still good and pissed over the house. She didn't know what the hell he wanted, what good he thought his hanging around here would do him, but he was up to something. There was no doubt about that. Maybe it was still guilt niggling at him for that perverted gag gift of his. But somehow she thought there was more to it than that.

You wouldn't know anything was bothering him at all, to watch him eat, though. He dug into Vidalia's hearty breakfast like a condemned man eating his last meal, pausing between bites to praise the skills of the cook.

The kiss-up, Edie thought. Trying to get in good with her mother, just to keep her on his side. Hell, if Vidalia knew about the handcuffs, she would box his ears until they bled.

When everyone finished eating, Vidalia pushed her chair away from the table, and that seemed to be the signal for everyone else to do the same. "Maya, you and Kara stay in here with the babies and take care of the cleanup chores. The rest of you, let's get on out to the barn. Um, except for you, Edie. You'll probably want to head up to your room and get your things there packed up."

Edie shook her head. "I did it last night."

Wade glanced at her sideways. "You didn't get home until after midnight," he observed.

"Now how would you know what time I got home?"

"Well, that's about the time the bar usually closes." He sent an innocent look at Vidalia. "Isn't it?"

"Yes, it is, most nights. Edie, are you telling me you were up all night?"

"I just... I was excited about the new house, is all. I couldn't sleep."

Great. Now all of them were looking at her oddly. Caleb sent Wade a worried, questioning glance. Wade shook his head very slightly from side to side, as if to say "just drop it." Vidalia probed with her eyes, but she said nothing.

Edie knew she would get the third degree from her mother the moment they were alone together, though. She wasn't looking forward to it.

The woman had more stuff than a department store, he thought as he loaded the Explorer for the second time that day. They had already taken one trip over to the new house, with his vehicle full of junk and Mel's full pickup right behind it. And none of it practical! Hardly any furniture, at least nothing usable like a couch or tables and chairs or a bed. Just foolish stuff. Paintings and ceramics and plant stands and lamps. A hammock, for heaven's sake, and a chair shaped like a giant bowl that would be impossible to get into or out of. Accent pieces, she called them. And boxes and boxes and more boxes. She had enough clothing to supply the population of a small country. The shoes alone would fill a closet.

It would take a year to get her unpacked.

Still, he worked steadily, loading the boxes, driving to the house, unloading them again. On the first trip over, Edie, Vidalia and Selene had stayed behind at the new place. By the time he, Caleb and Mel got the trucks reloaded and returned, several of the boxes were empty, stacked near the doors.

Wade blinked at the number of them.

"Amazing what the Brand women can get done when they put their minds to it, isn't it?" Caleb asked, slapping him on the back. Then he reached past Wade to open the back of the Explorer, grabbed a box and carried it into the house.

By lunchtime, everything had been moved in and the large open living room of the new place looked as if a bomb had gone off inside it. Vidalia had insisted they take the bed from Edie's room so she would have a proper place to sleep until she got one of her own.

With a nod of satisfaction, the matriarch brushed her palms against each other. "I say we break for lunch."

"I say you break permanently," Edie said. She was sitting

on the floor, her back against a tall box, knees drawn to her chest. "It's done. I'm moved. I can handle the rest."

"It'll take you a week to get all this stuff unpacked and put away," Vidalia argued.

"Yeah, but I'll enjoy it. I'll take my time, and when I get done, everything will be just the way I want it."

Her mother lifted her brows but finally nodded. "All right. If that's the way you want to do this."

"It is." Edie drew a breath, then used it to blow a strand of hair off her nose. When she did that it gave Wade a funny little hitch in his own breathing, but he ignored that. "Thank you all for your help. I really appreciate it. But you all have stuff to do, and I don't want to hold you up any longer."

"Are you trying to get rid of us, Edie?" Selene asked.

Edie shook her head in denial. "Of course not. I'm just tired out."

"Let's go," Vidalia instructed. "Let your sister have some time alone in her new place."

"I ought to do a house blessing on it," Selene muttered. "You can never tell what kind of energy might be hanging around."

"It can wait." Vidalia herded her daughters toward the door, and Caleb with them.

Wade stood where he was, near the massive windows that looked down over the falls. It was the view he'd fallen in love with and planned to make his own. Edie hadn't told him to get the hell out with the others, and he figured until she did, he would just stay where he was.

She sat still, not facing him, while they all trooped out and climbed into vehicles. She said nothing as the engines revved up and the convoy pulled out. He was beginning to wonder if she even realized he was still there.

"It's okay," she said finally. "You don't have to feel guilty anymore."

His brows bent in the middle, and he walked toward where

she sat. "Me feel guilty? You're the one who stole my house, remember?"

"You've worked your tail off today, Wade, and honestly, you've been a lot of help. Let's call it even, okay?"

He hunkered down in front of her, the better to try to figure out what was going on in her twisted little head. She seemed to think she was making perfect sense. "We aren't anywhere close to even."

"Sure we are. It was just a joke. You were pissed off, and I probably deserved it. You've more than made up for it, though. I'm not mad at you."

"For *what?*"

She smiled halfheartedly. "Stop playing the innocent already. I know." Shaking her head, she glanced away distractedly. "I wish the phones were hooked up. I'd order us something for lunch."

He tugged a cell phone from his shirt pocket. "Pizza?" he asked.

"That thing won't work around here."

"What, the phone? Oh, it's pretty useless in town and the surrounding areas. But it works great up here. You've got the elevation." As he spoke, he punched numbers. "What do you like, pepperoni?"

"Mushrooms," she said. "And peppers and onions and ham and extra cheese."

He lifted his eyebrows but rattled off the order, added a six-pack of soda and one of beer to the total, and told the person on the other end where to bring it. When he dropped the phone back into his pocket, he said, "If that arrives and you try to get away with nibbling a sliver-sized slice and calling it quits..."

"I'm going to eat at least two slices," she said, and she said it as if it were a threat. "Just because I can."

It made him smile. He thought it meant she didn't plan to go back to modeling, and that made him glad for some inane reason. It was stupid of him. He should be offering to drive her to the airport instead of hoping she would stay. That way he could get his house back.

He sat down, looked at the mess around them, then at her again. "Now that the food thing is settled, you have to tell me just what it is you think I did."

She frowned. "After lunch. While we're waiting, you can help me carry some of these bigger boxes upstairs, okay?"

He sighed his impatience but did what she wanted, sensing it was important for some reason. He moved boxes. They didn't unpack stuff, just shuffled the mess around, sorting it into its appropriate parts of the house.

The pizza arrived, and he paid Max, the delivery guy, told him to keep the change. They lugged the food and beverages into the kitchen, where they sat on the counter with the box between them. He flipped it open, took a piece out. It was good, as it always was. But for some reason, watching Edie eat became the highlight of the meal for Wade. They didn't speak, just ate. He drank a beer, she drank a soda, and they ate some more. He couldn't remember enjoying a meal this much.

Finally they finished. A few slices remained in the box. "Gee, you don't even have a fridge for the leftovers."

She shrugged. "You can take it home, if you want. It'll just spoil here."

He nodded. "So?"

"So…?"

"So what is it you think I did that made me feel guilty enough to put in a full day's work moving your stuff into a house that should have been mine?"

She sighed, rolled her eyes. "The gift," she said, and when he still looked at her blankly she went on. "The handcuffs? I'll admit it gave me a jolt, but then I realized how angry you must have been over the house thing—not that you didn't have every right to be. Hell, I deserved it."

He blinked at her, waiting for her to slow down, but she kept on talking about it being funny in retrospect, about not being mad at him, until he cut in. "Edie, stop."

She broke off in midsentence and looked up at him with eyes very round and very vulnerable somehow. As if his words had the power to hurt her in some way. He almost rethought them, but hell, he didn't want her thinking that of him. "Edie, I didn't send you those handcuffs. I already told you that. You know damn well it wasn't me."

She blew out a little breath of laughter and shook her head. "Of course you did. That's why you've been slaving away helping me all day. You felt badly because they shook me up so much. I mean, you had no way of knowing they would, after all. It wasn't your fault—"

"You really want me to tell you it was me, don't you?" he asked.

She met his eyes, held them, and, finally, she nodded.

"It wasn't. But I think you know who it was. And I think whoever he is, he's the reason you seemed so shaken up after you got them. And I also think he's the reason you changed your mind about the house, and maybe the reason you were in such a hurry to move, as well."

She shook her head from side to side as if denying every word he said.

"I helped out today because I was curious. I want to know what's going on with you. Who's got you so damn jumpy?"

Bracing her hands on the counter, she slid off it, landing on her feet on the floor. "No one."

"Who is he, Edie?"

"I told you, there's no one."

"No? The same no one who chased you out of L.A., out of your former career, and then out of your own mother's house?" He slid to the floor too, put his hands on her shoulders and made her face him. "I'm damned if I know why, Edie, but I'd like to help with this. I can, if you'll let me."

She shook her head. "I don't need any help."

"Did you tell your mother about that present? Hmm?"

"Look, why the hell do you care? Huh? Answer me that and I'll tell you everything you could want to know. Just answer me. Why are you even here?"

He licked his lips, seeing the anger in her eyes where there had been none before and wondering what the hell he had done to put it there. "I...I don't know, because I'm a decent guy."

"Bull."

He lifted his brows in stark surprise. "Well, then, why do you think I'm here?"

"Same reason every other guy has ever come around me. Including the one who sent the gift. To try to get into my pants."

He flinched as if she'd hit him, wondering if she were close to the truth. Was that his motivation? He knew he was a pig, but he kind of thought there was more to this.

"I'll tell you something, Wade Armstrong. I'm more than a pretty face and a decent body. A lot more. And I want no part of any man who doesn't know that, much less one who doesn't want to know. One who doesn't even care. I'm through with that, do you understand? I'm done."

He lifted his hands from her shoulders, held them up, palms facing her. "I got it. You're done."

"Would you be falling over yourself to help me out if I were fat? Hmm? If I were ugly? Bald? Flat chested? Would you?"

He backed away from her, feeling as if he were under attack. "Look, I don't know. Maybe, okay? I got the feeling you were in trouble when I saw the way you reacted to that package last night. That was what I was reacting to, and yeah, I'd like to think I'd react the same way to a less attractive woman if she were in trouble, but it wasn't a less attractive woman. It was you, the most drop-dead gorgeous creature

I've ever seen in my life. So how the hell am I supposed to know how I would have reacted to it being someone else?''

She stopped ranting. Her face softened a little, and her hands relaxed from their former fisted position. Sighing, she turned her gaze inward, looked at the floor. "I was really hoping it was you who sent the handcuffs," she said as if she hated like hell to admit it.

"Yeah?" he asked. He smiled a little at her. "Well, if you want, I can go get you some right now, and we could try them out."

She smacked him in the belly, and he faked a loud grunt and doubled over.

"You are such a pig."

"Thank you," he said, straightening.

"Take your leftovers and go home, will you? I've got unpacking to do."

He sighed. He didn't like it. He still hadn't gotten a straight answer out of her, but he didn't see that she was giving him a choice in the matter. So he took the leftover pizza and the beer, and he left.

But he didn't go home.

Edie was alone. Completely, utterly, alone in the big, strange, cluttered house. She wandered around for a while, unpacking boxes and amusing herself by deciding that the large, towering study off the living room was going to be her studio, and that the walk-in closet off the back of it would make a perfect dark room. But none of those things distracted her from the fact that she was all alone out here in the middle of nowhere. And her phone wasn't even hooked up yet.

"You're pathetic," she told herself. "It isn't even dark outside yet." The power was turned on. At least she would have lights. A little shiver went through her at the thought of having to spend the night without them. The big windows would be black as pitch. She would feel completely vulnerable. God, she needed to get some curtains!

With a sigh, she unloaded the last of her clothing into the smaller closet and the little dresser her mother had insisted she take with her. Then she got to her feet and brushed off her hands. "Might as well go into town. Get the word out that I'm here. No sense waiting."

She barely gave herself a cursory glance in the mirror before heading outside to her car and driving down the winding mountain road toward Big Falls proper. She figured she was about halfway down that deserted, winding mountain road when the front tire blew, sending her careening out of control. She gripped the wheel hard, forcing it into submission, and after a few terrifying seconds she managed to get the car stopped. Crosswise in the road, yes, but stopped. She sat there for a moment, stunned that a peaceful drive could turn into a roller coaster ride in a heartbeat. Then she blew her hair out of her eyes and inched the limping vehicle around until it was perpendicular to the road again and as far onto the shoulder as possible.

A truck pulled to a stop behind her. She glimpsed it in her mirror, and for just an instant she stiffened at the prospect of dealing with some stranger on this stretch of road, alone. But then she recognized the man jogging toward her car and relaxed. Wade.

He yanked open her door and leaned in. "You all right?"

"Yeah."

"You sure?"

She nodded.

He nodded back. "Sure you are. You can let go of the steering wheel now."

She looked at her hands on the wheel and realized she was gripping it so hard it hurt. Her knuckles were white, her fingers red. It actually took a minute to make her grip on the wheel loosen. Then she turned toward the door and started to get out, only to have the seat belt pull against her, holding her in.

"Hold on a sec," Wade said, leaning over her. He was too close, his face in her face, his big arm and part of his chest brushing her chest as he reached across her body to unfasten her seat belt. As he drew back, his hand moved to the switch. He turned the ignition off but left the key in. Then he straightened, and she could breathe again without inhaling his scent, which wasn't bad, just irritating.

She got more irritated yet when he took her hand to tug her gently out of the car as if she were some frightened child who needed guidance in something so simple.

"That was some piece of driving," he said.

Frowning, she looked at him in disbelief even as she put her feet on the gravel and stood upright. "What?"

"You kept the car in control. It's not easy when you have a blowout. Especially a front tire. Nice job."

She blinked, still not sure he was paying her a sincere compliment. "It didn't *feel* under control."

"It was. Otherwise you'd have ended up down there, instead of safely parked on the roadside." As he spoke, he nodded, and she turned to look at whatever the hell he was talking about.

On the far side of the road, the ground fell away sharply. She lifted her head a little to see the long, long distance to the wooded land below. Then her gaze slid to the road itself and froze on the tire tracks that marked the place where her car had come to a stop. So close to the drop. Only a couple of feet.

Her knees dissolved.

Wade's arms encircled her waist. "Whoa, hold on now. I've got you." And then, without even so much as asking permission, he turned her body and scooped her right up off her feet like some knight scooping up a damsel.

"What the hell are you doing?" she demanded.

"Putting you in my truck where you can sit down before you fall down."

"I don't want to be in your truck. I prefer my car."

"Your car has a flat."

"It also has a spare."

"And I suppose you're gonna change the tire yourself?"

"What, you think I'm incapable of changing a tire? Don't forget who raised me, Wade Armstrong."

He grinned down at her for some reason. But by then he was already standing beside his tow truck, and he'd somehow managed to open the door. He hefted her up onto the seat. "Just please sit here and let me take a look at the damage, hmm? I do this for a living, you know."

She pursed her lips and crossed her arms over her chest but didn't argue. He closed the door on her and strode back to her car. She watched him bending down to look at the front tire. He made a face and shook his head. God, she hoped someone else would come along. Anyone else. Being around him so much bothered her. He was still every bit as dangerous as he had always been. He was also as shallow as ever. And just as sexy, too. Maybe more so. And he knew it.

She glanced behind her, back up the road, hoping to see one of her sisters coming along, but no such luck. The big boom on the back of the pickup blocked most of her view, anyway.

The driver's door opened, and she jumped, startled, because she hadn't seen him coming back to the truck. He climbed in, turned the key, and the thing fired up loudly. "You have a bent rim on that front tire, and the axle needs checking, just in case. You can't drive it off this mountain like that without risking another accident."

"Then what do you suggest I do, carry it off?"

He rolled his eyes. "Honey, you have noticed you're sitting in a tow truck, right? I mean, this isn't totally lost on you, is it?"

She huffed. "So you're gonna tow my car to your garage, where you can hold it hostage to inept mechanics and inflated prices?"

"I have top-notch mechanics and perfectly competitive prices." He cleared his throat. "Not to mention the only garage in town." He put the truck into gear and drove it around to the front of her car. Then he moved the levers that controlled the equipment in the back, and she heard a mechanical hum as the boom lowered. He got out again and went around behind. She refused to watch for fear he would think she was even remotely interested in what he might be doing back there. But when he got back in, she did look, and her car was affixed, nose up in the air, to the back of his truck.

"Looks like they're mating," she muttered.

He swung his head toward her so fast she thought his neck should have snapped. *"What?"*

"The car, it's...hell, never mind."

He glanced in the rearview. "Oh. I get it." Then he looked her way again, a frown on his face. "Just never heard anyone put it like that before. Guess you just have a dirty mind."

She gaped at him, but he was ignoring her now, putting the truck into gear and into motion.

"Buckle up," he told her.

She did so, even though it burned her buns obeying orders from him. They were just rolling into town when it occurred to her to wonder and, finally, to ask, "Just what were you doing out on my road, anyway?"

## Chapter 6

It was after hours. No one was around in the garage, and that was good. He didn't particularly want Edie Brand in there, either. Not now. Not...yet. He hadn't had a chance to redecorate the place yet.

"Well?" she asked.

She'd been talking. He'd been preoccupied planning just what he was going to say when she walked in. If he couldn't keep her out.

"I'm sorry. What?"

"What were you doing on my road?" she repeated.

He lifted his brows and faked surprise. "You bought the *road,* too? My God, woman, you do have money to burn."

She looked utterly pained. He was good at pissing her off, he thought, enjoying it.

"I didn't buy the road. You know full well I didn't buy the freaking road. I mean, my road, as in, the road on which I live. What were doing out there?"

"Driving?"

She closed her eyes, sighed.

"Hey, just let me know if I'm supposed to file some kind

of formal request when I want to use the Falls Road, Edie. I'll be glad to comply if you tell me the regulations up front.''

"You're infuriating, you know that?''

He smiled. "I had a call. Errol Johnson's car died out that way, and he thought he needed a tow. Turns out he only needed a jump start. Okay?''

She looked as if she doubted him, which was pretty damned perceptive of her, since there had been no call. He'd wanted to drive by her place to check up on her, but he would never admit that. He'd taken the tow truck instead of the Explorer because it would give him a plausible excuse if he were spotted. Which was a good thing to have, he decided.

He pulled up to the front door of the garage, cut the engine, got out and started around to the rear.

"What are you doing?'' she asked.

He looked up fast, realizing she'd scrambled out, too, and followed him. "I'm going to lower the car and unhook it. Why?''

"Aren't you going to take it inside?''

"Not tonight, no.''

"Well…why not?'' She looked at the large garage doors, then at him.

"'Cause I've already locked up for the night. I'll put it inside first thing in the morning, don't worry.''

She was worried. She pursed her lips, hugged herself and lowered her head.

"What? You worried someone's gonna mess with your car out here overnight?''

Her head came up. "Frankly…yeah, I am.''

He frowned harder at her. "Why?''

She shrugged, looking away. "Let's just say it wouldn't be the first time and leave it at that, okay?''

Narrowing his eyes, he tried to search her face, but she didn't let him look long. It occurred to him that someone had really messed with her head to make her so paranoid. But it also occurred to him that she might have reasons to be cautious. "Fine," he said. "Fine, we'll put her inside for the night." He went to the main entrance, and she followed on his heels. He took out his keys and unlocked the door, opened it just a little and reached inside to flip a button.

The big overhead door groaned and began to rise slowly.

He licked his lips, looking around for a diversion, and finally said, "Look, your sisters are over at the Corral." He pointed down the street toward the bar, where a light was on in one of the windows.

"It's probably Mom. She spends way too much time at work. That place is like her baby."

"Why don't you go on over and say hello while I put the car in? It won't take a minute, and then I'll come pick you up and give you a ride home."

She looked at him oddly for a long moment, then finally she shrugged and turned toward the road. "Whatever."

He sighed his relief as she walked away from him. God, what a close call. She kept walking. Wade got into the truck and pulled it into the garage with the car still attached to the back, then shut it down. Getting out, he went back to the switches on the wall, flicking one to start the huge door on its way back down again and another to turn on the lights. He took just a moment to look around him.

Every wall sported pictures of Edie Brand in various states of undress, with pouty lips and bedroom eyes and wild hair. In spite of himself, he licked his lips. Damn, she was hot, if nothing else. She might be a hyper, snooty, arrogant pain in the backside, but she was hot. No doubt about that.

"Oh. My. God."

He whirled fast at the sound of her voice. She was standing just inside the doorway he had reached through to hit the button. Damn, he'd forgotten to lock it! He felt like the kid who'd been caught with his hand in someone else's cookie jar. But he resented feeling that way. He really resented it.

"What the hell is all this?"

Wade schooled his expression and his voice not to betray just how embarrassed he was right then. "All what?" he asked in a tone of complete innocence. Then he looked around the room. "Oh, you mean the pictures?"

She tilted her head and looked at him as if he were stupid. "No, I meant the wrenches. Yes, the pictures. What the hell are you doing with all these pictures of me, Wade?"

He shrugged. "The customers like them. So do the guys who work for me. And hell, I'm a red-blooded male myself. Have you ever seen a garage *without* a few nudie shots on the walls?"

She closed her eyes slowly. "They are not 'nudie shots,' as you so charmingly put it, Armstrong, they're lingerie ads. And yes, I have seen garages without them, though that's beside the point. They're all of me. Why is every one of them of me?"

"You're local. I always try to support local businesses, and it stood to reason I should do the same for our own local pinup girl."

She blinked. "You are a pervert." She said it as if it were some revelation she had just uncovered.

He turned it right back on her. "*I'm* a pervert? Hey, honey, you're the one who posed for them."

"They're underwear ads!" she shot back. "They're not meant to be used to fuel the libidos of sex-crazed grease monkeys!"

"No? What, not even this one here, where you're bent over fixing your shoe, with your ass toward the camera? What was the purpose of that shot, Edie, to show the full benefits of thong panties?"

She turned her back on him so fast he knew she was furious. And maybe embarrassed, too. Good. He walked right up behind her. "The ads are meant to tease and tantalize and titillate. Admit it."

She stiffened her spine, not facing him. "Sex sells, Wade."

"Damn right it does. And frankly, I saw nothing wrong with taking full advantage of your teasing, tempting photos as fantasy fodder when you were clear on the other side of the country."

"Fantasy fodder?"

"Hell yes. I'm human, you know."

When she turned to face him, her jaw was clenched, teeth grated, cheeks pink. "I'm not on the other side of the country anymore. And I have to live in this town."

"And I've been meaning to take the pictures down ever since you got back."

She studied his face as if trying to see through his lies. "You...you're going to take them down?"

"Yeah. Yeah, if they bother you so much, they'll be down by morning."

She pressed her lips tight together. "I appreciate it."

"You're welcome," he said.

She started to say something else. But he kept speaking. "But I refuse to take down the ones in my bedroom."

Her face went white, and she gaped at him.

"Hey, they're some of the best visual aids I've come across."

Her hand flashed toward his face, but he caught her wrist. "Will you chill? I'm teasing you. God, can't you take a joke?"

She couldn't; it was pretty clear by the high color that flooded her face, replacing the pallor that had been there before. That didn't bother him, though. What bothered him, way down deep where it shouldn't, was the moisture that sprang into her eyes.

She jerked her wrist free, turned and ran away from him. He sighed, called himself about a zillion nasty names, and then stepped outside to watch over her until she'd safely reached the bar and gone inside. Just like he'd been watching over her up there in her hilltop home.

The man was a Neanderthal. A jerk. A pig.

And if she had half a brain, she would sic the law on him. After all, she had a stalker who'd been hounding her constantly the last six months she'd been in L.A. And Wade Armstrong not only had photos of her wallpapering his garage, but he'd been very close by when the latest kinky little gift had been delivered to her.

"Well now, what are you doing here?" Vidalia asked when Edie stomped into the bar.

"Fuming, mostly. Did you know that horrible man—"

"You mean Wade Armstrong?"

"Yes, Wade Armstrong! Did you know he had magazine shots of me all over his garage?"

Her mother blinked, lifting her head from the books she'd been poring over. "What, still?"

"You mean you knew?"

"Everyone in town knew." She smiled to herself and shook her head slowly. "Mel threatened to break his face, of course, but only until I explained it to her. The man thinks he's got everyone fooled, you know. All that attitude."

Edie held up both hands in complete bewilderment. "What are you talking about?"

"Oh, Edie, come on now, don't tell me you haven't figured it out yet. That boy's been pining for you since high school."

She could have been hit by a falling house and felt less shock. "That's...ridiculous."

"He was gonna ask you to his senior prom, you know. The boy called me up and asked my permission. Can you believe that? Of course, by the time he worked up his nerve, you were already going with...Brad or Chad or one of those pretty boys."

"Matt," she corrected. "Matt McConnell."

"Whatever. Wade made me promise never to tell, but... well, things have their time."

Edie sat down hard. Fortunately there was a chair behind her. "He...he *liked* me? I didn't think he even *knew* me."

"He didn't think you knew him. Now he has all those photos. Tells folks it's to remind him he's risen above the people who brushed him off back then. The ones who saw him as unworthy of their time or notice. You seem to have become the poster girl for everyone who ever slighted him, Edie."

"But I never slighted him."

"Not the way he sees it."

Edie sighed, lowering her head, remembering the way Wade used to walk around school. He always had this "don't get too close" attitude, always exuded a sense of danger, and that was what kept people away. She'd been scared to death of him in high school. All the girls had.

It occurred to her then that high school wounds ran deep. Deeper than adults liked to acknowledge. Some kids never outgrew them. Which made sense when you put it into perspective. Some kids, tragically, didn't even *survive* them. She'd had no idea her behavior had caused Wade any pain. At the time, however, she'd been pretty wrapped up in her own little world, her own little dramas.

"Mom, did Wade leave town before I came back home?"

"Not that I know of, hon. In fact, that shop's open every single weekday, holidays included."

He would have had to be in and out of town a lot to have been responsible for all the harassment her stalker had doled out. Enough so that it would have been noticed. She could double-check, try to verify his exact whereabouts on the day the man had actually attacked her...but hell, deep down, she knew it wasn't him.

Her mother's hand covered hers. "You know, of course,

the real reason he kept all the pictures isn't resentment at all.
It's because he never got over you.''

Edie blinked fast, looking up at her mother. ''I think you're
way off base on that one, Mom.''

Her mother shrugged. ''Guess you'll figure it out, one way
or another.'' She slid the book into the desk drawer, closed
it and twisted a key in the lock. ''Come on, hon. I'll give you
a ride home.''

''All right.''

Edie didn't like the new house, she decided. She didn't like
it at all. Especially not that first night, with no phone hooked
up yet, and no car in the driveway. She locked the place up
tight but didn't sleep. She tried. She paced. She unpacked
some more. She set her minuscule portable television up on
cardboard boxes and got a fuzzy picture from a local station,
via the rabbit-ear antenna. She was going to need a satellite
dish out here, she mused. No cable ran this far out of town.

It was dark outside. Darker than hell, and with those huge
windows, she felt as exposed as a shooting-gallery duck.
Damn. She hated being afraid—especially when there was no
reason for it. The gift hadn't come from her stalker. Probably.
It could have been anyone in town. Just because Wade Armstrong denied it, that didn't mean he hadn't done it. And what
about Pete Dunnegan? She'd given him a hard time at the bar.
Granted, that was after she had received the gift, but he
seemed to have fixated on her before he ever arrived that
night. And there were others. There had to be lots of others.
Righteous, zealot-types who found her work offensive and
vulgar and wanted to put the fear of God into her. Oversexed
types who wanted to use her to fuel their fantasies.

She stopped there, closed her eyes. She had set a neatly
folded stack of towels and washcloths on a shelf in the bathroom attached to her bedroom, and now she just stood there
staring at them, her hands sinking into the plush fabric. She

really shouldn't be surprised at having picked up a sicko in
L.A., should she? Hell, she probably had several of them who
could be potentially dangerous. Maybe her agent had been
right when he'd said she should have expected it.

Sighing, she picked up a pretty bath towel in a deep forest-
green shade, and a hand towel and washcloth of soft mint
green, and moved to the hardwood rack on the wall to hang
them just so. She needed this place to feel like a home, not
like an empty shell full of boxes. Putting her bathroom together helped.

She wandered back downstairs, into the living room, located her bathroom supplies and refused to cast a shivery
glance toward the large black windows as she carried the box
back upstairs with her. She unwrapped a new bar of soap and
located a soap dish, setting both on the sink. She dug for her
toothbrush and hung it in the rack. It looked lonely there. Bit
by bit she unpacked her shampoos and conditioners and
makeup and facial-care creams and masks, and placed them
all around the bathroom. Hairbrushes, combs, hair dryer, curling iron, straightening iron, crimping iron, hot curlers, hot oil
treatments. She unpacked bath beads and salts and loofahs.
She found her favorite plush green rug for in front of the tub,
and a big white cotton robe, which she hung on the hook on
the inside of the bathroom door. She put her matching slippers
on the floor beside it. Then she looked around the bathroom.

The walls were bare. They needed something.

Thinking of that made her think of the walls at Wade Armstrong's garage and his choice of how to decorate them. It
had been mortifying to walk in there and see all those photos
of her. She'd felt as exposed as if he'd walked in on her
changing and caught her half dressed.

Why, though? She never felt that way with anyone else.
She had seen her calendar on walls before. She usually experienced a mixture of pride and discomfort at being on dis-
play that way—pride because someone had liked her work

enough to plunk down seventeen bucks for it. Discomfort at the thought of why they liked looking at her that much. Since the stalking had begun, the discomfort level had grown far larger than the pride. That really should have been her first clue that her time as a model was over.

Walking in and seeing her photos all over Wade Armstrong's garage had felt different, though. Different from anything in her experience. She'd been embarrassed. And more. Angry. He wasn't like those other men who had bought her calendar. He *knew* her. That was it, she realized slowly. He knew her in person, face-to-face. They had been in high school together. He *knew* her. To her mind, that ought to mean he didn't need the photos. Because he knew her, he should also know that they were not her. That they were little more than airbrushed, retouched, high-gloss personas she put on to do a job. That the real her was so much better, so much more.

At least, she had always hoped she was more. He didn't see that, though. He saw only the body, the face, the hair, the poses and the lighting.

Maybe he thought that was all she was. And maybe the reason that upset her so much was because she was afraid he might be right.

No. He wasn't. He was dead wrong.

Licking her lips, she sighed and turned to the tub to run a bath. The bathroom was looking more homey. She didn't even want to look at the bedroom yet. She was glad the bed was at least put together. Wade and Caleb had done that earlier in the day, under Vidalia's supervision. Pouring a generous amount of bath salts into the water, inhaling the sweet, soothing scents of lavender and chamomile, Edie stirred the water with her hand. It ran deeper and deeper, filling the room with warmth and steam and diffusing that soothing scent.

She rose from the edge of the tub, slid her clothes off and left them lying on the floor. She didn't have a hamper yet and made a mental note to get one. For now, her jeans on the floor just made the place seem more lived in. Finally she stepped into the still-running water and leaned back. The heat felt good, seeping into her bones, soothing her. It had been a long day. But, in a way, a good one. It could easily, she thought, have been the first day of the rest of her life. A new beginning for her.

If only that damn gift hadn't arrived.

What if it *had* been her stalker?

She closed her eyes tight, shook her head. She refused to believe it. It wasn't. It was that simple. It wasn't him. Someone in town was screwing with her head, and she would find out who. She banished the thought from her mind and relaxed into the water. The scents helped. Selene had made the bath salts for her, telling her they were a special blend designed to ease away stress and worries, to relax a person's mind, body and spirit. She believed her youngest sister was onto something, the way her muscles seemed to elongate and loosen as she rested in the water.

She let it happen, gave herself over to it, closed her eyes.

It occurred to her, for some inexplicable reason, to wonder what Wade Armstrong might be doing right now. And as she sank slowly into sleep, her mind asked the question again and again.

An image slowly took shape in her mind. An image of Wade Armstrong, lying alone in his bed, completely naked and completely erect as he looked at a magazine with her face on the cover. She saw it all very clearly. The way his eyes burned over her body on the page. The way he licked his lips. And then the way his hand slid down over his belly.

An irritating bleating sound drew her attention away from where it was utterly, mindlessly riveted. It came again and again. She popped her eyes open and sat upright in the tub, blinking in shock. She had fallen asleep, she realized slowly, and dreamed...

The sound came again. Damn, not a part of the dream.

Startled, she rose from the water, dripping, reached for her robe and pulled it on, then opened the bathroom door, wondering what the hell was ringing like that.

The sound was coming from her purse, which was in the bedroom, on the mattress. She made wet footprints on the hardwood as she hurried to it, dug around inside and found a cell phone that didn't belong to her.

Oh God, had someone been in here? Her stalker, was it him calling her now?

She pressed the green button on the keypad, brought the phone to her ear. "Hello?"

"What's wrong?" a voice asked.

The voice was Wade's, and it made that dream image flash before her eyes again. She blinked it away, but not before a little voice in her head wondered if he looked as good undressed in real life as he had in her dream. "Wade?" she asked.

"Yeah, it's me. What's the matter, Edie?"

"What makes you think anything's the matter?"

"You sounded funny when you answered. Scared or something."

She rolled her eyes. "Probably because I couldn't figure out who had come into my house to leave me a cell phone while I was in the bathtub!"

"You...you were in the tub?"

"Yes. Is this your phone, Wade?"

"Yeah. I dropped it in your purse earlier and just now realized I hadn't told you. So I figured I ought to call to let you know it was there, in case you needed it tonight. I know the regular line out there isn't hooked up yet, and I, uh... uh..." His voice trailed off. He cleared his throat. "So, are you *still* in the tub?"

"No, Wade, I am not still in the tub. I got out of the tub to answer the phone. I'm in the bedroom."

"Oh." Again a long stretch of silence. "So, um, what are you wearing?"

She closed her eyes, completely ignoring the little tingle that zipped through her when his voice lowered the way it had just then. She said, "The biggest, ugliest, rattiest flannel bathrobe you can imagine, with a collar that comes to my chin, and thirty buttons, all done up tight."

He sighed. "You couldn't lie, even a little bit?"

"No. Not even a little bit."

"Okay, we'll work with what we have, then."

"What?"

"Close your eyes, Edie." His voice had dropped again to that deep, whispery sound that brushed her nerve endings like sandpaper on velvet. "I'm unbuttoning the first button. With my teeth..."

"Stop it, Wade."

"Oh, come on, I was just teasing." His voice was normal again. Hers wasn't, and she was sorely afraid he could tell. "Listen, I wasn't just calling so you'd know the phone was there. I also wanted to apologize. For the pictures in the garage. I never intended for you to walk in there and see them. I mean it."

"You're apologizing?" She blinked at the phone in shock. "What are you up to, Wade?"

"Nothing. I took them down. They're gone, okay?"

She nodded slowly, thinking about what her mother had told her. "Let me ask you something. And give me an honest answer, will you?"

"Sure. Shoot."

"Why did you really have those pictures up there?"

He was silent for a long moment. Then he said, "Keeps the customers' minds off the long wait and the size of the bill."

"So would a TV," she said.

"Good idea. I'll get one."

She sighed, rolling her eyes.

"Look, I have to go. I just wanted to ease your mind about the pictures and let you know you had a phone."

"And make sure I was okay," she added.

"And ask what you were wearing," he returned. "If you need anything, or, you know, if you decide you want to have phone sex, feel free to call me back. Okay?"

"Right. Whatever."

"You have the number?"

"Oh, I've got your number all right, Armstrong."

"It's number one on the speed dial," he said.

"You have yourself on speed dial?"

"I programmed it in before I gave you the phone."

She blinked, shocked. The man was looking out for her. He was acting more like a guardian angel than a big bad dangerous sex maniac. "That was...that was nice of you. Thanks."

"You wanna thank me, just take the phone with you and slide back into that bathtub."

"Goodbye, Wade."

"Can't blame a guy for trying."

She clicked the cut-off button and tried to hold on to her anger and indignation. He was crude, ill mannered and had a one-track mind.

And that was all bull, wasn't it? A big act. Maybe he'd always been acting. Because if he was as sleazy as he pretended to be, he wouldn't have thought to leave his cell phone with her, just in case. It never would have occurred to him that she would be afraid up here all alone her first night.

Then again, it wouldn't have occurred to him if she had been an ordinary-looking woman. Would it? She blinked and felt her anger waning. She was too grateful to be as angry as his remarks and his attitude should have made her. She tucked the cell phone under her pillow, rolled onto her side and pulled a blanket up over her shoulders.

## Chapter 7

Something was wrong!

She came awake suddenly, her eyes flashing open and her heart leaping against her rib cage, though she had no idea why. Something had startled her awake.

It took a moment of blinking in the darkness to realize she wasn't in her bedroom at her mother's farmhouse anymore. She was in *her* house, her *new* house. Automatically, she reached for the lamp on the bedside stand, only to be reminded it wasn't there. The bedroom wasn't in order. The bedside stand was still sitting downstairs in the living room amid the boxes, and the lamp was on the floor, four feet away. She would have to get out of bed to reach it.

Then again, maybe that wasn't the best idea. If a light came on and there was someone here, it would be pretty clear where she was, wouldn't it?

She listened, sitting perfectly still and straining her ears. What the hell had shocked her out of a sound sleep like that?

There were sounds, of course. The wind up on a hilltop like this seemed to blow all the time, and with so much forest around, there was a singing in the air. The pitch changed, lower to higher, depending on how hard the wind blew. Branches moved at its touch, brushing each other and parting again like dancers in the trees. She heard that whisper now. And far beyond it, the distant, steady hoot of an owl came to her ears. But that was all. Nothing else. No other sounds. She looked around the room, straining her eyes.

The closet door was partway open.

Her heart slammed and her skin prickled. Had it been open before? Hadn't it been closed when she crawled into bed?

To hell with this. She had the cell phone in her hand, pressed the power button that made the light come on so she could see the panel and hit speed dial and 1 before she even got herself untangled from the covers and landed on the floor. The bed was between her and the closet door now. Her eyes were fixed on that darkened closet even as she crept toward the lamp. Her heart was pounding now, hammering so hard she thought it should be audible. There was someone in the house. She could feel it. The phone on the other end rang, and rang again.

Her hand shaking, she reached for the lamp, then froze when Wade's voice came into her ear with a sleepy, "Yeah?"

She licked her lips. If she spoke, and there was someone in her closet... She sprang to her feet and lunged for the bedroom door. Even as she sprinted through it, she said, "There's someone in the house!"

"Edie? Hold on. Just lock yourself in one of the rooms and hold on. I'll be there in five minutes."

"Hurry," she said, but the phone had already gone dead. She was standing at the top of the stairs in the dark house. She could see part of the wide-open area below, lit only by the thin beam of a crescent moon and a few stars shining through the huge, bare windows. She could see the shapes of all her boxes, the few steps down to the foyer, the closed front door that she wished she could just run through right now. But she couldn't. Anyone could be down there.

She knew she had heard something, something that woke her. And she still felt the presence. Her bedroom door stood open at the far end of the hall. The second bedroom was behind her, pitch dark, with no lamp in it and no bulb in the ceiling fixture. To her left was a linen closet. But there would be no lock on the inside of a closet door.

Which way to go, dammit?

A sound, a distinct sound, like a single footstep, galvanized her. It had come from her bedroom. She shot into the darkened guest room as if fired from a cannon, closed the door, locked it. And then she stood there, trying to listen to outside sounds over the pounding of blood in her temples and her own ragged breathing. She forced it slower. Wade would have pulled his clothes on by now. He was probably out the door, in his vehicle. She followed his actions in her mind. He was starting it up, driving out of his driveway. She wasn't sure where he lived. Somewhere in town, though. And it wasn't a big town. Even if he lived all the way at the far end, he could make it to the Falls road in a minute or two. Especially this late at night. No traffic.

She swallowed, tried to count in her mind. One, one thousand, two, one thousand... And even as she did it, she was straining, listening. Straining too hard, because now every breeze that caressed the siding sounded like a human moving. No more footfalls came, only a soft brushing, that might have been the trees outside or someone's trouser legs moving as he crept through her hall.

She thought of the gun Mike had given her. She had tucked it into the back of a dresser drawer and hadn't even thought to grab it. And she couldn't go back for it now.

She backed into the farthest corner of the room, sank onto the floor and drew her knees up to her chest. God, she was so afraid.

As he drove—not the tow truck, but his Explorer, which was a hell of a lot faster—he thought of a thousand things.

He should have called a cop before he left. He should have called Caleb. But he hadn't, and he didn't have his cell phone with him, so he couldn't. And he damned well wasn't going to stop the car to call anyone now.

She had sounded terrified. God, he had barely recognized her voice.

He drove wildly, recklessly, up the steep, winding road, taking curves so fast that if he met another vehicle on the way, one of them would end up in the brush, and it wasn't going to be him. He didn't have a weapon. He didn't think he would need one, the way his adrenaline was pumping.

He skidded to a dusty stop in her driveway only minutes after she had called—the faithful Explorer hadn't slowed to less than eighty until he hit the brakes. He jumped out, yanking a tire iron out of the back and striding toward the house, which was pitch dark. Damn, if she hadn't even turned on a light…

He headed for the front door. It was wide open, and he lifted the tire iron and strode through, reaching for the light switch just inside the door, flicking it on. Light flooded the foyer. He glanced around him, saw no one, and went on to the wide-open living area, turning its light on, as well. No one seemed to be there, either.

"Edie?" he called. "It's Wade. I'm here. You're okay now. Where are you?"

He heard movement, footsteps, soft and tentative, from above, and he headed for the stairs. "Edie?" He paused at the top.

A bedroom door opened slowly, and she looked out at him. She wore a white cotton robe, which she clutched around her middle. Her hair was as tangled as Medusa's, he thought—as if she had gone to sleep with it wet. And her eyes were bigger than he had ever seen them. She didn't look like his favorite pinup girl. She looked like a frightened child.

"Are you okay?"

She didn't answer that. "He was in my bedroom. In the closet, I think."

His hand gripped the tire iron more tightly, and something hot and ugly spread through his veins. If he found some son of a bitch hiding in Edie Brand's bedroom closet, he didn't plan to let him leave here under his own power. They would have to carry the bastard out. Possibly in more than one container.

He started toward the bedroom.

Edie lunged out of the room and gripped his arm. She didn't say "Don't leave me" but he heard it all the same. Her hands gripped his upper arm hard. He put his hand on her hip, nudging her behind him, but she still kept hold of his arm as he started forward. He spotted the switch for the hall light, snapped it on. Then he led her toward her bedroom. As he started through the door, he reached for the light switch.

"It doesn't work," she whispered, her voice near his ear. Warm breath did odd things to a man when it kissed his ear and his neck like that, even during times of great duress, he thought idly. "There's a lamp." She pointed.

Nodding, he walked to the lamp, with her still at his back; then he looked at the closet door. When he took his first step toward it, Edie released her grip on his arm, and he felt her heat fade. Glancing behind him, he saw that she had backed away, all the way to the opposite wall, and her gaze was fixed unblinkingly on the closet door.

His throat a little dry, he flicked on the lamp, lifted his tire iron and kept moving. He reached the door, yanked it open and stared inside at a dim, empty space. It wasn't a large closet, nor did it have its own light source, but he could see it clearly. Three bare walls, a clothes pole across the space at eye level, an empty shelf above it, and an empty floor below it.

He stepped aside, so she could see into the closet, too.

She shook her head slowly. "He was there."

"How do you know?"

She met Wade's eyes. "The closet door was open when I left this room and called you. It was open, Wade. It was open."

"And what about the front door?" he asked her.

She frowned at him, shaking her head. "The front door...I didn't go near it. It was closed and locked for the night."

"It was open when I got here," he said.

"Oh God..."

He saw the panic in her face as she swung her gaze left and right, fought to catch her breath as it came more rapidly than before. So he went to her, crossed the room, dropping the tire iron on the bed as he passed, and put his arms around Edie Brand. She didn't fight him. She hugged him instead. Hard. And he could feel her trembling down deep. "Whoever it was, he left. He probably heard you make that call and skinned out the front door. I'm gonna search the place top to bottom, just to be sure, and I want you to lock yourself in this room until I come back for you. Okay?"

She nodded, her head moving up and down against the front of his shoulder. "The b-bathroom first," she whispered.

He nodded and turned her around, set her down on the bed; then he went in to check the bathroom. She had left clothes on the floor in there, he noticed, and the water was still in the tub.

Assured the room was empty, he went back to her. "You still have the cell phone?"

She nodded.

"Great. Use it if you need to. I'll be back in ten."

"Make it five."

He sent her a teasing smile. "Can't live without me that long, huh? Okay, five, then. And when I get back, Edie, we are going to have a talk."

She blinked. "A talk?"

"Yeah. I think maybe it's about time you told me what's been going on with you," he said. He leaned past her, gripped his trusty tire iron. "Lock the door behind me."

She nodded as he opened it and stepped through. "Be careful, Wade."

He pulled the door closed, waiting to hear her turn the lock, and then he moved down the hall.

By the time Wade tapped on her bedroom door several minutes later and said, "It's okay, Edie, it's me," she had calmed down enough for the embarrassment to set in. Maybe, she thought, he wouldn't think too much about it. Maybe he wouldn't ask the questions she was dreading.

But he did. First, though, he took her arm and led her out of her room and down the stairs. "The house is clear. There's no one around. If anyone was here before, he's gone now."

She nodded, but she was still nervous as he took her into the kitchen. He dragged a couple of stools in from the living room. "You want me to get you anything?" he asked. "Cocoa, coffee?"

"There's nothing here. I...haven't even shopped for groceries yet."

Sighing, he sat on a stool—which did not match the one on which she sat, she noticed—and sat across from her. "So?" he asked.

"So...I guess I was just nervous. Probably imagined the whole thing."

"Uh-huh. Okay, we'll get to that. First things first. You called me."

She nodded. "Yes. And you came running. That was really good of you, Wade."

"Yeah, but that's beside the point."

"The point being?" she asked.

"That you called *me.* Not the cops. Not your brother-in-law, or your mom, or you sister Mel, who could probably handle any intruder smaller than roughly, oh, say, Godzilla. You didn't call any of them. You called me. And I think I know why."

She lifted her head and looked into his eyes, not sure what he was getting at. "Because you told me to?"

"Sorry?"

"You left me your cell phone. You called me on it and told me to call you if I needed anything. Remember? You said you had put yourself on speed dial. That was just about the last thing I heard before I fell asleep. So when I woke, it was the first thing I thought of. Speed dial."

"I see."

"It would have taken lots longer to call my mom or sister or Caleb. Even nine-one-one would have taken longer than just dialing one."

"So you ran all those options through your mind, and you decided it would be quicker to call me." It wasn't a question.

She nodded.

"Or maybe you still aren't ready for your family to know what's going on with you."

She lowered her eyes. Oh. That was what he was getting at. Not that maybe she felt drawn to him or anything ridiculous like that. "Well, yeah. There is that," she admitted, trying to keep the relief out of her voice.

"Well, then, you need to tell me."

She swallowed hard, lifting her head, meeting his eyes.

"And don't bother telling me there's nothing going on, either, Edie. You aren't the kind of woman to panic over nothing. You heard something tonight, and you have reason to be afraid. And that gift had something to do with that reason."

"You're right. I do have reason. And there is more going on."

"Well then…?"

"It's my business, Wade. I'm not trying to be rude, and I

really am grateful to you for helping me like this, but…it's
my problem. I'll deal with it."

He shook his head firmly. "Not anymore you won't.
You're gonna tell me. All of it. Starting right now. Or else
I'm going to make a phone call to my buddy Caleb and tell
him exactly what happened here tonight."

She blinked at him. "You're blackmailing me?"

"Blackmailing you?" He seemed shocked. "If I don't tell
him you think there's someone after you, and you end up
hurt— Look, he's my best friend. You're his family. I can't
do that, Edie. You need to come clean with me."

She grated her teeth in anger. "I'll tell Caleb myself."

"Yeah, well, I'd believe that if you had called Caleb over
here in the middle of the night to protect you from a phantom
in the closet. But you didn't. You called me. So what is it,
Edie? Old boyfriend who can't let go? Hmm? Abusive relationship? Bad breakup? What?"

She studied his face for a long moment and, finally, she
gave, sighing deeply, knowing by the stubborn set of his jaw
that he wasn't going to let up until she told him. "Obsessed
fan," she said at last.

"Obsessed fan?"

She nodded.

"As in…"

"As in stalker," she said.

He sat back in his seat as if pushed there. His breath came
out of him in a whoosh. "I didn't expect that."

"Neither did I. My agent said I should have, though. Considering what I did for a living."

"Sounds like a real understanding asshole," he said. "As
if you asked for this kind of bull."

She blinked at him, surprised, maybe, that he hadn't agreed
readily with her former agent's pronouncement.

"When did it start?"

She sighed. "Last summer. At first it was just fan mail.

Persistent, annoying, but not too scary. When I didn't answer it, it started getting weird.''

"Weird, how?''

She looked at him, watched his face. "He starting telling me about his sexual fantasies.''

"About you," he finished.

She nodded. "Yeah. And they got more and more descriptive, more and more detailed, and more and more...violent.''

"He wanted to hurt you?''

"Look, I don't want to—''

"Just tell me. What was it? Kinky? S and M type stuff?''

She nodded again, unable to look him in the eye. "He said he would teach me my place, that he would break me, make me completely submissive to him.'' She licked her lips. "And then the gifts started arriving.''

"Like the handcuffs," he asked.

She nodded. "Yeah. Like the handcuffs. With little notes telling me what he wanted me to wear, giving me daily orders as if he really expected me to do what he told me.''

"What kind of orders?''

She shrugged. "Stand by the back window and take off your blouse. Don't wear bras anymore. Sleep naked from now on. You name it.'' She shook her head. "It was creepy, because I knew he was watching me, to see if I would obey. And he seemed to get angrier and angrier when I didn't.''

He swore softly. "You went to the police?''

"They told me until he did something illegal, their hands were tied. Advised me to keep all the letters and gifts, along with a file on when they were received, the type of packing, mode of delivery and anything else I could think of. They also advised me to hire a bodyguard.''

Wade was listening, leaning forward, watching her face, literally hanging on her words, she thought. "And did you?''

"Yes. Mike was good, too. Just not quite good enough.''

His eyes flared wider. "This guy got to you?''

She nodded. "He got into the car with me after a party one night. Mike had gone back inside to get something I'd left behind. The valet had his back to the car. The next thing I knew, there was a blade to my throat, a hand over my mouth and hot breath in my ear telling me to stay perfectly still or die."

Wade got slowly to his feet. His face seemed to darken to the shade of blood. "Did he rape you?"

She shook her head slowly, left, then right. "No. He...his hands were all over me. Then I said the wrong thing, and he lost it. He started...choking me. Strangling me." She closed her eyes. "I thought it was over. But Mike came out, and he ran for it. But I knew he would come for me. To punish me for disobeying him."

Wade's face had betrayed a wealth of anger until, finally, he walked across the kitchen, putting his back to her. She wasn't sure why. "And that's why you decided to come home?"

"Yes. That happened just before Christmas. My contract was about to expire. I told no one other than Mike that I was leaving. I didn't want to spend another night in L.A. He made sure I didn't have to. He packed my things and hired a mover to ship them after I left, and he was very careful, everything in his name, nothing in mine. He leaked that I was in drug rehab to one reporter, and that I was having a facelift to another. No one, *no one,* knew where I was."

"Except Mike."

She looked up. Wade had turned briefly. "I'd trust him with my life."

"You did."

She licked her lips. "Yeah, I did." But she shook her head. "Still, I know he's not the stalker—because I saw them both together that day in the car. Mike came out, came running, and the other guy dove out the back and ran the other way."

Wade nodded as if in agreement. "And he'd have no reason to help this guy find you."

"None."

"Okay, we go with that for now. Though I'd still like to talk to this Mike."

"Wade, I told you about my problem. I didn't hand it over to you. You don't need to talk to anybody."

He sighed, then twisted his wrist and glanced at his watch. "There's still time enough left to catch a few hours sleep, you know."

She hugged her arms and shivered.

"Hey." He moved close to her chair, and, to her surprise, he put his hands on the outsides of her arms and rubbed up and down. "It's okay. I'll be right here."

"You don't have to stay."

"Don't even put up a token argument, Edie. I'm staying." He let his lips curve into a slight smile. "You know you want me to."

Reluctantly, she nodded. "As much as I hate to admit it, I really do."

His smile took full form. "Good. I'll take the floor. Unless you want me closer?"

"The floor will do?"

"Yeah, it'll do," he said. "For tonight, anyway."

She let him pull her to her feet, and she laughed a little. "You say that as if you're planning to be here longer."

"Only till we catch this guy," he said.

She stopped in her tracks, blinking up at him. "But... but..."

"You can help me move my stuff in tomorrow." He leaned down, pressed a kiss to her forehead. "Don't thank me."

"Thank you? Look, Wade, it was great of you to come rushing over here and all, but there is no way in *hell* you're moving in."

He stood back just a little, facing her squarely. "Look, I

hate to fight with you when you've had such a rough night,
but you really don't have any choice in the matter. And really,
when you think about it, it's the perfect solution. My place
is sold. Thanks to you, so is the one I was planning to buy
to replace it. By next weekend, I'll be bunking in the garage.''

''Look, that's not my fault.''

''It's *completely* your fault.''

''That doesn't mean I'm obligated to provide you with a
home.''

''Far easier on me to just bunk here than to come running
at all hours of the night. Hell, woman, you've seen the hazards
on that road. I took it at eighty, risking my neck to get here
as fast as humanly possible.''

''And I'm grateful, but—''

''Besides, someone's after you. I'm not comfortable leaving you all alone up here until we make sure that maniac is
behind bars.''

''It's probably not even him,'' she argued.

''Great. If we find out it's not him, the deal's off. But until
then, I'm staying.''

''No,'' she said. ''You're not.''

He drew a deep breath, blew it out again. ''Let's just wrap
this thing up once and for all. Here are your choices.'' He
held up fingers. ''One, you let me tell Caleb and your family
what's going on so they can help keep you safe.'' She was
already shaking her head no when he unbent another finger.
''Two, you report it to the sheriff and let him keep you safe,
which will result in your family finding out anyway. Three,
you call your old bodyguard and get him to come out here
and protect you.''

''He can't. His partner is sick. He can't leave now.''

Wade ticked off another finger. ''Four, you hire a new
bodyguard.''

''Right. There are so many of them in Big Falls, Oklahoma.''

"Exactly. So what remains is choice number five. You settle for me."

She crossed her arms over her chest. "Where do you get off telling me what to do?"

"What, you have other options that I don't know about?"

"Yes, as a matter of fact, I do. Six, I get myself a great big dog. And take some self-defense classes and…and…and…"

"Catch the guy yourself?" he asked. He tilted his head to one side, studying her face.

"Well, why not?"

"Because you'd get yourself killed, that's why not. Look, if you want to learn self-defense moves, I think that's a great idea. I'll teach you. And if you want a big dog, well, hell, I *have* a big dog."

She lowered her head, sighing.

"So?"

Lifting her gaze, she met his eyes. "I'm not what you think I am, Wade Armstrong."

His frown was swift and deep. "And what do I think you are?"

"An airhead. An empty-headed ditz with a pretty face and a decent figure. And probably something of a slut to boot."

"Hold on, now." He held up both hands.

"I'm not."

He shook his head slowly. "No. You're certainly not. If you were, I'd have had you in the sack by now. Hell, woman, you've been home almost six months."

She turned away. "I don't like men who only see me for my looks and my body. And you're one of them."

"You think so?"

"I know so. The photos in the garage said it all."

"The ones in the bedroom say more."

"Pig."

He smiled. "That's my girl. Got her spirit back. Come on, I'll take you to bed." He took her hand.

She yanked it away, gaping at him.

"I meant, I'll walk you up to your room. Sheesh, get your mind out of the gutter, will you?"

"You're infuriating."

"I know." He walked beside her up the stairs to her bedroom, checked the closet and bathroom one more time, and then stepped to the door to leave. "I know something else, too," he said, one hand on the doorknob.

"What's that?"

"Your name was on the honor roll every marking period in high school. You didn't hang out with the brainy kids— did your best not to let it show—but you were one of them all the same. I *never* thought you were an airhead. Except when it came to your opinion of me." He opened the door, stepped through it. "Good night, Edie."

Then he closed it behind him.

# Chapter 8

Despite the fact that she went to bed wondering just what he thought her opinion of him had been, Edie sank into sleep almost instantly, and she slept like a baby. When she woke to the sun streaming in through the uncurtained bedroom window, she wondered why that was. After the scare she'd had, she should have been jerking awake every hour or so. But she hadn't. Not once.

The idea whispered through her mind that maybe it was having Wade in the house that made her feel so safe. But she dismissed the thought as utterly ridiculous.

She wondered if he was awake yet. Was he up? Had he looked in on her while she was sleeping? For some reason, the idea of him standing over her bed in the dark, looking at her while she slept, sent a tingle up her spine. A forbidden one. Just like the ones she used to get in high school when the other girls talked about how dangerous he was. How experienced. How…*talented.*

She closed her eyes and told herself to knock it off. She was a grown woman now, and she knew perfectly well what kind of man he was. The kind who would date a model because of her looks, only to dump her for someone younger and prettier the minute she let her hair go gray or put on a few pounds. The kind who couldn't see any deeper than the surface. And just because he was still sexy as hell didn't change that.

A soft tap came on her bedroom door, followed by his voice. "You still in bed?"

"No, I'm up."

"Damn." The knob turned and the door opened. She sat in her bed where she had just said she wasn't. "You are such a liar," he said.

"Did you hear me invite you in?"

"No. Invite me louder next time."

She rolled her eyes. "I didn't invite you at all."

"Good thing I'm not a vampire, then." He grinned at her, coming farther inside. "You know, you lied last night, too. On the phone, when I asked you what you were wearing?"

She shrugged.

"That is not exactly an ugly flannel bathrobe," he said, nodding at the white cotton robe she still wore. His eyes burned her as they slid lower.

She looked down at herself and realized the robe was gaping open, exposing bare skin from her neck to her navel. The tie had loosened during the night. She grabbed it, yanked it together. "Don't look too close, Wade. You'll ruin your own illusions."

He smiled. "What do you mean?"

"Do you think I really look like those pictures all you perverts drool over?"

"I do not drool on them," he said. He tipped his head and looked up and to the left. "I *did* try licking one once, but the ink tasted terrible."

His words, though teasing, made a hot pool of lava form in her center. Damn him.

"Hey, I was kidding you. Come on, I'm not an idiot. I

know those things are airbrushed and retouched. But if you're worried that seeing that little birthmark just below your belly button or the V-shaped scar on your collarbone is going to shatter my illusions, forget it. Real women aren't perfect, Edie. Makes 'em more interesting."

She blinked at him in shock. He'd only had a momentary glimpse of her body, but he seemed to have seen every visible detail in that glimpse.

"So are you gonna get up, or are you waiting for me to slide in there with you? I gotta tell you, I think I would enjoy exploring your body for other imperfections."

"I'm getting up. And you really should stop with the sexual innuendo."

He didn't reply, just stood there as she slid out of the bed and started for the bathroom. He said, "Hey." She paused, turning back around to face him. "If it really bugs you, I'll cut it out. I'm just playing with you, Edie. I'm nothing like that maniac who's—"

"I know that." She saw in his eyes that he really was bothered by the idea she might think that. Pursing her lips, she drew a breath and decided to give an inch here. The man had come to her rescue last night, after all. "I'll tell you something I haven't told another soul, Wade. I called my agent a month ago. I was still up in the air about what I wanted to do about my career." She lowered her head, shook it slowly, embarrassed to admit what she was about to. "It took me three days to get him on the phone. Three days of leaving messages he didn't return. And when I finally did make contact, he told me the renewal offer from *Vanessa's Whisper* had been withdrawn. They found a hot young model to take my place. Then he told me my contract with his agency was being canceled, too."

Wade lowered his head swiftly. "If I might offer an opinion here—they're out of their freaking minds."

She smiled. "I'm not a kid anymore, Wade. Hell, I've been

modeling for over a decade. My age is starting to show. I
cost them more, I'm willing to do less for it. My taking off
without a word of warning and then dragging my feet on a
decision about renewing with them was the last straw. I
wasn't a hot enough commodity to be worth the trouble.''

"Out of their freaking minds, and blind to boot," he put
in.

She lowered her head. "It made me realize it was time for
me to figure out if there really is more to me than my good
looks. And even though I detest the fact that you don't seem
to know or care if there is—"

"Hey, I never said—"

She held up a hand, and he went quiet. "Despite that, I
have to admit, your lewd comments and constant flirting are
the only things keeping my ego from being completely de-
molished right now."

He blinked. Then, slowly, a smile spread across his face.
"Glad to be of service."

She shook her head at him. He looked more mischievous
than she had ever seen him look, and a little bit too pleased
with himself. "I'm gonna take a shower," she said.

"Great. You do that. I'll go get the whipped cream and be
right in."

She rolled her eyes, went into the bathroom and closed the
door.

The problem was, she really thought he was kidding.

The woman had no clue that he would quite possibly be
willing to drink her bathwater. Hell, up until very recently,
he had been pretty much convinced that his attraction to her
was purely physical, purely sexual, purely prurient.

He wasn't so sure anymore. Not since she had told him
about this stalker of hers. His reaction had been powerful, and
way over the top. He had actually caught himself thinking of
Edie Brand as *his* obsession. How dare some other man fixate

on her? Fantasize about her? She was *his* personal fantasy, and he didn't give a rat's backside how many glossy pages her body had graced.

The bastard was toast, whoever he was. His days were numbered. The thought of the guy putting his hands on her, holding a blade to her throat—well, hell, her story had shaken him more deeply than anything ever had. He hadn't known he was capable of the kind of feelings her words had stirred up in him.

So maybe there was a little bit more to his attraction to her than her body and the way it filled out a negligee. And maybe there always had been. Hell, there was the painting he kept hidden in his closet that no one—*no one*—had ever set eyes on besides himself and the artist who'd done it for him. He told himself at the time that it hadn't meant a thing. That it had been a whim.

Maybe he did care about more than the way she looked.

But he would be damned before he would admit that to her. She was still the same girl who'd held herself above him in high school, still the same girl who'd acted as if he was so far beneath her, he didn't even exist. He strongly suspected the second she got a clue he might have feelings for her that were more than sexual, she would throw him out like yesterday's fish.

So he would just keep that to himself. No sense making himself a target.

He heard the shower running, and his mouth went dry and his eyes slammed closed, his mind conjuring a picture of her standing naked under the spray. He pictured the water jetting powerfully from the spigot, hitting her breasts, making her nipples pebble. He would give a limb to go in there and lick them dry.

He was going to have that woman. Even if she had to believe it was a one-night stand with nothing more involved, he was going to have her. Oh, yes, he was. Or die with a hard-on.

He walked closer to the bathroom door, leaned close to it and listened. And after a while, he said, "Hey, Edie?"

Her movements stopped. But the water kept running. "You can't come in, Wade. The door's locked."

"You could unlock it."

She was silent for so long he knew she was thinking about it. Then he heard her moving again, returning her attention to her shower without even replying to his suggestion. But she'd heard him. And he wondered just how close she had come to turning the lock before she had chickened out.

He pulled his Explorer to a stop in the gravel road in front of the Brand family farmhouse. She looked at him, shaking her head. "I still don't think this is necessary. It's daylight now. No one would try anything in broad daylight."

He looked at her steadily, serious for once. "Up there, in the middle of nowhere, it might as well be night all the time. I have stuff to do at my place, not to mention the garage, and I wouldn't be able to do it if I knew you were up there alone all day, Edie. Just humor me, okay?"

She shook her head, narrowing her eyes on him. "You aren't at all who you pretend to be."

"No?"

"No," she said. "You're almost…heroic."

"Hell, woman, I'm just trying to keep you alive long enough to get you into bed. After that, you can do what you want."

He always had to ruin it, didn't he? She sighed and, turning, opened the passenger door and got out. Before she closed it again, he said, "Don't go back there alone, okay?"

She looked at his face for a long moment. "Okay."

"I'll call you later. Keep the phone on you."

She nodded. "See you later." Closing the door, she hurried

across the lawn to her family's house, opened the back door and stepped right on inside. The crew came in from the living room when they heard her. Edie looked from their curious expressions to the still-warm breakfast on the table and knew they'd been watching her through the front windows.

"So, why are you riding with Wade Armstrong this morning?" Kara asked with a lilt in her voice as she slid into her chair. Mel took the seat beside her and lifted her brows innocently as she watched Edie and awaited her answer. Selene lingered in the doorway but seemed pensive. Vidalia, of course, marched straight to the cupboard for another plate, filled it and set it on the table, instructing Edie to dig in.

Edie sighed, lowering her head and turning away from them all on the pretense of getting herself a cup of coffee. "My car had a blowout last night. No big deal, but I skidded on it for a little ways, and it damaged the rim. Wade had to tow it to his shop last night."

"Last night?" Vidalia asked. She blinked three times and stared at Edie. "And he's still with you this morning."

"I didn't say 'still.' Stop jumping to conclusions, Mom."

She lifted her brows higher, noting, no doubt, that Edie didn't deny it.

"Actually, though, he did make a proposition that I think I'm going to take him up on."

"I didn't *think* it would take Wade very long to get around to propositioning you," Mel said, elbowing Kara beside her and laughing.

"It's not like that at all," Edie lied. She carried her coffee to the table and sat down. "The thing is, he sold his house. He can't get out of the deal, and because of me buying the place he planned to buy himself, he has nowhere to go."

They said nothing. The four of them simply stared at her. Even Selene snapped out of whatever had been distracting her and came closer to listen.

"And, while I've been there, I've found several things that

need some work in the house. Loose floorboard, some tricky wiring in the basement, the gutters. Stuff like that." She shrugged. "And it *is* a huge place for one person."

Four sets of eyebrows rose.

"He's going to rent the spare bedroom from me for a couple of weeks. Just until he finds a place of his own. And while he's there, he's offered to help out with the odd jobs."

"Well, I'll be dipped in—" Mel broke off at a sharp glance from her mother.

Vidalia looked at Edie again. "Do you have any idea how that's going to look to folks around here?"

Edie blinked. "Mom, I've spent the last ten years posing for an underwear catalogue. Are you really worried about my reputation?"

"Don't you sass me," her mother snapped. The woman might be dead wrong, but she would never admit it.

"I think it's kind of sweet," Kara said. "He's always had a crush on you, Edie. Why, if you could see his garage—"

"Kara!" Vidalia warned.

Edie shook her head. "No need, Mom. I saw the garage last night. And I made him take all those pictures down. He even apologized."

Vidalia's eyes widened. Mel said, "Someone call Hell, will you? Ask if it's frozen over."

"Melusine Brand, you watch your mouth." Vidalia sighed in exasperation. "And as for you, Edain—you are keeping secrets. Now, you're a grown-up woman, and it's your right to keep your private things private, but you ought to know by now that you cannot fool your mother. I know when something's wrong, and I know something's wrong right now."

"Mom…"

She snapped up a stop-sign hand. "Don't you talk to me anymore until you're ready to tell me the truth." Vidalia got up from the table and strode out of the room.

Edie got up to go after her, but Selene came forward, stopping her. "Let her have her fit. It'll make her feel better. You just drink your coffee and relax."

Sighing, looking through the doorway in the direction her mother had gone, she finally obeyed. "Just so you all know, there's nothing going on between Wade Armstrong and me."

*Not yet, at least,* her mind added, startling her so much she almost gasped aloud.

Selene was looking at her in that way she had. "Something is wrong, though. Mom's right about that, isn't she?"

Edie sighed and reached out to take her sister's hand. "I'm fine. I promise." She looked at the other two, who were staring at Selene in alarm, and realized she needed to change the subject. "I need a crew of volunteers today to help me get my house in order. It's a royal mess. Who wants to help?"

Selene nodded hard, and Mel and Kara, too. Kara said, "Caleb said to tell you to just call him if you need any grunt work done. He has a light schedule at the office today."

"Great. That's great." She sipped her coffee faster, eager to get busy on her house, and knowing full well she would be safe with a crowd of sisters around her.

Hours later, they collapsed on various pillows and cushions in what would be the living room, when it had actual furniture. The place was finally taking shape. The telephone company had sent a man out to turn on the service. And Edain had figured out where her studio would be—in the area that had been designated a den or study. Like the living room, it had towering windows, but unlike it, it was closed off from the rest of the house. There was a door off the foyer that led right into it, too. She liked the idea of having some boundaries between business and home.

Even more, she liked the idea that she was beginning to look forward to getting this project under way.

Selene was perched in the room's only chair—a bowl-shaped rattan frame with a huge circular cushion of brown velvet. She sat at the chair's edge, because to lean back was to fall into the piece. It was a chair for snuggling into with a soft blanket and a good book. And Selene wasn't in a snuggling mood. She was tense, her face drawn.

"Well, sis," Mel said, "everything's put away, and the boxes are stacked in the garage. Until your sexy new housemate brings his own load of junk over, there's not a lot more to be done."

"He was going to bring a load tonight," Edie replied, not even bothering to argue over the "sexy" comment. He was. It was an indisputable fact.

"You ought to help him, Edie," Kara suggested. "Heck, he worked his tail off helping us move your stuff."

"He's probably still at the shop," Edie said.

Mel shook her head. "Nah, it closes at five. It's almost six already. And you know, it is kind of sad to think of him over there in that cracker-box house of his, packing all by himself. I mean, after all the help he was to us," she added.

"I'm all for it if it will get us out of here," Selene said softly.

They all looked at her. Kara seemed about to ask, so Edie interrupted. Mostly because she was afraid to have them all hear whatever Selene's answer would be. She was too perceptive. "So you want to drive over to Wade's place? Is that what you're saying?" she asked her sisters. "I'd have thought you'd be all in by now."

"Shoot," Mel said. "That wasn't anything. You'd think L.A. had made you soft to hear you talk now."

She shrugged. "Doesn't Mom need your help at the bar? What did she say when you called home earlier, Kara?"

"Maya and Caleb are helping her tonight," Kara explained with a smile. "Caleb's dad is playing grandpa/baby-sitter and loving every second of it."

"Let's get going, then." Selene got to her feet, pacing toward the door. "We should take both vehicles," she added, looking Edie right in the eye. "You can ride with me in the car."

"Sure." She knew she was in for it. Selene had that look in her eyes.

"Mel and I will follow along in the pickup, then. Selene, you know where Wade lives, right?"

"Yeah, Kara. I know. Come on, Edie. And be sure to lock up behind us."

They all trooped out and piled into the vehicles. The moment Selene had fastened her seat belt and started the engine of the compact car she drove, she turned and met Edie's eyes. "So who's been in that house?"

Edie didn't meet her eyes. "Lots of people. Me, Wade, the whole family, the real estate woman, anyone and everyone she's shown the house to, the previous owners, the phone company guy...."

"And that's all? You're sure?"

Edie nodded, pasting a false smile on her face. "Why, sis? You picking up strange vibrations? Think I have a ghost or something?"

Selene put the car into motion, shaking her head. "I don't know. There's something... It feels just like what I felt in our house the other night. As if someone had been there. Someone...messy."

"Messy?" She studied her sister's face. "I promise, Selene, the mess in that house was all mine."

"That's not what I mean. Emotionally messy. It's like someone walked through the place just dripping every feeling all over the place. Like tracking mud through the house."

"Emotional mud." Edie tilted her head. "Interesting concept."

"Don't humor me, Edie. And don't act like nothing's going on. We all know you're keeping something from us."

That brought Edie's head around. "Now you sound just

like Mom. So do you want to tell me what you mean by that?''

"Just what I said. It doesn't take an empath to see that something is going on with you. Mom thinks we should leave you alone, let you work through it. No one else thinks it's anything all that serious. But I think..."

She stopped there, biting her lip, focusing on the road.

"You think what, Selene?"

Selene licked her lips. "I think you're in danger, Edie. I don't want to scare you, but I doubt I will, since I think you already know it.'' She turned to look Edie in the eye again.

Edie held her gaze for a moment. Then she finally had to let her own fall.

"That's why Wade's moving in, isn't it?''

Rolling her eyes, sighing, Edie said, "Look, this is nothing for you to worry about. I don't want the family involved, Selene, so whatever you think you know, you need to keep quiet about it.''

Selene pursed her lips, and her hands gripped the wheel a little too tightly. "I'm glad Wade's there. He's good, you know. Everyone thinks he's so mean, so tough, so scary. But he is so far from those things it's almost laughable.''

Edie lowered her head. "You know him that well?''

"No.''

"Then how can you be so sure about his character?''

Selene smiled softly. "I saw him pull over one rainy night to rescue a puppy from a runoff ditch. The poor thing would've drowned. He didn't know anyone saw, of course. He tucked the little dog inside his coat just as I pulled up behind his truck to see if he needed help or anything.'' She shook her head slowly. "You should have seen him. He waved me off and got in his truck as if nothing was happening. He had no idea I'd seen the whole thing.''

Edie licked her lips. "He...has a puppy?''

"Well, not exactly a puppy anymore. I mean, it was two years ago."

"He did mention a dog."

"More like a small horse, but whatever." They drove through town and turned onto Oak Street just past Wade's garage on Main. "It's right over here."

He was sitting in the kitchen nursing a cup of hot, strong coffee, with a half-filled box of dishes in front of him. He'd been having second thoughts about hauling them to Edie's place. She probably had plenty of dishes of her own. She probably had plenty of everything of her own, if the number of boxes he'd helped haul over there for her was any indication. Maybe he should just put the bulk of his stuff in storage.

A heavy head bumped his shoulder as he tried to take a sip of coffee, sending hot spatters over his hand, and he looked down into the huge brown eyes and long, speckled face of his best girl. "What do you think? Huh, Sally?"

"Raou-roo-ra." She answered him in that Great Dane speak of hers. It sounded most of the time as if she were speaking in complete, if garbled, sentences. She spoke several more lines, and he grinned and rubbed her head. "What? Timmy's in the well?" he asked.

"Ree-raw!" She loped toward the front door, her tail swinging around like a wrecking ball, and nearly took out his coffee cup. He lifted it out of the way just in time. Then he got to his feet to follow her.

Two vehicles pulled up. One behind his in the driveway and the other alongside the road, since the driveway was full up. He recognized them both. And the women inside them. The Brand babes had come to pay him a visit. And his favorite one of the bunch was with them.

He scratched Sally's head, and she danced excitedly. Her head was high enough so she could see clearly out the glass upper portion of his front door without even craning her neck. "Guess she just couldn't stand to be away from me a minute longer," he told the dog.

She looked up at him, and if she'd had eyebrows, they would have been arched.

"Now, you stay," he told her firmly. She nodded, he thought, and sat obediently beside him. He opened the door. "What's this, the welcoming committee?"

Selene looked troubled and pensive, but she smiled a fake smile. She was a pretty thing, with her silvery-blond hair and angelic face. Mel and Kara got out of the pickup. Mel, with her deceptively pixielike frame and short dark hair, looked harmless. Many a man had found out otherwise, though. And Kara was so tall and lean she could have been a model like her sister, though she didn't seem as graceful.

His eyes brushed over all of them but fixed on Edain and, once there, seemed stuck. He couldn't look away.

She looked tired, a little tense, and she was looking at him a little differently, he thought. As if seeing something she hadn't before. She hadn't bothered with makeup today, he noted. Ponytail, jeans. Her gaze shifted down slightly to the dog at his side, and she suddenly smiled in a mushy way.

"Awwwww." She crouched a little.

Sally took her cue, springing forward like a linebacker at the snap. He tried to shout a warning, but there wasn't time. Sally hit, and Edie went right down on her backside. Wade tensed, lunging forward. But Edie's arms were around the dog's neck by then, and Sally was nuzzling her face and talking to her. As he watched, slightly amazed, Edie took the dog's face between her hands and looked her right in the eyes. "You sure do have a lot to say, don't you, girl? What's your name, huh?"

"Uh, she's Sally. And she's a little bit on the clumsy side."

"It's 'cause she's so tall," Kara said, speaking from experience.

"It's because she's young and hasn't learned how to manage her long, elegant limbs just yet. That's all," Edie corrected. He saw the look she sent her gangly sister and knew there had been a message there for her.

"So what are you all doing here?" he asked.

Edie got to her feet, brushed her hands over the seat of her pants, an action that had him riveted, and said, "We've come to help you move."

"Yep. We owe you one," Kara said with a smile.

"More than one," Selene added, but she didn't elaborate, even when he sent her a questioning glance.

He was more than surprised. But not being one to deny a gorgeous woman entry to his home—much less four of them—he held the door wide and waved them in. "Help yourself to coffee, if you need fortification before we get under way," he said. "To tell you the truth, I'm glad you're here. I was just debating how much I actually need to move in and how much I should just store."

"Move it all in," Selene said.

Edie sent her a look.

She shrugged innocently. "What? It's a huge place, and while you have truckloads of stuff, your actual supply of practical household equipment is sadly lacking. I have no idea how you got along in L.A." She glanced at Wade. "She doesn't even have a coffeepot."

"I was rarely home in L.A. And when I was, I drank instant."

Wade made a face. "Oh, woman, you are a sad case. Fill your cups, ladies. That coffeepot is going to be the first thing I pack, so get to work emptying it."

Mel laughingly obliged, filling a cup she found in the cupboard, passing it to Kara, then reaching for another. Then she peered around the corner into his living room. "Oh, boy. Oh, man, that is sweet."

Wade followed her gaze to his big-screen TV, his pride and

joy, and nodded. "Yeah. You can't watch Monday Night Football on anything else after having one of these babies." He saw Edie grimace and hastily added, "Uh, and you can't beat it for, uh, sappy, emotional chick-flicks, either."

"Chick-flicks?" Edie asked, brows raised.

"I have a satellite dish," he attempted, and when that didn't seem to get her excited, he added, "It carries that women's network thing."

"Oh, well, in that case…" She shook her head and looked down at Sally, who was, Wade noticed, still sticking tight to her side. That was odd. His dog usually stuck to him like glue. Sighing, he slugged back his coffee, rinsed his cup and stuck it into the box of dishes on the table. "Let's get this show on the road, then, shall we?"

They each tipped up their cups and followed his lead, although, he noted, they didn't just set them in the box. Selene looked around until she found a newspaper, then yanked it to pieces, wrapping his cups in the pages. He thought it was overkill. They were cups, not the Hope diamond. It wasn't that far to Edie's house, and if a few broke on the way, it would be no great loss.

Whatever.

"Let's load the big stuff," Mel said, starting toward his TV. "We want to take extra-special care with this baby."

He got a little quiver in the pit of his stomach. If someone had told him six months ago that come May he would be moving in with the woman he had spent the last ten years fantasizing about, he would have told them they were nuts.

But it was happening. He was moving in with Edie Brand. The girl who'd always been too good for him—in her eyes, at least. Hell, maybe if he could fix this little problem for her, she would realize he was up to her standards after all.

He gave himself a shake. Yeah, right, but who was to say he even *wanted* her to? he asked himself. She would probably fall into his arms in abject gratitude once he put her stalker away. And then, he thought, *he* would reject *her*. Oh, it would be sweet to give her a taste of her own medicine after all this time.

*Right,* a little voice in his head whispered in a cynical tone. *Sure you will.*

Wade and Mel were carrying the big-screen TV out to the truck, and Kara and Selene were packing dishes from his cupboards. So Edie took the opportunity to do what she had been dying to do since they had pulled up out front.

It was his fault. She refused to feel guilty for snooping. He was the one who kept taunting her about the pictures of her plastered all over his bedroom. She had to see for herself.

She slipped through the hallway, opening the first door she came to, only to see a room filled with exercise equipment. It was as good as a gym, with weights and a bench, a Nautilus machine, a treadmill, and a punching bag hanging from the ceiling. Wow. Where the hell were they going to put all this stuff? She thought of the room above the attached garage, the one she had no clue what to do with. It was big, roomy, wide open and airy. It would make a great exercise room.

Stepping back, she pulled the door closed. Sally nudged her hand until she petted the dog's head, then accompanied her to the door across the hall. Edie opened the door.

Wade Armstrong's bedroom was small, neat, not too imaginative. A bed, a dresser, a trunk, a closet, a mirror. There was a chair with a pair of jeans slung over the back of it, a hamper in the corner with clothes draping over its sides as if tossed there from across the room. And next to the bed, a small nightstand. She skimmed the walls for magazine pages with Scotch tape at the corners and saw none. He *had* been lying. He didn't have any pictures of her in his bedroom. She turned to go, then stopped and turned back again, her eye caught by something on the dressing table.

Slowly, she moved closer, eyes narrowing on the five by

seven color photo in the little gold frame. It sat between the alarm clock and the telephone. It was of her, and it had been taken more than ten years ago, at the senior prom. She'd been sixteen. She had gone with Matt McConnell, and he had tried to feel her up every time he got close enough.

A little sigh whispered out of her as she stared at the photo, wondering where he'd managed to find a copy. She and Matt had had shots taken by the photographer who had been there, and this looked like one of them, only Matt wasn't in it. It looked as if it had been professionally altered. Moving closer, she lifted the frame and squinted at the photo, and realized that was exactly what had been done.

She closed her eyes, recalling her mother's words at the saloon last night. *He wanted to ask you to the prom, you know. He called me, asked permission. He made me promise never to tell....*

She heard the front door and blinked away the inexplicable moisture that had gathered in her eyes. Quickly replacing the photo, she hurried out of his bedroom into the hall, pulled the door closed behind her and started down the hall.

He caught her before she had taken two steps. "What are you doing back here?" he asked, sounding for all the world as if it were an unimportant question.

"Checking out your weight room," she replied, hoping he couldn't see in her eyes the discovery she had just made.

"Oh. Hey, don't think I plan to clutter up your place with all that."

"Are you kidding me? I may have given up modeling for a living, Wade, but some habits are harder to break. I've been driving clear to the Tucker Lake YMCA three times a week."

"Yeah?" He looked surprised.

"Yeah. I was thinking that room above the garage would be perfect. What do you think about that?"

He nodded. "Sounds great. But, uh, you know, it's up to you. It's your house." He shrugged, trying to hide the pleasure that she saw anyway. "Besides, I won't be there all that long."

Those words pricked her just a little, made her flinch. She wondered about that. It was an odd reaction. "Well, we might as well enjoy all your cool possessions while you are there."

"I have a water bed," he said, regaining his composure.

"It didn't—" She bit her lip, cut herself off. She'd almost blurted that it hadn't looked like a water bed. But she didn't want him to know she'd been snooping in his bedroom. "Very funny, Wade." She tipped her head to one side. "Do you really have a water bed? That's such a cliché."

He shrugged. "No. I have a normal bed. But, hey, if you had taken the bait, I would have had one by morning."

She was supposed to be offended, she knew. But deep down, she was thinking this guy liked her. He had always liked her and never let her know it. But now she knew his secret. And maybe it wasn't just a sexual thing or he wouldn't keep that prom picture in his room. He would have half-naked pictures of her all over the place instead, wouldn't he?

Was it possible, she wondered, that Wade Armstrong really was still nursing a crush on her? And why did the idea make her feel almost giddy?

## Chapter 9

He was amazed at how quickly the packing and moving operation went with the help of the beautiful Brand sisters. Two pickup loads took care of the large items, and the smaller stuff fit into Selene's tiny trunk and back seat, and his own SUV. Sally sat on the passenger seat beside him on the last trip up the winding mountain road. Oh, he had a few more things to do. Odds and ends to retrieve. One final polish to slap on the place before Tommy and Sue moved in. But for the most part, his cracker-box house was empty.

Sally looked at him and mumbled in her row-roo-rah manner as if asking a question.

"I know, it's kind of scary. But it's a nice place. Lots of room. I don't get the feeling Edie's gonna be all squeamish about a few dog hairs on the furniture. And if we play our cards right, I might get lucky."

She barked. A short, sharp woof that sounded vaguely scolding.

"Oh, yeah, this from the woman I caught trying to hump the neighbor's poodle that summer before the operation."

She lowered her head. Sometimes he got the distinct impression she understood every word.

"Sorry, girl. I know I promised I'd never bring that up."
He petted her head, and she leaned over to lick his ear, a sure
sign he was forgiven. "Look, we'll only be at Edie's place
until we get rid of the idiot who's harassing her. By then, I'll
have found us a perfect place all our own. With a big yard
where you can run till your heart's content. Okay?"

They pulled into the driveway, and he stopped the vehicle.
Mel was backing the pickup into position near the front door,
and he parked out of the way. He got out, and Sally didn't
even wait for him to come around and open her door. She
just lunged across the seat and out his. She hit the ground and
loped to the smaller car, just as Edie and Selene were getting
out of it. It was a comical sight, his giant dog standing beside
that tiny car.

Edie smiled at her. "Here we are, girl. What do you
think?"

The dog looked toward the house, then back at Edie again.
Then she loped away at a full gallop, stretching her legs and
really letting loose.

Edie glanced at Wade, her eyes alarmed. He held up a hand.
"Not to worry. She'll be back. She tends to run in loops. The
bigger the better."

He kept his eye on things until Sally had lapped the house
and returned to the driveway to sit beside Edie again as if
nothing unusual had happened.

"Too many woods around here," Kara said. She was lowering the pickup's tailgate and climbing aboard. "You should
put up a fence to keep her from going too far."

"Just so long as it's a big one. A dog like that needs room
to run," Selene put in.

"Hey, let's get a key over here, huh?" Mel called. "We
can have doggie discussions later."

Edie stopped petting the dog and dug her keys out of her
pocket, tossing them to her sister. Mel caught them, turned
and unlocked the door.

They carried in furniture piece by piece. His bed frame and headboard went up the stairs into the room where he had found Edie hiding the night before. Every time he thought about someone having been in this house with her, he got angry all over again. There was one part of his brain telling him it might not even have been real. That she might have imagined the entire thing. But most of him believed her. She hadn't imagined that open front door, and it would be pretty tough, he thought, to forget to close it. Lock it, maybe, but not to close it.

It was eleven-thirty.

The living area of the big house was once again cluttered with furniture and boxes. The sisters were in the kitchen, drinking soda, ready to call it a night. His refrigerator stood now where there had been none before. He picked up the box of items taken from his bedroom, the box he did not want Edie to see, along with the large flat one that *no one* could see, and carried them upstairs. He took the big flat box into the bedroom and slid it under his bed. Then he carried the smaller one, the one that contained the old issues of the catalogue he just couldn't bear to part with, down the hall, to the smaller set of steps that led up to the attic. She probably hadn't even been up there yet. Not as nervous as she had been. Glancing behind him briefly, he saw no one. So he climbed the attic steps.

At the top he found a light switch, flicked it on. The attic was as dingy and dusty and full of cobwebs as an attic should be. It was also empty, except for one cardboard box that wasn't dust covered. It hadn't been up there long enough to be.

Wade set his own box down and, frowning, moved toward the other one. Could it be that Edie, too, had a box of belongings she didn't want anyone else to see? He licked his lips, wondering just how many commandments he was breaking as he reached out, tugged the lid open.

He realized what the box held at the first glance. The item on top was a black vinyl hood, its only opening a round one at the mouth. That opening could be sealed, though, with the large red ball dangling from a strap hanging to one side. A buckle on the other side would fasten it in place.

This, he realized, must be the box that held the "gifts" Edie had received from her stalker.

Swallowing bile, he moved the mask aside and looked beneath it. Countless leather straps and buckles filled the box. He didn't take them out one by one to determine their uses. Some were restraints; some were articles of clothing. There was an assortment of paddles and whips in the box, along with sex toys of various sizes and shapes. The handcuffs were there. At the bottom he saw a stack of envelopes and knew the letters the man had written would be inside them.

"Where did Wade go?" Edie asked, glancing into the living area and toward the stairs.

"I think he went upstairs," Mel said, sipping her Mountain Dew. "Probably getting his bed set up so he can get some sleep tonight."

Kara sent Edie an innocent look. "You sure do keep a close eye on him, sis."

"She doesn't like him too far away," Mel put in. "Not that I can blame her."

The three of them laughed softly, though Selene's smile was tainted by the worry in her eyes. "I'm glad he's here," she said. "I don't like the idea of you up here all alone."

"I managed in big, bad Los Angeles all alone, Selene. I think I can handle Big Falls."

Selene didn't look convinced. "Well, still, I didn't sleep at all last night. I kept getting this awful feeling you were in trouble. And I can tell you right now, if I didn't know Wade was going to be here with you tonight, I wouldn't leave at all."

Edie smiled and lowered her head to see Sally, lying at her feet, almost *on* her feet. "Not just Wade, either, but his faithful companion here."

"A pair of heroes, aren't they?" Kara asked, looking down. "Just like Batman and Robin."

"Robin Hood and Little John," Mel said.

"Scylla and Charybdis," Selene put in.

They all sent her a look, and she shrugged innocently.

"We'd better go. It's late, and Mom's going to want a full report." Mel rolled her eyes and stood up as if girding her loins. "I'll be sure and tell her there are separate bedrooms. And I'll make it a point to mention how hard Wade was working to get his bed put together in time to sleep on it."

"You think it'll help?" Edie asked.

"Not really."

Edie got to her feet to walk her sisters to the front door. Sally was on her feet, too, and keeping pace. She walked so close to Edie's side she brushed against her thigh with every step. They stood at the door, watching Selene's car and Mel's pickup pull away, and then Sally looked up at Edie and spoke what sounded like a complete sentence, probably a question, only in her own language.

"You need to go outside before we turn in, girl?"

At the word "outside" the dog sprang out the door. Edie ran after her, worried she might take off into the woods in spite of Wade's confidence that she wouldn't.

The dog loped around to the rear of the house, and Edie ran to keep up. Out back Sally ran the length of the lawn and back, then ran it again, before she finally stopped running laps and started sniffing around in the underbrush. She chose a bush and squatted underneath it. Edie shook her head and politely averted her eyes.

Something moved in the trees off to Edie's left. She went stiff, her head swinging around sharply. But she saw nothing. It was dark, the only light coming from the crescent moon, bigger than last night, but not by much. Stars dotted the cloud-less sky. Glittering.

A deep growling sound made her blood run cold, until she realized it was coming from right beside her. Sally had returned to Edie's side and, apparently, knew something was wrong. She was looking right at the spot where Edie thought she'd seen something.

Swallowing hard, Edie reached down and closed her hand on the dog's collar. "Come on, Sally. Let's just go back inside. Come on, girl."

She tried backing a few steps away, but the dog didn't cooperate. She pulled harder. "By God, you're strong. Come on, girl, please? Let's just go. It's probably a porcupine or... or a skunk or something."

The dog seemed to ease her stance a little. Edie pulled her toward the house. Then the thing in the brush moved once more, and Sally jumped forward so hard and so fast that Edie went down to her knees. She tried to hold on, but the dog yanked her collar, and some of Edie's skin, free and loped into the woods.

"Sally!" Edie cried. "Wade, get out here! Hurry up!"

The letters started out kinky. Then demanding. Then angry. And then they got brutal. Apparently when Edie hadn't done what her admirer told her to do—things like wear a certain item he'd sent to her at some public appearance or other—as a sign of her submission to his control, he had reacted with anger. His demands grew more preposterous with each letter. He would tell her to do things like take off her top and walk to a certain window in her house at a specific time of day, so he could look at her. And then the threats began. She hadn't obeyed. She'd worn a bra when he'd forbidden it. She hadn't put on the slave collar he bought for her to show her subservience to him. He was going to punish her now. To "break her," as he put it. The final letter, the most recent one, was the most frightening of all.

So close tonight, my pet. So close to you, and yet the bodyguard you hired to keep me from you interrupted. I wouldn't want to have to hurt him. The way I'm going to hurt you. The longer you elude me, the worse it will be when I finally get my hands on you, princess. I must mark you. I must disfigure you in a way that will remind you always of the consequences of rebelling against me. Perhaps a finger. Just one. The small one, I think. I'll put it on a chain and wear it around my neck, so you know who owns you. Be sure to keep your nails done for me, my pretty. And wear a ring, a special ring, on your little finger. The right hand, yes? You are right-handed. Yes. When I come to you, when I find you, I will bring my sharpest blade. And I'll slice off your little finger. And then you'll know. Then you'll know.

Evade me once more, my sweet, and I'll be forced to add to your punishment.

Wade felt his stomach turning, his blood boiling as he returned the letter to its envelope and the envelope to the box.

He heard Edie's voice then. Not everything she said, just two words—"Wade!" and "Hurry."

Wade Armstrong exploded out the back door of the house, shot across the lawn, snapped his powerful arms around her waist and pulled her off her feet. When he set her down again, a split second later, a large tree was at her back, and Wade turned, putting his back in front of her. He stood there with his arms slightly bent and held out at his sides, his feet wide apart, knees bent, his head turning slowly as he scanned the forest around them. "Where is he? Where is the son of a—" He broke off sharply, glancing over his shoulder at her. "Are you all right? Are you hurt?'' His gaze slid down her body and skidded to a halt at her hand, where his eyes widened. Whirling, he gripped her wrist, lifting her hand, and that was when she saw the blood. ''Oh sweet God, he didn't—''

''It's nothing.'' She turned her hand over, showing him where the skin had been scraped and how the creases of her fingers bled just slightly.

His gaze rose, locked onto hers. My God, the emotions racking him right now were enough to knock her flat. He was white. He was shaking. He looked like he was going to be sick. And she knew what he thought.

''Wade, it was just Sally. I called you because she took off into the woods. I tried to hold her collar, and when she pulled free she took a little skin with her. That's all.''

His lips parted, but only air came out. He closed his eyes slowly, opened them again, and looked marginally better. One hand rose to press itself to the tree trunk just beyond her head, and he leaned into it, letting his head fall forward. ''You scared the life out of me. So there was no one out here?''

''There was...something out here.'' She was looking at the top of his head, until he brought it up slowly, his eyes questioning. ''Something moved in the woods, over this way. I thought I was imagining it, until Sally started growling and snarling. I tried to pull her back, just get her into the house, but she pulled free and went charging off after it.''

He wasn't so relaxed anymore. His spine straightened, and he looked around again, eyes wary and alert. ''Which way?''

She pointed.

He aimed in that direction, put two fingers to his lips and cut loose with an ear-splitting whistle. ''Sally! Come!'' he shouted. Then he whistled again.

''Well, that ought to do it,'' Edie muttered. ''Any crazed killer in the vicinity will know right where we are.''

''No crazed killer could outrun that dog for more than a few yards. If it were a human she was chasing, we'd be able to hear the both of them from here. Him screaming and her chewing.'' He sent her a sidelong glance, a little smile. ''Which would be a picnic compared to what I'd do to him.''

The imagery made her feel better. His protectiveness made her feel...something else. ''I didn't think Sally had a mean bone in her body,'' she said, deciding to address the dog's reactions instead of Wade's. ''Until I heard her growling, at least.''

''She's as friendly as a pup,'' he said. ''But she's incredibly protective, too. And she's taken to you.''

''That's good to know.'' Edie swallowed, wondering if Wade had ''taken to her,'' as well. Was that why he'd come out here with fire in his eyes, looking like some battle-crazed berserker?

He wasn't looking at her now. He was looking into the woods, calling his dog.

Eventually she came loping through the underbrush, but she stopped every now and then to lower her nose to the ground and brush at it with her forepaws. Frowning, Wade hurried toward her and dropped down onto his haunches. Edie followed when she heard him cussing under his breath.

Porcupine quills were sticking out of Sally's snout. ''Oh, no!'' Edie said. ''Oh, poor girl. Poor baby.'' She stroked the dog's head and spoke softly.

''We'll need a vet. Poor damn dog,'' Wade muttered. He sounded heartsick. It touched her that he cared so much for the animal.

''In the morning. We can take care of the worst of it tonight,'' Edie said. ''Come on, let's get her into the house.''

They urged the dog inside. But something made Edie keep looking back over her shoulder. She didn't think it had been a porcupine lingering in the bushes out back. She'd felt something before she'd ever heard the bushes moving. A presence. Eyes on her.

Hell.

They coaxed Sally up the stairs and into Edie's bedroom, mainly because her bathroom supplies would be nearby. The poor dog whined and spoke in long rambling sentences about how badly her nose hurt, while Edie located an old, soft blanket and made her a bed on the floor. Then she looked up at Wade. "A pair of pliers. Just small ones."

He looked her in the eye, shook his head. "No. No way am I letting you rip those things out of my dog with a pair of pliers."

"Easy, Wade. Come on, I've done this a dozen times. When we were kids we had this coon dog who just wouldn't leave the porkies alone. He came home every other week all summer with a snout full of quills. I know what I'm doing here."

"It's going to hurt her."

"Not as much as you think. And we'll never get a vet to see her tonight. It's past eleven. You don't want her to have to suffer all night with those things in her snout, do you?"

He was sitting on the floor now, legs crossed, Sally's head resting on his lap. "You sure you know what you're doing?"

She nodded. "Just stay there. She's comfortable. Tell me where the pliers are and I'll get them."

He opened his mouth, then closed it again and gently slid himself out from under the dog. She whined in protest, but he soothed her. "They're out in the garage. I don't want you out there alone. I'll get them."

She nodded and watched him go. While he was gone, she gathered everything else she would need. A bowl of warm water and a soft cloth, some triple antibiotic ointment, a pair of scissors.

When he returned, he sat beside the dog, noticing the way her head was now resting on a pillow, sending Edie a look but not commenting.

"Now, she's not going to like it, but it won't hurt as much as she'll think it will. You'll have to hold her head."

Sighing, he put a hand on either side of the Great Dane's big head. She looked from him to Edie with trusting brown eyes.

"The thing with quills," Edie said, gently putting her fingers at the base of one to keep it from pulling as she worked. "Is that they're hollow, like straws. That makes a kind of vacuum." Holding the quill at its base, she lifted the scissors and snipped off the end. Sally flinched at the sound. "They come out much easier if you break the vacuum by snipping off the ends." She moved to the next quill, and the next. The dog flinched each time, but didn't fight or seem to be hurting any more than she had been already. When the quills were snipped, eight of them in all, it was time for the hard part. "Now this is gonna hurt a bit more, but I'll be quick. Hold her firmly, Wade."

He held the dog. Edie exchanged the scissors for the pliers and quickly plucked each quill from Sally's snout. She kept her fingers on the skin to keep from pulling unnecessarily. Sally whimpered at each tug but didn't cry out at all. When it was done, Edie took the soft, warm cloth from the basin of water and gently cleansed the dog's wounded snout. Tiny beads of blood welled from most of the punctures. She warmed the cloth once more and this time just let it rest over the sore, tender areas. "There, now, doesn't that feel better? Hmm?"

Sally sighed, her eyes falling closed as the warm, wet cloth soothed her pain away.

Edie looked up at Wade, and he quickly averted his eyes. But not in time. She saw how wet they were. The man was moved nearly to tears by seeing his dog suffer. She could barely believe it.

He reached past her for the ointment and lifted the washcloth long enough to daub some of it gently over each wound. Then he wrapped gauze around Sally's snout. "Just until the ointment has time to soak in a bit, girl," he promised. "I won't leave you muzzled all night. Can you stand it for an hour, do you think?''

She opened her eyes to look at him as he spoke, sighed loudly and lay back down again.

''She's feeling loads better already,'' Edie said.

''You're right, she is.''

Edie dropped the cloth into the basin, picked up the scissors and ointment and gauze, and got to her feet with her arms loaded.

Wade got to his feet, as well, took several items from her, and led the way into the bathroom. At the sink, he dumped the water, cleaned the basin, hung the washcloth over the edge of the hamper and then scrubbed his hands with soap. Then he stood there looking at Edie as she set the medicine and scissors back in the medicine cabinet.

''What?'' she asked.

''Your turn,'' he said.

She frowned, but even as she did, he reached for her hands, drawing them into the flowing water. He took the soap and then, holding her hands between his own, rubbed them into a lather. He washed each finger, ran his fingers between them, dragged them across her palms leaving soapy trails. And he paid close attention to the area where Sally's collar had skinned her up a bit.

Slowly he moved her hands beneath the faucets, letting the water rinse the suds away. Then he located the ointment she'd only just put away and applied it to the crease of each of her four fingers.

''I'm sorry Sally hurt you like that. She's usually very gentle.''

''It wasn't her fault,'' Edie said. She tried not to let her breath hitch the way it wanted to when his fingers danced over the insides of hers. ''Something in the woods frightened her.''

''When I saw your hand, the blood, I thought...'' He shook

his head, not looking her in the eyes. But his fingers caressed her smallest one in a way that told her he knew—he knew about her stalker's threats. He knew specifics.

"You went through my things, didn't you? You read the notes."

He met her eyes. "I was just stashing a box of my stuff in the attic," he said. "I didn't go looking for your cache of evidence against this pervert."

She pulled her hand from his. "But when you found it, you felt free to go through it. Read the letters..."

"I'm here to protect you from this idiot, aren't I? Don't you think I can do that better if I know all the facts?" He took the gauze from the cabinet and pulled her hand firmly back into his. She didn't fight him. She let him wrap the four fingers in a few layers, then tape them off. It would keep the ointment from rubbing off overnight.

"I think you should have asked me first."

He finished taping the gauze, and, to her surprise, he nodded. "Yeah, you're right. I probably should have. Look, Edie, this guy is dangerous."

"You think I don't know that?"

He lowered his head. "I think we should let the police know what's going on here. Let your family know."

"No." She shook her head firmly. "No, I don't want my sisters or my mother becoming this guy's targets. And I know they will, if they know. They'll be all over this thing, trying to protect me. It's bad enough you've muscled your way into this mess. He might very well attack you next, just for getting in his way."

"Yeah," he said slowly, walking away from the mirror and nodding. "Yeah, that would be perfect."

She frowned hard at him. "No, it wouldn't be perfect! Are you insane? I don't want your blood on my conscience."

He turned again, shaking off whatever insane thoughts he'd

been thinking. Instead he said, "You were great with Sally. Thanks for that."

"She's a great dog." She sighed, closing the medicine cabinet and walking back into the bedroom. She stared down at the now sleeping dog for several minutes. "You've had her since she was a pup?"

He nodded. "Yeah. We, uh, bumped into each other on the road one day, and the mutt followed me home. I couldn't get rid of her."

Not the story her sister had told her, she mused, but this version didn't rule the other one out, either. "You never had her ears or tail cropped?"

"Don't even get me started on that topic," he said, and he said it quickly.

She smiled. "What? A subject we agree on? You've got to be kidding."

He searched her eyes a little. "I think men have gotten pretty full of themselves when they think they can improve on nature and go about hacking up little puppies to prove it."

"Amen to that."

He lifted his brows. "You agree with me?"

"Yeah. I do."

"Huh. Well, gee, lemme push this theory a little. 'Cause it's not just dogs I don't like seeing surgically altered, you know. It applies to people, too."

She smiled at him. "Is this your roundabout way of asking if I've had work done, Wade?"

"You haven't," he said. "I saw the original, remember? I'd know."

"Photographic memory?"

"Where you're concerned, yeah."

She blinked, not quite sure how to respond to that. Instead, she turned away so he wouldn't see the color rushing into her face. "It's late," she said. "I...we should get some sleep."

She saw him nod in her peripheral vision. "Leave your

door open, Edie, so I can hear you if you call out. I'll do the
same. And we'll let Sally stay where she is, if you don't mind.
I have a feeling she wouldn't let that gauze stop her from
taking a bite outta crime if your maniac should show up.''

She nodded, daring to face him again now that they were
on a safer subject. ''When she wakes again, I'll take the gauze
off.''

''You won't have to,'' he said. ''Good night, Edie.''

''Night.''

He hesitated there by the door, looking at her. His eyes
fixed on her lips, and she knew what he was thinking, and
she thought he knew that she knew. Maybe he wanted her to
know. She licked them involuntarily and saw his eyes react.
Then they met hers. Full of messages, thoughts, images, sensations. She wondered if her mouth fascinated him as much
as his fascinated her.

Sighing, he left the room and walked down the hall.

She heard him for a few minutes. Wandering through the
house, checking the place, making sure the doors were locked,
shutting off the lights.

She felt good with him there. She felt safe.

## Chapter 10

Wade didn't sleep at all. Because up until tonight, he'd had no idea just how serious Edie Brand's trouble was. Not until he had read those letters, seen the box of gifts. She had glossed over it when she'd told him what had scared her back to Big Falls. An obsessed fan—the idea had seemed nightmarish, especially when she had described the man's physical attack in her car that night. But seeing the letters, reading their chilling words, made it more real. More immediate.

Things were far worse than she had made them sound. The man wasn't just obsessed, he was insane. It dripped from every word of his letters.

And he was utterly, completely, focused on Edie Brand. Having read the letters, Wade would have been surprised if the man *hadn't* followed her back here. He wouldn't give up until he'd tracked her down, no matter how difficult doing so might be.

Wade felt as if he had gotten himself in over his head. Edie needed more help than a small-town mechanic could give her. Damn, why hadn't she confided in anyone?

But she hadn't.

She'd confided in him.

*Trusted* him.

Asked *him* to help her. Reluctantly, yes, but it came down to the same thing. He had been handed the chance to be Edie Brand's hero. And he damned well wasn't going to screw it up. Screwing it up would only verify all the lousy things she had ever thought about him. It would convince her she'd been right all along to hold herself above him, aloof from him, to look right through him.

No. He had to do this. He had to show her he was equal to the task and ten times the man she had ever given him credit for being. And then she—and this whole town—would have to rethink their preconceived notions about Wade Armstrong.

His successful business hadn't accomplished that. At least, not enough to satisfy him. His decades of upstanding citizenship hadn't, either. But this would. Saving the local celebrity from a madman would show them all. It was a chance he had been waiting for his entire life.

And his attraction to Edie Brand had nothing to do with it. Yeah, he liked the way she looked. He'd always liked the way she looked. But that was the extent of it. There was nothing more. Or, if there was more…damn, if there was more, he was an idiot. But if there was more, it was unrelated to this.

He spent the night unpacking. He put his bed together and put his clothes away, and thought and thought about what he should be doing to put Edie's stalker out of commission. When he opened a box to find his laptop computer, which he normally used for keeping the books during his off hours, an idea occurred to him. He quickly located the nearest telephone jack, glad to find one right in his bedroom, and plugged the computer in. Then he went online.

A search under Edie B. turned up countless hits. Thousands. Her photos had been plastered on more Web sites than anyone else's ever, according to one site he read. A few claimed to have nude shots of her, but they really only displayed Edie's head on someone else's body.

Wade knew that at a glance. He had committed her body to memory—even the parts he'd never really seen. He knew what she would look like. He knew what she would *feel* like. You couldn't fool Wade Armstrong with a fake.

Eventually he found a reference to a tabloid article and located it in the magazine's archives. Nothing about the stalker. Nothing about the gifts or the attack. It was a sensationalistic bit of hype that consisted of a cover photo of Edie with a handsome, muscular hunk on her arm at some function or other, with the caption, "Edie B.'s Mystery Date Exposed!"

He studied the guy for a long moment, hating him, wondering if he could be the stalker. But when he clicked through to the article and read it, he realized the guy might be his best lead. It gave his name as Michael McKenny, and said he was a friend and a business associate of Edie's, but that nothing romantic was going on between them.

Just like a tabloid to scream promises of illicit information in the headline and then report inside that there was nothing to report.

He clicked back to the photo, copied it onto his hard drive, made a note of the man's name and saved the file. Then he ran a search on the name Michael McKenny and found, once again, dozens of sites, though it was clear that most of them had nothing to do with this particular Michael McKenny. Too many to go through in a single night to see if any *were* relevant, though, so he logged off and took a break. Time to make a pot of coffee.

As he stepped into the hall, he heard soft sounds from Edie's room, so he tiptoed closer and peered into the darkness through the open door.

The hall light was on. It spilled through, just enough so he could see clearly. Edie was lying in the bed. Her hair spilled over her pillow artlessly. It was messy, not carefully arranged by some photographer. Her nightgown was a big dorm shirt with a teddy bear on the front. She lay on her side, having kicked her covers free, and her long legs were drawn up nearly to her chest. She was almost in the fetal position. Which meant she was scared, even in her sleep. Insecure. Lonely.

His gaze slid slowly back up her body again, over the rise of her hips, the dip of her waist, to her arms and shoulders and neck and, finally, to her face.

Her eyes were open and looking straight into his.

He felt his widen and almost jerked in surprise, but he managed to hold it together. "You made a noise in your sleep," he said. "I was just checking on you."

She blinked at him and nodded once, when he'd fully expected her to scold. "You're still wearing clothes," she said, her voice thick.

"Sorry. I'll take them off, if you want."

She smiled at him. Didn't snap or call him a pig. Just smiled a crooked, sleepy little smile. "Not what I meant."

"I know."

She rolled onto her back, patted the mattress beside her. He almost choked but managed to walk steadily into the bedroom, to sit down where she indicated. He turned sideways, toward the head of the bed, so he could see her better.

"Why haven't you been to bed yet?" she asked softly.

"You haven't asked."

She gave him a look that told him he was pushing it. He shrugged innocently but amended his answer. "Just didn't feel sleepy."

She sat up a little, propped on her elbows. "I should take the gauze off Sally now," she said.

He shook his head, then pointed and watched her eyes follow his finger. The dog lay on the floor, head pillowed on her paws. The gauze that had been wrapped around her snout was a foot away, as if she'd tossed it aside.

Edie laughed softly.

"She's pretty good at getting rid of anything that needs getting rid of," he said. Then he saw the look in Edie's eyes and knew she was thinking the same thing he was. The stalker needed getting rid of. Sally might not be able to handle that, though.

She looked away, pulling the covers up over her as if she were cold.

"You looked like you were sleeping fairly well, considering."

She shook her head. "In fits and starts. I drift off, then just jerk awake all of a sudden with my heart racing." She rolled over and looked at the clock. "Thank God it's almost morning."

"You didn't get to bed until after midnight." He heard the tone of his own voice and winced at the worried, tender sound to it.

"You didn't get to bed at all," she said.

He would not tell her that part of the reason he hadn't slept was an irrational, gnawing fear that if he fell asleep, something bad would happen to her, and he wouldn't be able to prevent it.

It was stupid. He could hear her perfectly from his room. And Sally was in here with her, besides.

He looked at her, rolled his eyes, sighed and finally turned himself around and lay down on his back, beside her. He was on top of the covers. She was underneath. His head missed the pillow, but it didn't matter.

"What do you think you're doing, Wade?"

He glanced at her. "You've got three hours before decent people get out of bed. Go to sleep, Edie."

"Wade, we can't just—I mean, this isn't a very..."

He turned his head to the side and looked at her face. "Go to sleep."

She held his gaze for a heartbeat. Then she drew a breath, lowered her head onto the pillow, and sighed it out as she let her eyes fall closed.

Once again, she'd surprised him.

That was nothing, though, compared to the shock that shot through him when she rolled onto her side, facing him, nestling just a little closer. Her hands closed around his upper arm, and her face lay so close that her cheek just barely rested against his shoulder.

He closed his eyes and bit his lip to keep from groaning out loud.

He never touched her. He still lay there, flat on his back, in exactly the same position in the morning. Despite the fact that she was snuggled up to him much more closely than she had been when he'd come in mere hours earlier. He hadn't moved. Yet he had slept.

Was still sleeping.

She lifted her head carefully, so she wouldn't wake him, and just looked at him for a long time. She let her eyes trace the contours of his face. The harsh line of his brows, the straight, arrogant nose, the sculpted cheekbones and the firm jaw. His lips were full, softening the whole look of his face. Her eyes stayed riveted on them for a long while. What was so enticing about them? That dip at the top, maybe? She thought about pressing her own lips to them. Just to see what they would feel like. What he would taste like.

But, of course, she couldn't do that.

She'd slept like a baby with him close to her. She hadn't had another bad dream, hadn't started awake again, not once, since he'd come to her. Would it be wrong of her to ask him to do this every night? Probably, considering how badly he wanted to have sex with her. It would be almost cruel to make him lie there, night after night, on his honor not to lay a finger on her.

She was surprised he had managed to do that for a few hours of one night. And…maybe even a little disappointed.

Idiot.

She slid out the other side of the bed and padded across the floor to check on Sally. Her wounds were still puffy, but not as angry looking as they had been last night. She would call the town's only vet after eight. It was only quarter of. She would just have time for a quick shower first. She grabbed some clothes to wear, stepped into the bathroom, closed the door and reached back for the lock. Then, licking her lips, she drew her hand away. She told herself she wasn't really hoping he would just walk in on her. She wasn't. Of course not. She just…didn't see the need to lock him out. Not after he'd shown such remarkable restraint last night.

Wade spent a few hours helping her put the house in order. It still wasn't perfect. Lots of bare places on the walls, lots of missing pieces, but he personally felt that once his big-screen TV was set up in the living room, the place was damn near perfection. He hadn't had time to mount the satellite dish on the roof yet, but later.

They'd had to cut the work short in the middle of the day to take Sally to the vet. And while one or the other of them could easily have taken care of the task alone, Wade was hesitant to let Edie out of his sight. Which was why he was letting the guys handle the garage on their own today.

He tried to gauge his reasons as he drove his SUV down the twisting road with Edie beside him and Sally on the back seat with her head nearly hitting the roof. He figured it was partly his new awareness of the serious threat this guy stalking Edie represented. How dangerous he was. And partly because she hadn't locked the bathroom door this morning while she had taken her shower.

She probably thought he hadn't noticed. As if every nerve ending and every sensory receiver in his body didn't quiver to full awareness every time she moved a muscle or took a breath. He had been wide awake from the moment she'd lifted her head from his shoulder this morning. He had been lying there, striving not to move as she looked at him. And he knew she was looking, because he felt her breath on his face and her eyes burning into his skin. He heard her soft sigh, too, just before she turned away. Felt it waft over his lips. It had taken every bit of self-restraint in him to lie there like the dead and not reach for her.

And the second she went into the bathroom, he was on his feet, moving closer, listening. She closed the door, yes, but she didn't turn the lock.

There could be several reasons for that, of course, but the only one he cared to ponder was the one that said she was hoping he might walk in and join her. And that was enough fantasy grist to keep his imagination working overtime for a solid month.

He smiled to himself as he thought about it.

"What?" she asked.

He jerked his head sideways, wiping the smile off his face. "Nothing. Nothing. I was daydreaming."

"About what?"

He shook his head. "No way. You get pissy when I talk about stuff like that. Besides, it wouldn't be appropriate now that we're sleeping together."

She blinked as if stunned. "We are *not* sleeping together."

"We are so."

She pursed her lips as if to keep from speaking, leaned back in her seat and faced straight ahead. Another mile later, she said, "So you were daydreaming about us sleeping together?"

"No. But since you're so hot to know, I was daydreaming

about you in the shower this morning. And how you left the door unlocked for me.''

Her jaw fell open. She just gaped at him, and her cheeks got so pink and her eyes so wide, he almost laughed out loud. ''I wasn't sure, of course, if it was an invitation or just an oversight, though I suspect the former.''

''You are such a pig.''

''Whatever. If it's not an invitation, then you ought to lock the door.''

''I don't have to lock the door if I don't want to. It's my house.''

''That's true. It's your house. But if you leave it unlocked next time, I'll probably start to assume that it *is* an invitation, and I might walk in. I mean, if I tell you that up-front, and then you don't lock the door, you can't be mad at me if I walk in, right?''

''I most certainly *can* be mad at you if you walk in.''

''No, you can't. Because I told you in advance. I mean, gee, Edie, take a look at this from my point of view. If I say, 'Don't leave your doughnuts out, or I'll eat them,' and you say you're going to leave them out anyway, and I'm not supposed to eat them, and I say, 'Look, lady, I'm a doughnut-holic. If they're out, I'm eating them,' and then you leave them out and I eat them, how the hell can you blame me?''

She turned her head slowly as he spoke and stared at him with eyes that got so wide he thought he had maybe grown a second head. And when he finished she said, ''What the *hell* are you talking about?''

He closed his eyes, gave his head a shake. ''I don't know.'' The damned woman had him so hot for her he could barely think straight, he mused. He turned the wheel, pulled into the parking lot of the veterinary clinic and snapped Sally's leash onto her collar. ''Come on, girl.''

As he got out, the dog did, too. Edie got out her own side, and Sally damn near pulled his arm out of the socket, trying

to get to her. She walked close to the woman's side. He
scowled at his traitorous dog. She looked back at him and
wagged her tail.

"Did you see that? Did you?"

Edie asked the question even as she helped him transfer
bags of groceries into the back of the SUV from a shopping
cart. They had finished at the vet's office and stopped for
supplies on the way back.

"Did I see what?"

"Everyone in that store was looking at us. And whispering
as soon as we were out of earshot. God, it's all over town
already."

"What is? That we're sleeping together?"

"Shh!"

He grinned, took the last bag from her and placed it in the
back. She was looking around to see if anyone had heard that
remark. No one had.

"When is my car going to be done, anyway? At least we
wouldn't be joined at the hip if I had my car."

He shrugged. "We can stop at the garage and check on
it."

She got into the front. Sally was lying across the back seat,
waiting patiently. Edie closed her door, reached for her seat
belt and felt eyes on her. She whipped her head around, scanning the parking lot, even as Wade got in his side.

"Wade," she whispered.

He closed his door, glanced at her. "What's wrong?" For
once his voice wasn't sarcastic or teasing.

"Someone's watching us."

He nodded, reached over and smoothed a hand over her
hair. "Everyone's watching us, honey."

Her head turned slowly. The feel of his hand stroking her
hair like that—the heat, the friction of his calloused palm, the
pressure, the way his fingers threaded, tugging gently as they

moved through, then danced over her nape like hot wires...
made her shiver. "What...are you doing?"

"Do you think it's him?"

She nodded. "I do. I know it's foolish, but I do...."

He shrugged. "If you think he's watching, play along."
And as he said it, he leaned closer, brushed his mouth across
hers. Softly, barely touching. Then again.

"I don't get it," she muttered. But her hands had risen
already to close on his shoulders.

"Might flush him out to see you kissing another man," he
said. His lips brushed hers again. "Shake him up." And
again. "He makes a mistake, we nail his ass. Understand?"
He spoke with his mouth close to hers. Every breath, every
movement of his lips, sent a ripple of heat right down her
spine.

"I understand," she said.

"Good. Then kiss me. Like you mean it, Edie."

He did not have to ask her twice.

It didn't take any effort at all. All she had to do was stop
resisting the force that tugged her mouth to his like a magnet.
Once she did, their lips touched, parted briefly, then locked
together with some kind of erotic suction that she liked way
too much. And she forgot all about whoever might or might
not be watching. She forgot about her stalker. She forgot everything except that this was Wade Armstrong, the hottest,
baddest, most dangerous male creature she had ever known.
And that she had wanted to kiss him for as long as she could
remember.

It was every bit as exciting—and as frightening—as she
had always thought it would be. His tongue was devilish,
persistent, invasive, and it stroked paths of molten desire everywhere it touched her. His hands cupped the back of her
head to hold her at just the right angle for his kiss. He could
tip her slightly this way, or that way, or backward, to deepen
his access. All at his will. She didn't care.

Her heart hammered against her ribs, and her body melted. Her hands were splayed, one in his hair, one flat against his back, and she was kissing him now, too. Sucking gently at his tongue, then petting it with hers. God, he knew how to kiss.

He moaned real deep and pushed her back against her door, his body sliding over hers as his mouth plundered.

A sharp rapping sound came from the passenger-side window.

Suddenly Edie remembered the reason for the kiss and broke it, only to crush her face against Wade's chest.

His hands were on her back, soothing. His voice was near her ear. "It's okay, it's not him."

How did he do that? Know exactly what she was thinking?

Slowly she lifted her head, saw his eyes, the look in them as he helped her get upright again, and finally she turned to look at who stood outside the SUV.

Her mother looked back at her, her face drawn and tight. Beyond Vidalia, Edie saw Mel, fighting a grin, Selene, looking all knowing, and Kara, wide eyed with surprise.

A tap on the other side of the car made them both turn to look out the window beside Wade. Maya and her husband Caleb were looking back at them, each holding a baby.

Wade cleared his throat, rolled down his window. "Hey there, Caleb. How's it going?"

"Better for me than you, pal." He looked past him at Edie. "Best roll your window down and talk to your mother, hon."

Too late. Vidalia was already opening the door. "Are you goin' to sit there and pretend I'm not even here, child?"

"Mrs. Brand," Wade cut in. "It's not what you think."

"What I *think* is that my daughter is making out with a man in public. Which wouldn't be quite so bad except that the entire town knows the man is also living with her, under her roof, out of wedlock."

"We were just—"

"I'm a grown woman, Mom," Edie said, cutting him off.

"Then try acting like one."

"Just because I don't live up to your values, it doesn't mean—"

"*My* values? I'd be happy if you'd live up to *any* values at all, girl." She shook her head. "I knew there was a reason you were in such an all-fired hurry to get a place of your own, Edain Brand, but I never thought it was just so you could move in with the first man to strike your fancy."

"I didn't."

"And *you!*" Vidalia said, spearing Wade with her eyes so powerfully it made Edie wince. "If you had one ounce of respect for my daughter, much less for me or my family, you'd marry her."

"Mother..." Edie said again.

"Don't you 'mother' me, young lady. It's obvious now to the whole town what your living arrangements are with this man. Which would be just fine by me if you didn't feel the need to advertise it. Just how am I supposed to hold my head up in church on Sunday? Hmm?"

She slammed the door and strode away. Wade was out his door before Edie knew what the hell had happened. He said only, "Stay right here," as he left to go chasing after her mother.

## Chapter 11

Edie started to get out of the car. Mel leaned against the door from the outside and shook her head.

Edie cranked down the window. "What the hell do you think you're doing? Wade is talking to Mom, in case you haven't noticed." And God only knew what he might be saying, Edie thought.

"Ah, let him take a swing at it, sis," Mel said. "Hell, he can't be any worse at it than you are."

Edie crossed her arms over her chest and leaned hard into the back of the seat. "No one could get along with that woman!"

"The rest of us don't seem to have too much trouble," Maya said. She was on the opposite side, speaking through the open driver's window.

"Speak for yourself, Maya," Selene said softly. "Mom is easy for you because you're so much like her. Your values and hers mesh perfectly. It's not so easy for the rest of us."

Maya crooked her brows. "Oh, come on, Selene, you're exaggerating."

"No, she's not," Edie said. "If Mom disapproves of something, then it's forbidden. No leeway. No chance she could possibly be wrong. She's fine with you because you got married, didn't move far away and had a pair of babies. Exactly the way she had always planned.''

"That's not true. She gets along with me because I make an effort,'' Maya defended. "And so does Mel. Tell her, will you?''

Mel licked her lips. "Actually, I make an effort, too. But she still gripes about my Harley and feels she needs to lecture me at least three times a year on why a woman shouldn't kick a man's ass when it sorely needs kicking.''

"She's only stating her opinion,'' Kara said. She spoke softly, meekly, for the first time on the subject. "She doesn't make you get rid of the Harley or anything.''

"No. Because it's not *that* offensive. And because she's still distracted from my minor offenses by Edie's major ones. First posing in her underwear, and then living in sin with the town bad boy.''

"We are not living in sin.''

"Once she bends Edie and Wade to her will, she'll move on to me, I imagine,'' Mel went on.

"No, I think I'll probably be next,'' Selene said softly.

They all looked at her. She blinked the troubled look out of her eyes and forced a smile. "So you say you're not sleeping with him yet?'' she asked.

"No.''

"Honestly?''

"I haven't had sex with that man, Selene.''

Selene shrugged. "Sorry. Don't get so touchy. It's not my fault you need your head examined.''

"You got that right,'' Maya muttered.

Her husband sent her a shocked look. "What do you mean by that?'' he asked.

"Well, hon, I love you right to pieces, but I'm not blind. The man is hot.''

Caleb rolled his eyes and shot Edie a look. As if this were all her fault.

"Oh my *God*." Kara dropped the three words like lead weights, and everyone turned to see what she was gaping at.

Halfway across the parking lot, Vidalia Brand was hugging Wade Armstrong's neck. It was a halfhearted hug, but a hug all the same. Then she let him go and backed off a little, nodded firmly and, turning, came back to the SUV. When she stopped near Edie's door, everyone was staring at her. She didn't return anyone's look except Edie's. "I'll expect you for dinner tonight." She snapped her eyes to Wade's. "Both of you."

Then, turning, she strode away. Shrugging and shaking their heads in bemusement, the others left, too, Maya and Caleb to go into the grocery store where they had been heading in the first place, the rest heading to their cars. They'd stopped them along the roadside when they'd spotted Edie and Wade making out in the grocery store parking lot. They had been on their way to the bar, Edie surmised.

Wade got in, turned the key, fastened his seat belt.

She stared at him, waiting, but he didn't say a word, until finally she couldn't stand the silence another second. "Well?" she asked.

"Well what?" All innocence, those eyes of his.

"What did you say to my mother?"

He drew a breath, sighed. "Sorry, kid. But that's between me and your mother."

"Did you tell her about him?"

"Who? Your stalker?" He shot her a sideways glance while driving. "Come on, do you think she'd have walked away if I had? She'd have taken you home by the scruff of your neck and set a dozen bodyguards on you."

Pursing her lips, she relaxed in her seat just a little. "That still doesn't explain why she hugged you."

"Look, Edie. You're gonna have to tell her the truth sooner

or later. I can't cover this up forever. And when you do, whatever I told her just now will be entirely moot. So let's not hash it over.''

"No, let's hash it, Wade. What did you tell her? Why were we kissing?''

"I was kissing you to shake up your stalker. You, on the other hand, seemed to be attempting to swallow my tongue.''

"Which would have been impossible if you hadn't had it halfway down my throat,'' she shot back.

"Well, I try to give the ladies what they want.''

"And what gave you the idea I wanted that?''

"Well, there was the fact that you opened wide and said 'ahh.' And then there were these fingers digging into my skull to pull me closer.''

She punched him hard in the shoulder.

"Ow!'' He rubbed the spot. "Come on, Edie, I was just playing.''

"What did you tell my mother?'' she demanded.

He sighed, shook his head. "I told her you had a boyfriend in L.A. who gave you a hard time when you dumped him, and that you thought you caught a glimpse of him in town. I, hearing this, proceeded to kiss the living hell out of you, without your permission, in an effort to help you get rid of the guy once and for all. It was all an act. You fought me every step of the way, and that was all there was to it.''

She stared at him.

"It's the truth, I swear it. I was trying to give the ex-boyfriend a clear message on the off chance he really had come to call. You thought it was an idiotic idea and were in the process of shoving me off you when they interrupted.''

She lowered her head, feeling a twinge of guilt. "You took all the blame.''

"Yes.''

"Made it sound as if I wasn't even involved in the...the kiss.''

"Exactly. Although I want us to be real clear on this. It wasn't just a kiss. And you *were* involved."

He looked at her, waiting, she knew, for her to admit it. Slowly she lifted her head, met his eyes. "I got...a little... carried away. It's been a long time since I've...you know."

He tucked a loose strand of hair behind her ear. "No, I don't know," he said, his voice softer now. "How long?"

She shook her head, refusing to answer him.

"How long, Edie?"

She shrugged. "A year...or so."

He shook his head slowly, licked his lips, seemed to be thinking very deeply about something as he maneuvered the car along the narrow road to her house. He opened his mouth once but closed it again, and she could clearly see he was debating whether to say something or keep it to himself.

"What?" she asked.

"No. You don't want to know. Trust me."

She watched his face, weighed his words, but her curiosity got the best of her. "Yes, I do. Go on, say it."

He glanced at her, lifted his brows. Finally, he sighed. "Okay, I will. But you have to hear me out without interruption. And I'm serious now, I'm not playing with you like... like I have been up to now."

"All right," she said, waiting.

He cleared his throat. "You are clearly attracted to me," he began.

"Of all the arrogant, conceited—"

"Uh-uh-uh. No interruptions, remember?" She slammed her lips together, all but biting them to keep quiet. "I wasn't finished. I'm attracted to you, too. Now, us both being adults, responsible, unattached, disease free—unless there's something I don't know?"

"You son of a—"

"Okay, okay. Just asking. Sheesh." His eyes were damn

near twinkling. How he must love teasing her this way. "I was going to say there's no reason we couldn't end your little...dry spell."

She blinked at him, waiting to see if he was finished before she commented. "You're asking me to have sex with you?"

"Hell, no, I'm not asking. I'm offering."

She thought steam should be shooting out her ears.

"Look, you want to, I want to. It wouldn't mean anything. Just two adults, giving each other a little physical release." He turned to stare right into her eyes. "I'm very good, you know."

"Oh, are you?" she asked, putting all the sarcasm she could muster into the question.

"Yeah. I could make you scream."

"You're practically doing it already."

He shrugged, turned his attention back to the road. "Listen, it's up to you. I don't care one way or the other. Just know the offer's on the table, should you decide you want to take me up on it."

"Don't hold your breath, Wade."

He glanced at her and smiled. There was some kind of sexy fire in that look, in his eyes, and her blood heated in response to it.

But she would sooner die than admit it.

He carried in his share of the grocery bags, then went directly to his room when they got back to the house. Kicking the bedroom door closed behind him with one foot, he walked straight toward the small bathroom, peeling his shirt over his head as he went. By the time he'd reached the bathroom, he'd managed to heel off his shoes as well, and he crossed the threshold hopping on one foot while stripping the sock off the other. The jeans and shorts were next, and then he cranked on the taps, good and cold, and forced himself under the shower spray.

He had to bite his lip to keep from yelping out loud and giving himself away. He would be damned before he would tell her that the conversation they'd been having in the car had affected him far more than it seemed to have her.

The water cooled him down in a hurry. He stepped out of the flow, dripping on the floor as he reached for a towel, realized he hadn't unpacked any yet, and walked, shivering, back into the bedroom to paw through the few boxes still stacked in the corner. One of them contained towels. Beach towels, mostly. He liked them big and roomy, so he bought a lot of beach towels. He rubbed himself down briskly, then started to dress. All told, the entire operation hadn't taken more than ten minutes, he thought, zipping his jeans, looking for a shirt. Which was good, because he didn't want her to know about it. If she did, she might guess the reason.

No doubt about it, talking about sex with his lifetime fantasy girl was not a safe game to play.

Talking to her mother had been, he realized belatedly, even more dangerous. The things he'd said to the woman...

*"Wait, please, Mrs. Brand...Vidalia."*

*She stopped. She was halfway across the grocery store's medium-size strip of blacktop, standing in an empty slot near the yellow length of cement. An empty cart was at her elbow. "I don't want to discuss this with you, Wade Armstrong. In my day a man showed discretion. A man cared enough about a woman to want to protect her from gossip."*

*"It's because I care about her that I kissed her just now," he blurted. Then he paused, wondering why it had come out the way it had, but decided it was good. He would run with it. He just couldn't give away Edie's secrets in the process. He'd promised he wouldn't tell. "Look, she thought she saw someone she knew in L.A."*

*Vidalia's scowl eased. She narrowed her eyes. "Someone she didn't want to see?" she asked.*

*"Yes."*

*Her brows went up. "Is my daughter in some kind of trouble, Wade? Because if she is, and you don't tell me..."*

*"It's nothing like that. There was a guy, a boyfriend, you know. Nothing serious, at least, not as far as Edie was concerned. But he saw it differently. I guess he didn't take the break-up very well. For a while he kept bugging her, and when she thought she glimpsed him here, well..."*

*"She was afraid he had followed her home," she said slowly. "So you decided to send this fellow a message."*

*"Exactly. That's all that kiss was. An act, just a ploy." He shrugged. "One that probably wasn't even needed. I don't think it was who she thought it was in the first place."*

*"I see."*

*He nodded, watching her face, waiting. He didn't know what she was waiting for, but he got uncomfortable as he searched his brain for more to say to her. Words eluded him, though.*

*She finally sighed. "So there's nothing else you want to tell me?"*

*He looked her in the eye. She had pretty eyes. Dark, Spanish eyes. Her parents had been Mexican, and it showed in her face. She had the kind of looks that only got better with age. "No, ma'am, I can't think of anything else. I mean, except that we aren't, er, we haven't—"*

*"Slept together?"*

*He averted his eyes, because they* had *slept together. Just not in the way she meant. "Of course not."*

*"But you love her."*

*He felt as if he'd been electrocuted, her words sent such a jolt through him. There was a solid whap of impact, dead center of his chest, and then tremors of aftershocks shooting outward to his fingertips, to his toes. "We're just friends," he managed, and it sounded more false than anything he'd ever said in his life. He sounded about as convincing as he had when he'd been caught smoking in the boys' room at* thirteen. He ditched his butt as the principal walked up and said, "Wade Armstrong, have you been smoking?" And he said, "No, sir, I haven't," releasing the puff he'd been holding in his lungs with the words.

Vidalia Brand was speaking again. "I'm not a blind woman, Wade. And you don't have to worry about me saying anything. Your secrets are safe here."

That was irrelevant, he thought, since he didn't have any secrets other than Edie's.

"Frankly, I think she's plumb out of her mind not to return your feelings."

So did he. No, wait a minute, that wasn't right. He didn't have any feelings. He still thought she was nuts not to be all over him, but that was another matter.

"So what's holding her back, hmm? This old boyfriend? Or is she still harboring some damn fool notion about going back to L.A.?"

"Nah, she thinks she's above me, just like she always did."

He stood there for a second, looking at his feet, wondering who had just spoken for a split second before he realized it had been him. That last thought had emerged aloud, during some sort of psychotic break in time. He snapped his head up, met her eyes.

She was frowning at him. "Well now, Wade, are you sure? That just doesn't make any sense to me."

He opened his mouth, wondering how the hell to dig himself out of this hole, then realized anything he said at this point would only make it worse. "I—I really can't talk about this, Vidalia."

"Oh." She said it on a sigh, a look of stark pity coming into her eyes, and the next thing he knew she was hugging him to her. "Oh, poor Wade. I'm sorry." She let him go, looked him in the eyes and smiled. "I didn't raise any fools, you know. You be patient. Edie'll come around." She patted his cheek, gave him a wink, and turned to walk back to *the SUV, where she'd delivered her dinner invitation-cum-demand.*

Wade sighed, sinking onto his bed. So, he thought, let's review. Vidalia Brand was now under the impression that he, Wade Armstrong, the lone wolf of Big Falls, was pining away with unrequited love for her pinup-girl daughter. Furthermore, she had given him her blessing to pursue Edie's hand, and he wasn't quite sure but he *thought* perhaps the woman intended to *help.*

Could things be any worse?

The telephone rang. He hadn't plugged a phone into the jack in his bedroom yet, but it didn't matter. Edie got it downstairs on the kitchen extension. He got to his feet, went to the bedroom door and opened it, just out of curiosity. He'd left this number with the boys at the garage in case they needed him. He stepped to the top of the stairs and peered down. And he could see her.

She was standing with her back to him, just inside the arching doorway into the kitchen, holding the phone to her ear. He saw the way she stiffened, saw her move the phone away from her ear as she turned her head slowly to stare at it. Her face, her eyes, were stricken. She slammed the phone back into its wall cradle.

"Edie?" He ran down, taking the stairs by twos, reaching her, grabbing her shoulders.

She looked up at him, eyes wide, wet. "It…was him," she said. "It was him."

He pulled her to him, held her, surprised when she clung, pressed her face to his chest. He found himself rubbing her back with one hand, her hair with the other, muttering stupid phrases to reassure her—even knowing they were meaningless. It wasn't okay. She wasn't safe. And he wasn't at all comfortable with the black rage surging up from some deep hell pit inside him at the man who had shaken her up this badly.

The phone rang again, and she went so stiff he thought she would break in his arms. He set her gently aside, reached for it, picked it up and spoke in a voice he didn't recognize.

"News flash, dirtbag. You have a serious problem, because if you want her, you're gonna have to come through me. You understand that? Me. I'm in the way, and I'm not moving. Deal with me first, or you might as well quit right now."

There was silence on the other end of the phone. Then a voice said, "Wade?"

It was Caleb's voice. Wade closed his eyes, muttered a cuss word. "Caleb? You still there?"

"Yes. I'm coming over. Be ready to talk to me, because I'm not leaving until you do." There was a click as Caleb disconnected.

Wade licked his lips, put the phone down, turned to Edie. "I'm sorry. I...I blew it. Caleb heard all that and now he wants answers."

She was just looking at him, though. Staring at him as if she'd never seen him before in her life. She didn't look angry. And the fear that had clouded her eyes before was gone. There was something else there now. Something he'd never seen there before.

"I didn't mean to give it away."

"I know." She broke the hold of her eyes on his, looking at the floor, the walls, anywhere, it seemed, but at him. "It's all right. He's not going to want Maya and the babies dragged into this any more than I do. And if he tells her, she will be. And he can't tell the others without telling her."

He nodded. "Are you all right?"

"Uh-huh." She paced away from him now, back into the kitchen, but she gave the phone a wide berth, as if it were going to nip at her if she got too close. She'd been stacking canned goods into one of the cupboards, and she returned to that task.

"What did he say to you, Edie?"

She didn't turn, didn't look at him. "He said, 'How dare you betray me with another man? Don't you realize what you've done? You have to die now. You have to die.'" She just kept stacking cans in the cupboards. Mushrooms, vegetables, soups. "He never said that before. Always threatened to rape me, hurt me, dominate me. But never to kill me."

"He's not going to kill you. He's not going to lay a finger on you."

"Isn't he?"

"Not while I'm still drawing breath, lady."

Her movements stilled. Slowly, she turned, a can of creamed corn in one hand. "Why do you care?"

"Because I am Edie B.'s most obsessed fan. Me. The guy's way out of his league." He said it lightly, teasingly, with a little smile meant to ease the darkness from her eyes.

She said, "You're nothing like him. Nothing."

He lowered his head. "Glad you realize it."

"I do." She sighed, raising her head slowly. "You should leave, Wade. You shouldn't be anywhere near me until this maniac is caught. You're making yourself a target."

"I'm not going anywhere."

She licked her lips, holding his eyes with hers. "I've kept it to myself too long. I'm going to tell Caleb, go to the police, whatever I have to do. But I don't want you getting in the way."

"We've got no choice but to tell Caleb," he said, matter-of-factly. He picked up where she had left off, stacking groceries into cupboards. "But if we go to the police, it's liable to be all over town in no time flat. The cops are just local boys with badges pinned on them. They'll tell their wives, their drinking buddies. It'll get around."

He glanced at her. She was leaning on the counter, both arms braced straight, her head hanging between them.

"Edie?"

She lifted her head slowly but didn't look at him. "I'm tired. I'm so tired of this."

"I know."

"Selene already knows something's going on."

He thought about that. "She's sensitive."

"She's downright eerie."

He smiled, glad to hear her tone lightening up marginally. "Caleb will be here any minute. I'll put on some coffee."

"Yeah. God, I don't want to deal with this." She pressed two fingers to her temple as if it ached.

"Then don't."

Her head came up, hand frozen in place beside it.

"Go upstairs, run a hot bath, dump some of that sweet-smelling stuff in it. Soak and relax. I can talk to Caleb without you backing me up."

She closed her eyes, and he knew the suggestion was tempting her. "It's my mess," she said. "I shouldn't leave you cleaning up after me all by yourself."

"Caleb and I are friends. And it's not just your mess anymore. Hasn't been since you confided it to me."

She smiled with one side of her mouth. "You keep it up and I'm going to have to start doubting your badass image, Armstrong."

"Don't even go there, woman, or I'll be forced to prove otherwise."

She sighed, hesitated, looking longingly toward the stairs, but with wariness in her eyes. "Scared to go up there all alone?" he asked.

She met his eyes and almost nodded.

"Take Sally with you. Leave the door open so I can hear you if you call."

"I seem to recall someone telling me what would happen if I left the bathroom door unlocked again," she said, her voice lowering, along with her eyes.

"Hey, I'm not gonna ravage you with your overprotective

brother-in-law in the house. What do you think I am, a cave-man?''

"Uh-huh," she said, nodding emphatically. "Caveman."

"Ugh." He swatted her on the backside as she moved past him to go up the stairs. He watched her as she smacked her lips, making kisslike noises at the dog, who jumped to attention and trotted along beside her. Who the hell could blame her? The two vanished up the stairs, and he was still staring at the empty space where they'd been when Caleb came in without knocking and strode across the living room, stopping only when he stood facing Wade in the kitchen doorway.

He said, "Okay, I'm here. So tell me what the hell's going on, Wade."

Wade nodded distractedly. "I'm in trouble," he said softly. He dragged his gaze from the empty stairway and focused on his friend. "Damn, I never even saw it coming, but I am in serious trouble."

# Chapter 12

Edie soaked. Sally lay on the floor beside the bathtub and snoozed. It was almost as if the dog sensed Edie's need to have someone close by. She had been shaken right to the core by that phone call.

And shaken, too, but in a far different way, by Wade's behavior. The way he had grabbed the phone and spoken in a deep voice that was so menacing it scared *her*. There had been something in his tone, some emotion so tenuously held in check that every syllable vibrated with a tightly restrained violence.

She shivered when she thought about it now, dunked her head and rose from the water again. The bath was supposed to relax her. It didn't. It refreshed her, and as she sat there she began to feel cowardly for hiding up here while Wade dealt with Caleb, confessed that they had been keeping dangerous secrets. Caleb would be furious, no doubt about that.

She glanced at Sally, who lifted her head expectantly. "I should go face the music, too, shouldn't I?"

The dog said something that sounded like "Roo-rah-roo."

"Yeah, that's about what I thought. All right, then." She

got out of the tub, towelled down and put her bathrobe back on. It didn't take long. She didn't fuss. She hardly ever fussed anymore. Especially anytime she thought she would be around Wade. The less fuss the better, where he was concerned. She hadn't given it conscious thought before now, but she supposed it had been deliberate. A test, in a way.

It hadn't seemed to cool his attraction to her in the least. She had expected that it would. What surprised her was how much she was *enjoying* not fussing.

God, when she thought about how long a simple bath used to take her. She would exfoliate, wax and moisturize every inch of skin. She would wash and condition every bit of hair on her head. And the after-bath rituals took even longer than the bath itself. There was the scale to face—always with a deep dread in the pit of her stomach that she might see an extra pound or two on the dial. There was her hair. She would mousse it, flip it upside down to blow it dry, then spritz it stiff. After that, she would pull on a robe and sit down at the makeup stand for at least another twenty minutes of eyebrow plucking, lash curling and face painting.

For just a minute it hit her how good it was to take a bath just for the joy of it, and to get up and pull on a big soft robe, then towel-dry her hair and not worry about it. She honest to God didn't care. Wade might. But if he did, tough. He was the one who wanted to move in here and play big bad bodyguard. She'd warned him he might get his illusions shattered. And she hoped she'd been shattering them steadily. She stuck her feet into the scruffy slippers beside the bed, let the towel hang from her head like a nun's wimple and headed down the stairs, Sally at her side.

She heard only a single phrase, spoken by Wade, but it was enough to stop her dead in her tracks. He said, "I can't stay here indefinitely."

Edie backed up a step, waiting, listening.

"Sure you can," Caleb was saying.

"No, not the way things are. It's not sane. It's not healthy. She's deluding herself if she thinks I can live under the same roof with her and not touch her. And so am I."

"You'll manage." There was a clap. She imagined Caleb's hand smacking Wade's shoulder. "I'll get the P.I. here by tomorrow. He's good, and he's discreet."

"Thanks, pal."

"You're welcome."

Edie backed up some more as Caleb and Wade came out of the kitchen into the big open area that combined the dining and living rooms. Wade walked Caleb to the door as Edie stood on the stairs, hidden in shadow, trying to analyze what she had just heard. Wade wanted her, still. He wanted her so much it was difficult for him to stay here, despite the light-hearted teasing and flirting that seemed so cavalier. She wasn't sure how she felt about that. God, she hadn't been wearing makeup or doing anything more with her hair than pulling it into a ponytail. Look at her, she thought.

And yet part of her reacted with a longing that shouldn't have surprised her as much as it did. She'd always been attracted to him, drawn to him. Even in high school.

That wasn't important now. Two things were suddenly very clear to her. First and foremost was that she didn't want him to leave. She felt safe with him here, and she hadn't before. No, she wanted him to stay. So the second thing followed— she had to make it easier for him to be around her and not desire her. She glanced down at her attire, smiled slightly. Hell, she couldn't look much worse than she did right now. If he could look at her now and get turned on, he was hopeless.

Wade closed the door when Caleb left, and as he turned, Edie came the rest of the way down the stairs to hide the fact that she'd been lurking there. He caught sight of her immediately, sent her a reassuring smile. "He just left."

"I know. I was coming down to take my share of the fall-out."

"Guess I'm just too fast for you, Edie." He met her half-way across the floor. "Besides, there was no fallout."

"He wasn't angry that we kept him in the dark so long?" she asked, lifting a brow in doubt.

"Well, he was at first. But he knows we were just trying to keep the family out of it. He's cool with that."

"Is he?" She doubted it.

"Providing I let him help, now that he does know." Taking her elbow, he led Edie to the sitting area of the living room, where his couch now held court before the giant TV, and set her down. She far preferred the cozy, if eclectic, grouping they'd put together facing the fireplace. A few odd chairs, including an antique rocker from her mother's attic, her own bowl-shaped super-sized rattan one, and Wade's favorite re-cliner. A couple of end tables, a plant stand, and it looked almost homey.

Not without a fire crackling in the hearth, though.

She sat on the sofa at his urging, and he sat opposite her. "Caleb wants to bring a P.I. friend of his down here to help us out with this."

Edie pursed her lips. "I don't think—"

"Just let me finish."

She sighed but bit her lip and held her objections off, for the moment.

"You know Caleb's background. He comes from a long line of big money and political power. This guy he wants to bring in isn't some two-bit gumshoe, Edie. He's good. And he's discreet. Wouldn't stay in business long if he wasn't, not with the kind of clients he's had."

"So you think we can trust him to keep this quiet? I don't want my sisters getting in the way of any of this, Wade. Much less Mom."

"If Caleb says we can trust him, we can trust him. He's

gonna call the guy from his office, and he'll get back to us later. Let's at least see what the fellow has to say."

Rolling her eyes, she said, "It doesn't look as if we have much choice but to hear what he has to say."

"You're mad at me." He sighed. "Well, hell, be mad at me, then. If it'll keep you alive, you can be mad at me from now till hell freezes over."

He seemed almost petulant. That changed at the sound of a loud, rumbling motor outside. He surged to his feet then, instantly protective, and went to the door to peer outside. "It's a delivery truck," he said. "You ordered something?"

"Oh, it's my equipment!" She rushed up to the door beside him. Her towel had fallen from her head and was draped around her shoulders. Excitement surged in her veins. It was so good to have something positive to think about. "Let him in, Caleb."

She ran to the room off the foyer, the one that had been a den. It was a twin of the living room, except the floor-to-peak glass window was slightly smaller. "Have them bring everything in here!" As she spoke, she moved a few stray boxes out of the way. The one containing her camera and lenses, she carried into the living room, placing it on the coffee table, out of harm's way.

The deliveryman came in, carrying a large carton, and Wade came a few steps behind him with a smaller one. Then they both went back for more. On the final trip in, the man in his brown shorts and name tag shirt—Bill, it said—looked at her with a little frown in between his brows. "Aren't you...?"

Closing her eyes, she nodded. "Yeah, I am." She felt almost apologetic for her appearance. But if that part of her life was over, she would have to get over the feeling that she had to look picture perfect any time she was seen by anyone in public. Or even in private.

He smiled at her. "You look much prettier in person, Miz. B."

She blinked so rapidly that, for a minute, the man's smile appeared in strobe. "I—I—I—thank you." She heard Wade laugh softly, so low and muffled she knew it wasn't meant for her ears.

The deliveryman smiled and headed back out the door. Baffled, she turned around to see Wade in the doorway of her soon-to-be studio, arms crossed over his chest. "That guy shouldn't be driving without his glasses," she muttered, shaking her head.

"Oh, I don't know."

"What do you mean, you don't know? You're telling me you think I look good in a baggy bathrobe with uncombed hair?"

He seemed to take that as an invitation to look at her. And he did. From her head to her toes, then back again, and she swore his eyes burned every part of her they touched. "You know, it wasn't all the makeup and skimpy clothes and big hair that made you beautiful in those magazine shots, Edie. Besides, there's something…incredibly sexy about a woman without artifice. No makeup. No fancy hairstyles. You're not even wearing any jewelry, are you?"

His voice had dropped. Deepened to a soft, velvety caress that set her nerve endings tingling. She shook her head.

He was coming closer now. "You didn't dry your hair, did you?"

She shook her head, not moving. Unable to, for some reason. Her hair was still damp, half dry, maybe, and she imagined it looked like a rat's nest.

"It curls when you let it dry all by itself. Little waves that don't have any plan or pattern to them. Especially at the ends. And there's a little frizz."

She lifted a hand to self-consciously smooth her hair.

"And then there's the robe. Honey, I hate to tell you this, but it's sexy as hell."

"I thought...it was kind of ugly."

"Just bulky," he said. He was so close now that she could feel his breath on her face. His hands came up to the wide collar of the robe, touched it. He didn't try to open it, just slid his fingers over the soft material. "Makes a guy want to slide it off. And it's patently obvious you aren't wearing anything underneath."

"You're impossible. I thought this getup would turn you off like a lightbulb."

"Is that why you came down here wearing it?"

She pursed her lips, refusing to answer.

"Keep trying. I could get to like this game." His hands had wandered upward now, to her chin, which he caught between a thumb and forefinger. "We haven't talked about what happened in the truck this morning."

She lifted her eyes to his. Big mistake. They were too intense right now. "You mean...the kiss?" Her tongue darted out to moisten her lips.

His luscious mouth curved very slightly. A sort of smile. "I liked it."

"It was an act."

He shook his head. "You liked it, too."

Yes, she had more than liked it. "No," she said. "I wasn't—"

"You liked it, too," he repeated. He moved closer, and still closer. "Say it, Edie. Tell the truth. Tell me." His lips were so close to hers now that they brushed her mouth with every word, sending shivers right up her spine.

"I liked it, too," she whispered.

"Good. 'Cause I'm gonna do it again."

"Yes."

He kissed her. At first it was just their mouths in contact, and his hand on her chin, holding her to his mouth. But then, as he tasted her, probed her with his hungry tongue, she felt him shiver. His hands moved to her shoulders, slid down her outer arms, and then locked with her hands, fingers interlacing. She felt the wall at her back. His hands pressed hers to it. And he kept on kissing her. Licking her mouth. His hips pressed against hers, and she felt him. Then he slid one leg between hers, nudging her thighs apart, the robe with them, and moved his hips against her again. His arousal pressed right into her now. She was exposed down there. And open. And damp. And he was hard and insistent, encumbered only by the jeans he wore. Rough denim. He rubbed it against her, over her.

He broke the kiss, his eyes open and blazing into hers. She saw the question he didn't voice. She didn't know the answer.

He released her hands and moved his to her hips, pushing the robe even wider to do so. Then he held her to him, grinding against her as he slid his palms up her waist, over her rib cage, until his thumbs touched the undersides of her breasts.

She was shivering, shaking with need.

"How long," he whispered, "since a man has touched you here?" His thumbs moved upward, over her nipples, then down again, up and down again. She felt them tighten and ache.

"Too long." Her voice was broken and hoarse.

"It's a crying shame." He drew his thumb and forefinger together on them. Pressure, then more. Squeezing the distended buds tight, he rolled them, pulled at them, pressing a little harder, and a little harder. "Too much?" he asked softly, his mouth at her ear, hips moving against her still.

She knew his eyes were on her face. She didn't care. It felt so good. She didn't answer; instead, she arched toward his hands, every inch of her centered where his calloused fingers held her nipples captive.

He gave a sharp pinch that made her suck in her breath as a bolt of pleasure bit through her. Then he did it again, and

she would have gone to her knees if he hadn't been holding
her up.

Very suddenly, though, he let go. His hands shot to her
sides, capturing her hands, lifting them. She was burning up,
and she didn't argue. When he placed her hands under her
breasts, lifting them, she didn't ask why. And when he
stepped away just slightly and looked at her breasts held up
that way, as if in offering, and licked his lips, her knees buckled.

"Oh, no, you don't." He slid a hand between her legs,
cupping her there to hold her upright. "Keep your hands
where they are," he told her. Then he wrapped his free arm
around her waist and tugged her away from the wall. In an
instant he was on the couch, her body across his lap. He bent
his head and latched on to one of her proffered breasts with
his mouth even as he shoved her thighs wider and drove a
finger inside her. She gasped for breath, but he didn't let up,
and she sure as hell wasn't going to ask him to. The sensations coursing through her were so intense she could barely
think or breathe. She existed for his fingers, for his mouth.
He was sucking hard now, scraping her nipple with his teeth
as his fingers moved in and out of her. And then his thumb
found her most sensitive place and pressed, rubbed, rolled,
until she was shaking all over. He kept it up, took her to the
very brink of exploding; then he pinched her pulsing kernel
between thumb and forefinger, and bit down on her nipple at
the same time. Harder, she said, out loud or in her head, she
wasn't sure, but he complied. She felt his teeth, his pinching
fingers, and she exploded in pleasure so intense she thought
she might die with it.

And then he folded her up in his arms, and he held her.
Just held her, while the ripples and waves of mind-numbing
bliss washed through her, leaving her limp and shaken and
feeling utterly vulnerable. As if he knew, he held her. Pulled

her robe tight around her body, let her curl around him and against him, and held her. No demands. Nothing.

And he hadn't even…

"Wade, you didn't—"

"Shh. Rest now. Be still."

She closed her eyes, the languor of afterglow completely enveloping her. He was so warm, his arms so strong around her. Her eyes were heavy. Leaden. "You make me feel…"

He was stroking her back, holding her close. He said nothing. He didn't have to. He wouldn't let her go; she knew it without him saying it aloud.

She wasn't sure how to finish her sentence as she drifted off to sleep. He made her feel…safe? Yes. Good? Oh God, yes. But something else. He made her feel…cherished. In a way no one else had ever done.

"Oh, yeah," Wade muttered softly as she slept in his arms. "I'm in trouble." Very gently, he managed to get off the couch without disturbing her sleep. She was really out. He didn't imagine she'd been sleeping all that much lately, with all that had been going on.

He looked at her there for a minute; then he had to close his eyes to resist waking her up in some creative fashion. Gently, he pulled her robe together around her, so she wouldn't be cold. Then he walked into the den, where all her boxes waited to be opened. He ought to be at the garage, taking care of business. Or going through his house one last time to retrieve any remnants of the life that seemed to have dissolved like sugar in hot coffee. But he wasn't going to. He unpacked her boxes instead.

He lost track of the time as he got into his task whole-heartedly. He had to go out to the truck twice for tools. He had both his toolboxes in here with him now, along with a stepladder and nail apron. He was actually enjoying figuring out how to put various lighting fixtures together, guessing what other items were for, looking around the room to try to guess where Edie would want things.

He wasn't aware he'd been at it for over two hours, and was even less aware that he was being watched—at first. Then he felt her eyes on him like a touch.

He was on a stepladder, fixing a bracket to the wall with a screwdriver, when he felt her and stopped, then turned to stare down at her. "You're dressed," he said. And of course he wanted to take the stupid statement back the minute it left his lips, but it was too late.

"You were expecting me not to be?"

He licked his lips. She wasn't quite meeting his eyes when he looked at her, and he detected the heightened color in her cheeks. He wasn't sure what to say about what had happened between them. So he decided to act as if it hadn't happened at all. "These brackets here are for those screens you ordered. You know, the ones with the various background designs on them?"

She nodded, looking around the room. "The backdrops." He wasn't sure if he saw approval in her eyes or not. She kept her expression blank. Of course, there were torn boxes and brown paper strewn everywhere. Hunks of foam packing and plastic wrap littered the floor. Long-necked poles with light fixtures on them stood in every corner of the room. They were bendable beasts that looked like something out of a vintage science fiction film, especially with the collars some of them wore. Removable, interchangeable, they ranged from shiny tinfoil to actual mirrors. And there were shades, too, like hats the lights could wear. They came in silk and other materials he hadn't identified, and in all the colors you could imagine. There was a tripod, probably for her camera, along with a case of new lenses and a supply of film. Beside that box were a pair of others he hadn't even opened. Their labels read "Dark Room Equipment."

"I didn't mess with that stuff," he said as she looked at it. "I figured it was probably chemicals and such."

She nodded, still saying nothing.

He bit his lip, waiting. Had he overstepped? Did she hate where he was putting the brackets? "Hey, I can move these if you want them in some other spot. Just say the word, it's no big deal."

"They're fine. Perfect, actually. That's exactly where I was thinking of putting them."

"Oh. Okay, then." He frowned, but she didn't speak. Finally he shrugged. "Hey, now that you're awake, I can get the power tools. This hand screwdriving action is for the birds." He dropped the small screwdriver into its slot on his tool belt and came down the stepladder.

"Wade, don't you think we ought to talk about what happened between us a little while ago?"

He stopped, on the floor now, hands on the ladder, his back to her. "I don't see any need."

"Well, I do."

He pursed his lips, tried to come up with an answer that would neither embarrass nor insult her, while protecting his own secrets. "Look, you were tense, Edie."

"I was *tense?*" The emphasis she put on the word made him cringe.

He forced himself to turn, to face her. "Are you sorry it happened?"

"Yes. No." She threw her hands up. "I don't know. Why? Are you?"

"Not in this lifetime."

Her eyes shot to his, but he looked away fast. Damn. Why couldn't he censor himself around her? "Listen, we are both attracted to each other. You've been scared to death day and night for way too long, and you were on edge. I know for a fact that a good healthy orgasm is the best thing in the world for easing tension."

Her brows went up high. "Oh, you know that for a fact, do you?"

"Well, sure I do."

"Done a lot of research on the subject, I suppose?"

He shrugged. "Some. You know, in the past, doctors used to get their female patients off as a treatment for nervous conditions."

"Did they now? Well, my goodness, this is just getting more fascinating by the minute." She leaned sideways, resting her shoulder against the wall. "Do tell."

"Well...well, it's true. I mean, women weren't expected to enjoy sex back then, so their husbands rarely took the time to try to see to it that they did. After a while the frustration would...well, hell, it was a common thing for a doctor to..." His face was getting hotter by the minute, and he couldn't even think of how the hell he'd gotten onto the subject. Much less how to get off it.

"So, in this case, you were just...playing doctor?"

He regained his composure in a hurry. "I wasn't *playing* anything."

She blinked, straightened away from the wall, and it was her turn to look uncomfortable, to avoid his eyes. "Then you were serious?"

He looked at her, opened his mouth, closed it again, and finally lifted his hands, palms up. "I don't even know what you're asking me here."

Her eyes shot to his like arrows. Stabbed just as deeply. "What did it mean, Wade?"

"What do you want it to mean?" It was a lousy answer; he knew that.

She made fists and sort of growled at him. "You're infuriating!"

"I know. Look, we both wanted it, and it happened."

"Oh, come on. You couldn't have gotten anything out of that, it was all...one-sided."

He was stunned at that statement, and for a second he said nothing at all. Then he drummed up his courage and moved closer to her. He reached out, his hand brushing her cheek, gently turning her face to his. "If you really believe that," he said, very softly, "then you are sorely deluded, lady. I was in heaven." He swallowed hard. Her eyes softened and pulled at his, and he almost leaned closer before thinking better of it. Finally he turned away. "Now I have to go get those power tools."

He strode out of the room without another word.

Hours later, she still could not believe the man. She wanted to know what the hell he was thinking, what he was feeling, besides lust. Maybe nothing. Maybe that was why he had nothing to say on the matter, because there was nothing else there. And she wanted to know why he hadn't taken the opportunity to have sex with her, when he'd been pretty damned open about the fact that he wanted to. He'd had the chance and hadn't done it, and what did that mean?

She was feeling so many things, she couldn't even begin to sort them out. She tingled every time she met his eyes, or touched him. Even a casual, accidental brush of his hand sent shivers up her spine. She was mortified at the thought of having let herself go so completely under his masterful touch, while he had apparently been in complete control the entire time. God, what must she have looked like? Sounded like? She couldn't believe she could act that way in front of him.

That would probably seem odd to him, if she said it out loud, she thought. But it shouldn't. Oh, sure, she'd been spread all over in various states of undress, in front of millions. But she'd always been in control. She had known exactly what emotions her face conveyed. She had been safely hidden behind her makeup and her image. And she had known that any flaws, no matter how slight, would be airbrushed away before anyone could see them.

This man had seen her soul, naked.

And maybe he didn't even realize it. Which made it even more humiliating.

"You're awfully quiet," Wade said as he walked beside her up the path to the back door of her family's farmhouse.

She could already hear the noise spilling from inside. Warm noise, happy noise. It flowed out with the comforting yellow light from the windows. "I just can't believe my mother invited you to dinner. She knew about your little wallpaper design at the garage, you know."

"Did she?"

He had the gall to seem unconcerned.

"Uh-huh. She didn't like it."

"Neither did Mel. She threatened to kick my ass once, unless I took your pictures down."

"She did?" The thought made her smile for some reason. "But you didn't comply, did you?"

"Nope."

"And yet all I had to do was ask you."

He shrugged. "They were your pictures."

The back door opened, preventing her from demanding a more satisfying answer, or from wondering too long just what she would consider satisfying. What did she want from him? Was she hoping he *did* feel something for her, or praying he didn't?

"Oh, they're here! Hi, you two!" Maya called from the doorway. She didn't have a baby in her arms, but that wasn't unusual. When her sisters and mother were around, Maya was rarely allowed to hold the twins for more than a moment at a time.

"Hi, Maya," Edie returned, trying to sound light, casual. "What's for dinner?"

"A nice ham, with the works. Mamma made gravy, I did the biscuits, and there's pie for dessert."

"Be still my heart," Wade muttered.

"Careful what you say, Wade," Maya said, grinning. "We have enough cholesterol here tonight to make your heart think you mean it literally."

He laughed, and the sound was so warm, so genuine, that it startled Edie. She glanced up at him sharply, because it occurred to her to wonder if she'd heard his laugh before. If she had, it hadn't been this one. This one was real.

"Hey, is that Sally out in the car?" Maya asked.

"Yeah. She hates to be left home alone," Wade said.

"Well, bring her on in. She's welcome here."

"I'll get her," Edie said. She saw Maya take Wade's arm, tugging him into the house. She saw her sisters send him warm smiles, and her mother's eyes looking genuinely glad to see him.

What the hell was up with all of this?

Sighing, she trudged back along the walk to the SUV, unlocked the back door and took the leash from the floor. "Come on, Sally girl. You've been invited to dinner."

"Roof!" Sally said, sounding overjoyed at the prospect.

Edie reached in and snapped the leash to her collar, took the end in her hand and led the dog out of the SUV. Despite the vehicle's size, Sally's forefeet hit the ground before her rear ones left the seat. Edie closed the door and started forward.

Then she stopped as a chill slid up her spine. Like a finger of ice on her back.

She quickly glanced down at the dog, hoping to see Sally looking utterly relaxed so she could tell herself she was imagining things.

Sally had gone still, too, though. Her ears were cocked forward, as much as unclipped Great Dane ears could be. Her eyes were alert, her stance stiff and tight. She was sniffing the air, and growling deep and low in her throat.

"It's all right, girl."

She looked around, the lawn, the road, the woods on the

opposite side. He could be anywhere. Sighing, she led the
dog forward, tried to shake off the feeling of impending
doom. Aloud, in a voice intended to project, she said, "One
of these times, I'll just let you go tear the bastard to bits. It
would make my life simpler."

Sally kept looking back toward the road, growling, tugging
a little.

"Or maybe I'll just buy an Uzi and start peppering the
entire area. What do you think, girl? You just look toward
the sick bastard and growl, and I'll point and shoot. Hmm?"

"Edie?"

It was Caleb. He'd come out the back door and was heading
toward her. She met him halfway. "Hi, Caleb. What's up?"

"Everything okay out here?" As he asked the question, he
looked past her, toward the woods across the road.

Whatever had been there was gone now. That sense, that
prickling awareness, had vanished as soon as Caleb had come
outside. Sally had stopped growling, too. "I just get jittery
sometimes," she said. She did not want to see Caleb go loping off into the woods, unarmed, after a lunatic. "But there's
no one around out here."

"You sure?"

She nodded.

Caleb took her arm and led her toward the house. "Wade
was pretty much under siege from the second he got in, but
he sent me out after you."

"Under siege?"

"He's suddenly a very popular guy with our family." He
opened the door, and she stepped inside, saw everyone gathered in the living room, all cozy, chatting like old friends.

"I noticed that," Edie said softly as Caleb came in and
closed the door. "Any idea why?"

"Maya won't say a thing. She doesn't need to, though. It's
fairly obvious they have him picked out as the next Brand-
in-law."

Her jaw dropped, and she blinked rapidly. He was right; that was exactly the way the family was acting. "Oh my God," she whispered.

"What did you expect them to think?" Caleb asked. "Short of telling them the real reason you two are living together, I don't see how you can change this. Might as well play along."

"This has to end," she muttered. "This absolutely has to end."

# *Chapter 13*

Edie hadn't liked it when Wade had refused to leave her home alone the next morning. He had to go into town, he said. The garage needed his attention. Her car was probably done, and he also had to be sure his house was ready for its new owners, who would be moving in within a couple of days.

He wanted her to go with him. She wanted to stay home and try out her new equipment. Ever since it had arrived, she'd been getting a steady stream of ideas, and suddenly she was excited about the new direction in her life.

But, of course, Wade had been stubborn, and no, leaving Sally there to guard her would not be sufficient. Fortunately Kara had shown up in the nick of time, saving her from any further arguments. Wade wasn't fully satisfied with Kara's presence. But it seemed to ease his mind marginally. He promised to be back soon, made Edie promise to call if anything felt off. And then he left.

Kara wore jeans with tapered ankles and a sweatshirt that read Where In The World Is Big Falls, Oklahoma? Her long, dark hair was caught up in its usual ponytail, and she looked rather troubled as she watched Wade's oversize tow truck wheel out the driveway.

"He's so protective of you," she said. "It's just about the sweetest thing I've ever seen."

"Yeah, he's a real sweetheart." Kara sent her an odd look, and Edie covered quickly, grabbed her sister's hand and tugged her toward her studio. "Come here, you've got to see this."

Kara came along, then paused and looked around the room. "Wow. You're really gonna do it, aren't you?"

"Yeah. Yeah, I think I am. I've always loved taking pictures. I mean, it was only a hobby, but I couldn't help but learn a lot about photography with all the time I spent in front of the camera. And...and you know, I think I'm pretty good."

Kara smiled at her. "Is Mom ever wrong about anything?"

Edie sighed. "No, not really. Irritating as hell, isn't it?"

"Watch your mouth, young lady," Kara said, her tone mimicking her mother's.

They both laughed. Kara's smile died first, though, and she looked pensive and nervous again.

"Okay, so you wanna tell me what's wrong, or do I have to guess?"

Her sister shook her head. "Nothing, really. I just...thought maybe you could help me figure out what's wrong with me."

Edie blinked. "What's wrong with you? Kara, there's nothing wrong with you. What are you talking about?"

Kara shook her head, then lifted her arms expressively and looked down at herself. "I'm like the ugly duckling in a family of swans. I trip over my feet. I look horrible in everything I put on. I'm too tall, too skinny and too clumsy. I'm sick of it."

Smiling slowly, Edie took Kara's hand in hers and led her out of the studio, back into the living room and then up the stairs to her bedroom. Sally lifted her head to watch them walk past but didn't get up from her spot on the rug in front of the fireplace. In the bedroom, Edie marched Kara up to a full-length mirror and stood beside her. "Now look in that mirror."

Kara looked; then she grimaced.

"Kara. Come on, stand up straight. You slouch all the time. Come on."

She straightened slowly.

"See that? You and I are just about the exact same height. I think I may be a half inch taller. That's all."

Kara blinked. "We are, aren't we?"

"Uh-huh. And you're not too skinny. I'll bet we weigh close to the same amount. And I've put on weight since I was modeling. So now, tell me you're too tall and too skinny when you are the height and weight of a famous ex-lingerie model."

Kara frowned. "I don't understand."

"Of course you don't. That's because you see yourself as gangly and unattractive, not because you are. Look at our faces. Look at me. I'm not wearing any makeup. Look at you. Your nose. Your eyes. Your cheekbones. Anyone could tell from fifty feet away that we're sisters. Except for coloring, we're very similar."

Lifting a tentative hand, Kara touched her own cheek, staring at her reflection intently now.

"Wanna have some fun, Kara?"

Kara looked at her uncertainly.

"Let's make you a model for a day, hmm?"

"Oh, I couldn't...."

"It'll be just like playing dress up when we were kids. And it'll give me a chance to try out my new studio. Come on, Kara, please?"

Kara sighed, and Edie knew she had won.

She gave her sister the full treatment, hair, makeup. Then, on a whim, she made herself up, as well. She dug through her closets, pulling all the high-fashion suits and dresses and accessories from the depths, and hauling all of it down to the studio. And then she posed Kara, and shot frame after frame. She shot Kara alone, Kara with Sally, and herself and Kara side by side. That was so much fun they did it again and again, changing outfits and hairstyles, adding wigs and hats, posing in silly, crazy ways, while Edie experimented with the lighting. They even put a feather boa and a wide-brimmed hat on Sally, and shot her over and over.

They had a blast, and by the time they finished, several rolls of film were used up, and they were both exhausted from laughing so hard. They picked up the studio, then collapsed on the sofa in the living room.

"Wait till you see them, Kara. You'll realize you're a full-blown beauty."

"That won't change the fact that I trip over my feet."

"So you take a ballet class or yoga or something. If you even need to. My own theory is, once you stop thinking of yourself as an unattractive klutz, you'll be as graceful as anyone."

Kara sighed, thinking hard about that. "And what about the jinx thing?"

"There is no jinx thing, Kara. It's all in your head."

"Every man who gets close to me gets seriously injured in a freak accident of some sort! That's not in my head."

Drawing a deep breath, Edie sighed. "Probably just a string of bad luck, or coincidences, then. And even if it wasn't, Selene could probably fix you up with some kind of charm or talisman that would help."

"So she keeps saying," Kara said.

Edie sighed. She glanced at her sister. "You like that outfit?"

"It's gorgeous," Kara said. She was wearing a floral print summer dress with a flared skirt and draping V-neck collar. "It makes me feel almost...petite."

"The right clothes will make a world of difference. We

should go shopping, you and I. Get you a whole new ward-
robe.''

"I shouldn't need one," Kara said. "You don't. You look
as good in jeans and a T-shirt as you do in designer clothes.''

"That's only because I feel just as good in jeans as I do
in designer wear. It's because I have confidence. When you
look good enough for long enough, you will, too. You just
have to build up your self-esteem.''

"Really?''

Edie nodded. "Yeah. And remember that it isn't what's on
the outside that counts. I had all that licked years ago, and
here I am, starting all over, trying to figure out who I am
underneath it. And what that person wants to do with the rest
of her life.''

Sighing, Kara looked at her watch. The morning had rushed
past, Edie realized. It was early afternoon. "You can go, if
you want. Wade will be back any minute.''

"You sure? He didn't seem to think you should be by
yourself today.''

"He's nuts. I was by myself for years in L.A. Go ahead,
if you need to.''

"I did tell Mel I'd help her wash the cars this afternoon.''

"Not in that dress, I hope.''

"No way.'' Kara got to her feet, started rushing for the
door.

"Slow down, sis,'' Edie said. And when Kara glanced back
at her, she went on. "You're always hurrying everywhere. No
wonder you trip yourself up a lot. Walk slowly, deliberately,
as if you know exactly where you're going and have all the
time in the world to get there. And stand up straight.''

Sighing, Kara straightened and walked slowly toward the
door. She was stiff in the heels, a little wobbly, but she would
get it in time. She paused by a chair where the clothes she'd
arrived in were piled and picked them up. Edie would rather

have burned them, but she couldn't say so. A little at a time, she thought.

She watched her sister get into her car and pull away, and smiled, thinking she now had two projects going. Her studio and her sister's new image.

Halfway down the twisting, mountain road from Edie's house, Kara saw a car off the side of the road and a man standing in the middle, waving his arms. She stopped to see if she could help.

Wade had spent two hours getting up to speed at the shop, and another three at the house, where he wound up helping Tommy move some of his larger items in, including a pretty little baby bassinet. White wicker, with a frilly hood. Tiny mattress pad inside.

Cute.

He couldn't believe, however, that his weight room was about to become a nursery.

He got home at five. Home? He told himself to knock it off already and focused on parking Edie's car. He'd decided to drive it back from the shop, since the repairs were finished. She could drive him into town the next morning and drop him off, and then he could bring his own vehicle home tomorrow night.

Home. Hell, there he went again. It was a little soon to be thinking of Edie's house that way, wasn't it? But it felt like home.

He tensed a little when he didn't see the car Kara had been driving earlier in the driveway. Maybe she'd only just left. He hoped so.

He shut the car off and walked inside. The door was locked, so that was a good sign. At least Edie was exercising a hint of caution. Not that he'd expected otherwise. She was scared half to death.

Using his key, he opened the door, stepped inside, looked around. "Edie?"

There were clothes scattered around. On the furniture, on the floor. Edie didn't answer. "Hon, where are you?"

Still no answer. He moved through the house quickly, his heart in his throat. Her studio was empty, as were the other rooms on this floor. He ran upstairs and searched it in about a minute flat. Still no sign of her. Pounding back down the stairs, he ran for the phone, halfway to dialing nine-one-one, when he heard a thump that seemed to be coming from her studio.

He set the phone down and ran in there. And finally he noticed the red scarf tied to the doorknob of the closet she had said she was going to use as a darkroom.

Sighing, he walked up to the door, tapped on it. "Edie? You in there?"

"Yeah, just a sec."

He waited patiently for his heart to return to its normal rhythm. Then she opened the door.

The closet was big, formerly a walk-in number, but the fumes were terrible, and he resolved to get some kind of ventilation system installed before another day passed. She was wearing a painter's mask that probably did very little good. She had pans full of chemicals on a shelf, and photos hanging everywhere. She'd been busy.

"You're later than I expected," she said, reaching past him to flip on a light switch.

"So you decided to scare me half to death so I'd call next time?"

She frowned at him.

"I searched the entire house, Edie. When I couldn't find you, I was afraid..."

Her frown vanished. "Oh, Wade. I'm sorry, I didn't think. I was just so excited to see how I did. Look at this, look." She pointed at a photo hanging to dry. He looked. It was his

Sally, wearing a goofy hat and feather boa. And he'd be damned if she didn't look as if she were mugging for the camera.

"That's pretty undignified," he grumbled.

"It's gorgeous. She's a natural. I took a bunch of her. And Kara, too. Look."

He did, and then he looked again, squinting this time. "That's Kara?"

"Of course that's Kara. She's gorgeous. She just doesn't know it."

"She looks more like you than I realized." He smiled. "Has she seen these?"

"Not yet. I can't wait to show her."

"It's gonna change the way she sees herself, I'll bet."

Edie tilted her head, studied his face. "You think?"

"Sure."

"In what way?"

He shrugged. "Well, she doesn't seem to think of herself as particularly beautiful or sexy." Then he shook his head. "Of course, I would expect any younger sister of yours to have trouble with her self-image."

Her brows went up; her lips parted.

"Don't be offended," he said. "It's just that you're a lot to live up to. You know?"

"There's more to me than the way I look."

"You still think I don't know that?"

"Do you?"

He frowned at her. "Can we get out of here? It stinks to high heaven."

She nodded, looking back at her photos. The phone rang. "In a minute. Get that for me, will you?"

He headed out of the little darkroom, through the studio and into the living room, thinking on the way that she would need a phone in her studio. Probably a separate line. She should have space for an office, and a red light for that dark room so people would know when not to open the door. Also that ventilation he'd been thinking about. Hell, there was enough work here to keep him busy for months.

He picked up the phone. Vidalia Brand said, "Well, hello, Wade, hon. How are you?"

"Just fine, Vi, just fine. Yourself?"

"Couldn't be better, but I seem to be short a daughter. Is Kara still there?"

"Nope. She must be on her way home."

"All right, then, I suppose she'll get here shortly. You give Edie my love, all right?"

"Will do, Vi."

He could almost see her smile through the phone lines. The woman liked him. It made him feel kind of warm and mushy. She disconnected, and he headed back to the dark-room.

"It was your mother," he said. "She was looking for Kara."

Edie backed away from the photo she'd been staring at. "She isn't home yet?"

"No. Why? When did she leave here?"

"Two hours ag—oh, no."

"What? What is it?" He didn't like the way her voice had gone soft, or the way her eyes had widened and were fixed now on the photo.

"Look, look at this!"

He leaned over her and looked. It was a photo of Kara and Edie, posing in full makeup and big hair, back to back, facing the camera, arms crossed over their chests. It was a great shot. A fantastic shot. "I don't see—"

"The window behind us. Look."

He looked. A man's face peered through the window in the background of the photograph.

"He was here," she said softly. "He was here, and now Kara is missing." Her eyes shot to Wade's. "Oh God, Wade, what if—"

The doorbell chimed. He took Edie's hand, held it tight in his, drew her close to him and looked her dead in the eye. "I'm not gonna let anything happen to your sister. You hear me?"

She nodded, but he wasn't sure if it helped. The doorbell rang again, so he drew her with him through the studio to the front door. When he whipped it open, he was ready for a fight.

Caleb stood there, though, a tall stranger at his side.

"Hey, Wade. This is the P.I. I told you about," Caleb said. "Alexander Stone, Wade Armstrong."

"Thank God," Edie said. "You're just in time."

It was, Alex Stone assured her, too late for discretion. Edie agreed with the slate-eyed stranger, and fifteen minutes later the State Police were in the driveway and her entire family was in her living room. All of them demanding answers.

"I can't believe you had some lunatic after you and you didn't tell us," Vidalia said. Her eyes were wet with worry, her tone harsh. "Especially once you realized he'd followed you back here."

"I know. I'm sorry. I should have...I just..."

"Hold on now," Wade said, drawing Edie close to his side, his arm around her shoulders almost protectively. "Edie bought the house and moved into it because she thought it would draw this guy away from the rest of the family. She didn't tell you because she knew you'd want to get involved, and she was afraid you'd be at risk if you did."

"They would have been better off knowing," Edie said softly, her head hanging, eyes burning. "If Kara had known there was a risk..."

"He's not going to hurt her," Selene said. She had been sitting silently in the rocking chair until now. She looked up with her round, pale blue eyes. "It's Edie he wants. Not Kara. He has no problem with Kara."

"This is ridiculous. Why are we just sitting here?" Mel barked. She was pacing, pushing one hand over and over through her short dark hair. "We should be out there looking for her!"

Alex Stone glanced up from the front door, where he stood speaking to a uniformed cop. He nodded to the man, who left; then he came up the shallow steps from the foyer into the living room with the others. "You left someone at your house, ma'am, in case Kara shows up there or tries to call?"

Vidalia nodded. "Maya's there with the babies. Caleb went back over to join her."

"Good." He looked at Edie, who stood, restless and frightened, then at Mel, who was wearing a rut in the floor with her pacing. "Look, the State Police have set up roadblocks. This man has no reason to harm Kara."

"This man has no *reason,* period," Mel snapped. "He's a maniac."

The man nodded. "Yes, but a maniac with a goal. He wants Edie."

"He'll contact her," Selene said softly.

Everyone looked at her. The second she said it, the phone rang, and Edie was so startled she thought her heart would explode at the sound. Wade held her tighter, searched her face. "I can get it...."

"No," Edie said. "It's me. I..." Swallowing hard as the shrill sound came again, Edie went and picked it up. The police were supposed to be putting wiretaps on her phone lines, but they hadn't had time yet. They wouldn't be able to trace...

"Hello?"

"Ms. Brand? This is Lieutenant Daniels. We've found your sister's car."

She blinked, shocked at the sound of the male voice—it wasn't the one she had expected. Then she realized what he'd said and looked toward Wade. "They...found Kara's car."

Wade took the phone from her hand, spoke briefly, then hung up. "Okay, they found Kara's car hidden along the edge of one of the side roads. About halfway down. It had been driven into the brush there."

Edie couldn't speak. She couldn't form the question in her mind.

"Was there anything in the car?" Vidalia asked. "Or anyone?"

"No, nothing."

"I'm going to head down there, take a look for myself," Alex Stone said, heading for the door.

"I'm going with you."

He glanced back at Mel. "There's nothing you can do, Miss—"

"But there's something *you* can do?" Mel shook her head. "If the police miss anything, Stone, I'm far more likely to spot it than some buttoned-up city slicker."

His face hardened a little. "I'm a trained professional, Ms. Brand. I know how to study a crime scene."

"I know the woods. I know the car. I know the road. I know my sister." She strode to the door, yanked it open. "So are you driving or am I?"

He sighed, giving up, shook his head and walked to the door. "I am."

Sighing, Edie turned and went into her studio without a word to anyone. She saw her mother send Wade a glance as she left, and she knew he was coming after her.

"Where are you going?" he asked softly, catching up, hands on her shoulders.

"I can't face them. My God, Wade, this is my fault."

"How the hell do you figure that?" His eyes searched hers, and she saw the worry in them, the caring.

"I'm the one who posed for those magazine shots. I'm the one who drove this man over the edge, made myself a target, put myself right in front of him."

"It's your fault he became obsessed with you? Well, hell, then we may as well blame every rape victim and every battered wife, while we're at it."

"It's different."

"No, it's not. No one is responsible for this guy's behavior but him. Dammit, Edie, there is no man on the planet who fell for you harder than I did, and you don't see me going around kidnapping your sisters, do you?"

She blinked, staring up at him, shocked by his words, and not fully understanding what he meant by them.

He lowered his head, turning away. "I shouldn't have said that. Not now. I'm sorry."

"Wade, I—"

"Don't. Just...where were you going?"

"To the darkroom. I thought I'd try to enhance the photo. See if I could get a better look at his face, or..."

"Good idea. You do that. I'll handle things out here."

"But...don't you think we should—" Then she shook her head. "No, you're right. We...later."

"Yell if you need me. I'll leave the studio door open." He walked in with her, checked the windows to be sure they were locked, then called Sally in, as well. "Stay," he told the dog.

She obediently lay down near the door. Edie watched him moving around the studio. She didn't want him to go. She wanted to make him explain what the hell he'd meant by that remark he'd made moments ago. But she couldn't ask. Not now, with her sister in danger. Not now, when she didn't know how he would answer her and was even less sure how she wanted him to answer.

She stood there, hand on the darkroom door. He looked at her as if about to say something. Then he seemed to think better of it and started out of the room.

She lurched forward, caught his upper arm and spun him around. He looked at her, a frown bending his brows. Edie rose up and pressed her mouth to his. He reacted with a start of surprise; then his arms curled around her waist, and he bent a little, kissed her back, held her close.

She didn't want to let go, but eventually she released her grip on his neck. Lifting his head, he stared down at her face. "What was all that about?"

"I..." She closed her eyes, stepping away from him. "I'm just so glad you're here right now."

He lifted his brows a little but quickly hid any other response before it could show on his face. "I'm here. And I'm not going anywhere."

She swallowed hard, looking away quickly, because she knew she wasn't as good at hiding her emotions as he was.

Too late, though. "What? What is it?"

She drew a breath. "I heard you telling Caleb you couldn't stay here indefinitely."

He smiled a little self-deprecatingly. "Call me fickle. I'm here for as long as you need me to be, Edie."

"Even if it's unhealthy? Insane?"

"Even if." He leaned in, kissed her on the tip of her nose. "Now go play with your photo and see what you can do."

She nodded, turned and hurried into the darkroom. Once inside, she leaned back against the door. He touched her with the most incredible tenderness—as if he cherished her. He treated her intimately. Maybe he did feel something more than desire for her after all.

Sighing, she got to work on the photo.

A long while later, she was staring at the blown-up shot she'd isolated of the stalker's head. He wore a black ski mask. It was too blurred to make out details, but that didn't matter. What did matter was that his hand was beside his head, and in his hand was a white square that looked like a folded piece of paper. The way he held it, the way those eyes from behind his black ski mask seemed to be looking directly into the camera lens; it was almost as if he were posing. As if he *wanted* her to know he was there. Along with the paper.

She went to work again, focusing on it and it alone, blowing it up until she could barely make out the lines of blue ink on its surface. Lines that seemed to spell out the first two letters of her name.

It was a note, and it was for her. Blinking, she flipped on her light and opened the darkroom door. Sally lifted her head and looked at her expectantly. Glancing to the left, Edie saw the open studio door, the steps up and the living room beyond. Wade was out there, holding hands with her mother, speaking softly to Selene. They were drinking something, and she smelled cocoa and realized he was doing everything he could think of to comfort her mother and her sister. God, he was something.

She stepped into the studio, ducked past the open door quickly, silently, and went to the far window, where she had captured the image of her stalker. Leaning close, she looked outside. It would be dark very soon. But it was still light enough for her to see the white square of paper. He'd tucked it into the window frame. She opened the window carefully, reached out and pulled the paper free, careful to touch as little of it as possible.

Then, unfolding it with hands that shook so much she could barely control them, she read the note.

Hello, my pet. It's been a long time. You've made me very angry, you know. Letting another man be with you. Touch you. You've been a very bad girl, but I suppose you know that. Maybe you crave the punishment I am now forced to apply. Maybe you're simply foolish. Either way, you've left me with no choice, pet. I'm going to have to hurt you. Badly. I'm going to have to inflict a great deal of pain and suffering on you. I wouldn't be doing my job if I did less.

You belong to me. You have violated my trust. You will be punished. And you will submit to the suffering you have earned and you will thank me for it, or your sister will have to bear it in your place. And I won't be as careful with her. Permanent damage is irrelevant where she's concerned. She's not my property. You are.

I will be waiting for you at midnight. There's an old barn on the road that runs past the falls. I'm sure you know the one. You will be alone there. You'll wear the black teddy—you know the one I mean. I will know if anyone else is there. And if you disobey so much as a single order I give you, your sister will suffer beyond anything you can imagine.

Always,
Your loving Owner

Edie blinked down at the note as tears rose up to distort her vision. She wasn't afraid, not for herself, not anymore. She was scared to death for Kara, though. Lifting her head at the sound of Wade's voice, she glanced back out toward the living room. How the hell was she going to do this? Get out of here, alone, without letting anyone know her reasons why? Wade would never let her do this alone. No more than her mother or her sisters would.

She quickly folded the paper, tucked it into her jeans pocket. Then she hurried back into the darkroom and took the photographs that had shown her the note, tore them into tiny bits and dropped them into a wastebasket. Finally she drew a breath, lifted her chin, and walked back into the foyer and up to the living room.

Wade met her at the top of the steps, his expression warm, his hands familiar as they touched her arms. "Any luck?"

"No. I didn't find anything at all."

"It was worth a try."

She nodded, looking around the room and wondering if the man was watching her even now. She felt exposed. Vulnerable.

"You're shivering," Wade said, pulling her into a gentle hug, warming her with his body. "It'll be okay. I promise it will."

She nodded against his chest. "It has to be."

## Chapter 14

It was killing Wade not to be *doing* something. He wanted to join the cops at one of the roadblocks, search the vehicles that came by, hand out flyers with Kara's face on them, something. Anything.

Alexander Stone, the designer-suit-clad P.I., and Mel had returned to the house. Selene and Vidalia Brand had gone back to their own, exhausted and worried to the point of being physically sick with it. Damn, Wade wanted to help them. To make it better for them. But he felt impotent.

The four of them were huddled in the kitchen, warming themselves at their coffee mugs like refugees from a blizzard. It didn't matter that it was spring outside. What was happening was cold. Brutally so.

"I don't understand why he hasn't contacted you by now," Alex said. Wade noticed the way he was watching Edie's face as he spoke. Carefully, and closely.

"I'm afraid I don't follow," she said, but she looked away. Averted her eyes in a very un-Edie-like manner.

"Sure you do. He took your sister to get to you. That's only gonna work if he contacts you to tell you what you have to do to get her back."

"Well, he hasn't."

"Are you sure?"

Edie shot her eyes to Alex's. "Are you calling me a liar, Mr. Stone?"

"Whoa, whoa, hold on a minute here," Wade said, cutting in. "Stone, you don't have any way of knowing this, but you're looking at one tight family here. Edie would cut off a limb for any one of her sisters."

"That's what I'm afraid of."

Wade blinked. Mel, who'd been glaring at Alex, suddenly shifted her eyes to Edie. "You keeping secrets, sis?"

"How can you ask me that?" Edie said. And it occurred to Wade that it wasn't an answer.

"How can I not? You kept this whole thing to yourself until you had no other choice. It makes me wonder what else you aren't telling the family, you know?"

Edie shot to her feet, and so did Mel. They glared at each other across the table. Edie blinked first, turned away. "I'm going up to my room." She shoved her chair out of the way and stomped out of the kitchen.

"The hell you are," Mel shot back, shoving her own chair aside and lunging after her.

Wade and Alex got to their feet, too. Wade made it to the living room in time to see Mel grip Edie's upper arm and jerk her around.

"You tell me what you're keeping from me, Edie, or I swear I'll—"

Wade was there in a heartbeat. He put his hand on Mel's, removed it from Edie's arm. "Leave her alone."

"You stay out of this, Armstrong. This is a family matter." She shot a look at Edie. "Kara is my sister too, dammit."

"Yeah. But the guy who took her is *my* stalker."

"What the hell difference does that make?"

Edie set her jaw, turned her back on Mel and strode away up the stairs.

"Damn you, Edain Brand!" Mel shouted after her.

Wade squeezed Mel's shoulder. "Just let her be. She's shaken up. She needs time."

Turning slowly to face him, Mel shook her head. "She's hiding something! Dammit, Wade, can't you see that in her face?" Wade said nothing, so Mel looked beyond him, seeking help from the stranger. "You wanna back me up on this, or are you just gonna stand there taking up space?"

Alex Stone cleared his throat, stepped forward. "I would watch her very closely tonight if I were you, Wade. I don't know the girl well enough to know if she's lying, but her sister certainly ought to."

"Right through her teeth," Mel said.

"Go home. I'll deal with it."

Crossing her arms over her chest, Melusine Brand lifted her chin. "I'm not going anywhere, Armstrong. If she decides to go off on some half-baked rescue mission all by herself, you're gonna need all the help you can get."

"I'll watch her all night. She's not going anywhere."

"You're underestimating her. If she has her mind set to do it, she'll find a way."

Behind him, Alex made a sound that was a cross between a snort and a laugh. Mel's attention shot to him. "Sorry," he said quickly. "I'm not—you make her sound like some kind of superhero or something. What do you think she is, Wonder Woman?"

"She's a Brand woman," Mel said. "And that's plenty."

Stone stopped smiling, swallowed hard.

"You can have the sofa," Mel said to Alex. "Not to sleep on, just to relax while you keep the front door under watch. I'll go find a comfortable spot near the back door." Even as she said it, she yanked a blanket and a throw pillow off the sofa, and strode away.

Alex met Wade's eyes. "Man," Alex muttered, "I pity the poor slob who winds up with *that* woman someday."

Wade shook his head. "Mel? She's not at all like she seems."

"No?"

"Nope. She's worse." Then he smiled a little. "But she grows on you."

"Fortunately I won't be here that long."

Sighing, Wade changed the subject. "You really think Edie's keeping something from us?"

"The perp should have made contact by now. Is there any way he could have called her without you knowing it?"

Wade thought carefully, finally shaking his head. "No, that phone hasn't rung once that I didn't know who was on the other end."

"E-mail?"

"She doesn't have a computer. I do, but she hasn't used it."

Alex shook his head slowly. "There was no note in Kara Brand's car. I'd have expected him to leave one there, if nothing else. But nada." He shrugged. "Maybe she's telling the truth. Either way, Wade, stay close to her tonight. And stay awake, just in case."

"Will do."

Feeling as if he were facing the longest night of his life, Wade headed up the stairs. He didn't even bother going to his own bedroom. He went, instead, to Edie's. And her door wasn't locked, so he opened it and stepped inside.

Edie was sitting on the floor in front of her open chest of drawers, a pile of lacy fabric beside her. She had to dig. She didn't own the pieces she wore in the shoots. But she had been given many items from the catalogue over the years. She'd bought others. Never had much call to wear them, however.

She finally found what she was looking for. A black teddy

similar to the one she'd worn in the shoot that seemed to be her lunatic's focus. She hoped it would be close enough.

"You okay?"

The deep voice—Wade's voice—came from behind her. Her back was to him. She shoved the black teddy underneath her blouse, wrapped her arms around her waist to hide it there and turned to look up at him. "Yeah. I'm okay."

His eyes looked doubtful. Then curious as they skimmed over the pile of lingerie on the floor. "Dare I hope you're getting dressed up just for me?" He said it lightly, an attempt to tease her into a smile or a little banter.

"That's not who I am," she muttered.

"And you still think I don't know that." It wasn't a question. He moved closer, finally sitting himself down on the floor opposite her. "You probably haven't even worn most of these things. Oh, you might someday, for the love of your life, in the privacy of your bedroom. But the sex kitten in the pages of *Vanessa's Whisper* was a role you played. Like an actress. And maybe you were a little too convincing for this nutcase out there to understand that it wasn't real. But you have to remember, Edie, I knew you before."

She met his eyes. "Yeah," she said very softly. "You did. Tell me something. Truthfully, Wade, what did you think of me back then?"

He looked a little alarmed. "What do you mean?"

She sighed, a deep, tired sigh. "I've been playing that role for so long, I started to forget what else I was. It's coming back to me now. Now that I'm home, with my family. This house, and the photography, and...and you. But I want to know—maybe I even *need* to know—how you really see me."

He licked his lips, drew a deep breath. "In high school, I thought you were damn near perfect. Not just the way you looked. The sound of your voice. Your laugh. Your walk. But I also thought you were full of yourself. Hanging out with the popular crowd. Looking right through me. I wasn't even sure you knew I existed.''

She stared at him for a long moment, realizing that the admission hadn't been an easy one for him. "I did, you know.''

He shook his head.

"All the girls in my crowd did. You...well, you had this reputation.''

"Of being trash. The son of trash. The guy most likely to fail. A loser.''

"Is that what you think?''

He nodded.

"It's not what we thought of you.''

"No?''

She shook her head slowly. They were sitting on the floor, legs crossed, facing each other. "You were considered the hottest guy in town. But also the most dangerous.''

"By whom?'' he asked her, his eyes fixed to hers.

She lowered hers. "My crowd. My friends.'' She paused. "Me.''

His brows were arched when she peered up at him.

"It was rumored you could convince any girl to have sex with you and you only needed one date to do it. It was common knowledge that no girl could say no to you.''

He smiled widely. "And you believed that?''

She shrugged. "I was raised to believe keeping my virginity intact until graduation, if not marriage, was essential if I wanted to get into heaven. And I was sure that if I spent any time with you at all, I'd be doomed to hell.''

Her voice had softened. Deepened. His smile died.

"So I looked at you. God, I looked at you a lot. But only when you weren't looking back. And I avoided you in every way I could think of. And then I went home and dreamed about what it might be like if I weren't such a good girl.''

When he spoke, his voice was hoarse and choked. "I thought you detested me."

"I didn't. In a way, you were my sexual fantasy long before I was yours."

"Not quite, hon. You were already mine. Way before you posed for any magazine ad." He reached out and tugged the teddy from underneath her blouse. "And you don't need this. Not for me."

"No?"

He hesitated for a long moment. Then he finally said, "Do you really want to know how I see you, Edie?"

She nodded wordlessly.

"Maybe it's time I showed you, then." He rose slowly to his feet. Reached a hand down to her. "Come with me for a second."

She took his hand and let him pull her to her feet. He led her out of the room, into the hall, down it to his bedroom, and then inside. He took her to the bed and nodded at her to sit down. She did. He knelt in front of her and reached underneath the bed. He pulled out a large, rectangular cardboard box, only an inch or two deep. Then he stood it up on one end and peeled the front away, revealing a canvas, a painting.

It was a painting she should recognize, she thought. A classic image of a beautiful woman standing magically on the surface of a dark sea. She was nude, except for the sheer fabric draped over her thighs and billowing out behind her in the sea wind. She had seen this piece before. Everything in it was the same...except for the woman. The woman wasn't the woman in the original piece. It was her. It was Edie.

She blinked in complete shock, her gaze shooting to his. "What...how...?"

"The original was called *Evening Mood.* It's by Bouguereau. A print of it used to hang in the library in town. It always struck me. One of your layouts made me think of this painting. And something about the tilt of your head—" He gave his own head a shake. "I couldn't get the idea out of my mind. So I found an artist and hired him to do this."

She was still not saying anything. She couldn't find words.

"No one knew. No one's ever seen it but me." Then he lowered his head. "I guess it seems pretty foolish. Call it a whim. But this is how I see you. How I've always seen you. As something...more."

She was still staring at the woman in the portrait. She was beautiful, her nudity awe-inspiring and lovely. Not dirty.

Shifting his weight from one foot to the other, Wade leaned the painting against the wall and started to put the cardboard cover on it again.

Edie reached out and caught his wrist, tugged him toward her. She slid her arms around his neck, then leaned up and kissed him.

He kissed her back, twisting his arms around her waist and holding her close. But then he stopped, lifted his head away, frowning at her. "You're crying...."

"No, I'm not." She leaned in again.

He held her off. "Yes, you are. Why, Edie?"

Sniffling, she shook her head. "I don't know. A hundred reasons. I don't know."

"Is it Kara?"

She shook her head. "Kara's going to be fine." She was sure of that now. She glanced at the clock on his nightstand. An hour and a half until midnight. It wasn't long enough. Why the hell had she waited so long?

Pulling herself gently from his arms, she walked back across his bedroom, closed the door, turned the lock.

He stared at her, and she knew he was confused by her changed attitude toward him. She wasn't sure what was behind it herself, but she knew that later tonight she might very well have to bear the hands of some other man on her. A man who saw her only as the sum total of all her airbrushed images on glossy pages. Even if she gave him what he wanted, he would hurt her, but he would let her sister go. So she would do what she had to.

But first she wanted to know the touch of a man who saw her as something more. And finally she realized without any doubt that this man did see her as something more. And maybe he always had.

She took her clothes off, piece by piece, as she walked back toward Wade. Her blouse. Her bra. She was bold, utterly unconcerned. She slid out of her jeans, her panties. His breaths came shorter and faster as she walked up to him, tugged his shirt from his jeans and started on the buttons.

He put his hands on her shoulders. Breathed her name and let her undress him, in between kissing her face, her neck, her shoulders. When his chest was bare, he scooped her up in his arms, and then he laid her on the bed. She lay naked, on her back, and he stretched out beside her on his side, head propped on his hand, elbow to the mattress, so he could look at her. Look at every part of her.

"No fake tan," she said softly. "No double-stick tape keeping my breasts standing at attention even when I'm lying on my back. No baby oil coating my skin."

"Thank God," he whispered, leaning down, kissing her breasts, tasting them.

"You're not disappointed?"

He trailed a hand over her chest, down her belly, dragged his fingers across her thighs and brushed them over her center. Then he lingered there, touching, parting. "Know why I kept those pictures all this time, Edie Brand?" he asked her. He stroked, and she shivered. "Because the real thing was out of reach. Like staring at glass and wishing for a diamond. The glass is perfectly clear. It's the flaws in the diamond that let you know it's real." He stroked again, his breath wafting over her nipple as he spoke. "Perfection is boring."

Her breath stuttered out of her as he touched her, played her like an instrument.

"Relax, baby. Let me take care of you." His fingers slid inside her, and he bent to nurse at her breast.

Edie shook with longing but opened her eyes, pushed him away. "I want you to make love to me."

"I am."

She rolled onto her side, facing him, slid her hand down to the front of his jeans. She rubbed his arousal through the denim. "I want you inside me," she told him.

His eyes widened a little. As if maybe he were just the tiniest bit afraid. Edie popped his button fly, lowered his zipper and slipped her hand inside his jeans. When she found him there, she closed her hand around him, teasing and taunting.

"Why don't you want to make love to me, Wade?"

He rolled onto his back, shuddering now, and she rose above him, shoving his jeans and shorts down, out of the way, so her hands could continue to torment him. She leaned low, used her mouth on his chest to add to the sensations. His eyes were closed, his head shifting from side to side.

"Why?" Her thumb ran over the tip of him, and when he shivered in reaction, she did it again.

With a deep groan, he gave up. His hands snapped around her waist, moved her until he was nudging at her wet opening, and then he pulled her down onto him, driving deep inside her. She bit her lip to keep from crying out at the fullness, the stretching, even as he lifted her and brought her down again, arching his hips to thrust into her even more deeply than before. Over and over he moved into her, and she felt the intensity move through her, center in the very core of her and begin to build. Every move he made, every whisper, every touch of his lips, his hands, his skin on hers, intensified it. And she was moving, too, over him, around him, with him. Until finally she exploded. She cried his name, quivered and shook around him, felt his answering climax in every part of him.

As their bodies relaxed, she lay down on top of him.

He wrapped his arms around her, kissed her long and languorously, rolled her onto her back without separating from her and began to move inside her again.

It was, he realized, the biggest mistake he had ever made as he held her close to him in his bed, spooning against her, listening to her breathing. He had known it would be a mistake, and that was why he hadn't wanted to make love to her. Not that way, at least. What the hell did a man do when he realized his fondest dream? It could only be downhill from there on. He would never equal this, never have sex this good, or that meant this much, ever again. No other woman was ever going to measure up to Edie Brand. How could they? She had been his fantasy, his first crush, his obsession....

And hell, it wasn't as if he could keep her.

Well...then again...

She slid out of his bed at twenty-five minutes to midnight. Waiting that long had almost killed her, but he hadn't fallen asleep right away. She forced herself to wait for his even, steady breathing, and then she slid out of the bed, taking a spare blanket to wrap around her, and tiptoed to her own room. She did a quick washup in the bathroom, then put on the black teddy, adding a sweater and jeans over top of it. She slid her feet into sensible suede walking shoes and threaded a long sharp hat pin into their laces. Going into the bathroom, she turned on the shower. She locked the door from the inside, then stepped into the bedroom and closed it.

Perfect.

Her everyday jacket was downstairs, and she couldn't go down there. So she took a silky warm-up number from her bedroom closet and put it on. Lastly she dug through her dresser drawer for the handgun Mike had given her. She checked it, fumbling for a moment before she managed to release the catch and make the cylinder open. He'd shown her, but it had been a long time.

The bullets were in place. Six of them. She clapped the cylinder closed again, mentally reviewing what Mike had told her. There was no safety. You just thumbed back the hammer, took aim and pulled the trigger. She pulled everything he'd told her from the depths of memory. How to hold the gun, using both hands, one to support the other. How to look down the barrel and use the notch on the end to sight on the target. How to hold the gun down a bit as you pulled the trigger, to compensate for the recoil.

Biting her lips, scared half to death, she dropped the gun into her jacket pocket, then changed her mind. He would take her jacket off, or insist she do it. No, she needed to hide the gun better.

She rummaged around, found some masking tape, and shimmied out of her jacket, and then her sweater. She taped the gun to her side, where she could cover it with an arm, if necessary. Then she dressed again, quickly. Finally, opening her bedroom window, she climbed out.

# Chapter 15

Edie shimmied her way from the second-floor bedroom window to the ground by way of an obliging maple tree, scraping her hands raw on the bark and wishing she'd thought to pull on some gloves. At the bottom, she brushed her stinging palms against each other and looked around.

It was pitch dark tonight. She had no idea what phase the moon was in, waxing or waning, although she would lay odds Selene would know. It had been a crescent last night. Maybe tonight it was gone. Or maybe it was bigger. Not that it mattered. If it was out there anywhere, it was obliterated by clouds. There was no light.

She needed a flashlight. She damn well wasn't going anywhere without a flashlight.

She glanced toward the front of the house. Wade would have a flashlight in his truck, and if not there, then maybe in the garage, where he'd put all his miscellaneous guy-paraphernalia. She headed to the truck first, opened the door, winced when the interior light came on. No buzzer, at least, thank goodness. She glanced nervously back toward the house, saw no movement inside and, sighing in relief, pro-

ceeded to ransack Wade's truck. She found a small Mini Mag-
lite flashlight in the glove compartment. It was deep red, and
heavy for its size.

Nodding, she backed butt-first out of the truck and closed
the door as quietly as she could. Then, squaring her shoulders,
she headed down her driveway on foot. There was a path that
cut kitty corner through the woods and came out on the dirt
road about 100 yards from the old barn where the maniac had
told her to meet him. It occurred to her that that might be
why he chose the place. It was close to her, within walking
distance via a concealed route. Maybe he'd been staying there
the entire time he had been in town.

She flicked on her light as soon as she stepped onto the
trail. The ground was soft, no crackling dry leaves as there
would be in the fall. It was still moist, and the grasses were
young and silent. Her footsteps were whispers as she moved
along the path, her flashlight beam arcing back and forth in
front of her. Once she thought she heard answering whispers.
She stopped, spun around, aimed her light like a weapon,
stabbed at the darkness with it.

But she saw nothing. No one.

It must have been the wind.

Swallowing, she turned again and continued on her trek.

It took twenty minutes, by her best guess. She was worried
that she was late. It had to be midnight already, she thought,
when the forest around her fell away and opened onto the
narrow, winding dirt road. The barn stood in the distance, a
darker shadow against the coal sky.

Her sister was in there.

Stiffening her spine, lifting her chin, she flicked off her tiny
flashlight. She walked a little faster. And finally she was
standing there, facing the barn door. It was big and square
and hinged. A cross piece made of a two-by-four held it
closed. Edie lifted it slowly and pulled the door open.

The hinges groaned like the souls of the damned. She clenched her jaw, ducking backwards, expecting an attack.

Nothing. Nothing happened. No one came bursting out the door onto her. She didn't delude herself into believing he hadn't heard her or didn't know she was there. He knew. He was calling all the shots here.

Squaring her shoulders, she stepped into the darkness. "I'm here."

And then he was there, behind her and around her, and her arms were pinned to her sides. She cried out in shock and surprise, and then his breath was hot in her ear. "Ten minutes late, too," he rasped. "You must *really* want to be punished."

Edie tried to calm her breathing. Tried to halt the trembling that was rising up from the depths of her. "Where is my sister?"

"Safe. She's beautiful, you know. If you hadn't come, I just might have kept her."

Swallowing against the bile that rose in her throat, Edie said, "Where is she?"

He tightened his arms crushingly around her. "Don't be cocky, young lady. Don't forget your place." His arms held hers pinned hard to her sides, and the gun taped there pressed its shape into her inner arm hard enough to bruise. And yet it was comforting, somehow.

Now one of her captor's hands slid lower, caught her wrist, and she felt cold metal snapping tight around it. She sucked in a breath.

"Give me your other hand."

"No. Let go of me."

He let go. She was shocked and surprised, and she whirled to face him.

He stood there facing her in the darkness as she panted. She could barely see him. An outline. A dark mask. A white shirt. He lifted a hand toward his breast pocket and took something from it. It was too dark to see what. A box of some kind.

"What...what is that? What are you doing?"

"Oh, poor baby can't see? No matter. Listen."

His thumb moved on the box, and there was a scream. Kara, somewhere in the barn, crying out in pain. Horror shot through Edie, and she swung her head around, looking for her sister. But the sound died quickly, and there was only darkness.

"Kara! Kara, where are you?"

There was no answer.

"She won't reply," the man said in a rasping whisper. "She knows she'll get another jolt if she does."

"You bastard, what the hell are you doing to her?"

"Oh, it's not nearly as bad as she makes it sound. Only a few volts, really."

"You electrocuted her?"

"Don't worry, pet, your turn will come. Now let's see if we understand each other. Put your wrists together."

She hesitated. He thumbed the control again, and again Kara cried out in anguish. "No, don't! Don't. I'm doing it, all right, I'm doing it." She slammed her wrists together, and held them out to him.

He dropped the device into his pocket, put the other cuff on her, took hold of the chain in between and led her deeper into the darkness. She couldn't see. Not his face or his expression, only his outline. She felt straw under her feet and smelled mustiness. He lifted her arms over her head, draped the chain over some sort of hook. Then he stepped away, grabbing a rope and pulling.

The hook rose, pulling her up onto her tiptoes. The cuffs bit into her wrists. He tied it off there. When he came back to her, he ran something cold and sharp over her neck. "Now, let's see if you wore the black, like I told you." He started slicing away her clothes.

\* \* \*

Wade knew when she left the bed. His heart knotted up in his chest, because he so didn't want Alex to have been right in his theory that Edie was lying to them all. Damned if he knew why. No, that was a lie, and he'd been telling himself way too many of those lately. Honesty was what he needed here. The bald, unvarnished truth. And that truth was that he wanted to believe Edie trusted him more than she trusted anyone else. He wanted to believe that she would tell him the truth, even if she kept it from every other soul in the universe.

But she hadn't told him.

And now she was up, sneaking around the house. He could hear her moving around in her bedroom, padding to the bathroom, then back out again. He could hear the shower running. He was so tuned in he could almost see her through the walls that stood between them.

Sighing, he slid out of bed, moved closer to the wall, listened.

He heard something that sounded like...

Holy God, the window?

Wade lunged to his own bedroom window in time to see her clambering around in the tree outside like some kind of monkey-girl. He could barely believe his eyes. When she landed on the ground and looked back up at the house, he pulled back just in time. When he looked again, he saw her disappear around the corner.

Hell.

He pulled on his jeans, left his room and paused at the top of the stairs. Did he really want to alert Alex and Mel to what was happening? Would Edie want that? She wouldn't, and maybe she had solid reasons for striking out on her own. She obviously knew something the rest of them didn't.

Maybe he should trust her just a little bit here.

Okay. But he had to go after her.

Swallowing hard, he turned toward her bedroom and, with a sigh, walked into it. The bathroom door was closed, the shower running. But he knew that was a ruse. He was going to have to take the same route Edie had. And fast, before she got out of sight.

"Alex!"

Alexander Stone woke to the sound of an irritated female voice and an elbow in his rib cage. Opening his eyes, he saw an agent of Satan glaring at him. Then his memory returned, and he realized it was only Mel Brand. Yeah. Okay, correct on both counts.

"Something's going on!" she hissed.

He lifted his brows and sat up straighter on the sofa, where he'd fallen sound asleep. "Define 'something.'"

"The light just came on in Wade's truck outside. I couldn't see who was in it. Then it went out again."

He came more fully alert then. What the hell would a sexually depraved stalker want with Wade Armstrong's tow truck? "Did you go upstairs to check on your sister?"

"No." She turned and started for the stairs, and he went with her, just in case. When they got to the top, she paused, staring through an open door into an empty room.

"What is it?" Alex asked.

"Well...that's Wade's room. But it's empty."

"And this surprises you?"

She shot him a look. "Shouldn't it?"

"Not if you saw the way he was looking at your sister it shouldn't." He took her arm. "Come on, let's look in her room."

"Wait a minute." Mel jerked her arm free and strode into Wade's room, flicking on the light switch. "Those are Edie's clothes on the floor!" She pointed at them as if shocked.

Alex bit his lip to keep from commenting, gripped her arm again and tugged her along into the hall to Edie's room. That door was closed, and he knocked gently. When there was no answer, he tried again.

"Oh, get out of the way," Mel said, shouldering him aside. She whipped the door open and strode right in, flicking the light switch.

The empty bed was the first surprise. The open window the second.

"Holy..."

"Edie? Wade?" Mel called. She looked at the bathroom. The door was closed and the shower was running. She didn't even hesitate before going to it, trying the door, and then shouldering it open despite the fact that it was apparently locked. "Edie!" she shouted. She rushed into the bathroom. A second later the water stopped running and she came out again. Then she looked at him. "It's empty. Where are they?"

He shrugged. "My best guess is that one or both of them had a communication from the man who took Kara today and kept it from us. They've probably gone off to try to meet his demands."

"But where?"

Alex shrugged. Then he glanced up at her. "Those clothes on Wade's floor, they're the ones your sister was wearing today?"

She nodded.

He turned and went down the hall, back to Wade's room, snatched up the blouse from the floor and ran the fabric between his hands. It had no pockets to check. Then he picked up the jeans and turned the pockets inside out, one by one. As he shoved his hand into the final pocket, he found the folded-up piece of paper, pulled it out, held it up.

"Oh my God," Mel said. "Read it. Hurry."

He unfolded the note, read it aloud, then frowned at Mel. "You know this barn he's referring to?"

"I know it."

Her face had gone stony. He'd never seen anything quite like it. Stony. Pale and hard. She just walked past him, down the stairs into the kitchen, where she picked up the phone and dialed. He didn't know who she was talking to when she gave the location of the barn. But he clearly heard her say, "Bring my shotgun. The twelve gauge. And a box of slugs. No, not birdshot. Slugs. This son of a bitch is going down."

She hung up the phone, strode into the living room and jerked an iron fire poker from the rack near the fireplace. She hefted it in her hand, and Alex felt his stomach clench. Then she went to the door, yanked it open and finally glanced over her shoulder at him with the coldest, most dangerous eyes he'd ever seen. Those eyes didn't fit in such a pretty face. "So are you coming or what?"

Wade followed her, but keeping up wasn't easy. She had a light, and she knew the path. He had neither advantage on his side, and every time she went around a curve in the trail and her light blinked out of his line of vision, he found himself stumbling through the brush, struggling to keep on course.

By the time he got to the road on the far side of the trail, he had lost her. But he heard a scream that galvanized him. And it came from the abandoned-looking barn hulking like a shadow in the distance.

"Wade, just what the hell is going on?" a voice said, damn near making Wade jump out of his skin. Mel and Alex Stone emerged from the path through the woods just behind him.

"I don't know," he said. "She took off, and I followed. I think they're in that barn." He started forward.

Alex put a hand on his shoulder. "We should make a plan."

"Screw the plan," Mel said. She slapped her poker into her palm and strode toward the barn.

"She's right," Wade agreed. "A second ago, I heard a woman scream."

Alex nodded, his jaw firm. The two turned and caught up to Mel. They went right up to the front door, opened it slowly, cringing at the groan of the hinges, and stepped into the dark barn. In the distance, a light flickered, and Wade saw a dark form hunched over a kerosene lantern, just lowering the globe into place. As the light flared brighter, he saw Edie.

She was standing on tiptoe, wearing nothing more than a skimpy black lace teddy, her arms stretched over her head and anchored there. She looked up, as if she felt him there, saw him, and shook her head from side to side rapidly.

He stopped, holding a hand out to stop the others.

Edie said, "Listen, mister, you—"

"Master. You address me as Master, and you speak only when I tell you to." The man turned to face her.

"Master," Edie said, and damned if she didn't sound totally submissive. "Please take those electrodes off my sister now. You don't need to hurt her anymore with that little remote control you have in your shirt pocket. I'll do whatever you say."

She was telling them the situation, explaining why they couldn't just burst in. Kara would suffer for it if they did.

"I ought to give her a little jolt right now, just to teach you not to speak unless you're told to!" He strode up to Edie and smacked her hard across the face. "I can gag you. Don't make me do that."

Wade stiffened, but Alex gripped his shoulder, tugged him backward until the three of them were outside again. "We have to find Kara, get those electrodes off her."

"But he's hurting Edie," Wade argued.

"Edie's tough," Mel said. "She can handle it for a few minutes. Let's just skirt around the barn and find Kara."

Wade shook his head. "I'm staying put. I'll wait as long as I can, give you guys time to find Kara and get her safe. But if he gets too rough…"

Alex and Mel nodded their understanding and took off around the barn. Wade crept back inside, on hands and knees, crawling closer now.

Edie's eyes were on his, riveted to his. The man had bared her breasts now, though the teddy remained in place. He was walking around her, speaking slowly, and he had a short, whiplike tool in his hands, with multiple tendrils on the ends.

"So, you're ready now to receive your punishment?" He looked at her. "You may answer."

"I will be ready," she told him. "As soon as you let my sister go."

Smiling, the man reached into his pocket, and a second later, Kara screamed somewhere in the depths of the barn. Edie's eyes welled with tears, and Wade's stomach turned. Still, he realized the sound would lead Alex and Mel straight to Kara.

"Every time you ask me to let her go, I'll hurt her a little more."

Then he lifted his whip and brought it down hard across Edie's thigh.

She never made a sound. Just held Wade's eyes.

The man whipped her again, and then again. When he lifted the lash again, Wade lurched at him. He leapt onto the man's back and knocked him face first into the musty hay on the floor. The kerosene lamp fell over and smashed, and fire swam through the hay.

Wade and the maniac rolled on the floor, amid the flames, Wade pounding the man mercilessly and taking a few solid blows himself. When he managed to glimpse Edie, she was clinging to the hook above her with both hands and pulling her legs upward, as the flames danced higher and higher beneath her.

Then the man landed a blow Wade hadn't seen coming. He saw stars, tried to get up, dropped to his knees again. Edie shouted a warning, and he ducked just as the bastard swung a board at his head. The fire was burning higher. He drove his head into the maniac's belly, and while the guy was doubled over, Wade reached out and snatched the leather hood off his head.

He looked up, and Wade recognized him. He was older, fatter than he had been in high school. But he hadn't changed that much in thirteen years.

"Matt McConnell," Wade said. And he smiled as he drove his fist into the guy's face with everything he had.

The hook above Edie was attached to a rope, and she had managed to climb it all the way up to the beam over which it was flung. Now, as she pulled herself up onto that beam, still handcuffed, she saw Wade hit the man hard, knocking him onto his back. He didn't get up again.

Then Wade turned, looking for her. She wasn't where he'd last seen her. "Edie?" he called.

"I'm up here. I'm okay!"

He looked up at her, shielding his eyes against the flames that were leaping between them. And at that moment she saw the man rising up behind Wade. He had a board in his hands, and was lifting it. "Look out!" Edie cried.

She moved her cuffed hands to her side and tore the little gun free from under the teddy. It was in her hands then, tape still dangling from it as she leveled it, thumbed the hammer back and squeezed the trigger.

The recoil knocked her off balance, and she fell from the rafter into the burning hay below, having no idea if her shot had hit its target. There was smoke, heat, she was burning, and her head was spinning from the impact, when someone bent over her.

She flinched until she heard his voice. "I've got you. It's okay, baby, I've got you." Gently, Wade scooped her up into his arms, and he carried her out of the smoke-filled barn into the night.

"Kara," she whispered. "Wade, what about Kara?"

"We got her, Edie! We got her!"

Edie turned to see Mel running toward her. Beyond Mel, Kara stood, wrapped in Alex Stone's jacket, looking bewildered and shocky.

"She's okay," Edie whispered. She tipped her head up to look into Wade's eyes. He was sooty and bleeding.

As he dropped to his knees, he said, "Everything's okay now, Edie. Everything's okay."

Then she found herself on the ground as Wade just sort of tipped over and went still.

Wade woke in his bed at Edie's house.

Women seemed to be everywhere. Vidalia Brand was clucking around like a mother hen, giving orders to the others. Mel and Selene were running in and out of his room, fetching things. Selene was arguing with her mother over which ointment to put on his cuts. Sally was pacing back and forth, looking as worried as a Great Dane could look.

And Edie was there. She sat beside his bed, a cool damp cloth in her hands as she ran it over his wounded face. "Finally awake," she said softly. "How do you feel, Wade?"

Vidalia turned to see him, sent him a wink and a nod, and then hustled her other two daughters out of the room and closed the door behind them. Sally rushed to the bed and licked his face. Edie gently moved her away, and Sally finally sighed and padded to the foot of the bed to lie down.

Wade closed his eyes, wiped his cheek dry. "I feel like I just went a few rounds with the high school football star. Oh, wait. That's because I did."

Edie lowered her head. "I can't believe it was Matt McConnell." She swallowed hard. "The police said my gunshot only nicked him. It was the fire that did him in."

"He got what he deserved. He was always a jerk." Wade lifted a hand, cupped her face. "Are you okay?"

"You're the one with the burns and cuts and bruises. I'm fine."

"And Kara?"

"She's all right. No serious damage."

"Thank God," he said, closing his eyes slowly.

Edie licked her lips. "Wade...I'm sorry I tried to go after her on my own."

"You were doing what you thought you had to," he said.

"I didn't tell you because I didn't want you to get hurt. I thought I—I thought I might have to give him what he wanted in order to save Kara. And I knew you'd get yourself killed before you would let that happen."

He studied her face for a long time. "You're right. I would have. And I'm glad you know I would have. But do you know why?"

She smiled down at him. Very slowly, she nodded. "I knew as soon as I saw that painting, Wade. You love me."

His own smile hurt his face, but he couldn't help it. "I do," he said. "And it wouldn't matter what you looked like. You know that, too, right? I didn't fall in love with the lingerie model. I fell in love with the little sophomore who always ignored me."

"Pretended to ignore you," she corrected him. "The truth is, I was probably a little bit in love with you even then."

"Yeah? And what about now?"

She lowered her eyes, licked her lips. "Now I'm just wondering if it's healthy to love someone as much as I love you."

He sat up in the bed, despite the fact that it hurt to do so, cupped her head and drew her close for a kiss. "It is when they love you back just as much." He kissed her again, tasted tears on her lips. When he drew back again, he said, "Why don't you go ask your mother how she feels about a June wedding?"

"Is that your idea of a proposal?"

"Nope. This is." He got out of the bed with effort, even as she jumped to her feet in protest. Then he dropped down on one knee in front of her, gently pushing her back into her chair. "Edain Brand, you are the love of my life. If you won't marry me, I'll be a lonely, lonely bachelor, pining away over pictures of you until the day I die—just like I have been for the last decade or so. Will you be my wife, Edie? Please?"

She slid out of the chair and sank to her knees, nodding and crying, kissing his lips through her tears. "Yes, Wade. Yes. Yes."

He pulled her close and kissed her. Sally barked and lunged at them, hitting them bodily and knocking them both sideways onto the floor. Then she danced over them, speaking volumes in her own little language.

"I think she's congratulating us," Edie said, laughing.

"No. She's asking if this means we get to keep the house after all," Wade said. He kissed her, and they managed to get to their feet. When they did, he looked toward the door and saw Vidalia standing in the doorway, sniffling, eyes wet. Her daughters surrounded her, smiling and sniffling, as well.

"June," Vidalia said. "My goodness, my daughters don't believe in long engagements, do they?"

"Thank God for that," Wade said. He looked deeply into Edie's eyes and said it again, in a whisper. "Thank God."

\*   \*   \*   \*   \*

On sale now

# girls' night in

21 of today's hottest female authors

1 fabulous short-story collection

And all for a good cause.

## Featuring *New York Times* bestselling authors

**Jennifer Weiner** (author of *Good in Bed*),

**Sophie Kinsella** (author of *Confessions of a Shopaholic*),

**Meg Cabot** (author of *The Princess Diaries*)

Net proceeds to benefit War Child, a network of organizations dedicated to helping children affected by war.

### Also featuring bestselling authors...

Carole Matthews, Sarah Mlynowski, Isabel Wolff, Lynda Curnyn, Chris Manby, Alisa Valdes-Rodriguez, Jill A. Davis, Megan McCafferty, Emily Barr, Jessica Adams, Lisa Jewell, Lauren Henderson, Stella Duffy, Jenny Colgan, Anna Maxted, Adèle Lang, Marian Keyes and Louise Bagshawe

www.RedDressInk.com    www.WarChildusa.org

*Available wherever trade paperbacks are sold.*

# eHARLEQUIN.com

## The Ultimate Destination for Women's Fiction

### Visit eHarlequin.com's Bookstore today for today's most popular books at great prices.

- An extensive selection of romance books by top authors!

- Choose our convenient "bill me" option. No credit card required.

- New releases, Themed Collections and hard-to-find backlist.

- A sneak peek at upcoming books.

- Check out book excerpts, book summaries and Reader Recommendations from other members and post your own too.

- Find out what everybody's reading in Bestsellers.

- Save BIG with everyday discounts and exclusive online offers!

- Our Category Legend will help you select reading that's exactly right for you!

- Visit our Bargain Outlet often for huge savings and special offers!

- Sweepstakes offers. Enter for your chance to win special prizes, autographed books and more.

**Your purchases are 100% guaranteed—so shop online at www.eHarlequin.com today!**

INTBB104-TR

# DYNASTIES: THE DANFORTHS

### introduces an exciting new family saga with

## A family of prominence... tested by scandal, sustained by passion!

**THE CINDERELLA SCANDAL by Barbara McCauley**
(Silhouette Desire #1555, available January 2004)

**MAN BENEATH THE UNIFORM by Maureen Child**
(Silhouette Desire #1561, available February 2004)

**SIN CITY WEDDING by Katherine Garbera**
(Silhouette Desire #1567, available March 2004)

**SCANDAL BETWEEN THE SHEETS by Brenda Jackson**
(Silhouette Desire #1573, available April 2004)

**THE BOSS MAN'S FORTUNE by Kathryn Jensen**
(Silhouette Desire #1579, available May 2004)

**CHALLENGED BY THE SHEIKH by Kristi Gold**
(Silhouette Desire #1585, available June 2004)

**COWBOY CRESCENDO by Cathleen Galitz**
(Silhouette Desire #1591, available July 2004)

**STEAMY SAVANNAH NIGHTS by Sheri WhiteFeather**
(Silhouette Desire #1597, available August 2004)

**THE ENEMY'S DAUGHTER by Anne Marie Winston**
(Silhouette Desire #1603, available September 2004)

**LAWS OF PASSION by Linda Conrad**
(Silhouette Desire #1609, available October 2004)

**TERMS OF SURRENDER by Shirley Rogers**
(Silhouette Desire #1615, available November 2004)

**SHOCKING THE SENATOR by Leanne Banks**
(Silhouette Desire #1621, available December 2004)

*Available at your favorite retail outlet.*